Helen

TRAGEDY AND MIRACLES

In this dramatic and inspiring novel we follow the upswing of a man's spiritual growth as he learns to break through the barriers of convention to a richer life illuminated by faith and hope.

Paul Forrester is the minister to the church of All Saints in the small city of Mapleton, where he experiences all the trials that beset a young clergyman—from economy-minded vestrymen to the attentions of spinster parishioners with matrimony on their mind.

The most serious crisis of Paul's life arises when his failure to save a boy from ultimate tragedy drives him to question the reality of his own faith. Ironically, he becomes most deeply indebted to a woman of whom he has intensely and vocally disapproved—Burnett McNeill. Through Burnett he learns of a way to help others as he has always longed to do.

The unfolding of Paul's story is an experience which leaves the reader with a heightened awareness of the ironies, the humor, the pathos, and follies of everyday life. The reader also comes to share the author's reverent conviction that the foundation of life is living faith.

Lost
Shepherd

Lost Shepherd

AGNES SANFORD

By The Author Of

Dreams Are For Tomorrow
The Second Mrs. Wu
The Healing Light
Behold Your God
Healing Power Of The Bible
The Healing Gifts Of The Spirit
Oh, Watchman!

Logos International
Plainfield, New Jersey

Printed by arrangement
with Agnes Sanford
Logos pocket-sized edition
© March 1971

Logos Books Are Published By
Logos International
Plainfield, New Jersey

Printed In The United States Of America

To

My father, the Reverend Hugh W. White,

and

My father-in-law, the Reverend David L. Sanford,

and

To their fathers and their fathers' fathers, all ministers,

This book is lovingly dedicated

Lost
Shepherd

1

Clouds hung low over All Saints. The Reverend Paul Forrester felt a vague depression as he drew his car into the deeper gloom beneath the maple trees. Usually he was comforted by his ancient church, overhung with ivy and surrounded by ferns. Usually the faint sag of his spirits on entering Mapleton lifted as he neared All Saints. But today he had driven the thundering highways of New Jersey in great good humor. He had looked with joy on the yellow light of afternoon brightening the woods and cornfields. And the brief unconscious sigh with which he had slowed down for the shadowy streets of Mapleton was lighter than usual, for he was still upheld by the day's retreat.

At times one was lonely, being a priest. The vast world was so appallingly filled with those who did not know the Church. A man could not help wondering, as he stepped before the high altar of a Sunday morning, that so few out of the crowded town came there to worship God. But what could one do? If one filled the church with beauty and with reverence and people were too blind to see it, what more could one do?

Just the same, it was a lonely business. Therefore he had been greatly strengthened by the meeting together of other clergymen like himself.

> "Brother clasps the hand of brother,
> Stepping forward through the night . . ."

So they chanted all together at Matins, two score of them, in the stalwart black vestments of the Church.

But here he was at Mapleton, and he must slow down.

Everything slowed down for Mapleton. Life moved sedately upon its stately streets. Its wide lawns were unbroken by the frivolity of flowers, its massive houses set well back among correctly chosen trees. Even Main Street, Paul reflected as he turned into it, seemed to move at a quieter pace than the main streets of other towns. The quietness, however, was an intangible thing, for the main street of Mapleton was like any other main street in these United States: the Asco and the A&P, drugstores, vanity shoppes and gift shoppes, all the churches among them as though to say, "Here am I. You cannot pretend to have forgotten me."

All the churches. And his own, standing in wide lawns, so much more attractive than any of them, even when gray clouds darkened its gray stones. Paul disregarded the shabbiness of wooden rectory and parish house and rested his eyes upon the beauty of his church: stone and slate, Gothic windows and flying buttresses, as correct and as conventional as its minister.

Paul strode across the grass to the rectory and slammed the front door shut in his usual quick, nervous way.

"Oh, hello!" shouted Janet from the kitchen. She appeared in the front hall and turned on the light, for the faded wallpaper and dark woodwork did not make for brightness. His sister's voice was brisk and cheerful, but trouble was written upon the open book of her face.

"How's everything?" asked Paul, picking up his mail from the hall table. Paul Forrester had lived always behind a barricade of reticence. He did not leap over it lightly and say, "What is the matter?"

"Oh, all right," Janet smiled, but her brown eyes were solemn like the eyes of a frightened child.

"Any messages?"

"Well—Jack Fenton said he couldn't serve on Sunday, and Doris crawled out of the Altar Guild as usual and Hannah McGhann called up about some dishes the Woman's Auxiliary lent to the Baptists—"

I shouldn't have asked, thought Paul, and he closed his ears as he had learned to do and read his mail, an occasional phrase about Baptists and teacups reaching his ears from the kitchen.

"So I told 'em where they could all go," shouted Janet cheerily.

Paul Forrester, established now in his easy chair in the

living room, froze suddenly to attention.

"Who? Mrs. McGhann?" he called.

"No, Priscilla."

Paul was relieved. True, Priscilla was the sister of the senior warden, and Hannah was his wife. But Janet's feud with Priscilla was an ancient and honorable one and he surmised on the basis of former skirmishes that Priscilla would hold her own.

"But I thought you were talking about Hannah McGhann and the Baptists," he said, his eyes returning to his letter.

"I was, ten minutes ago." Janet stood accusingly in the doorway, a wooden spoon in her large capable hand. She was rather a pretty woman, with curly black and silver hair, up-tilted nose and a shapely mouth. Even her solid figure was pleasantly curved beneath the housedress that she wore with an air, as she wore all her clothes. "You're always asking me something and then not listening to me. That's your worst fault."

I'd never get any work done if I did listen, thought Paul. But he lifted questioning brown eyes to his sister and asked, "What was the matter with Priscilla this time?"

"Oh, she was poking around the church wanting to know why Ambrose didn't dust the wood carving," fussed Janet. "First place, Ambrose can't get up there to dust the wood carving, what with his crooked back and all. Second place, you need the dust there anyway, to give it a look of age. So I told her, I said—"

"Is that what you're so worried about?" asked Paul suddenly.

But Janet only murmured that her stew was boiling over and darted away.

She would soon tell him. She could never keep a secret very long. And a smile played about the corners of his mouth, for with all her vagaries his elder sister amused him. Paul's lips were well-formed and pleasant like hers, but there were lines around them and his smile was chained, turning down a little as though he did not dare release it that it might turn up. Someone was passing the rectory window, and Paul, who knew every man, woman and child in his parish, glanced out to see who it was.

"What's that woman doing in the parish house?" he called to Janet, scowling at the figure in bluejeans and white sweat shirt marching down the flagstone walk.

To all Mapleton, "that woman" signified always the young artist with the coiled black hair who lived a somewhat questionable life in her little house on Main Street. By day she lived alone and worked as was right and meet for her to do. But by night strange characters of every sort went in and out of her front door, and Mapleton wondered . . .

"She's still working on your angels' costumes," said Janet.

"If the women of this parish ever get done appointing this person and that person without consulting me . . ." muttered Paul.

"Now listen," said Janet firmly, appearing at the living-room door. "There isn't another person in town who could make anything like that: Fra Angelico angels with great tall wings. Just wait till next Christmas when you see them in the pageant and you'll be thrilled."

"Oh, I suppose so," sighed Paul. "But it starts a bad precedent just the same, getting all kinds of dubious people to do the church's work."

"What's dubious about her?"

"What's dubious?" echoed Paul. "With every Tom, Dick and Harry in and out of her house?"

"She's a healer," stated Janet. "Women aren't the only people who need help."

"A healer, for heaven's sake," muttered Paul in disgust. He settled his head against the back of his chair to rest until dinner was ready. It was good to have Janet and her son Skip living with him. They had been his family for five years, ever since Janet's husband had died. And in all probability they would remain his family. He sighed, remembering briefly a girl whom he might have married years ago if she had lived. And here in his kitchen where she might have been was Janet, incorrigible, contentious, but always cheerful, filling the big dark rectory with life. Then there was Skip, whose rambunctious youth annoyed the vestry and warmed the coldest corners of the rectory.

"Where's Skip?" asked Paul as the two of them entered the dining room. Paul sat opposite the window. He liked to look out on the cut stone of his church walls, gray and mauve and cream and gray again, fitted and balanced by an artist's eye. "Where's Skip?" he repeated, as Janet did not answer.

"Oh—out with the gang I guess," she said evasively.

Paul sighed.

"Oh, all right, I'll tell you," Janet burst out. "There was a mix-up at Tony's last night—you know, that roadhouse the gang goes to nowadays—Frank and Skip and all of them. Frank's been queer, lately—"

A picture flitted through Paul's mind: Frank, sitting in the big leather chair in his study where he always put the troubled members of his little flock; he saw again Frank's white face and heard him say, "I can't go on! I tell you, *I can't go on!*" And he remembered his own halting words about the comfort of religion, about the peace to be found at the altar, about patience and courage and the value of suffering. Useless words, for they had not reached the boy's heart and he had gone away with bleak, helpless eyes. "Well—I guess there's nothing anyone can do," he had sighed.

"Frank had had a few too many," Janet was saying. "He picked a quarrel with Buddy because Buddy was getting too sweet on Jean to suit him. Then he got to waving a gun around. Why he was carrying a gun I don't know—"

(Paul knew.)

"Well, they got into a sort of a free-for-all, and the gun went off and—it was Jean."

"Dead?"

"Not yet, but—"

"Where's Frank?"

"In jail. They've been trying to call you all day. . . But I *did* want you at least to get some food in you before you charged into the middle of all this!"

The telephone on the hall table shattered the stillness.

"I know," said Paul in his most consoling tones to the broken voice on the other end of the line. "I've just heard. I'll be right there."

"Vestry meeting!" called Janet.

"Not until eight-thirty."

"Then *eat your dinner!*"

But Paul could not eat. He pushed aside his plate and with a small, apologetic smile slammed out the front door to his car.

Janet was waiting when he came back. "Jean?" she asked as though she did not dare put her question into words.

"Still living," said Paul briefly. "No, thanks. I've really had all the dinner I need." And in ten strides he was across the bit of lawn that connected rectory with parish house.

Paul disliked the parish house. It was built lugubriously of yellow painted wood after the style of the nondescript buildings that lined Main Street. One half expected to find a delicatessen store on its lower floor with a hall dedicated to Oddfellows or Moose above it. Instead, one went down the dark hall, with a chapel and three classrooms on the left-hand side, choir room and secretary's office on the other, to the rector's study. It was a comfortable room, with two shabby leather chairs, desk overflowing with mail and notebooks, yellowed prints of cathedrals and a crucifix upon the one faded brown wall that was not lined with bookshelves. Behind the parish house the old cemetery brooded in the misty evening light. It had overflowed into the bit of lawn between parish house and church, so that all the study windows gave upon it, and for this Paul was glad. For the cemetery with its grave dignity matched the church, built years ago under an ambitious rector by an architect of some esteem. On the back shelves of the study closet Paul had discovered blueprints cracked with age, hopefully laying out a parish house and rectory to match the church. But the ambitious rector had gone away, the town's woolen mills had moved South and the declining church remained in lonely beauty amid the tawdriness of its companion buildings. Paul dreamed sometimes of building a parish house and rectory in the same Gothic style, exquisitely united by cloisters, and of himself pacing them in cassock and biretta . . .

But tonight he dreamed no dreams. He went past the parish house, into the side door of the church and through the sacristy to the chancel. Paul loved his church: the simple and gracious lines, the deep chancel with its stone altar and choir-canopies of wrought iron, the stone pillars down the side aisles with angels carved above them as though they upheld the towering roof-beams with their wings. Paul did not notice darkness or chill. To him the austerity of dim light and cold stone was heaven and the mystical Presence on the white stone altar was a reality:

light from another world, flickering dimly amid the darkness of the earth.

He came away strengthened, as always. But before he had gained his study, fumbling footsteps sounded in the cloister and Miss Hattie Burroughs tottered to the sacristy door.

"I've come to church," she quavered in the high, uncertain voice of one very old and very deaf. "And I can't find anybody. I can't find anybody at all."

"There isn't any service on Tuesday night, Miss Hattie," shouted Paul as gently as he could.

"Oh dear. I thought it was time for church. I can't remember very well, you know. I'm getting old and I just can't remember . . ."

The old woman stood forlornly before the closed door of God's house. Her white hair straggled from under a moth-eaten black hat and her petticoat dragged to her skinny ankles, one in a brown cotton stocking and one in black.

"Come into the church, Miss Hattie," said Paul, taking her by the arm. "Let's have Evening Prayer, just you and me."

"Then it *is* time for church?"

"Yes, it is. I was just wanting someone to come and have church with me." And Paul ushered Miss Hattie with all dignity to her own pew, donned his cassock and read a shortened Evening Prayer.

"Now I feel good," sighed Miss Hattie as Paul steered her toward her home. "I feel like myself again. It's terrible, you know, not to feel like yourself. That was funny, though. Nobody came to church but you and me. Nobody else at all. Just you and me."

"Oh, I don't know." Paul smiled, his pleasant, undistinguished face suddenly beautiful. "'Therefore with angels and arch-angels,'" he quoted. "Who knows how many angels may have had Evening Prayer with us?"

"So they might!" quavered Miss Hattie delightedly. "Oh my, you always make me feel so *good!*"

There was someone he could help anyway, Paul reflected. All the old Church words and symbols were life to Miss Hattie. This was his medium. These were the tools in which he was trained. Could he help it if Frank was too dim of spirit and too dull of wit to understand them? Frank had no Church background or he would have understood. He had come to Paul out of a godless family only because of Skip. "I don't know about this God business," Skip had said. "But Paul's a good guy. People are always trotting into his office and they seem to feel better when they come out."

Just as Skip used to bring lost puppies home, so he brought Frank, picking him up, Paul thought grimly, from God knows where. "He went haywire in Korea," Skip had explained anxiously to his uncle. "You'll know what to say to the guy, won't you, Paul?"

Paul had not known what to say. He was a priest, not a psychiatrist. He could no more be expected to heal the mentally ill than to operate for appendicitis. Nevertheless he was sad, for he was troubled by a tender heart.

It was this compassion that had drawn him into the narrow confines of the ministry. He had grown up under the shadow of the Church, tied about with the bonds of rectory life. A minister's son might not go to dances on Friday night or to baseball games during Lent. He must not fight or play small gambling games with marbles lest he set a bad example to other boys. And always and forever, whenever the church doors were open, he must go to church. Moreover, Paul was the youngest of the rectory children, and five domineering brothers and sisters took part in his upbringing. So when the first chance to escape came his way, he had leaped at it and was gone. His mother's brother was a topographer. From the age of fourteen onward, the small boy with the wiry body and the dark, eager eyes acted as rodman, as chainman, and finally during his college vacations, as chief of party. It was a life of open spaces and of freedom, and Paul rejoiced in it like a flower blossoming in the sun. It pleased him to do the work of a man, to prove that his deceptively thin body could stand the strain of hacking down brush with a machete under the broiling sun, of tramping through swamps and establishing markers upon the mountaintops. When his uncle had moved to the West Coast, Paul's joy had been unbounded. For a year after his graduation he had worked over a thousand miles of desert. There he had known the passionate peace of unimaginable beauty. The radiance of high skies had been his, blue over violet-blue, burning with an electric intensity that the East has never seen.

Paul remembered it and sighed. Why had he ever imagined that by giving up this radiance and this peace he could bring peace and radiance to other men? He had relinquished a great deal to help people such as Frank and he had failed. And Skip—what would Skip say?

Skip would say, "Failed, heck! The guy isn't dead, is he? Then what's the idea of quitting?"

Right. He would not quit. He would see Frank tomorrow and every day and he would not let him go till he was well. More than that, he would use this tragedy to emphasize to the vestry a need that he had long recognized. For he was not content with a church for worship. He wanted more than that: a refuge, a home for those who were young and lost, like Frank. He had worked out a plan and presented it to the vestry and tonight they would make their decision.

Paul went into the sacristy and arranged twelve chairs expectantly about the long oak table.

Twelve good men and true . . . but on this June evening they were not happy. Angus McGhann, the senior warden, was iron-gray and handsome with cold blue eyes and an impressive frame. He would have done nicely on a billboard, thought Paul, advertising some particularly fine automobile. His keen eyes and cocksure mouth would make anyone rush to buy whatever he recommended. He was aware of this fact, was Angus McGhann, and he conducted his church work with the zest of a big businessman laboring over a stamp collection. But tonight his face was heavy with displeasure. Little Sammy Birdsong, warden for some fifty years, was mumbling with excitement, his shaky mouth quivering like a rabbit's. Large, grave Harold Lindstrom camped behind his legal barriers; his usual vast smile said nothing. Thayer Tewksbury's expressive face was troubled, his bright eyes perplexed, his florid coloring dimmed.

In ominous solemnity, the meeting was called to order, minutes were read and old business was considered. Harold Lindstrom, chairman of the committee on Paul's new plan, read a careful estimate: so much for bowling alleys to be built in the parish house basement, so much for a game room made of unused classrooms thrown together.

There was silence around the table.

"It seems to me, gentlemen," Paul began, "that this is little enough to pay in order to achieve our objective."

"Would you care to state, quite definitely, the nature of our objective?" Angus McGhann was using his best business-executive voice and a shudder went up Paul's spine at the sound.

"It is, to fit our church to the need of the times," said Paul. "We may not like the change in our world, but—there it is. Life is keyed too high—too high. Even we who are older feel the need of continual amusement." His eyes rested on a certain young vestryman who squirmed, for on the previous Sunday he had worshipped God on the golf course. "Our young people rush about in herds, feverishly active, trying to forget a life that has somehow become unendurable." Paul's voice was low and grave, for he was not thinking at the moment of the twelve vestrymen. For a split second he was behind cold bars with one who had seen more agony than he could take and whose rocking mind had slipped its moorings and was fast carrying him out to sea.

"Therefore," finished Paul, "our objective is to provide an opportunity for games and fun here, in the very shadow of the church. Then those who have no home for their restless souls will find a home with us. The church will seem cozy and warm and friendly to them, and habit itself will draw them here on Sunday. God is love," he added in a less certain tone, for he found it difficult to speak of God except in church. "And having found love and friendliness here all week, they will find God in the church on Sunday."

Paul was an able speaker. Most of his vestrymen were older and larger than he, but he was often able to gather them into his hands and sway them according to his will. Tonight, however, something had broken his hold. They were measuring him with their eyes. And suddenly he saw himself as they saw him, an unimpressive fellow in black clericals that had shrunk a bit, his nervous Adam's apple riding above his dog collar, his face pleasant and perennially youthful, but not the face of one whom they intended to follow.

"Well, gentlemen?" asked Paul, for silence had settled upon the vestry of All Saints.

At this Angus McGhann drew the evening paper from his

pocket and laid it on the table in front of Paul. Staring back from the front page was the face of his nephew Skip. A news photographer had been at Tony's roadhouse on the preceding evening. There was a picture of Frank, head half-turned away, gun still in his hand; but Skip's broad shoulders, handsome face and horrified eyes dominated the picture.

"If my plan had been in effect ten years ago, this might have been avoided," Paul said. "I have just pointed out to you a need—there it is." And he tapped the picture of Frank.

"And *there*," growled Mr. McGhann, "is the block to your plan." And he in turn tapped the picture of Skip.

"That's the truth, that's the truth!" piped up Sammy Birdsong. Old Sammy slept through much of the vestry's proceedings, years lying heavy upon him and his eyes being dim. But seeing the pictures, he caught the gist of the conversation and entered into it with zest. "Can't have that young one around the rectory!" he quavered, shaking an ineffective fist at the picture of Skip. "Leading 'em astray just as fast as he can lead 'em! He's got no business running with that Frank, anyway. Poor kind of folks that Frank comes from. Mighty poor kind of folks. His father works in a garage."

"Jesus Christ worked in a carpenter's shop," said Paul.

"What's that? What's he talking about, Jesus Christ?" Birdsong demanded of the vestry. "I didn't say anything about Jesus Christ! I'm talking about Richard Anderson, that there Skip, as they call him. Yes, and his mother, too. Always picking fights with other folks and messing into their business. Mighty poor set-up for a rectory. Mighty poor."

Paul Forrester had a temper and at this point it rose and beat in his throat. But he had learned to sway his vestry by keeping that temper under control. So he said nothing and waited.

"We've warned you before, Forrester, about that nephew of yours." This from the far end of the table.

"Does your son never go to a roadhouse?" asked Paul, his voice reined in and cold.

"Sure he does! And who does he go with? Skip! The whole gang follows Skip. But I've not noticed him leading them to church on Sunday on account of its being a home for his soul."

"The boy's a ringleader. No question about it," stated McGhann.

Skip, Paul knew, was merely a bit more adventurous than the average young man emerging from adolescence. His restlessness was the vigor of his eighteen years, lit by the joy of childhood and unweighted as yet by maturity. But unquestionably he was restless; not even the dark fragrant lakes of the piny countryside nor the foam-ringed Atlantic satisfied his roaming spirit; he must also investigate road-houses and wrestling matches and all the life of the tawdry city. But there was no evil in his adventuring; there was only curiosity and a great, gay lust for life. "Aw, nuts, it's only a show, Mom!" he would say to Janet. "And the crowd is funnier than the wrestlers. If you could see 'em, hopping around like lunatics and throwing chairs into the ring, you'd laugh yourself sick."

Perhaps he should have been stricter with the boy, thought Paul, as he kept silence for a moment and the murmurs of his vestry sounded about him. But he remembered his own repressed childhood too clearly. There was no real reason why the child of the rectory should be forced to a standard that was not expected of other boys. And in spite of everything he trusted Skip.

"He'll find himself," Paul would say to Janet. "He's just exuberant with life, that's all." And so it was. Skip brought light and laughter wherever he went. Even the click of his latchkey in the front door was a prelude to merriment.

Paul smiled to himself. "Do you seriously think," he asked the vestry, "that it is a deadly sin for a young man to visit a roadhouse?"

There was a shocked silence.

"What's that?" shrilled little Sammy, his hand to his ear. "What's that he says?"

But nobody answered him.

"It was 2 a.m.," said Lindstrom at last in his precise, legal voice. "And he was in the company of this Frank."

"That's it!" blurted Thayer, Paul's best friend upon the vestry.

"He is sorry for him," and even before the words were out of his mouth Paul was aware of the silent scorn with which they were received. He did not add, "Skip wanted to help him." How strange, he thought with sadness, that no one would believe the things that were quite simply true! "He sent Frank to me, hoping that I could help him," said Paul Forrester in a voice edged with pain. "And I failed."

"Doubtless because you had no bowling alley—" this from the far end of the table.

"Doubtless," said Paul, lifting his chin. "The church meant nothing to Frank. If for years it had signified to him friendliness and home, he might have absorbed the feeling behind the things I tried to say."

"Skip rather gives the lie to that, doesn't he?" murmured Angus McGhann.

"By no means," replied Paul steadily. "On the contrary, he demonstrates it. I consider him an average adolescent— no better, no worse, than your own sons." And at this he glared at his vestry. "Nevertheless, he attends church every Sunday and is faithful in his duties on the Servers' Guild . . ."

"With some encouragement from his uncle, no doubt," added McGhann, an edge to his voice.

"No doubt," Paul agreed. "I have always felt that religious education is just as important as secular education. If children can be required to go to school, they can also be required to go to Sunday school or church. Being forced to go to public school does not necessarily prevent them from learning the lessons taught there . . . And my nephew, although attending church at my order, nevertheless has learned a certain appreciation of religious values. For instance, he met this Frank at the garage where he works, saw that he was in trouble and brought him here, hoping that I could help him."

"If his effort was a genuine one, it was apparently unsuccessful," said Harold Lindstrom in his precise and slightly lisping voice.

There was an approving murmur about the table and the vestry settled back on their haunches like a wolf pack. They did not believe him and they would not believe him. They had fastened the name of ringleader to Skip and they would hold him to the pattern they had made for him.

Paul looked past the twelve men to the cemetery gradually darkening in the late June evening. He fixed his gaze on the lone star in the deep electric blue of the twilight sky and steeled himself against the words that came from one after another as from infancy he had learned to steel himself against older brothers and sisters.

"And now, with all this coming out," McGhann was saying, thumping the paper with his fist, "everybody in town will know what kind of an influence their young people have in the rectory."

"Will the meeting please come to order," Paul interrupted dryly. "I call for the reports of the various committees."

"As chairman of the committee on social service," said Harold Lindstrom, showing all his teeth in a deprecating smile, "I will report our conclusion reached last night: we believe the rector's plan worth trying but only under the most favorable circumstances. It will involve a great deal of money and personal sacrifice on the part of all of us..." He coughed delicately and looked about the circle of gravely nodding heads, his gaze resting a trifle longer on those owning ground rents and first mortgages. "Therefore we do not feel that we can undertake this project under the present living arrangements in the rectory."

"Are you proposing, gentlemen, that I send my sister and her son away from the rectory?" Paul asked, incredulously.

"Not at all," said Lindstrom smoothly, lifting an authoritative hand. "You are of course free to order your own personal life. We are only pointing out that some arrangements encourage certain types of parish activity more than do other arrangements."

"Nine thousand dollars is a considerable sum," McGhann stated, having spent twenty thousand that same day on the purchase of a house at the seashore. "We do not propose to throw it away. That's all."

And another added, "No matter who is appointed to organize your youth activity, you know good and well who *will* organize it—Skip."

And still another, a dark-browed sombre man who until now had been still, "Moreover, your sister is not in every respect the most suitable—er—hostess—for All Saints. This very afternoon the chairwoman of the Guild's Church Committee was here inspecting the buildings, and Mrs. Anderson, if I understand correctly, was extremely rude."

"I will—speak to my sister," murmured Paul, not for the first time.

"There's no question of her finding something else to do," said Thayer, with sympathy in his voice. "She is a capable person."

"Too capable," grunted McGhann with admirable understatement. "She is wasted on All Saints."

Sorrow descended upon Paul as darkness blotted out the little cemetery beyond the window, enfolding all its quiet gravestones. Paul saw himself coming in the front door to a cold house full of loneliness, no longer needing to listen for Skip's latchkey in the front door, waking alone in the silent house and Skip's door standing open ... Skip's room alone and desolate, save perhaps for a few discarded Boy Scout books and an antler or two hanging dismally upon the wall ... He *would not do it!*

And yet he knew that he must.

"I would suggest, gentlemen," said Paul, keeping a very tight hold on his voice, "that we lay the matter of the youth program upon the table, to be considered at our next meeting. Is there any new business?"

And the vestry, squirming a little under his dark, harried eyes, proceeded with the order of the day.

An hour later Paul snapped off the light in sacristy and cloister and went swiftly to the rectory. He glanced up from habit at the lovely tower of the church, its four delicate pinnacles outlined against the dark sky. But tonight its beauty did not touch him. He entered the dining room with unusual quietness, hoping to gain his room before Janet should hear him. But there she was in the hall.

"How was it?" she whispered, fear in her round eyes.

"They were pretty upset about the picture of Skip. You—didn't tell me."

"Couldn't quite get the words out," muttered Janet, a slow red creeping into her cheeks. "Well—what are they going to do about it?"

"It's put the lid on my youth program," Paul sighed, setting himself in the big chair in the living room while Janet charged about the kitchen making cocoa and shouting her opinions of a bunch of busybodies.

To come home at night to nothing, to no one ...

But Paul had been reared in the unyielding concept that

God's will came first.

He finished his cocoa and rose to go to bed. "Where's Skip?"

"Oh, I don't know. He said he wouldn't be too late."

Not too late. That probably meant between one and two.

He did not want to see the boy until his decision was made. *But it was already made,* the voice within him said. God's will came first. In spite of his inner rebellion he had entered the ministry, as his father had done and his grandfather and grandfathers before him as long as anyone knew. When one had mapped all the mountains and all the deserts in the country, what had one really done? The world was as sad as ever, full of people who needed God and could not find Him. To keep the altar candles lit, that those who could discern God in His Holy Temple might come and be at rest—this had meaning unto eternity, when all surveying would be done and at an end. And if Skip and Janet were the price of doing this, what right had he to refuse to pay? He lay in bed and tossed, wondering. Could he drop the matter of his youth program till fall, when Skip would go to college? Could he manage to send the boy far away instead of to the University across the river, from which he would come home every night? But as he worried the subject, chewing every angle of it as a dog chews a bone, he knew that there was no escape. If he postponed the plan for his own pleasure it would forever lose its force. If he did not care enough about his young people to make a sacrifice for them, why should the parish do so? This argument had already been presented by his vestry, politely veiled but undeniable.

It was not Janet who lay upon his heart. There were times when Janet chafed under the restrictions of her confining life and longed to be free of them. And there were times when Paul wearied of her older-sister solicitude and wondered for a disloyal moment whether a housekeeper that he might hire or fire would be a better adjunct to his home. In certain grim moments, after he had reminded Janet of his oft-repeated request that she divorce her attention from parish affairs, he would find her coldly studying the want ads. Once, dressed in her home-tailored suit with its well-chosen and becoming accessories, she had sallied into the city, returning round-eyed, sober, and secretive. But it was beyond the bounds of possibility for Janet to keep any secret very long. When Paul came home from the study that night she said abruptly, "They offered me a job."

"Good for you!" Paul had cried encouragingly. "Come into the living room and tell me about it."

"It's—to be a saleswoman at Forsythe and West's," Janet had said.

But although Paul had encouraged her, speaking highly and quite truthfully of her wisdom concerning women's clothes and of the certainty that she would rise to a position of authority in that excellent store, Janet had remained solemn.

"But I didn't take it, of course," she said.

"Why?"

"Now, listen, Paul: even if you do make me mad sometimes I'm not going to leave you to batch it all by yourself or to contend with some incompetent hired woman either. If you had gumption enough to get married like any other man, that would be a different matter."

"Nonsense!" Paul had replied somewhat testily, for he did not consider his unmarried state the result of a lack of gumption. "The Church is full of celibates. What do you suppose they do? They don't all have an older sister to dry nurse them."

"That's just too bad."

"But why in the name of sense did you go and apply for a job if you didn't mean to take it?"

"Just to see if I could land one," said the exasperating woman.

"You'd make more money," said Paul. "There's no future in being a clergyman's housekeeper."

But Janet, brought up on a minister's salary and clever enough to dress herself exquisitely out of odds and ends, was not to be moved by any words concerning salary. "Bob Anderson wasn't a millionaire, but he left me enough so that I don't have to scramble and scrape to make ends meet. I can do what I want, and as long as you're unmarried I want to stay here, so that's that," she concluded, and Paul did not know whether to be relieved or disappointed. "Besides," she added, "there's Skip. This is his home."

"This could still be his home—and yours. You could

come back in the evenings and keep your hand on things."

"That wouldn't be fair," Janet had said. "I wouldn't do right by either job."

So the matter had ended. And Paul could not decide whether Janet stayed on from a sense of duty, a thought which embarrassed him greatly, or whether she really preferred the life of the rectory. One thing was clear and plain however: it would not trouble Janet unduly to loose her hold upon the rectory of All Saints and find herself work in the city.

But Skip—what had Janet said? "This is his home..." And the boy had grown into his heart as his own son. What would happen to Skip if he were thrown out? Would Paul's own father have dealt so with him?

Paul smiled wryly to himself. For in his imagination he could hear his father's voice: "What that boy needs is to be pushed out of the nest and made to use his own wings. Best thing in the world for him. Best thing in the world."

There was no help there.

And there was no real decision to be made. He had made it fifteen years ago, when he had turned his theodolyte and his alidade back to the company and had entered the ministry of the Protestant Episcopal Church.

2

Paul did not need to send for Skip the next morning. Skip came to him as soon as he had finished breakfast, bursting into the study with a light unanswered knock.

"Jean's still hanging on," he said, his brown eyes solemn, level eyebrows knit with anxiety. "What do we do next?"

"I'm going to see Frank this morning," Paul replied.

Paul usually placed his visitors in a leather chair lower than his own, feeling a slight advantage in being above them. But one did not place Skip. He established himself where he pleased, this time on the edge of Paul's desk, swinging one big foot carelessly shod in an ancient loafer topped by a violent sock of red and green. His mouth was generously curved, a bit truculent in repose but beautiful in laughter, curving over white, even teeth. And he laughed a great deal. But this morning there was no joy in him. Paul looked up and found himself thinking, to his surprise, not of Skip's failings but of his own.

"I'm sorry about Frank," he said.

"So'm I," agreed Skip sombrely. "I asked him why the heck he was packing a gun. He said he forgot it was in his pocket. I said, why did he ever put it in his pocket? And he mumbled something about there were times when he figured he's lived long enough."

"But why did he own a gun in the first place?"

"Oh, Frank's always played with guns. Target practice and so on. He's a crack shot. But I sure hope somebody'll take his guns away from his after this."

"They will. But I wouldn't worry about—the other. People who threaten to shoot themselves never do it."

"Yeah?" asked Skip dubiously, picking up a bit of string from the desk and twisting it around his forefinger. "You believe that, or is it just some more parental psychology?"

And he grinned at Paul with a loving, teasing look that tugged at his uncle's heart.

"I believe it," said Paul, wondering whether he did or not.

"That's good, anyway," muttered Skip, brooding over his string. Then he glanced up suddenly. "There really isn't anything to this God business, is there?"

"Skip!"

"Then where the heck is He? Why doesn't He *do* something? Why doesn't He help Frank when Frank really needs help and asks for it? Or why doesn't He crack down on me for talking against Him?"

"Don't say that!" Paul cried sharply.

But Skip only flung out inquiring hands. "Why?"

"Because He has made us with minds of our own and He doesn't interfere with our affairs..." The Reverend Paul Forrester then delivered a lecture on free will versus predestination. Just as he was warming up to a more or less convincing close, Skip interrupted him.

"Nuts," said that young one, more in sorrow than in anger. He strode over to the window, where his square shoulders blocked out the light. "The only person that ever told me anything sensible about God was Burnett McNeill," he muttered.

"That woman! When did she talk to you?"

"Oh, every now and then. I jump over her garden fence and chew the rag with her while she's weeding. I like her little house. It's different; flowers all over it."

"But Skip, she's—she's—where did you meet her?"

"Here," said Skip calmly. "In the back classroom, making those angels' wings for the Christmas pageant. Boy, what a job! Great, tall frames and here she was sewing that shiny rayon stuff on them in folds—gold to green and green to blue, like painting. So I wandered in and got to kidding her along, and, boy, I think she's swell!"

"Don't you know that she is not even a member of any church—that she—"

"Sure I know it. I asked her why. She said, well, if church helped people get hold of God's power so that it really worked, why, O.K. But she couldn't see that it did."

Sudden wrath held Paul speechless. It was bad enough for Miss McNeill to invade his parish house, even if some other woman did ask her to do so. But to proselytize his nephew into her unchurchly ideas about God—that was too much. Apparently she had no conception whatsoever of professional ethics.

"But Paul, about God," Skip persisted. "Why doesn't He take a hand in our affairs? You would, wouldn't you? When I'm unhappy, you help me. You want to help me. Well, you call Him 'Our Father...' If He really is a father, then why could He possibly *will* something like Frank's shooting Jean? How could He?"

Paul had no answer. "I don't know," he said in a whisper. Then sitting down in his revolving chair and pulling himself together: "It is not given us to know all of God's ways... wait! Don't go, Skip. There's something else I want to talk about." And he pointed the boy to the leather chair. "You know I—care a lot about you, don't you Skip?"

"Oh-oh," observed Skip warily. "That takeoff usually means trouble."

"I'm afraid it does... the same kind of trouble that I've often discussed with you... You know, Skip, I have never forbidden you to run around with the gang. But time and again I have requested you, for my sake, to—er—restrict their activities; just to say, 'Time to go home now' instead of saying, 'Let's go on to Tony's.' "

"Yeah, I know," admitted Skip, collapsing in the leather chair. "And I guess I should do better. I've tried to, once or twice, but then they say, 'Skip's got to get home to Morning Prayer' or something like that, and—"

"Aren't you rather cowardly to be afraid of a little kidding?"

"Yes," muttered Skip, elbows on knees, chin in hands. "And it worries me sometimes. You're a good egg, Paul, and I don't want to be a pain to you. You know, I do try to help around the place some—" He paused, embarrassed. "I'm a louse even to mention it. The truth is, I'm not too proud of myself, the way I am. And that picture in the paper—that was a bad break."

"A very bad break. And it came on the night of vestry meeting."

"Ouch," observed Skip. "I'm sorry, Paul. Afraid I kind of made things tough for you."

"It has made things tough for *you*," said Paul. "In fact, the vestry told me very plainly that they—they would prefer—for you to live elsewhere."

"So they want me to clear out? That's a laugh! Don't they know this is my home?"

The interview was going to be even more difficult than Paul had thought. "Skip," he stammered pleadingly, "would it matter so very much to you if—you were to live somewhere else for a while? You'll be going to college... You—you could go—out West somewhere—see the world—"

He saw the color drain from the boy's face and his lips settle into hard lines. Perhaps, he thought weakly, perhaps this threat would challenge Skip to mend his ways and the vestry would reconsider... After all, the matter had been laid on the table until July.

"Don't you see," he went on, swallowing hard, "that you're not setting a good example for other young people?"

"What am I supposed to do?" asked Skip, a knife-edge on his voice. "Go to the Boy Scout Jamboree and get an ice cream soda and then read the Bible quietly until bedtime?"

"You could certainly do something more constructive than running around to roadhouses every night," said Paul, sternly. "You could work, for instance. Sometimes I wish your father had left you no money—"

"I *am* looking for a counsellor job in a boys' camp, but—"

"But you won't get it. Not with your reputation. You are considered a—ringleader."

"Ringleader, heck," the boy scoffed. "It's just that I think of things before the other guys get around to it. I don't like to be bored, that's all. When the fellows get to just sitting on their butts chewing the rag, then I have to dream up something or I'd go nuts. I can't be like these guys that stand on street corners in front of drugstores and gawk at dames all day."

"Precisely," agreed Paul. "But that doesn't solve the immediate problem: it is perfectly true that a minister who cannot order his own household any better than I have done would be somewhat hampered in a youth program."

"So you're going to throw me out," Skip said in a flat voice. He looked at Paul, and then looked quickly away.

There was a dazed expression on his face, as if he had suddenly seen a stranger sitting there in Paul's chair.

"I guess I got it wrong," sighed the boy. He rose and groped for the door. "I thought you were—like my father, almost—"

"Skip!"

But the door banged shut. Skip was gone.

Paul told himself it would work out somehow—it must! Until now he had said too little perhaps, remembering the chains on his own boyhood and wanting the boy to go unchained and find his own way. He would change his methods. They could work it out, as a thousand other fathers and sons had worked it out.

A knock at the door brought him out of his reverie.

It was Ambrose-of-All-Saints, poking an unwary head into the study door. Ambrose was the sexton, or as he preferred to call himself, the verger. Never was a man who so appreciated his own position before his fellowmen. "This is Ambrose-of-All-Saints," he would intone gently into the telephone, a slight rising inflection on the "Saints" as though to say, "I do not wish to boast or to brag, but there it is: you *do* notice who is answering you, do you not? Ambrose—of-All-Saints?"

"That's too darn many saints," Skip would object. "I'd like it better if it was Some Saints and a Few Sinners."

Ambrose would chuckle delightedly, for he adored Skip. Janet also he adored. She teased him, yelled at him and treated him altogether as a friend and ally.

"Now, Ambrose, you remind me when it's time to vote," she would shout above her cake mixer when he prowled into the kitchen after hot water for the Altar Guild. "That's up to you, you know. If I don't vote and the country's lost, you've no one to blame but yourself."

Ambrose would fold his face into a big grin and say, "Not if you're going to vote Democratic, I won't."

But Paul was apt to make his sexton work. And Ambrose did not care for work. His back was humped, which was a mercy of the Lord to him. The vestry hired a woman to do the heavy cleaning and Ambrose concentrated on swinging open the folding sacristy doors of a Sunday morning, elegant in his silken verger's gown. And when a parish function reared its ugly head on the horizon and committees of ladies invaded the parish house, wanting to know where the flower baskets had been hidden and who had used their dishtowels and why there was dust on the piano, then Ambrose would discreetly disappear. There were two schools of thought concerning this vanishing act. Some claimed that on such menacing occasions Ambrose sneaked home to his wife. But as that lady was apt to seize upon him and cause him to run the washing machine, the said plan of action would seem to belie his usual policy, which he summed up thus: "If you can just keep clear of the womenfolk in this world, you'll get by all right." The other theory was that when the danger of work threatened, he would duck into the back room of Doc's drugstore and there sit on a stool and air his opinions upon the world in general until the crisis had passed. Paul himself leaned toward this latter hypothesis. Paul, moreover, was brought up in the grim New England tradition that if a man would not work, neither should he eat. This ideology was naturally distasteful to Ambrose, whose feelings toward The Boss were therefore somewhat mixed.

He took one look at Paul on this June morning and apparently perceived that the time was not good for consultation. So having poked his head into the door, he removed it as unobtrusively as possible.

"Oh no, you don't," thought Paul, and summoned him sternly into the room.

"Ambrose, how long is it since you've washed the parish car?" Paul had not inspected the car that morning. But this was an issue of long standing and he asked the question in every confidence that the matter was worth his attention.

"Can't wash it," chirped Ambrose sturdily.

"What do you mean, can't wash it?"

"Can't do it." Ambrose looked mysterious.

"Why?"

"Because you haven't backed the car up to the faucet for me," explained Ambrose, confident of victory, as usual.

"How often do I have to tell you: when you're ready to wash the car, ask Skip to put it where you want it?"

"Can't ask Skip. He's gone."

"Gone—where?"

"Lord knows. Like a bat out of h— he went, his old jalopy about to rattle to pieces—like a bat out of h—. He'll come to no good, driving like that." And before Paul could reply, Ambrose had departed leaving the door gingerly ajar behind him. "Better watch your step," Paul heard him say gloomily to the parishioner doing a bit of secretarial work in the office.

"Like a bat out of h--," Ambrose had said.

But he could not skulk in his study and moon about Skip, Paul told himself. He sighed, picked up the telephone and called the Morses' home.

"We've got him out on bail," said James. "Jean's getting well, you know... well, it took a lot of wangling, but we live next door to the police, and the chief's a pal of ours and—anyway, he's home. But he's kind of down in the dumps."

"I'll come around," promised Paul.

The boy's mother met him at the door, her face dark with suspicion.

"He's in the backyard," she said, and slammed the door in his face.

Paul gathered together his courage and trudged down the drive between the Morses' weather-beaten house and the old red brick police station. There was Frank, beside the garage, polishing his father's car.

"You're doing a good job there," observed Paul. Paul was neither a brilliant man nor a brave man and well he knew it. But he had a compassionate heart. Therefore when he entered with all simplicity into the washing of a car, there was a reality in his voice that one could not doubt.

Frank whirled about to face him, his gray-blue eyes frightened, his freckled face set and drawn. He looked like a crouching animal, waiting, its ears back, not knowing whether to run or to fight. "I guess I—let you down," he muttered.

"I guess I let *you* down," Paul replied. It never occurred to Paul to utter pompous words in order to cover his failures. What he believed, that he said: "I *know* that there is power in the Church. I *know* that a man can get help at the altar. But apparently I do not know how to get it across to you. All I can say is, if you'll keep on trying, I'll keep on trying."

Frank's drawn face relaxed a little. "Jean—if she dies— Gee, how I wish I'd shot myself instead! Parson, you don't think God could want Jean to die, do you?"

"I do not."

"Then pray for her, will you, Parson?"

"I will," promised Paul, the prayer for All Conditions of Men running through his mind: "Especially Jean, for whom our prayers are desired: that it may please Thee to comfort and relieve them according to their several necessities, giving them patience under their sufferings and a happy issue out of all their afflictions."

"You know I never meant to do no harm, don't you?" asked Frank, his frozen face suddenly breaking, as though on the verge of tears.

"Of course I know that, Frank!"

"But I can't understand it—what it is that comes over a fellow! Ever since I was in Korea it's as if another guy's sitting in here" and he thumped his chest "grinning at me like, and making me do things I don't want to do. Sometimes I wonder, am I going nuts? But I'm not, am I?"

"I don't think so," said Paul. "But you know, there are mind doctors just as there are body doctors. I'm not sick, myself. But sometimes I go to a doctor just to get my sinuses cleared out. You aren't nuts. But maybe a mind doctor could clear out this queer feeling inside of you."

"Uh-uh." And with a grunt of rejection Frank turned away from him and began once more to polish the car. "I've seen guys go to them mental hospitals and have them shock treatments. I've seen 'em. Nothing doing. If God can't help me, then after all, there are ways "

Paul sighed. He had often suggested psychiatric help to Frank's family, but they had fixed him with stony eyes and with one accord refused. "Well, then," pleaded Paul, "will you keep coming to the communion services so as to give God a chance to reach you?"

He spoke in all sincerity, for so he had learned to apprehend the Almighty. His churchly soul, grounded on the "realities," grasped nothing of the splendor of the Creator in light and air, in the vital earth renewing itself unfailingly from season to season, in the far stars swinging together in the harmony of eternity. "Sermons in stones, books in the running brooks" meant to Paul only excuses to stay away from church and play golf. He knew but one way to see the eternal glory of God, and that was in the face of Jesus Christ his Lord. "God of God, Light of Light, Very God of Very God": if ever Paul knew rapture, it was when he intoned those words before the altar in the hushed church. The processional cross was to him a symbol of this Reality, and his heart bowed with the congregation as they bent their heads before it. The clear tones of the organ proclaimed to him the footsteps of the entering Christ, and he stilled himself with wonder to receive Him. So when he asked the young man to come to church, he was not uttering platitudes. He was holding out in humble wistfulness the way of life that he felt most real . . . the way of the Great Shepherd, leading His flock in paths of peace.

"You don't want me in your church *now*, do you?" cried Frank, amazement in his scared blue eyes. "I wouldn't even go to the garage today. I was afraid they'd kick me out."

"Of course I want you in church!" said Paul firmly. He could see Angus McGhann, his bushy eyebrows knit in a fierce line of disapproval. He could see Priscilla peering delightedly about her, hardly able to wait for the sevenfold Amen in order to rush about and acquaint people with the rector's new goings-on: "My dear, we have *never* had people like that in our church . . ." He could hear Opal, his most twittering spinster, "Oh, Father Forrester, *who* do you think I saw in church? That *dreadful* young man! Oh, *dear!*"

"I kind of wish I'd kept on now," murmured Frank.

"Kept on—what?"

"Don't you remember? My brother Jim and me come to some of them talks of yours, a couple years ago, just to see if—if—" He coughed apologetically and finished, "But we couldn't make head or tail of it."

Paul remembered. They had attended three confirmation lectures and had dropped away, as people so often did, unable to comprehend the mysteries of the Church.

"Yes, I wish you had kept on," sighed Paul. "But it's not too late. We'll have some more confirmation lectures soon. Meanwhile, come to the church anyway, even if you do not receive." And without waiting for Frank to say yes or no, he went away.

The moment he was out of Frank's sight he remembered Skip, and his heart sank. Surely there would be word from him by dinnertime! But when Paul had lunched with a diocesan committee on the Church and finished an afternoon of calls, he did not see Skip's souped-up jalopy parked at its usual rakish angle on the patch of cinders beside the garage.

Janet met him at the kitchen door, her mouth pulled down in taut lines, her eyes big and sober. "Skip's been away all day and I haven't heard a word from him," she announced.

"Don't get hysterical," Paul snapped. "Skip often stays away as long as this. I can think of any number of places where he might be."

"But he usually *tells* me," insisted Janet.

Paul trudged up the stairs and the open door of Skip's room filled him with a quite unreasonable desolation. Skip might be anywhere, at the seashore in Buddy's sailboat, watching a doubleheader at the baseball park, swimming in a still pool among the pines. At dinner Janet looked at him reproachfully and asked, "What did you say to Skip this morning about that picture in the paper?"

"Very little." He remembered Skip's words: "I thought you were—like my father, almost—" And he went out to make his evening calls with those words ringing in his mind.

"No use waiting up for him," said Janet grimly when Paul returned. "I'm going to bed."

"Buzz the buzzer for me when he comes," said Paul.

He knew that his mounting uneasiness would not let him sleep. So as long as he could, he forced his mind to work. Twelve o'clock came and passed, one o'clock, one-thirty, while Paul balanced the church accounts and his own with his meticulous double-entry bookkeeping, while he answered letters and filled out parish reports. At last his tired mind faltered and he could work no longer. Perhaps Skip had come home, he thought, and Janet had forgotten to call him. He turned off the lights, put on the deadlatch, banged the door behind him and strode to the rectory. He knew without looking at Skip's room that it was empty.

He went to bed and read a detective story. Two o'clock . . .

Janet's door opened and he snapped out his light so that she might not come and speak to him—

Again he read and dozed a little, book in hand. He awoke with a sick plunge of the heart and looked at his watch . .

three-fifteen. Paul leaped out of bed. He must do something, he thought. But what could he do? Call Buddy's house or Al's or Pinky's in this dead hour before the dawn? "Where's Skip?" And he imagined sleepy voices replying, "Why, I don't know . . . " Or should he ask the police to trace him? That would indeed put the final touch on Skip's disgust. Just the same, he opened his door and started downstairs with a blind urge toward action. At the same moment Janet stepped out of her room and they faced each other.

"Something's happened," whispered Janet with white lips.

"Nonsense! If there'd been an accident the police would have phoned us, wouldn't they?"

Even as he spoke, the telephone split the silence of the front hall.

"There he is!" breathed Paul, with a vast sigh of relief. It would be Skip's voice: "Paul, I'm terribly sorry, but here I am, stuck on Route 29—flat tire—yes, I tried to, but my spare's shot too—" Or, "I meant to be home ages ago, but, gosh, we ran out of gas in the pines. Had to walk eight miles to this phone—"

"Yes?" answered Paul eagerly.

"Is this the Reverend?"

Paul felt blindly for the chair beside the hall table and sat down.

"This is the State Police," said a deep, grave voice. "Afraid I have bad news for you. There's been an accident. The license gives the Rectory of All Saints, Mapleton, as the address."

"My—nephew." Paul could hardly get the words out.

Janet, as white as her nightgown, leaned against the wall, her hands spread out against it as though for support.

"The car apparently went off the road, head on into a tree. We have him here at Brookside Hospital."

"I'll come immediately."

"Reverend—" the grave voice hesitated. "Sorry to tell you this. Come, of course, but—"

"Is he dead?"

"Not—yet. But the doctor doubts if he can live until you get here."

Paul hung up the phone and dashed upstairs, jerking out

to Janet the state trooper's words. He hauled on a pair of pants, flung a coat over his pajamas, shoved his feet into bedroom slippers and made for the car. By the time he had started the engine, Janet was with him in dress and loafers.

In dead silence they shot along the ten miles of empty highway, screeched into the side road to the hospital and drew up at the accident entrance. Two state troopers, solemnly awaiting them, escorted them to the emergency ward. There was Skip, stretched fully clothed upon a bed, covered with blood and cinders, his face swollen, his body contorted and still.

"Is he dead?" asked Paul.

The officer only said again, "Not yet."

"Well, *get somebody!*" ordered Paul.

At this a nurse appeared reproachfully from down the ward. "There's nothing we can do for him . . . I'm sorry."

"But *there is!*" cried Paul. And he added as though to himself, "I've stood by enough deathbeds so I ought to know! You can always manage to prolong life somehow."

The nurse looked at Skip and shook her head. "It would be no use," she said, compassionately.

"You call your head surgeon or I will!" thundered Paul.

"Call the doctor," growled the trooper out of the corner of his mouth as he jerked his thumb toward the door.

The nurse departed. Moments later or hours later the doctor arrived. He felt the boy over with practiced hands and shook his head. "I'm sorry."

"You mean it's hopeless?" asked Paul.

"I'm afraid so. Internal injuries, bleeding from the mouth, God knows how many bones fractured, skull crushed in . . . I'm sorry."

Janet had been standing like a statue, eyes glued to her son. But on this she broke, and being Janet, broke into fury and not into tears. "Hopeless or not, you people are going to find a room and a bed and wash this muck off him!" she stormed.

"Can't you give him something—a stimulant or something—just to keep him alive a little while?" her brother pleaded.

They humored him, respecting perhaps his office as a priest, and the crushed body that had been Skip was taken to a private room. And still the laboring heart beat on.

Paul held his cold hand, fearsomely still, and whispered, "Skip! Skip!" calling him, calling him, while the tears ran unheeded down his cheeks.

Janet on the other side of the bed awoke as from a trance to cry, "Paul!" her eyes blazing with sudden life. "He's not going to die!" said Janet. "I won't have it!" Then her own face quivered into tears and she dropped Skip's hand and dashed out of the room.

When she returned, her face once more was still. But the frozen look had left it. "Are you praying for life?" she demanded fiercely. "Or are you praying for the repose of his soul?"

Paul could only shake his head. He was not praying at all, only calling in a whisper, "Skip! Skip!"

"Then pray!" ordered Janet. "Why do you think you're a minister?"

Paul tried to pray. "Oh God, give him back and I'll do better. Oh God, what a fool I am—what a fool—to think of sending him away so that I could teach other boys to be good, when I can't teach my own! Oh God, give him back, give him back!"

But these wild words did not befit a minister who prayed. "Heavenly Father, give me strength to say, 'Thy will be done.'" No, no! He could not pray as he knew he should! He could only look at the battered face that had once been Skip and say, "Oh God, give him back, give him back!" And all the while something within him said, "It's too late."

3

Gray dawns and golden sunsets came and passed, and the boy still lived.

Dr. Cameron would stand by the bed, his hand on the strengthening pulse, and shake his head in bewilderment. "Never saw anything like it," he would murmur.

"There's nothing strange about it," Janet told the doctor one day, while Paul on the other side of the bed lifted sorrowing eyes and said nothing. "Skip's getting well, that's all."

Dr. Cameron smiled and sighed. There was sadness in his gentle, fatherly face, yet one saw beneath its wrinkles the roadbeds of old smiles. He studied the boy, recognizable again in spite of bruises and blackened eye sockets, with the compassion of one whose life is spent among the sorrowing. He who loves a few can break his heart when those few die. He who loves humanity can watch while many die and still be grounded in serenity.

"Mrs. Anderson, I've told you, haven't I—" began the doctor in the voice of a father to a small child.

"Yes, you've told me, Dr. Cameron," said Janet in her decisive way. "Now you listen while I tell you: *Skip's going to live.* Don't you believe God can do anything around here?"

"I do, my dear, I do," the doctor answered mildly. "But I think man can be presumptuous and ask too much. My question is: if Skip does live, how much mind will he have left? The skull was crushed into the brain, you know."

"I notice you say 'was.' " Paul's voice was low and hesitating.

"Yes. We elevated the depressed fragments of course. It seems to be—shaping out," murmured the doctor, his own voice uncertain as he looked at Skip. For the boy's whole body, sunk as it was in a profound coma, nevertheless seemed to draw itself back into the shape and form of life.

"If God can do that, why can't He restore life too?" demanded Janet, and it must be confessed that her tones were belligerent rather than devotional.

Dr. Cameron laid his hand on hers. "Dear lady," he said with a pleading note in his voice, "you keep right on praying and God bless you. But as a doctor, it is my duty to tell you what I know: nature does not rebuild brain cells. If a part of the brain is really destroyed, then—Skip will not be the same person again."

As the days went by, the swelling left Skip's face and he looked like himself: very pale beneath his fading sunburn, very black under the eyes, but himself, lying in a heavy sleep that might have been death.

"Can't you see that he is getting well?" demanded Janet of the doctor two weeks later.

"I do not know how to interpret what I see," Dr. Cameron assured her. And he added in a lower voice, "Or—how to credit it—unless—" He studied Janet speculatively and said no more.

"Well?" demanded that lady. "What do you see?"

"The incisions are healing," admitted the doctor. "The shoulders appear to be knitting with amazing speed. As for the internal injuries that we feared, apparently there are none. So far as we can tell, considering that all his food is taken intravenously, his body is functioning normally—except, of course, for the brain—"

"What makes you think anything is wrong with his brain?" Janet asked him in embattled tones. "People recover from concussion."

But the doctor only smiled his gentle smile.

"I'm willing to bet you," said Janet, tightening her lips, "that he'll wake up one of these days, just as if he had been asleep."

Dr. Cameron looked at the boy again and shook his head. "I suppose anything is possible," he said doubtfully. "The brain may, after all, be intact."

"He's going to get well," said Janet to her brother for the hundredth time when she went home that evening.

But Paul did not believe her.

He went about his duties with the hand of death upon his heart. He had failed Frank. He had failed Skip. Years ago, desiring to help people such as these, he had given up money and freedom, he had given up the shining desert with its icy peaks touching the stars—only that he might serve the Lord and feed His sheep. And here were His sheep, His lambs—lost. "Don't be a quitter," whispered Paul as he drove home from the hospital on a July morning dark with thunderstorms. "Even if you've lost Skip, you've still got to take care of Frank—for Skip's sake." He should have been encouraged, thinking of Frank, for the girl Jean was making a recovery. But Paul's heart did not lift as he remembered the bewildered young man with the freckled, frozen face, sitting hour after hour in his home watching a merciful television. Paul had given him much advice, and Paul was completely right. Yet in another way he was completely wrong, for his words were based on reality and Frank was drifting away from reality. His eyes told the story: blue eyes that had lost their life, like blue skies darkening and sombre after the sun has gone. Paul had no way of following Frank into this world of unreality. There was One, Paul thought, Who could follow. But how could he open pious lips and say, "God will help you," when heavy day followed heavy day and God did not help? How could Paul say, "Trust in the Lord," when Skip lay in a hospital room harshly bright, since light and dark were alike to him, and Paul had no way of knowing whether his wandering soul was yet in this life or whether it was not?

Paul drove past drugstores and radio shops, past closed churches standing lonely among the filling stations, and drawing up beside the sheltering gray stone of All Saints, knew that he had lost Frank, too.

He entered the shuddering loneliness of the rectory and closed the door against the rain that cracked down on the roof. If only it would rain like this tomorrow, he thought grimly, maybe the congregation would stay at home. But just the same, he would have to preach. In rain or sunshine, in life or death, still he must climb into the pulpit on a Sunday and utter words concerning God and man, time and eternity. And what did he know more than another that he should open his mouth? "As for man, his days are as grass; as a flower of the field, so he flourisheth. For the wind passeth over it, and it is gone, and the place thereof shall know it no more." On that he could preach with conviction. With a wry smile he imagined himself doing so, the ladies of his congregation dabbing at their eyes, the men with knit brows thinking, "Tough luck, but after all, the young one brought it on himself." No one had said these words to his face, but Paul had felt them strike against his heart. Even old Ambrose, every fold of his ancient face sagging with woe, was known to mutter to himself, "I told him no good would come of all that running around. I told him—" He would preach on Church history, Paul decided.

And so he did, getting through it the best way he could as for the past two weeks he had gritted his teeth and forced himself through all his parish work. He had omitted only one small thing: on the past Sunday he had not stood at the front door, sweltering in the heat of sun on stone, to shake hands with the congregation. But on this Sunday he returned to his post. After all, he told himself grimly, pulling his surplice over his head and handing it to the ever-present Priscilla, he could not skulk in the study the rest of his days. So he marched down the side aisle to the front door where the congregation filtered out into the June sun.

"Good morning, Mrs. Bragg, glad to see you out this morning. Yes indeed, it's a hot day. Oh, much the same, thank you. Morning, Bert. Missing your golf this morning? Won't St. Peter be surprised! Oh, much the same, thank you, much the same...Well, Sally, you kept your doll nice and quiet in church, didn't you? Yes indeed, I remember. I told you she ought to come to church. Well now, wasn't that a good idea, huh? She didn't say a word, did she? Yes indeed, Mrs. Mitchell, we like to have the children come....Much the same, Mrs. Mitchell, thank you. No, not conscious—no."

Paul's voice was hearty and his handclasp strong. He had been brought up among a people who set their faces and did their work, come what might.

The line thinned out. Paul sighed and fumbled in his pocket for a handkerchief. Then just as he turned to go, there was a scuttling and a twittering beside him and Opal Oldershaw, his nemesis, untangled herself from two other lingering females and descended upon him.

"Oh, Mr. Forrester," she breathed, clutching his hand in both of hers and looking up at him with melting eyes. "Oh, I do think you are so brave and wonderful! Oh yes, I do! Oh, dear Mr. Forrester, you don't know how much I've thought of you!"

"I bet I do too," thought Paul.

"Oh, I've just prayed for that boy to get well for your sake—only for your sake! Oh, Mr. Forrester, I do think drink is the most terrible thing, don't you?" And she drew her mouth into a small "o" above her retreating chin.

"My nephew was not drunk," Paul said stiffly, after he had digested this remark.

"Oh, but Mr. Forrester, how can you *tell*? I mean—I mean—"

"I can tell very well, Miss Oldershaw. Because I know Skip."

And with the heat of anger flooding a face already hot enough, Paul fled before her following remarks and drew the sacristy door closed behind him. "Darn fool woman," he thought most reprehensibly. Then he realized with a wave of grief that no doubt all his congregation thought that Skip had been intoxicated . . . He stood still for a moment, gazing out into the cemetery, green and steaming under the June sun.

Nevertheless, he knew it was not so. "I'm not a sap, Paul," Skip had told him. "And I like to live, same as anybody. So don't worry. Takes more than a couple of beers to make me drunk." And he had patted his strong stomach with pride.

No, Skip had not been drunk. But—the boy was a superb driver, managing the car as if it were part of his own person. . .*Then what had happened?*

He would never know.

He drew in his breath with a sharp sigh and turned away from the window. Priscilla McGhann was billowing about the sacristy with every sail set, like a ship on the high seas. There was none today to stand between her and that ordering of the house of the Lord which was her delight. Usually Janet, grim upon the threshold, scanned her activities with a critical eye and offered advice as soothing to Priscilla's overstuffed bosom as a red rag to a bull. There was a variance of opinion between these two embattled females. Both considered themselves the handmaids of the Lord, presiding over the sacred vestments by divine right. Paul, with a finesse worthy of an international diplomat, had persuaded the two to alternate their laudable services. But the difference in their opinions still reared its ugly head to confound them. For Priscilla from time immemorial had ironed vestments in the office, both ears cocked toward the keyhole of the study door. Janet on the other hand deemed the choir room a more seemly place for her labors and from time to time removed the ironing board thither.

Priscilla moved it to the office.

Janet moved it back.

And when the battle reached its height, both ladies, exhausted, carried the ironing board only as far as the hallway, where it sat irately against the wall, announcing to all and sundry that the feud was on.

But since Skip's accident the ironing board had remained in the office, or the workroom, as Priscilla preferred to call it.

Paul glanced briefly at his worthy servitor and noted with certain qualms the triumphant gleam in her eye. "What's she up to now?" he wondered.

Ambrose, seeing Paul, slunk away down the corridor with the smug expression of one who has just heard a particularly juicy bit of gossip. Had Paul been less preoccupied he would have known immediately that the two of them had been in conference. And remembering that Priscilla was the sister of his senior warden, he might have guessed the subject of their talk. But Paul's soul was in a hospital room. Paul removed his cassock and hung it casually on a hook inside the vestment closet.

"*Mr. Forrester!*" boomed Priscilla, not unkindly but nevertheless with considerable fervor. "How often must I ask you to use a *hanger?* The way you sling your cassock on that hook, it can fall off just as well as it can stay on! Now please—"

But Paul, meekly putting the cassock into her outstretched hand, retreated out the door toward his home. There stood Janet in the hall, in her fighting pose, arms akimbo, chin up and lips pulled down.

"I've just heard that you threw Skip out of the rectory," she announced without preamble. "Is that true?"

"Who's been talking to you?"

"Ambrose. Priscilla told him . . . and her brother told her."

Naturally. Inevitably. He might have foreseen this.

"So now I know why he crashed!" cried Janet, her eyes bright with anger and tears. "I *wondered!* Because Skip drives better than you walk."

"Janet, Janet!" Paul's voice sounded strange even to himself. "You don't mean—you can't mean that Skip—"

"Of course he didn't do it on purpose, if that's what you're trying to say. But he *was* mad and upset, and so . . . And if he dies . . ." She broke off abruptly and her face changed. "Don't—don't look like that," she muttered hastily, the lightning of her wrath ending in tears.

Paul could feel the blood drain out of his face, leaving it prickly and cold.

"I'm sorry," faltered Janet. "I shouldn't have said that."

But she had said it.

"Well, don't just stand there looking like a scared rabbit!" cried his sister. Demonstration was not encouraged among the Forresters. So Janet did not kiss him, although he thought for a startled moment that she would. But she took him by both arms and gave him a friendly little shake. "Come and lie down while I get dinner ready," she pleaded. "And I'll promise not to shoot off my mouth anymore. You're white as a sheet."

Paul lay down as ordered, putting a newspaper over his head, but he did not rest. The thought that she had suggested was not new. He had been trying to push it away from him. Now it was here. He would never know to what extent he was responsible for his nephew's death. Unless Skip roused for some brief, lucid moment before departing, he would never know.

Paul could not sleep that night. Hour after hour crept by and still he lay awake, listening to the swish and roar of traffic that jammed the town's main street. He heard every bus that churned up to the corner and hissed and spat and paused. He heard the loud laughter of those who waited for the bus in the dead of night. As night wore on and traffic thinned, even an occasional footstep down the sidewalk smote his drifting consciousness and called him back from the fringe of uneasy slumber. Through his sorrow drifted a vague uneasiness, an expectancy.

"It's just a hangover from the old days," he muttered to himself, remembering many a night when he had lain awake waiting for the click of Skip's latchkey in the front door.

From the hall below he heard a small, tinkering sound. A latchkey. The front door opened. Had Janet been out? No . . .

There was no question about it. He heard footsteps.

Paul knew stories of those whose spirits in departing had found a way back to their homes. But he did not believe such childish tales.

There are no ghosts, he told himself, stiff with terror.

But there were footsteps in the hall, footsteps that he knew, coming toward the staircase. Up the steps—across the hall—then the footsteps paused.

"Hey! Where's everybody?"

As Paul leaped out of bed his door opened and there stood Skip; not a ghost, Skip, black around the eyes and very pale but quite alive. Paul's mind went blank for a moment. The next he knew he was clutching the boy to him, comforting his heart with the warm, live feel of him, even comforting his nostrils with the smell of the young body perspiring a little of a summer's night.

"Here! What the heck! You'd think I was dead or something!" laughed Skip, patting his uncle on the back.

Janet burst into the room, her curly hair on end. "*Skip!* How'd you get here?" she cried.

"Hitchhiked," Skip said casually.

Janet, who never reacted as anyone would expect, leaned back against the door and laughed until the tears stood in her eyes. "Well, you dumb cluck," she said at last, pulling his face down to hers and kissing him, "you'd better get to bed before you have a relapse."

"Bed, heck," said Skip. "I'm hungry."

He swayed a little, and Janet pushed him firmly into a chair. "How on earth did you manage to get out of there?" she gasped, still laughing a little and crying at the same time.

"Walked out," grinned Skip, leaning his head against the back of the chair. "How else could I?"

"But—your clothes—"

"Looked in the closet and there they were. Somebody

had swiped my wallet. Oh, well. Nothing in it anyway. But my latchkey was in the inside coat pocket where it always stays, so I was O.K."

"And—you just *walked out?*" asked Paul recovering his voice. He drew up a chair and sat down beside Skip, his hand on the boy's shoulder as if to reassure himself that the tall, gaunt body was really alive. "Didn't anybody stop you?"

"Nobody around up there. I heard a lot of commotion so I went downstairs to the basement and there was everybody running around like mad. Cops—stretchers—all kinds of bums that looked a lot worse than I did. So if anybody saw me they didn't pay any attention and I skint out and picked up a ride on the street corner."

Before anyone could speak, the telephone rang, and Paul stepped to the extension in the upstairs hall. "It's all right. He's here," he said to the excited voice that cracked into the phone. "Hitchhiked . . . I'm sorry you can't believe it, but it is true. No, it's not necessary for you to speak to anyone else. This is Mr. Forrester speaking, and I assure you that I am in my right mind ... No, it ... it doesn't seem necessary for you to send an ambulance ... I'm sorry it will make trouble for you ... Yes, yes, I understand ... I will come to the hospital in the morning and see the superintendent ..."

"Let me take over." Skip wove his way to the phone and grabbed the receiver out of his uncle's hand. "Hi there—this is me, and I'm not coming back. I didn't like that place. You can keep it. 'Bye now." And having disposed of that matter, he hung up the phone and sat down, a little white about the lips. "When do we eat?" he demanded.

"Right away! Right away!" And Janet, still laughing, threw on her kimono and dashed down to the kitchen.

Skip leaned forward and peered at his image in Paul's mirror. "Who's been hitting me?" he demanded. "I sure have got one beaut of a shiner."

"There was an accident," Paul said gently, one hand on the boy's knee. "Don't you remember?"

"Makes me dizzy to try to remember," muttered Skip, lying back and closing his eyes.

"Never mind it then."

But Skip went on haltingly: "I was in a bad mood, I

don't know why. Driving kind of fast. Along zoomed a car, flying low, oh boy, really flying low, all over the road. I jerked the wheel once—that's all. Say, where's Jemima?" he cried, sitting up and opening his eyes.

"On the junk heap," Paul told him grimly, thinking of that driver flying low and not stopping to see what lay beneath the crushed car at the bottom of the steep bank.

"Aw, heck," mourned Skip. "She was a good old bus, Jemima was."

"Never mind. It's enough that you are alive," said Paul in a choked voice. And he shuddered suddenly.

"Put on something for Pete's sake," advised Skip.

Paul was not cold. But he went to the closet obediently, and found his robe.

"I was far away," murmured Skip, his head against the chair back, his eyes closed. "Way off somewhere." Skip's voice was a thin thread. "It was funny. Like a dream. I can't quite—explain—the way it was. But she kept calling me. 'Skip! Come back!' And finally somebody said, 'O.K., Skip, you'd better go back. She's calling you.'"

"Who was calling you?"

"Burnett."

Paul, in the act of putting on his bathrobe, stopped as if he had been shot, one sleeve off and one sleeve on. *"Who?"*

"Burnett McNeill. She came to see me every day. They thought I was asleep, but something inside of me would always wake up when she was there. Then it would make a fight for it, trying to get back. Boy, it was tough going, too," he added meditatively.

Burnett McNeill. That woman, who without his permission had sat in his own parish house, making angels' wings and teaching his nephew strange things about God ... whose door, of an evening, was open to all kinds of unknown men ... that unacceptable person had been to see Skip every day behind his back! Murmuring something about helping Janet, Paul dragged his bathrobe sleeve on to his other arm and ran down to the kitchen. He closed the kitchen door behind him and leaned against it, trembling a little.

"Janet," he panted. "Do you know anything about that woman going to see Skip?"

"What woman?" asked Janet coolly, lifting a saucepan from the stove.

"Burnett McNeill," snapped Paul, and he thought, a name like a whiplash. Women should be named Anne or Mary or at worst Rosamund. *Burnett*, indeed!

"Certainly," Janet replied, lifting her chin defiantly. "I phoned her that first night."

"Why, for heaven's sake? You know what I think of her."

"And I don't care a snap of my finger what you think of her. Skip had to get well. That's why."

Paul's little world of church and prayer book whirled around his ears. "Now listen, Janet," he pleaded. "You can't possibly think that Skip got well because *she* prayed for him."

"But I do."

"Janet!"

"There was Georgie," said Janet firmly, pouring out a glass of milk. "Nobody expected him to live until Burnett went to see him. And there was Mrs. Stockly and that young Perry fellow and—"

"But why would God answer her prayers and not answer mine?" demanded Paul.

"You didn't believe," said Janet. "Move out of the way now. I've got to take this tray up to Skip before he charges down here after his food."

"She can't come to the rectory!"

Janet set the tray on the kitchen table and faced her brother. "Unless Skip can go to see her, Burnett is coming here," she announced.

"But what would people say?" And Paul imagined with horror the round "o" of Opal Oldershaw's mouth if she should see that woman darkening the rectory door.

"I don't give a continental what they say. I'm not risking Skip's having a relapse just because we've made an act of faith and then gone back on it."

"The parish is upset enough about Skip without this," worried Paul. "They want him to leave . . . now don't get excited! He won't leave. I would leave myself before I would send him away now. And I hope he will never remember..." A small fear shivered in Paul's heart as he said this, for he knew that some day Skip would—remember.

"Now you're showing a little spunk for once in your

life," said Janet. "Just use some of that same courage about Burnett. Heck with what anybody says. If there's something in religion that you don't know, it's up to you to find it out."

"But the whole New Thought idea is revolting to me!" cried Paul, leaning with both hands on the white enamel table. "All this God in you and God in me and God in everybody—all this you're Christ and I'm Christ and everybody's Christ—it's not *sound!* There's no dignity in it, no reverence, no understanding of redemption or salvation! It—it outrages everything I have been taught!"

"And how do you know she thinks that way?" Janet asked.

"Well—"

"And what have you been taught?" demanded Janet.

"Well, after all, I have been to seminary for three years."

"Yeah, so you know all about religion except how to make it work." And with this parting shot, Janet picked up her tray and marched upstairs.

4

Burnett McNeill was painting with the fierce concentration that was her power. June sunlight shone clear and cold through the great north window of her studio, but she was not aware of it. Burnett lived in an old house, the small front yard clinging to Main Street, the backyard sloping sharply down into the meadows and orchards of the Jersey countryside. The studio, boldly constructed of cement and glass, had been added to the back of the house, above the garage. It was plain and bare, furnished only with easels and worktables, high stool and a single wicker chair, adorned with nothing except the paintings that leaned against the walls and formed a casual and brilliant panelling beneath the windows. Bird songs floated in through the open eastern windows, but Burnett did not hear them. She did not even notice the lilting melody of a thrush singing in the ancient apple tree whose branches touched the window-pane. She would lean forward and paint and then lean back, studying her work. Scarlet bird-of-paradise flowers lit the foreground of the painting. Its background was a dark jungle of matted vines and a tree trunk bent over shadows deep and black. A panther crouched beneath the tree trunk, its green eyes burning, its face mysterious, immobile, hauntingly still.

"More red in the shadow," decided Burnett, her lips drawn together with the intentness of her thought.

She did not hear the doorbell ring nor the footsteps of her helper nor even the opening of the studio door.

"Miss Burnett, it's that minister—Skip's uncle," said Madeleine.

Burnett whirled about. "Heavens!" she cried, hastily slipping off her paint-smudged smock. "Do you suppose he's found out?"

"He looks kind of worried." Madeleine's voice was rich and sweet, as Negro voices are, but her pronunciation differed little from Burnett's own. Like Burnett, she had been born in Mapleton.

"Then pray that I don't get mad and yell at him," said Burnett, and she added, "I'm glad he came on the day you're here." She clicked down the narrow hall in scarlet sandals, her red printed skirt rippling as she walked, its palm trees and Mexicans, burros and cactus waving in the wind of her swift motion.

The minister rose hastily as she entered the little living room. Then at her request he sat down again in the rocking chair that had been her grandmother's, primly upholstered in black with a sprigged pattern of small flowers. Burnett's living room, and indeed all of the original house, was as old-fashioned as the studio was new. It had grown after that manner, upon that spot. No spinning wheels and churns cluttered the room, no iron pots hung in the fireplace, no oil lamps adorned the mantelpiece. The furniture remained where it had always been, comfortable and a bit shabby. The ruffled white curtains were tied back as Burnett's grandmother had tied them back. Burnett herself, in the Windsor rocking chair with the high back, fitted into this room as truly as she did in the studio. Perhaps it was because she made no effort to be one thing or another, but was merely herself. Her hair was drawn back rather sternly from her broad forehead and coiled mysteriously into a smooth black crown, blue where the sunlight shone on it through the small-paned windows. She sat erect and with folded hands as her grandmother might have sat, waiting for the nervous minister to announce the subject of his call. And she thought, "I should have asked Madeleine to pray for my heart to be still."

What was there about this man that touched her heart? She did not know. But so it had been since she saw him first at the christening of her brother's baby. She had stood, stiff and cold in the sanctimonious dim light, resenting the absurd medieval works of the baptismal service, when her eyes had fixed themselves upon the minister. He was looking down at the infant, folded lovingly in his white vestments. Soft light from the stained-glass window touched his face. Or was it a light that shone from within? And suddenly, to Burnett, he was beautiful; his brown eyes with their dark, level brows, still for once, instead of drawn together as now in an unconscious frown of tension; his features, somewhat nondescript but rather delicately modeled; his lips, gently curved in relaxation . . . Burnett had forgotten the cold stone church and the jarring words of the prayer book and had watched Paul Forrester. He took the baby to the high stone altar and held her there, then lifted her up to the cross. What was he saying? "Patricia, this is Jesus! Jesus, this is Patricia—"

Burnett, erect in her grandmother's chair, wished that her flighty imagination would not bring such notions to her mind. She wished that she did not see beneath the minister's stern face a wistfulness that moved her. She wished that she had not made the angels' wings for his midnight service, leaping at the suggestion because it would bring her into his parish house. It had done no good. He had only drawn his brows together and glared at her as he was doing now.

The minister, clearing his throat, was apparently through with his few rambling remarks and was about to state his real concern.

"Skip came home last night," said Paul Forrester abruptly.

"Skip—*came home?*" Burnett was startled out of her studied calm.

"About three o'clock," Paul said. "The front door opened and in he came. Hitchhiked."

"But—he might have got lost—he might have been run over—"

"I gather that you did not expect this particular development."

"Good heavens, no!" cried Burnett, wondering whether the minister, who evidently knew of her visits to Skip, had come to thank or to blame her. "How ever did he manage to get away?"

"Just walked out," said Paul grimly. "I hear that you went to see him every day," he added, turning a little red.

"I did."

"Do you think it was quite—ethical—to do that without my knowledge?"

"I don't give a darn whether it's ethical or not. I love Skip. I wanted him to get well. So I went." And Burnett's heart said, "And I love *you*. I could not bear for you to break your heart over the boy." Did she? Absurd! A country minister, with worried eyebrows and droopy shoulders?

"Do you seriously think," Paul said, "that he got well because you prayed for him?"

Burnett's eyes were wide with astonishment. "Do you doubt it?" she asked. "What does his doctor say?"

"That it was a miracle," Paul said reluctantly.

"All right then."

"But why should you assume that *your* prayers saved him? After all, I prayed too. All of us did."

"And how?" Burnett interrupted, furious, for this man who could move her to tenderness could also sting her into rage. "Give him patience under his sufferings—nevertheless, not my will but Thy will—"

"What's wrong with that?"

"Nothing, except that it doesn't work!" On a sudden impulse she rose and led him into her studio. "Look at that," she commanded, pointing to her painting. "Suppose I said, 'Let it be a panther—or a tabby cat—or a tea cozy; whatever You like, Lord.' And suppose I looked at a tea cozy while I painted it?" she demanded.

"I don't understand," said Paul, blinking in the strong light and looking with bewilderment at the panther.

"Prayer is a creative art," Burnett explained. "One of the laws of creativity is that a person must fix his attention on the thing that he desires to create and believe that it is going to be accomplished. Did you think of Skip as well and believe that he was going to recover?"

"No," Paul admitted.

"Well, then."

"Are you actually trying to say that my prayers for him were of no avail and that yours made him well?"

Burnett nodded. "Mine opened the way for God to make him well. Yours did not. And yet, I know it sounds terrible to you! As if I were talking a foreign language."

"It certainly does."

"Just the same, it's true. And the key is that I have learned some of the laws of prayer and you have not."

"But Our Lord said—"

"He said, when people came to Him for help, 'Do you believe that you can get well?' And you admitted that you didn't believe Skip could get well. Obviously the first thing you need to learn is how much you may dare to believe." She dropped down on the stool beside the easel, her skirts wide and gay, her head outlined against the smouldering colors on the canvas. Paul, at the suggestion of her swift, expressive hand, perched gingerly on a straight chair near the door.

"But I wouldn't dare," Paul explained. "What if it were not God's will?"

"Nonsense!" cried Burnett briskly. "What kind of a God do you have, anyway?"

At this heresy Paul rose, trembling a little, and made for the door. "I'm sorry," he muttered through tight lips. "But I cannot cooperate with that kind of—theology, if it deserves such a name. And I will appreciate it if you respect my desires and discontinue your calls on Skip."

He was hopeless, completely hopeless, thought Burnett, and she was an idiot ever to have seen anything in him. "What about that Frank Morse?" she asked. "What about Jean? You don't know how to help them and you just don't care, do you? No concern of yours whether they die or commit suicide. It's more important to keep your ideas of God neatly packaged and labeled."

"How do you know anything about Frank and Jean?"

"I don't feel it necessary to explain my prayer life to you..." ("Hold everything, my girl," said Burnett to herself. "You're stirring up a fight unnecessarily—") And in gentler tones she said, "All I mean is: wouldn't you like to know how to help them?"

But she was not the only one who had a temper. "Yes, but I shall choose my instructor with some care," said the minister. "Skip is now in the rectory, and there I have jurisdiction. And I repeat—*stay away*."

He started out of the door, but with a swirl of her skirts Burnett was in front of him. "I suppose you are afraid of what people will say," she stormed. "'That woman, with all kinds of strange people in and out of her house—'"

"The point had not occurred to me," said Paul, his face very red. "But now that you mention it, there is an added reason for my request."

He pounded down the hall, grabbed his hat from the table and made a flying exit, closing the door behind him with a crack that was almost a slam.

"Blast, oh blast!" cried Burnett, standing in the studio door, half laughing, half crying. "Madeleine," she added, turning toward the dining room, "Didn't I tell you to pray for me not to get mad? Well, you're a fizzle of a pray-er, just like I am. But honestly, he is the most insufferable two-for-a-cent pipsqueak I ever saw."

"Now, Miss Burnett, he's not that bad. Men must have things their own way, that's all."

"But Skip—" sighed Burnett. Then she lifted a determined chin and said, "If Skip needs me, I'll see him, whether that nincompoop stands in the way or not."

"Miss Burnett, you taught me to see people as God made them, and you aren't doing it."

"Oh, yes I am. That's the way God made him—I can't think why."

Burnett charged into the bedroom, flung her skirt on the spool bed that had been her great grandmother's, dragged on a pair of faded bluejeans and stormed out into her garden, spade in hand. Here the sunlight comforted her, and the warm, fragrant earth slipping through her fingers gave her peace. Burnett would not wear gloves for gardening. "But you *should,*" her sister-in-law would tell her. "After all, you teach with your hands. And they are the prettiest part of you, really." She would look askance at Burnett's high cheekbones and her straight, narrow lips. "If the art class doesn't like my hands," Burnett would reply, "that's just too bad."

Even her feet rejoiced in the feeling of the cool earth. She kicked off her sandals and waded luxuriously into the flower bed. "It's a little early to move you," she whispered to her lemon lilies. "But you're crowded here by the house. So come on. You're going over beside the brick walk. You'll like that."

The traffic roared by on Main Street as she separated the lilies and planted them beside the moss-grown walk. But Burnett did not hear it. Sunlight and flowers quieted her anger and her thoughts drifted away from Paul to that other one whom she had loved so long ago. Long ago, in another country, in another world: Alan. She had had no other playmates in the Chinese city of her childhood. Her brother had been sent away to boarding school while she remained alone amid the teakwood and Peking rugs of her father's home. So the shabby missionary compound where she went to school was fairyland to her. Classes were casually conducted anywhere that Alan's mother, Mrs. Whitacre, saw fit: in the big, barn-like house, smelling of boys and cabbage; on the porch, where she might watch the Christians trooping in and out of Mr. Whitacre's study; or under the wisteria arbor with the yellow cat sitting in Mrs. Whitacre's lap while she heard the multiplication table. Burnett's education had been careless, gay and free. And in all her youthful world, Alan had been her only friend.

Why, after so many years, should all this buried past return so vividly to her mind today? Perhaps it was the Canterbury bells that tossed their pink and purple heads beside the picket fence. There had been Canterbury bells in Mrs. Whitacre's garden, beside the high clay walls that separated the mission compound from the execution grounds beside the city wall. There had been certain holidays in Burnett's schooling, not because George Washington or Abraham Lincoln had been born but because the execution grounds were in use. On other days goats wandered over them and villagers trudged across them, singing high, weird songs to scare away the ghosts of those who had perished there.

No one but the missionaries would have dared to build in such a place. But then, of course, missionaries did not believe in ghosts. And the land was cheap.

So there were Canterbury bells beside the wall, as though to shield the compound from the ghastliness of life beyond. And though no one else could see them except herself and Alan, within their lovely bells the fairies lived . . .

"What an imagination I must have had," thought Burnett, patting the dirt firm around a lily plant. "But then, Alan saw them too."

Alan was dead. At least, so Burnett had heard and so she hoped. She wished to learn no details of a life that had been too hard for him. She had known, as the years passed, the terror that more and more tormented him, the black cloud deepening over his adolescent mind. Even now in the June sunlight she shuddered, remembering: cold wind over the city wall, wailing down from hilltops full of graves; and Alan's thin, white face, once so ruddy and full of life; Alan's blue eyes, frightened, frightening; Alan's shaky whisper: "No, I can't tell you! I can't!"

"But somebody ought to *do* something about it," the helpless little girl had said.

And Alan had replied: "There's nothing to do. It would only worry them. Oh well, maybe it's just this digestive trouble I've picked up. Maybe I'll get over it."

He seemed to get over it, indeed, when the two of them went to school in Shanghai.

Burnett could not remember the time when she had not loved Alan. From earliest childhood she had accepted him as she accepted the Chinese city where they lived, with its quaintness and its horror: its moss-grown water gates, and its pagoda-ed hills; and the beggars, crawling with vermin and infested with sores, who lined the paths up to the temple doors. Alan was part of herself, and there was no one to draw him away from her. But when they went to school, Alan no longer belonged exclusively to her. He was, in fact, the idol of the school. His extraordinary good looks, his keen and brilliant mind, even his physical prowess exceeded that of the other students. Long legs and a magnificent physique made up for the years of physical weakness now overcome; and since he was competing only with other youngsters like himself, brought up in mission compounds, he surpassed them all in basketball and soccer as he surpassed them in his scholastic work.

Burnett in those days was small and plain. Her loving spirit had not yet softened the angular contours of her face, and the piquant charm that later was to be hers had not begun to shine in her. She was only a little girl with skinny legs, straight black hair, and an abrupt manner that sat ill on her adolescent awkwardness. She was glad her beloved Alan was so adored and followed. Yet at the same time she was lonely, and tormented by a fury of jealousy.

Burnett would never forget the agony of that hurt. She could feel it now as she planted lilies with the traffic of Main Street reverberating in her ears. But on a certain day all the hurt had gone away from her, and remembering it, Burnett smiled. It was toward the end of their senior year, when the thought of being separated by the width of a continent had added sorrow to her loneliness. The school, rejoicing in an English teacher whose zeal outran her discretion, was topping off a year of Shakespeare by staging *Romeo and Juliet*. Alan was the immortal Romeo. And Burnett, quite appropriately, was backstage shifting the balconies and tree trunks which she had painted. She would peer through the curtains to see Alan, tall and handsome in blue and gold, lost in his part as one who loves the sea might abandon himself to the great rush of its passionate beauty. In studying the poets Alan had learned that he himself was a poet, and the love of beauty that was no longer satisfied with flowers and sunsets found its vent in blank verse. He would read to Burnett bits of his own plays and even act them for her on the city wall during those vacation days when for a blissful interval she had him all to herself again . . .

He stood in the synthetic moonlight of the stage, holding out his arms to the beautiful blonde Juliet upon the balcony Burnett had painted and repeating the old impassioned words of the immortal lover:

> "But, soft! What light through yonder window breaks?
> It is the east, and Juliet is the sun!"

The small, plain girl back of the curtains had watched him with a smudge of paint on her nose and the tears hot in her eyes.

At this point Alan for the first time made a mistake. He turned away from Juliet, leaving her languishing over her balcony, and addressing himself apparently toward a crack in the green curtain, he said with all the tenderness of his heart:

> "With love's light wings did I o'erperch these walls;
> For stony limits cannot hold love out,
> And what love can do, that dares love attempt . . ."

"Alan!" mouthed the English teacher from her prompter's stool.

And Alan obediently turned back to the neglected Juliet. But there was a smile on his lips that did not belong to the house of Capulet, thought Burnett, smiling herself after so many years, while she planted lilies and thought of him.

"Why did you do that?" she asked him the next day,

intercepting him on the bit of campus behind the high walls of the school.

"Because I love you and nobody else. And I always will," replied Alan steadily. For the first time he swept her into his arms and she clung to him, dizzy and blinded with the rapture of his lips upon her own.

"Mother says that people shouldn't be engaged until they are eighteen," she said after a while, innocently assuming that by this kiss they were bound to each other forever—as indeed they were.

"We've always been engaged," Alan had replied. "Always. Promise me."

So Burnett had promised.

The agony of parting, when she went to college in the East and Alan remained on the West Coast, was comforted by the knowledge that she was his.

"I'll come and get you just as soon as I can," he whispered as they stood together in the great roaring railway station of San Francisco, terrified, both of them, by a life they had never known. "Only one thing bothers me; that old shadow—you know—I thought it had gone away, but all this—all this—" and he looked around him with frightened eyes.

"Of course it's gone!" Burnett had replied. But fear touched her with a cold finger as she spoke. Even now, Burnett shuddered as she thought of that old shadow. For it had not gone. Alan had plunged into college life as a glad swimmer into breakers. He played football, he ran, he danced, he studied—and all the while the Thing sat on his bedpost and he played and studied harder that he might not see it.

The time came when he could no longer stand the strain. The wheels of his thinking had grown slow. The letters that came to Burnett faltered and grew thin. Then they ceased entirely and Burnett could only wonder, taut with a fear that was no longer groundless. For a letter from Mrs. Whitacre, vague and wandering though it was, confirmed to her the very worst of all her fears.

Alan was in a mental hospital.

For a little while Burnett had heard from him—broken bits of notes, sometimes in his own words and sometimes not. Then silence had closed over him and he was gone—so far away, so desperately far away, that when Mrs. Whitacre had written of his departure into another world, the news had been release.

And now at long last the bitterness had faded out of her memories and she no longer thought of him by night, by day, until her mind was weary with the weight of it. No longer. Only sometimes of a bright June morning, seeing Canterbury bells and remembering . . . Burnett sighed, pushed away a straggling lock of hair and brought her mind back to the lilies she was transplanting.

"Hi," called a laughing voice behind her back.

"Skip!" cried Burnett, sitting flat on the grass in her astonishment.

There he stood, casual and gay, in a blue sweatshirt, laughing down at her.

"How'd you get out of hock, you crazy kid?" demanded Burnett, her face breaking into merriment.

"Walked out." Usually Skip leaped over the fence, but today he opened the little gate and sat beside her on the grass. "Didn't you expect me to get well?"

"Not this fast."

"You look cute in that rig," Skip said irrelevantly, tickling her bare feet with a blade of grass.

"I'm not usually considered cute. That implies prettiness and I'm not pretty."

"Not exactly," Skip agreed candidly. "You're the kind of girl a fellow keeps looking at, trying to decide whether she's ugly or beautiful. That's more fun than just being pretty."

"Thank you, Skip." Burnett patted his hand. "But you shouldn't be prancing about like this, should you?"

"They said not to, but heck," explained Skip lucidly, "nobody was around and I got bored, so I came here. I didn't know exactly where I was going. Feels funny, somehow, as if part of me was far away . . . But I wandered down the street and here you are. Say, Burnett, where was I the last time you saw me?"

"In the hospital," murmured Burnett.

"No, I don't mean that. I wasn't there really—I was way off somewhere. You know," he added, "it's funny about God. I guess He got tired of hearing me talk against Him."

"You don't think God crashed your car, do you?" asked

Burnett. "He wouldn't be that mean."

"Well, it's funny, though," Skip said thoughtfully. "Anyway, now I know He's real. Because if He wasn't, I wouldn't be here." He reached for Burnett's hand and held it in both of his. "What made you learn to pray?" he asked. "You don't look like a praying female, at all."

"Come into the house," parried Burnett. "Too much noise and light out here."

She led him into the studio, knowing that he felt at ease among her canvases and paints.

"Getting a little woozy," murmured Skip, and he leaned back in the wicker chair and closed his eyes.

"You'll be all right soon," Burnett said quietly. And as was her way, she visioned the Life from the air all around entering into him and restoring life.

"Sure I will, with you here." And once more Skip held her hand, his brown fists unimpassioned, trusting, like those of a child. "Now tell me," he insisted, his eyes still closed, "why did you learn to pray?"

"To try to help someone I loved," said Burnett. Briefly and simply she told him about Alan, quite as if the two of them had been the same age. "I tried to find help in the Church and there was none," she ended.

"That's how you got down on churches," added Skip.

"Well, yes. All they did was to say, 'God's will be done,' and if it was God's will to torment an innocent person as Alan was tormented, then I have no use for that kind of a God. And they prayed for me to have courage to say, 'God's will be done.' " Burnett's voice went deep and cold with bitterness as she repeated the words.

"You don't believe in giving God that much leeway, do you?" smiled the boy.

"No, I don't!" said Burnett, and she was not smiling. "That is not what He wants of us—to leave everything in His hands. There is a power that He has given us, and He is waiting for us to use it." She stared out the window at the ancient apple tree, her face vivid with longing. "Why won't people realize?" she sighed. "He wanted Alan to be well, as much as I did!"

"Then why didn't He make him well?" asked Skip.

"Because His power is geared to work through His people," replied Burnett. And she quoted, " 'He that believeth on Me, the works that I do shall he do also.' We're trying to do them, but we have so much to learn, such a long way to go. So I studied philosophy and psychology and all the rest of it, trying to find the way to help Alan. But—I failed."

"Too tough a case for a first try, huh?"

Burnett nodded. She said, "Skip, you've got sense."

There was silence in the studio for a while. Burnett in her bluejeans and sweater looked into the apple tree and saw not green leaves and singing birds but Alan's face. "Why am I thinking so much of him today?" she wondered. "After all these years—after all these years—"

"You were a good sport to go on helping other people when you couldn't help him," said Skip suddenly.

"Oh, well. They popped up." Burnett sighed. "People seemed to feel something in me that might help them, I don't know why."

"I know," Skip said. "I can feel it right now. Like sunshine inside of me."

Burnett suddenly remembered Paul, who did not know that God was near and real like sunshine. "We ought to phone your uncle," she said, turning toward the door. "He's probably having fits by this time."

"Nuts!" said Skip, his face darkening and his ethereal mood flying out of the window. "I'm not going to be tied to his apron strings the rest of my life. Let him worry! I'm mad with him anyway, only I can't remember why. Maybe it's about Frank Morse. He sure did let Frank down."

"Do you really like Frank?" asked Burnett, pausing in the doorway.

"He's a good guy. Besides, you can't help feeling sorry for him. He didn't mean to hurt anybody," Skip explained. "He was drunk, see, and he'd been moping for a long time and all of a sudden he just went wild. So Jean's *got to get well!* Are you working on that, Burnett?"

"I am," nodded Burnett. "Madeleine and I, every morning at the same time. And she's getting well."

"Well, then, what's the matter with Frank? I made Buddy drop me off there yesterday. He just sits. Won't talk, won't go anywhere, won't do anything. He's so scared he's frozen stiff. No wonder, either. If Jean dies—"

"I told you, she won't! Now I'm going to phone your

uncle, so you just keep still."

"Oh, all right," said Skip disgustedly.

Burnett returned from the telephone to report with a rather wicked smile that the Reverend Paul Forrester was en route to rescue his nephew.

"What'd I tell you?" murmured Skip. And when his uncle came he rose, sullen and wordless, to go with him.

"Get in the car, Skip," Paul ordered, after a chilly acknowledgment of Miss McNeill's presence. "I'm already late for an appointment."

"Well, why did you come? I got myself up here. I can get myself back."

"Don't you remember?" asked Paul sternly. "The doctor said you were to keep absolutely quiet."

"No, I don't remember. Did the doctor come to see me?"

Paul turned a little white. And Burnett, knowing what the doctor had told him about Skip's brain, understood the reason for his fear. "He will never be the same again," the doctor had said . . .

"But he *is* the same," Burnett told herself, clinging to the Power that could make him so. "The real Skip, with a perfect memory, is *right here*. In spirit this is already so, and it will soon be so in the flesh."

Paul went to Skip and laid his hand on the boy's shoulder.

"Of course you don't remember," he said, his voice as gentle as a mother's. "I'm sorry. I forgot. It will take a little while for your memory to come back. We must both be patient, that's all." He smiled, his face softened into the gentleness that Burnett had once seen in him long ago.

He does not know himself, she thought. Within the narrow minister there was a great and gentle spirit, half asleep, never fully expressing itself in this life . . .

Skip trailed sulkily out of the room and Paul turned to her in a constrained goodbye. "Ah, your painting," he murmured, glancing at the panther and apparently feeling that he should say something besides good-day and good-bye. "Very nice, very nice." Then he started and gazed at it attentively.

"Yes, it is," said Burnett quickly, before she could stop herself.

"What is—what?" asked Paul, turning to her in surprise.

"The panther is like me," replied Burnett. "You see, he *is* me—in certain moods."

Paul gazed at the panther, crouched, darkness behind him, the sunlight striking his silky curves with blue light. He looked at the triangular face, cryptic, brooding, immobile, with the gray-green eyes that burned in silence. "Yes. I was thinking that," he said slowly. "But *how did you know it?*"

"Oh, just a sort of a hunch, I guess," murmured Burnett.

"Can you look into everyone like that?"

"Not everyone," replied Burnett. And the voice within her added, "Only those I love."

5

When on the next Sunday Paul gave thanks at the altar for the restoration of his nephew Richard, rapture lit a flame in his brown eyes and deepened the rich timbre of his voice. Priscilla McGhann, steaming about the sacristy after the service, beamed upon him with a smile that almost beautified her heavy face.

The whole congregation was touched with joy, the uncritical kindness of heart that is peculiarly American overcoming, at least for the moment, any reservations concerning Skip. Skip himself attended Morning Prayer, for Paul said that since he would not stay in bed but insisted on wandering about town to the great perturbation of everyone, he could just get himself to church. And with a rather bad grace Skip slipped through the side door while everyone craned furtive necks to see him.

"Yes, indeed," said Paul, perspiring in his cassock at the tower door, "it's wonderful! Yes indeed! Good morning, Mrs. Mulcahy. Yes indeed, it certainly is wonderful—"

Even Angus McGhann, lifting his gray moustache in a broad smile, managed to say, "Good news, Forrester. Glad to hear it!" And if the cocking of one bushy eyebrow signalled squalls ahead, Paul did not notice it.

So the Lord's Day passed in robes of light. Even the children gathering at sunset time to sing Evensong wore above their tiny vestments the faces of angels. Paul loved Evensong, as he did every one of the services of the Church. He loved the ancient prayers breathing dignity and beauty, the chants like strong bulwarks withstanding the centuries, the hymns that were the heartbeats of the saints. Somehow, without words, the children entered into this love. Paul had a way with children; a quaint way, speaking to them, half-amused yet wholly understanding, as if they were his partners in the house of the Lord, as indeed he assured them that they were. "We are ministers, all of us," he told them with grave simplicity. "That is why we do not whisper or smile or look around at the congregation. We are busy worshipping God and being His ministers." The congregation marvelled that their rector, who had no children of his own, should have such gentle and perfect control of these their children. There they sat, little hands folded on their laps, responding to the thrill of the Lord's house just as the minister did. Each child was allowed one look at the nave, to see Father or Mother; no more. After that they kept their eyes in front of them, for all the world like the small angels that most certainly they were not. On the Sunday after Skip's return, the love Paul felt for Skip spread itself out over all his little choir and the delight on his face as he shepherded them out on the recessional was beautiful to see. Within that delight there lurked a bit of amusement. For a certain chorister, Joe McGhann, had introduced a variation into the ritual of the service. The organist had informed Paul plaintively that this small seeker after God was quite unable to carry a tune. "And he's a pain in the neck anyway," he had burst forth. "Always teasing the girls and throwing spitballs and making faces."

Paul found it difficult to understand why the organist, who was much larger than the offending Joe, should be unable to restrain the child's antics. But he replied, "I'll come to rehearsals and see that he behaves. It's very important for him to have this training."

"Oh, well—he's your senior warden's nephew, so—"

"I hadn't thought of that," said Paul rather sharply. "Let's see now. You say he can't sing?"

"Not a note. He throws them all off, bellowing and squawking."

So Paul had made one of his nimble compromises, persuading Joe that the younger children needed a crucifer of their own to follow after the great brazen cross had disappeared around the chancel steps. "And I think you're just the fellow for that job," he had assured the boy gravely. "You can be trusted with it, can't you, Joe?"

Joe had consented to keep his mouth shut during the services, on the theory that crucifers do not sing. But on this particular evening Joe's thoughts were elsewhere and the choir made their way out of the chancel while he sat daydreaming. Nothing daunted, Joe seized his small wooden cross, tucked it under his arm and forged through the choristers as through a huddle on the football field. Then he took the cross out from under his arm and once more held it reverently aloft.

"You big dope!" screamed the other children as soon as the church door was shut behind them.

"Now, now," said Paul mildly. "When we have been to church it makes us feel kind to everybody, especially to those who make mistakes. We have just been singing about Jesus who is eager to help those who do wrong. So we will not get excited because Joe daydreamed a minute and forgot." He put his hand on Joe's shoulder. "I've done that myself," he informed them. "Do you know what happened to me last Sunday? I was thinking of my sermon so hard that I started to go into the church in my surplice and stole and without any cassock—only my trouser legs showing beneath!"

They forgot all about Joe in their delight at being given a grown-up target for their mirth.

"Thank you, Mr. Forrester," Joe said gravely.

But on Monday morning reaction set in, and in spite of everything he found himself worrying. What were they to do with Skip, who continually wandered away and forgot where he was going? Mercifully, he had no car in which to disappear. But even that blessing had its tormenting aspect, for he could not understand why he was refused the parish car and became more sullen at each refusal.

"What's the matter with you, Skip?" Paul finally asked at lunchtime, when the boy sat silent and heavy-eyed over his plate. "Are you angry with me about something?"

And Skip answered, "Yeah, but I can't remember what." Then he muttered to his soup plate, "I get pretty darn tired of not remembering anything."

"Now, Skip, you know you remember more every day," Janet assured him cheerfully. "Burnett says you're going to be all right."

Skip's face cleared a little. "If it wasn't for her, I'd go nuts," he said.

Paul dropped his fork with a slight click upon his salad

plate. He could feel his face grow red. "Do you see that woman very often?" he asked, his voice edged with distaste.

"Sure. Seems like I can always remember how to get to her house. Why?"

"You are living in a rectory. It seems to me very strange that you should choose as your—spiritual counsellor—someone who is not even a member of a church."

"What the heck's that got to do with it?" shouted Skip. "All you ministers, pussy-footing around playing church, and she's the only one that could show me there's a God!" And he got up and slammed out of the front door.

"For heaven's sake, where's he going now?" muttered Janet, watching him out of the dining-room window. Then she rounded on her brother: "Now listen here, Paul, Burnett is helping Skip get well. Dr. Cameron said so himself. So your best bet is just to keep your mouth shut. You hear? You wait till you can deliver the goods yourself, and then you'll have a right to talk."

"I can't believe that Dr. Cameron said—"

"Ask him!"

The suggestion suited Paul, for certain disquieting doubts had entered into his feelings about Miss McNeill. He felt a slight discomfort when he remembered his own words: "Every Tom, Dick and Harry in and out of her house." An incongruity, unnoticed in the tense moments of his visit with her, was forcing itself into his mind. If this woman were leading a loose life there would be signs that one like himself, trained in the understanding of humanity, would have noticed—the odor of cigarette butts and stale beer, and something more subtle about the woman herself. On the contrary, Burnett's living room was as clean and cool as the nave of his own church. And the woman who sat and faced him, her eyes remote and shining and her face still, was a woman of dignity and of restraint. Paul had never really looked at her until those moments when he had sat across the living room and asked her to stay out of his home. It disturbed him to find his concept of her shifting.

When Paul talked about Skip and Burnett, the doctor listened intently, his arms upon the desk, his hands clasped.

"May I ask you, Bill," finished Paul, "what is your explanation of Skip's recovery?"

"There is only one possible explanation," answered Dr.

Cameron. "Skip recovered by supernatural power."

True enough. Even Paul was inclined to believe that God had intervened to save Skip's life. But...."Do you know that Miss McNeill went to see him every day?" asked Paul with a spark in his eyes.

"Skip was in a private room," parried the doctor primly. "And since he was in a deep coma, no ruling against visitors was necessary."

But Paul, who was no fool in understanding men, studied the doctor's inexpressive face and saw that he knew. "What do you think of her?" he asked.

"There was a baby who screamed for two days," the doctor said meditatively. "Polio or meningitis: confused symptoms. The mother told me that she had asked Miss McNeill to come and pray for the child. I said, 'Good.' What right had I, as a Christian doctor, to forbid prayers? Miss McNeill did nothing but hold the baby in her arms. What she thought, I do not know. Ten minutes later, the infant stopped crying and from then on was well."

"Then your theory is—"

The doctor held up one large hand restrainingly. "I am not talking about theories," said Dr. Cameron. "Only about facts. As a man of science, I cannot refuse to face facts when I see them. I had a melancholic patient who attempted suicide with gas. This woman was taken by a friend to see Miss McNeill and later attended a group that Miss McNeill holds in her studio for study and prayer. The patient is not only well, she is—reborn."

Frank! The thought of him shot like a knife through Paul's heart. Frank, with his scared eyes and his frozen face—could she help Frank? But he hastily put out of his mind the fantastic thought of sending Frank to Miss McNeill.

"But—*why?*" he asked the doctor. "How do you explain those incidents?"

"Why does God answer her prayers more readily than yours?" Dr. Cameron smiled. "I couldn't tell you. *She* says that there are ways of prayer that can be learned."

"Skip sees her every day." The words were out before he could stop them.

"Then thank God and keep your mouth shut."

"But the congregation will think—"

"It will do them a lot of good to think—for once."

On this discouraging note Paul drove home.

He did not like it.

It displeased him to think that a mere human being could in some mysterious way twist the will of God and turn it to his own ends. "You must *see it so,*" that woman had said, pointing to her weird panther and talking about tea cozies. What if a man could thus by his own concentration bring to pass the thing that he desired? What then of Jehovah the Almighty who dealt with man according to His will, meting to him good or ill for the chastisement of his soul? Should a man depart from the obedient worship of his God merely to exercise a dubious power of mind over matter? Paul slowed down to let a trio of boys, bathing suits in hand, dash across the street and climb into a rattletrap car. Passersby smiled at him as he paused: "Good afternoon, Father.". . ."Hello, Mr. Forrester . . ." But he did not see them. Most of all, he thought, as he drove past the small town's sleepy stores, what did this make of Jesus Christ his Lord? If one needed only to see the perfect thing in order to produce it, then why should He have come into a darkening world and submitted Himself to every anguish known to man? "They have taken away my Lord, and I know not where they have laid Him . . ." Paul felt within his heart the tears of the woman who had wept on that resurrection day because she could no longer see the body of the Christ. True, the woman had wept useless tears. Her Lord had not been taken away from her, but had only risen to a higher way of life. For a moment he wavered, as he wove between the shoppers' cars that backed away from the grocery stores. Could there be an analogy between himself and that unseeing woman? Could it be possible that Miss McNeill was tapping a higher current of the life of that same Lord of his? But this also displeased him. He had learned to discern the body of Christ in the sacraments of his church: the very center and focus of his life. Could that Christ have risen into a more universal place and could He from thence befriend such people as Burnett McNeill? Surely that would be most unbecoming of Him . . .

"No!" decided Paul, parking his car in front of the rectory. "No!" That his own Lord Jesus Christ would work for this strange woman with her haunting face and her gray

eyes in a way that He would not work for him, Paul? "No!"
If the doctor was right and she had really helped Skip to
recover, it must be through a hypnotic power of her own,
and he would have none of it.

He snapped the front door shut behind him and asked as
usual, "Where's Skip?"

"Gone swimming with the gang," answered Janet,
appearing from the kitchen door.

"Good!" cried Paul. Skip, the color coming back into his
face, going swimming with the gang when only three weeks
ago he had been lying at the gates of death ... With a sense
of deep thankfulness Paul said, "They'll see that he gets
safely home, won't they?"

"Sure. I've told them they are never to leave him until
they get him home. Come on in the kitchen. I'm making
cookies."

But Paul did not feel like chatting with his sister. An
uncomfortable thought followed his wave of gratitude, and
after fortifying himself with a cookie or two, he went over
to the study to contend with it. If this woman, Burnett,
had restored his boy to him, then no matter how much he
disapproved of her ideas, he still was in her debt. Instead of
expressing thanks or gratitude, he had been very rude. But
if he apologized to her and thanked her, then how could he
refuse to learn from her? And how could he harbor her
ideas without doing violence to his faith and to his Church?

Finding no answer, he sighed and tried to put the
questions away from him. But there was a nervousness
upon him, a pressure from within, as of a voice trying to
reach him. And as he stilled himself and said a prayer for
guidance, there came to him the thought of Frank.

If he could learn from Miss McNeill something that
would help Frank, should he not learn at any cost? The
idea pricked him into restlessness. He leaped up from his
desk and stood for a moment at the window, where the
midsummer grass was turning brown; then he whirled about
as though pushed by an unseen hand, climbed into his car
again and went back up Main Street to the rambling old
house next to the police station.

"Frank at home?" he asked of the stringy-haired woman
who came to the door.

With infinite relief he heard that Frank was in. Why was

- 75 -

he so overwhelmingly relieved? What had he feared? He did not know . . .

There was Frank as usual, slumped down in the big chair before the television set, and from the look on his face, not seeing it. He did not rise or speak as Paul sat down beside him.

"Jean's getting well," said Paul. "God is helping her . . ." He was silent for a moment. The picture of Burnett with her strange, secret face and that Power behind her gray eyes stood before his mind's eye and he had to push it aside before he could continue. "So now, we must just believe that God is going to help you, too," he finished lamely. For as he studied Frank's unresponsive face a cold fear crept down his spine. "After all," he went on more vigorously, "God is helping you already. Now the whole thing will be settled very quickly and you can go back to work and forget it."

Frank made no reply.

"Well, isn't that true?" asked Paul rather sharply.

"It's too late," Frank muttered.

At this point Paul delivered a brief lecture, true and well expressed, on the value of taking hold on one's own life and directing it. "You might at least come to church," he finished.

A shudder passed through Frank's body. "No!" he said, more strongly.

This was strange, for hitherto his reply had been, "I'll show up some day." What had happened?

"Every Sunday I look down in the congregation and expect to see you there," Paul told him soberly.

"There's something in me pushing two ways," muttered Frank. "Pushing me to church—then saying, 'But it'll get you, when you do go—' "

"*What* will get you?" And Paul thought to himself, "Good heavens, the boy is crazy."

Frank was silent for a while, his chin sunk on his chest. "I've always been scared of churches," he said at last. "Ever since I was a little boy and went to Grandpa's funeral."

"Oh, is *that* all?" Paul smiled, relieved. "Well, then, I tell you what: come some time when the church is empty and see if you don't get a good, peaceful feeling. That way you'll get over being scared of church."

"I might just once," agreed Frank. "Then if that didn't work—"

"Then what?"

But Frank did not answer.

Once more the picture of Burnett rose into Paul's mind, and he pushed it aside determinedly. What could that panther-woman in red sandals say to Frank that he, Paul, could not say? "Why don't you go to see a doctor?" he asked.

"I have. He said I was O.K. He said I'd been worrying too much about Jean, that was all . . ."

"Well, he's right," Paul declared stoutly. "The doctor knows. You *will* be all right. You just wait and see."

"Oh, yeah?"

Paul went home ill at ease, only to be met by a belligerent Skip in the front hall.

"I've remembered," Skip began, and Paul did not need to ask, "What have you remembered?" "You were going to chuck me out. *That's* what had me so upset that night. Well, all right—when do I go?"

Paul laid his hand on the boy's shoulder. "Nobody's going to chuck you out, Skip," he said gently. "Come and sit down and let's talk about it."

Skip strode into the living room, his big mouth set in sullen lines. As usual, he marched straight to Paul's easy chair beside the round table and flung himself into it. Paul established himself in the cheap modern rocker on the other side of the table and hitched it a little nearer to the boy. He turned on the table lamp, for the living room with its faded wallpaper was darkening early, as it always did. It was a large square room with handed-down odds and ends and yet shabbily comfortable.

Paul's gaze rested anxiously on the young man sprawled in the big chair. "You know, you didn't exactly set a good example to the parish," he began.

And Skip broke in, "Yeah, I know. Had a couple of beers every now and then. Went out with the girls just like any other guy. So I'm a bad lot. Sure."

"No, you're not, Skip," said Paul gently. "You're really good. I know that."

"That's parental psychology," observed Skip. "It goes over all right with your junior choir, but it doesn't fool me any. However, go ahead."

Paul sighed and went ahead. "You never lie and you never purposely hurt anyone," he said earnestly. "And you always want to help people in trouble. It's just that you refuse to adjust to life in a rectory." And he endeavored once more to explain to Skip the vestry's position in this matter, and his own. "Just the same," he finished, "I'm sorry I told you that you—that you couldn't stay here any longer. And now, no matter what happens, I'll never ask you to leave. I promise you that, Skip."

"You might as well," growled Skip. "Because I'm going to leave anyway, as soon as I can remember whether I'm going or coming."

"Skip—"

"You don't like anything I do," the boy went on morosely. "You don't like it when I'm a playboy, and then when I go to see Burnett and find out a little bit about God, you don't like that either."

Paul rose from his chair, driven by the unexplained restlessness that had dogged him all day long, and leaned his elbow on the mantelpiece, looking into the empty fireplace and seeing in his mind Burnett's face—and Frank's. "As for your seeing Miss McNeill," he decided at last, "I have nothing to say. I do not understand her—theology. But Dr. Cameron believes that she really did help you. So—"

"You weren't very nice to her," said Skip as Paul hesitated.

"Did she say that?"

"*Of course not!*" Skip drummed with his fingers on the worn arm of the chair and raised his voice a little as he spoke. "But—didn't you come up there to get me once, or did I dream it? Well, then"—as Paul nodded—"I saw you, screwing up your eyebrows and scowling at her. Seems to me you ought to go and say, 'Thank you.'"

"Maybe I ought," said Paul, soothingly. "But right now, I'm talking about *you.*" He turned away from the fireplace and sat down again by Skip.

"I thought I was doing the right thing, Skip, when I told you of the vestry's stand and—my decision. I was brought up to believe that the more difficult choice is always the right choice. So the more I agonized about it, the more I figured that it must be God's will. Now I wonder: how dumb can you get?" he murmured, slipping into his nephew's vernacular. "I—I think this is an apology, Skip," he added rather shyly, with a small one-sided smile.

"Oh well, I guess I had it coming to me," Skip admitted in a gentler voice. "Only—I didn't have it figured out just right. I kind of thought this was my home."

"*It is!* Wherever I live is your home, always." And Paul added, surprising even himself, "Did it ever occur to you that I love you, Skip?"

"I wondered." The words came slowly and the brown eyes rested on Paul with trouble in their depths. "I've always been kind of a nuisance to you. I'm sorry. From now on I'll try to—to give you a fifty-fifty break." And he added with his old warm loving smile, "I guess that's an apology too."

Paul leaned forward and laid his hand on the boy's knee and there was silence in the rectory of All Saints.

"What do the vestry say about me now?" asked Skip suddenly.

"They haven't said anything," Paul answered. "And they won't. I'll do the talking—tomorrow night."

"Can they really make trouble for you?"

And Paul responded, smiling, "No indeed!"

But he wished he felt sure of it.

Uneasiness pursued him through his dreams that night, and a sense of urgency pressed behind them. "Don't be an idiot," he would tell himself, awakening with a start. And he would give thanks for the returning friendliness of Skip and try to go to sleep again. But once more the dream would return, and he would rouse and try to catch it before it sank out of his memory...*what was it*...dark sand slipping, slipping, over something shining and hard...and somehow, back of it all, Frank.

As soon as he had finished breakfast, Paul went to the telephone and called Frank's home: "How's Frank?"

"Oh, fine," answered James, in his pleasant, drawling voice. "Went out to see if he could get his job back."

"He *did?*"

"Well, we had to push him some, but he went."

"Did he—did he feel all right?"

"Oh, sure. He's bound to feel all right. Jean's getting well, isn't she? He wasn't kicking up his heels any, but that's just because he's gotten so dopey, sitting there worrying. He'll be all right. There's nothing wrong with Frank, only that he's been worrying."

Paul hung up the phone and sighed. He should have been comforted, but he was not. That had been the Morses' theory from first to last: there was nothing wrong with Frank; he was only worrying. It would take more than a restatement of this theory to allay Paul's fears.

Footsteps sounded on the stairs and Skip appeared, negligently clad in a pair of khaki shorts.

"Thought I'd get out there and wash your car," he said. "Show old Ambrose what a real wash-job is like."

"Swell idea." And Paul thought with tenderness, "He's giving me that fifty-fifty break . . ."

It was one of those frustrating mornings when a man does everything and nothing. Nevertheless Paul soothed troubled parents and looked up lost baptismal certificates, filled in diocesan reports and answered the ever-shrieking telephone with light in his eyes and a smile on his lips. No matter what dark dreams might linger on the threshold of his mind, he was happy, for his boy had come back to him.

But as the day wore on, his joy grew thin and the dark dreams came once more into the foreground of his mind.

"What on earth's the matter with you, Paul?" cried Janet at dinnertime. "You're as jumpy as three old women. You aren't worrying over vestry meeting, are you?"

"I don't think so." Paul laughed a little shamefacedly. "No! I know I'm not. I'm all right."

"That's what you say," retorted Janet rudely. "All shut up inside of yourself, as usual. If anything's eating you, will you tell a body? No, you won't—" and she grumbled all the way out to the kitchen.

Something was indeed "eating him." He felt a brooding heaviness and at the same time a restlessness, as though he should burst out of his study and do *something*—but what that thing might be he did not know.

Perhaps it was the vestry meeting after all that lay on his mind. There was no telling what they might have heard about Skip and Miss McNeill . . . Paul paused en route to the study and threw a clod of dirt at the doves upon the church roof. There was a diversity of opinions between Paul and those doves concerning the ownership of the chimes.

To the eye of a dove the church was a predestined bird sanctuary and the choir seemed to fall in with this opinion. "The sparrow hath found an house," they sang at times, "and the swallow a nest where she may lay her young, even thine altars, O Lord of Hosts." No doubt, thought Paul, and he appreciated the cry to the Almighty with which the chant closed, although if he himself had been moved to poesy he would have rhapsodized upon some other subject. "O that I had wings like a dove," the choir would further carol. And Paul would think gloomily, "You'd all be up on the church roof if you did." Nevertheless Paul still joined battle with the doves and chucked clods of dirt at them as they strutted complacently back and forth on the gray tiles or circled with a great beating of wings about the tower. He may have shouted at them more vigorously than usual today, his mind being rather stormily fixed upon his vestry.

The rector suspected that the twelve good men and true would take a dim view of miracles.

"That woman," Opal Oldershaw had breathed into his face one day, seizing him in the cloister and clasping his hand fervently in both of hers. "I saw dear Richard in her yard one day, and *my dear—"* She caught herself on this and dimpled coyly, rolling her eyes up at him. "She was quite barefooted, I do assure you, and in *very* short shorts! But, dear Mr. Forrester, we know that you do not countenance such queer people. Why, they do say she has *seances,* no less!"

Opal was an idiot, thought Paul crossly. And what did he care if the vestry looked askance at Miss McNeill? So did he, for that matter. No, it was not the vestry who oppressed him. Maybe it was only the weather, heavy and foreboding and pregnant with thunderstorms. He would go into the church and try to get hold of himself.

But as he reached out his hand to the great oaken door, the telephone rang. "Oh, let it ring!" Paul muttered, for suddenly he felt an overwhelming need to enter that church. But the habit of years was too strong. Wouldn't he *please* do something about old Hattie Burroughs, asked the local restaurant keeper. Wandering into the restaurant in all kinds of weather, looking simply *terrible!* A nightgown over her slip, one day ... wouldn't he please do *something?* He had found three housekeepers for Miss Hattie and she had always dismissed them. Well, but wouldn't he please find another one right away? Perhaps he could persuade this person or that person to look after Miss Hattie. The agitated voice held him until the vestry gathered, and the way was no longer clear into the church.

He never forgot how near he came to entering that oaken door.

Paul presided at one end of the long table. McGhann sat at his right hand as usual, Old Sammy on his left, one hand cupped over his ear. Smiling faces, kind faces, all of them, thought Paul. "How's your nephew, Forrester? Splendid news! Splendid!"

Paul called the meeting to order. Harold Lindstrom read the minutes in his precise, legal voice and old business was considered. The question of the sexton's pay arose, together with a consideration of work accomplished by said sexton. This was a perennial question, concerning which parish feeling was sharply divided into two opposite camps. The question of the bowling alley was next brought before the group, bringing in its wake the rector's social service plan for youth.

"Concerning that," said Paul clearing his throat and lifting his chin, "I have come to a decision. My nephew stays here. He is my first responsibility, and I expect no further questions about his remaining in the rectory which according to Church law is at present my home. If you feel, gentlemen, that this makes my youth program impractical, I cannot but appreciate your point of view. I am content to relinquish it for the present."

Polite silence wrapped the twelve men.

"There's always the possibility," said Lindstrom gently, "that Richard will lead a more quiet life from this time on."

Various others consented to this opinion, murmuring hopeful words about the youth program, and old Sammy chirped, "What's that? What's he talking about?"

Only McGhann, drumming on the table with his well-manicured fingers, looked dour and said nothing.

"Gentlemen, I move that we raise the money for the rector's youth program without delay—and that we leave the control of his nephew to his discretion," said Thayer at last, his blue eyes full of kindliness. And behind his gratitude, Paul knew uneasiness. For suddenly he realized that he not longer cared about the bowling alley.

The finest recreational center in the world could not have saved Skip's life or brought back light to the darkened mind of Frank Morse. One needed not a program but a power, and where could one go to find it?

But he did not know how to say these things to his vestry. So he thanked them, and a committee was appointed to look again into the price of altering the parish house basement. Since the last estimate, costs had risen . . .

For the moment Paul had forgotten the shadow that had followed him, the restlessness that had driven him here and there. Just as that disquiet seized him once again, the thing happened—and immediately Paul knew that it was this and nothing else that he had been dreading all day long.

A shot crashed and reverberated in the church.

The men leaped to their feet. Paul reached the door first and flung it wide. Darkness within—a terrifying darkness—then someone reached the switch and an explosion of light shattered the gloom.

There was the church, with its high rafters flanked by tall, still angels, their heavenly faces calm; with its woodcarving and its great stone pillars and its oaken pews—there it was, empty and still.

Or—was it empty?

There came a loud cry from the far end of the church, next to the street door. Lindstrom, his heavy face as white as death, pointed to the floor beneath a pew.

Frank. He had come to the church at long last, seeking for the help Paul had told him he would find there . . . With the painful slowness of a nightmare Paul got his stiff limbs down the church to the nave door. There on the floor, half-hidden by a pew, lay Frank, his glazed eyes staring into the bland face of the Archangel Michael, who gazed serenely back at him from the vaulted roof.

Paul dropped on his knees beside him.

He was breathing, with a faint, rattling sound that chilled the heart.

"The doctor—" and McGhann charged down the side aisle to the telephone.

At that moment Skip and Janet burst into the side door of the church.

Paul looked up at Skip and with lips that hardly seemed to move in his drawn face he whispered, "Get Burnett."

Now at long last, now when it was too late, his lips had said the thing that all day long his heart had longed to say: "Get Burnett."·

Paul Forrester knelt on the flagstoned floor, the blood from Frank's twisted body soaking into his clericals, and bowed his head beneath the greatest of all heartbreaks: the knowledge that this thing need not have been. If only he had followed his impulse yesterday and had sent the boy to Burnett! If only he had let the telephone ring this very evening and had opened the door and found him here! If only he had known the way to lighten Frank's mind as Burnett had awakened Skip, calling him back from the shadows into life!

"Oh, God, don't!" he prayed in desperation. "Don't let him die before she gets here! Oh God, don't!"

But even as he prayed, the labored breathing broke and faltered and was gone.

6

Burnett McNeill sat uneasily in her studio on this same July evening listening, and thinking of Paul. *"What's the matter?"* she called out to him in her mind. All morning, while teaching her art class, Paul's face had stood before her mind, and in the afternoon as she worked on a portrait, her fierce concentration was broken now and then by a strangely troubled thought of him. "It's almost as if he were calling me," she told herself. Then she brought her mind back to the man sitting across from her in the studio and reminded herself that her feeling about Paul could not be true.

Burnett was apt to see her visitors in the studio for the living room thundered with the traffic of Main Street. All Burnett's visitors were limited to the evening. "But can't I see you in the morning?" they would ask, and Burnett would reply sternly, "In the mornings I work, earning my living." Those who came to the little old house were usually the gaunt and fragile ones, or those with the haunted faces of the mentally ill. And the greatest problem of Burnett's life was the ordering and the limiting of those who came. "Why don't you go professional?" her friends on the West Coast would ask her. "Get some cards printed and call yourself a healer or something. Then you could charge for your services and give your whole time to this thing."

But Burnett had shuddered away from the thought. The word "healer" revolted her. She did not consider herself a healer, but only one who helped others to find the healing power of God. And, although she knew that many people charged a fee, she could not have followed that pattern herself. When people asked, "What can I do for you?" she would reply flippantly, "Nothing. This is my avocation, that's all. It's more fun than playing bridge." When her words were received with gratitude, then she was happy, and the warmth within her heart released more of the power of God's love. This gratitude was sometimes expressed by a gift of vegetables or of a handkerchief, or a check tactfully sent by mail. Burnett used the checks to pay for help, and in the time that Madeleine released for her she slipped into homes and hospitals with her priceless gift of life, as she had gone to the hospital to see Skip. But Madeleine's day did not cover the time that Burnett spent in this service, and the gifts did not cover the money she lost through delaying or refusing commissions. And always there was the problem of a schedule filled while others waited their turn.

The man who sat with his head in his hands and his eyes on the floor and jerked out the story of a troubled mind was a veteran. He was one of the Toms and Dicks and Harrys continually in and out of her house. Burnett realized that seeing these men alone in her studio put her in an awkward position, but she accepted it as part of the price of doing this work. She loved independence and solitude and could not bear the thought of sharing her home with a companion to act as chaperone. Burnett was aware of no sacrifice in deciding to risk her reputation in the small town in order to help those who needed her. She had thrown away a less valuable thing for one of more value, that was all, like discarding an old dress and buying a new one.

"It's funny I'm talking to you like this," muttered the man.

Burnett calmly replied, "No, it isn't. Everybody talks to me like that."

"But I'm saying things that I've never said out loud in my life."

"Of course," said Burnett in a voice so gentle that Paul Forrester would have been surprised if he could have heard it. "You know it's all right to say them, because the man you're showing me is not the real you. And I know the real one. He's right there, not hurt at all, and as soon as all these troublesome things have gone away, he will be set free. You'll feel like yourself again."

"When you say that I really believe you."

"Because I'm so sure of it," replied Burnett, using to the full her one tool of faith. She had forgotten Paul, forcing her mind into a one-pointed concentration upon the man in front of her. But at that moment the telephone rang.

Skip's voice. And Paul's face leaped into Burnett's mind as all day long she had seen it: white, stricken, pleading.

"Come quick!" panted Skip. "Frank's shot himself in the church. He's still breathing. Quick!"

So that was the trouble. Her spirit, seeing further than her eyes, had known it all day long.

"But Skip! Does your uncle want me?"

"He said *come!*"

"Right away."

"It's—an emergency," gasped Burnett. "Wait for me. Or come again." She banged out of the studio's back door and ran down the cement steps. Then she started the ancient Ford in the garage beneath the studio, churned up the winding drive and shot down the four blocks to the church.

She drew up behind a police car. Skip was waiting for her on the sidewalk. She glanced at his white face and followed him into the church, asking no questions.

People were gathering on the sidewalk. Ambrose of All Saints stood on the wide stone steps, his face carefully folded into sombre and impressive lines, broadcasting explanations and enjoying himself not a little. A policeman guarded the church door, forbidding it to the curious. But when he saw Burnett and Skip, he stepped aside.

Policemen, doctor, Janet, but who were these others? Burnett had not expected to find the small and humble body of Frank surrounded by a group of leading citizens, as if he had stumbled into a directors' meeting. They motioned her to the central block of pews at the rear of the nave. There lay Frank. And Burnett knew in one glance that he was dead. Beside him knelt Paul, his head still bowed.

"She's here," said Skip.

Paul raised his head and Burnett's heart stood still.

"It's too late," said Paul, his voice emotionless, his face white and set.

Burnett dropped on her knees beside him and laid her hand on his arm. "You did everything you could," she said, her voice deep with sympathy. "Frank will know that." Unconsciously she had used the future tense, as though Frank's spirit, in passing, had not yet opened eyes in the new world to which he had gone.

"Not everything," replied Paul Forrester. "No."

"All of us think that when it's—when it's too late," murmured Burnett. "It's happened to me, too. There's always more that we could have done. But we don't look back and grieve over it because we must go on. We must get on our feet so that we can help the next one." It was grief that made her words falter; grief and love.

"Life is hard," she added abruptly. "Nobody ever said that it was not."

Paul straightened his shoulders, drew his hand across his eyes in the gesture of a man awakening from sleep, and rose to his feet.

"That's right," said Skip consolingly. "Come on, Paul. Let's go home."

Janet murmured to the chief of police "Do you need him here?"

The chief shook his head. "We'll take care of everything," he said. "You'd better take the Father home and give him a stiff drink."

But before anyone could act upon this kindly advice there was a clamor of voices from the door and James Morse burst into the church, followed by a stunned father and a mother full of lamentations.

"Does he have to go through this too?" thought Burnett, and she whispered fiercely to Skip, *"Get him away!"*

But Skip looked at her blankly. Paul was a minister. It was not for him to escape from any situation. It was his duty to meet it and master it. But what could he say to Frank's family? "God knows best...We must trust our Heavenly Father..." For the first time Burnett understood how a minister might be driven to say such things. She found herself almost hoping that Paul would cleverly shift the responsibility into the hands of God.

But Paul was not clever. He said nothing at all. He only laid one hand on the shoulder of each parent and stood with bowed head between them, deeply identified with their grief.

"You were going to help him!" screamed Mrs. Morse, suddenly finding release in rage. "'Come down to the church,' you was always saying. 'God's there, and He'll help you.' And he come, and now—look, look!" Her shaking

- 88 -

hand pointed to the body on the floor.

"God is here," Paul began.

"Listen to him! Getting Frank down here and then saying Frank killed himself! How do we know but what *he* killed him?" She shook her fist in Paul's face. "Saying our Frank's crazy—maybe he's the one that's crazy!"

Several vestrymen closed in on her and the policeman said, "None of that, now," and took her by the arm.

But Paul silenced them all with a lift of his hand. "God is with us," he repeated, ignoring her remark about himself. "And His power is real. It is we who fail to make it effective. We who are older and wiser should have known how to help Frank." And he added, his quiet voice sharp with pain, "I mean—I should have known."

Mrs. Morse looked at him blankly for a moment and then her anger melted into tears.

"Now, Mom," said James in his gentle voice, "you know the Parson didn't want to look after Frank all by himself. He was always telling us to take him to a psychiatrist, and we wouldn't."

"Our Mame—" sobbed Mrs. Morse.

"Yeah. You were afraid he'd be like our Mame. And I was just dumb. I had it doped out wrong. If Jean got well he'd be O.K., I thought. So there's no use blaming Mr. Forrester."

Paul looked at him gratefully. "I tried," he said. "I guess I'm just not big enough . . . You know, Mrs. Morse," he went on, intent in his earnestness, "the real Frank isn't dead, and God will take care of him—the real Frank."

Frank's father, kneeling beside the body, looked up and spoke for the first time. "Yeah, but—he done it himself," he said in a voice heavy with grief.

"No, he didn't!" answered the minister. "Because he wasn't himself when he did it! It was something else, not himself, that came over him."

"Then you don't think he'll go to hell?"

Paul dropped down beside him and put one arm around his shoulders. "God loves him," he said gently. "He's God's boy. What would you do if you were God?"

"I'd take him home and straighten him out somehow."

"Well, then," said Paul, giving him a little shake, "isn't God as kind and as sensible as you are?"

"How does he do it?" thought Burnett. And she decided that he did not know how he did it. He had no technique. He was only honest, and truthfully, painfully loving, so that it broke the heart to see him standing beside Frank's body.

Then Burnett became aware again of the others in the church. Dr. Cameron, bending over Frank, Janet, hushed for once into silence, policemen, the coroner entering the door with an air of importance, and beyond them a dozen men, knotted together in the center aisle. She looked inquiringly at Skip.

"This would happen in the middle of vestry meeting," muttered the boy, with a grim twist to his mouth.

"Very kind of you to come," said Thayer Tewksbury, stepping to her side. "Very good. Now you'll want to be getting home I imagine. There's nothing that any of us can do."

So Burnett departed, blown out as it were by the chill wind of their aloofness and without a single glance from Paul.

"Thank you for coming," said Skip. "It helped Paul a lot. I know it did."

But Paul had not thanked her. Would he ever come, Burnett wondered, or would he forget her entirely? It would not be the first time that had happened.

Day after day passed by. The great white clouds of midsummer marched across the sky and away to the far sea, and still he did not come. Burnett made plans for a vacation on the West Coast. But there was a loneliness that none of those who trooped in and out of her house could drive away. Even Skip had gone to visit friends on the seashore. By the time he came home he too would have forgotten her, thought Burnett.

She had given all that she had to both of them, and discreetly, coldly, Paul had pushed her out of his way. It was wise—it was right for him—but bitterness closed upon her as she thought of it. Never once in any way, not by word or look, had he expressed gratitude for her many hours of labor over Skip. Of course he did not know what she had done, she told herself, but nevertheless her mind went back to those dark days in the hospital and brooded over them.

Hour after hour she had sat beside the bed, connecting herself by faith to that torrent of energy that came from God and by her loving imagination pouring it into Skip, as though she were giving him a spiritual blood-transfusion. She had looked away from the boy's battered face that she might see his spirit perfect and eternal. Up and beyond him she had looked, into the blank ceiling of the hospital room, as if his spirit lingered there just outside its broken home of flesh. *"Come back!"* she called to this spirit again and again. "You aren't ready to go on. You don't know the way. Come back! I know it's hard, but come back! Skip! I call you—"

Then she had thought of that One Triumphant, Whose human voice had troubled death itself and had brought forth Lazarus out of corruption and the tomb. His spirit was alive, as Skip's spirit, whether or not it would come back into the body, was alive. So she spoke the name of Christ aloud and called on Him for help.

Gray light had announced the dawn as she said the words, gray light where the black windowpanes had been. The night nurse had departed and the day nurse, heavy-eyed, came and took the boy's temperature, as if there could be any fever in that cold body awash on the chilly brink of death . . .

Something had stirred in the sterile air as Burnett spoke that Word. Something had changed in the laboring body before her, its tiny hold on life tightening—strengthening.

The day nurse looked askance at Burnett but she stayed on, protected by the doctor's orders that she should be left alone. She remained until she no longer sensed the departing spirit straining on the cord of life. Then Burnett had spoken to the living Skip, seeing beneath his crushed face the boy who had vaulted over her garden fence and sat beside her on the grass. "You'll be all right now," she had said. "Just hold everything, and you'll come through." And with a rush of tears she laid her cheek for a moment upon his hand.

Burnett did not have Paul's sympathy with childhood nor his tenderness for age. But the young who verged on manhood touched her heart with a passion of tenderness, and she grieved over them as she had grieved over Alan Whitacre so many years ago.

Time and the melancholy passing of the years had

softened her sorrow over Alan. But on these slow days while she waited, hoping against hope that Paul would come, memories of Alan moved and stirred within her mind. Could she love Paul, she wondered, as she had loved Alan? Or was her real self forever buried with the beloved of her youth? She had felt passing fancies, for this man and for that one. But none of them had led her into marriage or into any kind of an affair. Those whom she might conceivably have loved, had not loved her. Those who had loved her had failed to awaken the slumbering depths of her nature and she had guarded the bright doors of her spirit against their approaches, lest she do violence to her objective of finding and using thy power of God.

"I should never have let myself go like that, never!" thought Burnett on a day in late July as she looked over her clothes preparatory to her vacation. "Thinking about Paul as if I could really fall in love again after all these years."

Then for no reason that she knew, she glanced out of her bedroom window and saw Paul himself coming up her walk.

Burnett's heart stood still with a great shock of joy. She darted to the mirror, pushed back a few stray hairs and went to the front door.

He stood on the doorstep, the sun on his brown hair and his forehead drawn up into its accustomed worried frown.

"Come in," Burnett said casually.

"I should have called sooner," said Paul uneasily, sitting on the edge of his chair, "to thank you for answering my S.O.S. that night. But—there were—a lot of things to—think about."

"And a lot of fears to allay, I suppose," replied Burnett from her grandmother's rocking chair. Her full-skirted dress had small gay flowers on a white background, and Burnett sat as erect and still as her grandmother might have sat.

"I—do want to say," Paul forced out the words with obvious difficulty, "that it's only your ideas that I question, not—you. I know that the rumors—the things that people say are—not true. And if in my first conversation with you I gave an opposite impression, then I—I apologize."

He should apologize for a great deal more than that, thought Burnett. And she said, "How do you know those things aren't true?"

Paul was unable to tell her. He merely repeated, "I just know. But your—your pseudoscientific ideas about prayer—"

The "pseudoscientific" was a red rag to a bull.

"In spite of those *pseudoscientific* ideas you sent for me," she reminded him.

"In an emergency, one grabs at any straw," replied the minister with a certain lack of tact.

What an insufferable man! "So I'm a straw," she snapped, tossing her head and darting a withering glance at him. "To be grabbed and thrown away again when no longer needed. Thanks."

"I'm sorry." Paul had the grace to blush. "I didn't mean that the way it sounded."

"Just what did you mean?"

The annoying minister was not cowed. "Since you ask me," he replied, with a flash of his own eyes, "I mean, explicitly, that except in an emergency I hesitate to call upon your somewhat dubious power because I do not understand it and I am a little afraid of it."

"Nevertheless, in an emergency you will call," said Burnett, "without any regard at all for *me*—how much I may have to give up or to overcome in order to answer you. I am merely an institution, dubious, as you say, to be avoided whenever possible."

"I'm sorry," Paul said again. He looked at her as though seeing her for the first time. "I—guess I have been so concerned with your ideas that I have not really considered—you," he admitted.

"Well, I'm here," Burnett said grimly.

"You went to the hospital a great many times to see Skip," Paul stated, forcing out the words with difficulty. "It was as I told you, without my knowledge. However, if you helped him, I should express my thanks."

Burnett rose. "I'm very busy," she said, and turned abruptly away to hide the tears in her eyes. "It is obvious that we have nothing to say to each other. So if I may be excused—"

"No—no!" cried Paul, rising in his turn and stepping between her and the door. "I'm a blundering fool. Forgive me. I'm rigid, like a poker. I don't mean to be. So many years of stiffening myself to meet life that I just don't know—how to unbend. Forgive me. You *did* help Skip. The truth is that you have done such a great thing for me that I—don't quite dare to think about it . . ."

Burnett, having forced a thank-you out of him, was suddenly ashamed of herself. "That's all right," she murmured, motioning him back to his chair and sinking down again in hers. "I shouldn't have obtruded myself."

Paul's face cleared, and he sighed as if with relief. "I really would like to ask you some questions," he said rather diffidently. "In spite of my fear of new ideas, I must learn, in order to help people like Frank. So will you bear with my clumsiness and tell me: what is this power? And what do you do in order to release it?"

Burnett tried to explain matters too great to be framed in words. "So, first of all I *know* that God's power is real, like electricity or any other flow of energy," she concluded. "Then I make in my own mind the image, clear and bright and definite, of the thing that I desire, so creating a form for that power to enter. And finally I accept the power, saying by faith, 'Let it be so.' "

"But isn't that rather presumptuous?"

"It's only saying Amen in English words."

"But what if it isn't God's will?" the minister puzzled.

"If it isn't God's will, I don't work for it in the first place," replied Burnett. "First of all I ask Him if it's His will."

"But when Skip was dying, I prayed continually, 'Thy will be done,' " insisted Paul. "What's wrong with that kind of prayer?"

"Nothing. Except that it doesn't work."

"But didn't Our Lord—"

" 'Arise and walk if it be God's will'?" Burnett misquoted. " 'Lazarus come forth if it be God's will'? I can't remember that He did."

"But in the Garden of Gethsemane He said, 'Nevertheless, not my will but Thy will be done.' "

"So did you, in a smaller way, when you came here this afternoon." Burnett smiled and there was tenderness in the warm planes of her face. "You thought, 'I don't want to go to see that woman, but if she can teach me anything that might help people like Frank, I will.'"

"That's right," agreed Paul, smiling in his turn.

"That's the decision prayer," explained Burnett. "That's not the healing prayer. Go through the New Testament and see what He really did say for a healing prayer."

"I know the New Testament pretty well," said Paul, tightening his lips a little. "Only I thought—well, we were taught in seminary that we live under a new dispensation; that the age of miracles is past."

"Which are you going to believe: the seminary or—*Him?*" asked Burnett. "He said that we were to do His works."

"I—I don't quite know," muttered Paul.

Burnett, watching him in silence, knew that she had said enough for one afternoon. "I hope that it won't make trouble for you, coming here to see me," she said.

"That's as may be," replied Paul absently. And Burnett saw that his hesitance about her was a matter of convictions and not of personal fear. When he thought it right to come he did come, in full daylight and in view of the whole town.

"I'm sorry that your vestry saw me that night," she said abruptly.

Paul waved that aside with an impatient gesture. "We can't concern ourselves about that," he said. Then he added with a lopsided smile, "There are certain people in my congregation who would make secrecy practically impossible." As Burnett considered this he burst out, gathering his courage, "What does all this mind-over-matter theory do to Jesus Christ Our Lord? If this is true, why the Cross? Why didn't He just see the Pharisees and Pontius Pilate as perfect? Surely He could do that if *you* can! If we can step into the place of God and act, why do we need any redemption? Moreover, if this is carried logically through to the end, why do we die?"

"Maybe we won't always," said Burnett, answering the last question first. "The last enemy that shall be overcome is death," she quoted.

"Oh, come now, you don't think that means—"

"What it says?" interrupted Burnett. "Perhaps it does. And for the rest, I suggest that we set aside your questions about theology and just begin. After you are familiar with the working of the power, you will be better able to understand the theories concerning it. So why don't you pretend that God's promises are true and act on them, as a scientist adopts a certain theory and acts on it?"

"Is that what you did?"

Burnett nodded.

"What made you start?" asked the minister abruptly.

"A tragedy. Like Frank, only—worse."

"How could it be worse?"

"Well—he lived longer—It was a boy with whom I grew up in China. My parents were missionaries, you see. He was my only friend. And I saw him grow more and more sad, the darkness around him deepening and deepening, and no one could do anything about it. Then he swung toward a manic stage, becoming overstimulated. That was when we were in the Shanghai-American school—and the next year he went home, and his letters became wild and confused, and then I heard that he was in a mental institution and—died."

"How?"

"I don't know. I couldn't bear to ask."

Paul had no words.

"I couldn't do anything for him—not anything," said Burnett, looking out of the window and far away into the past. "And when I asked why, I was told that I must accept the will of God."

"And it wasn't the will of God," said Paul, remembering Frank dying on the floor of the church where he had come looking for help.

"And I asked why we didn't do miracles as Christ said we were to do. 'Verily, verily I say unto you,' " she quoted, her voice deep and throbbing, " 'He that believeth on me, the works that I do shall he do also, and greater works than these shall he do—' But they told me that this was a new dispensation and the age of miracles was past."

Paul nodded. He had heard that also, and although somewhat uneasily, he had accepted it. "Then what happened?" he asked gently.

"A miracle!" said Burnett, light coming into her eyes as she spoke. "I was in the hospital supposed to be dying with peritonitis—this was after I had come up here to teach art in the public schools—and the chaplain put his hands on me and prayed for healing, and the next day I was perfectly well! All my life I had known that it should be this way— all my life! And though I still belonged to the church, and taught Sunday school and all the rest of it, something inside me was never satisfied until a miracle actually happened to me. I was so happy I couldn't keep still, just as I can't keep still now when I tell you about it!" cried Burnett, rising and walking about the room. "So I told my Sunday school class, and those kids were as thrilled as I was! Naturally we had to find out how to do these things. So I decided that for the time being I would set aside all that I had been taught, and pay no attention to what anyone said in the Bible or out of the Bible—not St. Paul nor the minister nor anybody—and just study the four Gospels and see what Jesus Christ really said to do—and do it. And we began to see miracles —even the children— little miracles of answered prayer. But—" She sat down again and flung out her hands in a gesture of hopelessness.

"What happened then?" asked Paul breathlessly, his heart sinking, for he guessed it and grieved.

"The children told their parents about it, naturally, and the parents began complaining to the minister that I was teaching heresy, and that the children were becoming overexcited on the subject of religion, and the session met and—they threw me out."

"What?"

Burnett nodded. "Of course they couldn't exactly excommunicate me—one can't when there isn't any communion, only a memorial service about once a year— but they asked me to give up my class and to resign from the women's guild and to take no part in church activities, and—they said it as plainly as they could—to leave."

Paul sat with his head in his hands, deeply stricken and wondering. Would he have done the same? He had no answer.

"But you kept on, going to people, as you did to Skip—"

Burnett nodded. "By that time I found out that I could help them," she said simply. "So what else can one do? I don't mean that I try to help everyone! Just those that I feel especially sorry for—"

"And Jesus was moved by compassion," quoted Paul softly.

"Some of those who were helped were also eager to learn," said Burnett. "And they said they had to see me from time to time in order to keep themselves from drowning, as it were, in the sea of life. So I have a little prayer group or Bible class or whatever you might call it, here. We do need each other, you know—we do need each other! So if there's no place for us in a church, we just get together and do the best we can."

"Did you ever try another church?"

"I went to two or three confirmation classes in Philadelphia several years ago."

"What were you taught?" asked Paul, swallowing hard in embarrassment, for he could guess.

"The first class was on the history and meaning of the ministers' vestments," said Burnett without expression. "The next was on the names and symbolism of the various things about the church. The third was on finding one's way through the prayer book—"

"Don't go on," said Paul, remembering a young woman who had said after the last confirmation lecture, "Oh, Mr. Forrester—I've been meaning for a long time to ask you— do you think there really is any God?" Paul concluded sadly to Burnett, "I know."

"I had to search where I could search," Burnett went on. "It's all there in the Bible, of course, but I didn't know how to find it. So I read all kinds of books on prayer and meditation and mysteries and miracles. I tested them in two ways: first, did they check with what I found in the Gospels, and second, did they work? I may have made mistakes, but I had to learn the best way I could, even though it was too late for the young man I loved when we were both so young—so very young."

"Have you never loved anyone since?" For a moment Paul spoke as a man and a lonely man, not as a minister.

Burnett's heart missed a beat, "Not really," she said briefly. "Little flames, now and then. Soon dying."

Paul was looking at her in a new way, seeing her as herself, as a person. "You were very brave to go on helping others after you lost him," he said.

"The more courage one puts into a project, the more apt it is to work." And she added, "It took courage for you to come here this afternoon. And you'd better not make a habit of it. People will criticize you."

"That I can bear," said Paul with a smile. "It's not fear of criticism that makes this thing hard for me. It is—well, I am a minister. I'm supposed to know the rudiments of prayer and to teach them to others. So I confess, it is a bit upsetting to my—"

"Pride," finished Burnett.

"Yes." Paul sat forward on his chair, elbows on knees, hands clasped. Then he murmured, looking toward the floor at his feet, "But it has already been humbled. Into the dust—into the dust." There was no melodrama in the words. They were too quietly spoken; hardly more than a whisper, hardly more than a sigh.

The barrier around Burnett's heart broke and melted in a great rush of tenderness. She saw once more the minister's white, stricken face, as he knelt beside Frank's body. Here was a grief great and overwhelming, but unshared, uncomforted. Not for a single day had Paul taken time to withdraw from life that he might fortify himself against the sorrow of his heart. He had proceeded with his normal duties, unfaltering. It had not even occurred to him to do otherwise. Meanwhile that picture of the dying boy who had trusted him burned itself deep into his consciousness, a wound he would always carry, a burden he would always bear.

Burnett was a person of impulse. Without plan or volition she crossed the room and dropped on the floor beside him, touching his clasped hands. *"Don't. Don't!"* she pleaded, her voice, that could be winged with fire and touched with steel, now tender, deeply comforting. "Don't reproach yourself like that! Grief we can bear, but self-reproach is such a burden—and we don't need to carry it. I have learned that. After all, I failed too. And I had time and more time and all the time there was. Still, I failed—"

"There was nothing else that you knew to do," whispered Paul, his eyes upon the floor. "I did know something else to do: I should have sent him to you. Something in me tried to make me do it. I even dreamed about dark sand slipping, slipping in an hourglass—and I was too proud."

"Maybe that wouldn't have worked after all," pleaded Burnett. "Anyway, it's past. The only thing to do with possible mistakes is to turn them into power; to use them as stepping-stones to greater things."

"Can that be done?" asked Paul, in a voice so low that Burnett could hardly hear the words.

"You're doing it now," said Burnett, and quite unconsciously she held his hands in both of hers and looked up with her eyes full of tears. In concern for him she had forgotten to draw the veil upon her face, and her love shone through it like a flame.

Paul looked sharply into her eyes. She felt him stiffen and withdraw his hands. "Now you've done it," she thought. And she rose and walked away from him. He had seen that she loved him, and she knew it. But with everything in her, she would deny it. She stood, still and cold, while he excused himself rather breathlessly, and fled.

She watched him from the window as he hurried around the corner of the fence and flung himself into his car. Now that he had seen her love, he would never again enter her house. Between them stood all the world: God and the seminary, the church and the vestry, Priscilla McGhann and a hundred like her.

Nevertheless Burnett knew as she watched him with the ache of tears in her throat that she loved Paul Forrester as she had loved no other man since Alan.

7

What a strange person, thought Paul Forrester. At one moment prim in her grandmother's chair, with her hands clasped on her lap and her face as still and remote as the bland countenance of a Chinese lady in an old print; then in a flash, kneeling beside him on the floor, her voice as tender as sweet music, her eyes full of—Paul reined in his thoughts sharply, tightening his grip on the car wheel as he drove down Main Street. For he had almost used the word "love."

That was impossible, he told himself firmly, rounding the corner into the wide street that slumbered beneath the misty August sunlight. As he drove past the stately residences and out to the dank Jersey countryside he assured himself that the light he had seen in Burnett's eyes was not the glow of love. She was, after all, a genius in her own strange way—a woman of fire and ice and power. She would not fall in love with a small-time minister who would never be anything more important. The beauty of vestments and the softening light of the chancel had no allure for her. She was not, thank heaven, of the same vintage as Opal Oldershaw and the other sentimental virgins of his church—and he would with all promptness put her out of his mind.

But this proved difficult.

He looked at the cabbage fields, purple and gray-blue in the sun, and wondered whether she had ever painted them. Paul was not altogether ignorant of her paintings. He had gone on hesitant feet to an art museum in the city and, cringing past much modern surrealism, had found her pictures, clear and cool in the quietness of beauty. As he rattled over a cedar-water creek, he remembered a study that she had made of dark waters, brooding beneath the gaiety of lacy trees. How could she do it? How could she make one know that her water was deep and cold and that her trees were full of singing birds? How could she paint water and trees and within them a thought and a mood, as surely as his sermons held a thought and mood, and far more beautifully? Thank God she was not a surrealist, he thought, and then wondered what difference it could possibly make to him. She did not paint squiggles and whorls and say, "This means something else." She did not draw deformed and lumpish people. Her people looked like people. Yet every careful portrait showed not only features but a soul and a mood as well, and even, mysteriously, the artist's sympathetic appreciation of that soul and that mood. And every landscape translated into beauty a feeling so deep that he who looked must sense it, yet so elusive that no words encompassed it. What was there in this woman, he wondered, his thoughts taking another turn, that brooded beneath her bright and flippant manner; what mysteries, what unknown depths?

"This will never do," the Reverend Paul Forrester told himself. "Get your mind on your work, for heaven's sake."

He pushed Burnett away from his aroused consciousness and turned his thoughts toward the mental hospital where he was bound with vestment case and communion set. He would not admit to himself how much he disliked going into the midst of that hopelessness, bearing in his hands the sacred Life that no longer resurrected but only comforted. At least it did comfort, he told himself, sighing. Wandering minds that grasped no words felt somehow the eternal message of the Eucharist and were still. Eyes dark with hopelessness brightened to a brief, uneasy life. Those to whom he ministered could live for a moment at least in that real world where eternity reaches out to time.

What would Burnett do, he wondered, as he turned from the country road into the vast, roaring highway. "See them well," perhaps, assuring herself that such was God's will. *And so it was.* Suddenly Paul knew that, with a deep, impassioned knowing, as if his own inner spirit arose and shouted the knowledge into his flabby thoughts. Death might be a blessed release or the fulfillment of a divine purpose; illness might be a purposeful chastisement; but that a living being should decay into filthiness or should be tormented by unholiness, no, such as this could not possibly be the will of God.

Why, then, he asked himself, did God not intervene and make these people well? And to this question he had no answer.

Burnett had said, "Maybe the answers will come to you as you act." Could she be right? He did not know. But there was one way of finding out—to try her way of creative visioning and observe the results. He would give it just one try. Paul decided, in the midst of the demoniac noise of Route 1. He would choose one person in the mental hospital and for that person he would make an act of faith, persistently conceiving of that one as well—and he would see what happened.

Ancient words of beauty and dignity floated into his mind: "That it may please thee to succour, help, and comfort, all who are in danger, necessity, and tribulation; *we beseech Thee to hear us, good Lord.*"

All of them. What did that make of his own small childish thought of choosing one?

He did not know. But with a rueful smile he told himself, as he cut across the battle-tide of traffic, that he was not big enough to pray with real power for all of them, so he might as well start where he was and try with humility to pray for one; and perhaps some day he would grow up to the measure of the stature of that great prayer-book prayer.

He wound through wide lawns and parked beside the red brick Home that tried so hard to be a home. There he found his way to chapel and robing room and vested, making ready to minister the Holy Communion to the wanderers who came to him.

As he lit the candles on the altar he glanced at the shipwrecked souls washed up by the cold waves of life upon this bit of shore: old women with restless fingers and blank eyes, a man or two, sitting apart, eyes on the floor; one girl who looked about and giggled vacantly at the group; more old women, more old women. They were no more crazy than his own great-aunt had been, he thought, remembering the old lady who had rocked upon the back porch and told stories to the rectory children. A bit childish, Aunt Lucy had been, her ancient mind, weary of life, wandering from time to time. There had been room in the rambling dwellings of those days for the Aunt Lucys. But now there was no room. Tiny cottages and flats crammed with television sets and pet dogs had driven the Aunt Lucys of the world to this uncertain refuge where they waited for the long brightness of eternity to lift the shadows from their minds. His heart softened with compassion as he looked at them. He would have given everything that he had to restore them to peace. But he did not see here one whom he could visualize as well.

A man whom Paul had never seen before lingered at the door of the chapel. Accustomed to the wary ones, too timid to come in, Paul went to the door and spoke to him: "Won't you join us?" Then he saw from the elegance of the man's attire and from a certain look of authority about him that this was not a patient. Nevertheless, he said, "We would be glad to have you with us."

The man shook his bald head. "But will you pray for my daughter, Judith?" he said. And he added, sorrowingly, "She is here."

"I will remember her in the service," promised Paul. "And I would be glad to see her—"

But the man broke in with a shudder, "No—no!" And he added more quietly, "You cannot see her. She is in solitary."

"I understand," said Paul.

And he prayed in the Prayer for All Conditions of Men "Also thy servant Judith, for whom our prayers are desired . . ."

Could this be the one whom he should take for his experiment in prayer? he wondered. But no. He could not see her, that he might imagine her perfect. And besides, he knew from her father's looks that she was Jewish. No. He would look about for someone else.

So he did the one thing that he could do. He comforted the aged and the helpless; a smile here and there, words of humor and of gentleness. From ward to ward and from room to room he went, and wherever he entered he brought the joy of friendliness and of an interest that was real and deep.

Then as he left the hospital his eyes fell upon a man weeding one of the flowerbeds. "An inmate or an employee?" he asked himself. He did not look like an employee. His face, as he turned toward Paul, was intelligent and arrestingly beautiful, with a noble forehead, a well-shaped mouth and eyes of a deep blue. It was not the face of a gardener. Yet he was out in the sun and air, with no guard watching him.

"Oh Lord, if you want me to help this man, tell me what to say," prayed Paul, standing still on the driveway.

The man went on weeding the scarlet sage and zinnias. A yellow bloom among these common summer flowers caught Paul's eye. He had not seen that little flower except in the rectory garden of his childhood. "Saint-John's-wort, that's what it is," murmured Paul, hardly knowing that he spoke out loud.

The young man started and raised his head. Then he rose and faced Paul, looking full at him with eyes a bit too clear and wide to be quite sane. "Saint-John's-wort, that's what it is," he repeated. "My mother said that once. Just those words." And he smiled. There was charm in his smile, but there was also an indefinable uncertainty.

"That's funny," said Paul. "My mother grew it too, in the rectory garden." And he leaned down and touched the fluffy yellow flower with its golden stamens. "Do you work here?" he asked, not looking up.

"I'm an inmate," the man said simply.

"Oh. I don't remember seeing you—"

"I have just come. My family moved East, so—I—I visit them sometimes—for a little while."

He made no explanation of this, but Paul could read its meaning in his bent head and in the sadness of his voice. This man could not long endure the confusion of freedom, the burden of real life. His mind would presently buckle under the strain of it and he would be glad once more to find shelter here where nothing was required of him. Without knowing how he knew this, Paul knew. So when the man said, not lifting his head, "I've been in places like this for quite some time," Paul simply replied, "I know."

The man looked down at Paul from his great height and smiled. "You seemed to understand."

Paul said, "I come here often. Forrester is my name, Paul Forrester. And as you see, I am a minister."

The man's eyes fastened themselves on Paul's clerical collar as though they had not noticed it before and as though they grasped its implication with some difficulty. "I'm Alan Whitacre," he said. "Al, they call me here."

They sat together upon a bench beneath an oak that dropped its acorns now and then with small thuds upon the brittle summer grass. And as they talked Paul knew: *this is the one.* So he practiced seeing Alan with all strain gone from his intense blue eyes, all nervousness from his smile, all fear from his heart. He visioned him relaxed, at ease, integrated, whole. It made Paul feel very strange and awkward. But every now and then he would say in the midst of it, "Oh God, let this be so." Then he would try to picture a light from God shining into Al's mind.

Should he ask Burnett to help in this? he wondered, as the conversation drifted from one theme to another. And he decided, no. This was his experiment. He would see what he could do alone and thus he would find out whether Burnett's words were true.

"Come again," Alan said as Paul climbed into his car. And there was a real desire in his voice.

Could he develop, Paul wondered, the power of channeling the healing love of God to these defenseless ones? *"Oh-h-h,"* he sighed aloud, as he turned into Route 1. His heart leaped into life as he thought of it, quite as if for all his days he had longed for this very thing.

Perhaps he had.

Happiness stayed with him all week. He found himself smiling at anything and nothing—at Skip, at Janet's loud, cheerful chatter and Ambrose's gloomy observations concerning the state of politics—even at the ironing board, when he found it standing crossly in the hall.

Two people lingered just below his consciousness, and the thought of either one filled him with a warm glow. One was Burnett McNeill, and the other was Alan Whitacre.

He entered his church on Sunday with a high heart, after being firmly vested by Priscilla while Janet glowered at her from the sacristy door. Ambrose, his face solemn over his verger's robe, swung open the heavy doors of the sacristy and the choir marched in, "flinging out the banner," with loud, holy voices as they went. Last of all went Paul, just behind the impressive rear of Angus McGhann. There were no servers this morning, for the service was Morning Prayer. Paul deplored this fact, for the gracious sacrament was so beautiful to him that he longed to celebrate it at every morning service. But this his sturdy congregation would not accept. Paul entered the chancel alone and in due course read the Lesson for the Day.

Paul did not lift his voice in the Episcopal howl, nor did he gabble or mumble. He loved the Bible for its beauty and for the fire that glowed beneath its stately words, illumining them with the rhythm of poetry. And the manner of his reading, grave and beautiful, showed that he loved it. The Second Lesson was from the fourth chapter of St. Luke's Gospel, beginning at the fortieth verse. "Now when the sun was setting," read Paul in his pleasant, resonant voice, "All they that had any sick with divers diseases brought them unto Him; and He laid His hands on every one of them and healed them."

Paul lifted his eyes and looked at the congregation. And he saw before him in the seventh pew the face of Burnett McNeill. There she sat, as still and as expressionless as a Chinese Buddha, with that smile that was hardly a smile upon her face. She was in the yellow linen dress which he had seen once before, and a white hat, severely plain, framed her shining blue-black hair.

Without the shadow of a pause he bent his head again over the Book and read steadily on. He closed the Book and returned to his seat. And he wondered, while the choir was being joyful in the Lord, why all the lights in the church should have brightened when he saw her face. He should have been perturbed rather than rejoicing, he told himself, for undoubtedly certain ones among his flock would be displeased. He glanced uneasily toward the sopranos. There stood Opal Oldershaw, piping valiantly away and stealing a sideways glance at the congregation—undoubtedly at the seventh pew. Was her little rabbit mouth a rounder "o" than usual as she went her way into His gates with thanksgiving and into His courts with praise? Then he caught Priscilla's grim glance as she bellowed among the contraltos. There was no question about the look of her bushy, uplifted eyebrows and her meat-chopper mouth.

Paul should have been disturbed. But he was not. Anyone has a right to come to church, he told himself, and a minister should, like the angels of heaven, be uncommonly rejoiced at one home-staying sinner that repented and came to worship. Then he coughed slightly and covered his mouth to hide a smile. For Burnett, as cool as an iceberg in a shining sea, did not in the least resemble a sinner that repented.

The great words of the Apostles' Creed brought Paul out of his wandering. He crossed himself mentally in a wordless prayer for forgiveness, and said with sincerity, not looking at Burnett, "The Lord be with you."

"And with thy spirit," answered the congregation. And Paul led them in those prayers that have for centuries brought peace to the wandering hearts of men. During the prayers he was supported by the liturgy and upheld by his sense of the protecting Church. But when he entered the pulpit and knew that he was talking about the mighty things of God to one who had more faith in mighty things than he had, his heart failed. A minister, however, delivers his sermon whether he wants to or not. So Paul fixed his gaze sturdily on those back pews where Frank had lain on one dark night and preached about the Kingdom of Heaven.

But the congregation was not with him. He could feel them far away and dragging. What was the matter? *Burnett!* He could almost hear them whispering, "What's that woman doing here?"

"God help me," thought Paul, and went on preaching. "Make them forget her," he prayed. But he could not forget her himself. Why was she here? To make trouble for him? To pray for him? Or could it possibly be, only to look on him with that light in her eyes that he had seen once . . .

"So we are commanded," he told his congregation, "to go into all the world and preach the Gospel to every creature . . ." And suddenly his mind presented him with the neglected words that follow these, and without knowing that he was going to do so, he said them aloud: "Heal the sick, cleanse the lepers, raise the dead." What had got into him? "And He healed all manner of disease," he went on, stumbling a little, for now that he had said so much he must say more. "And we are—are told—to do so too. But the Church has neglected this power and it has become a lost art. Just the same, although so few people realize it, the authority to heal the sick is vested in God's Church and the gift of healing is an integral part of that gift of the Holy Spirit conferred upon every priest at his ordination.

- 108 -

Therefore, as we set ourselves to bring in God's kingdom on earth, let us not forget that this is part of so doing. And since we know nothing of this mysterious work of faith, let us humble ourselves and ask God to illumine our spirits, so that we will know." And after this deviation from his manuscript, Paul hastily ducked into it again and finished the sermon that he had prepared to preach.

He could feel the congregation swinging toward him. Every good preacher knows the mind of his people and gathers them into his own mind, sensing and swaying their reactions as he talks to them. Paul drew them to him, with his humble honesty and with a certain fire that burned within him more brightly than ever before. *"She* is praying for me," he thought. And the knowledge brought him no dismay.

His heart sang as he rested during the anthem. "Unto us a child is given." Ah yes, he remembered. There had been words about that anthem. Angus McGhann had dubbed it a Christmas theme and had fought the singing of it at this time. But his sister Priscilla, glaring her brother down, had declared that He is given to us at all times and that we should sing about it at frequent intervals. Especially, she contended, since there was little chance to sing this anthem at Christmas time, when the Carol Service with its costumed choir swept everything else out of the way. Opal sided with Priscilla, chirping brightly, "For unto us a Son is born" to show how pretty the tune could be, then ducking her head and dimpling, "Oh, silly little me." The organist, hastily following the line of least resistance, had decided in favor of singing it. So here it was. "Unto us a child is born," declared Opal, her soulful eyes upon the wrought iron of the canopy. "Unto us a child is born," announced Miss McGhann to the prophet Jeremiah dolefully carved in wood upon the roof-beams. A chorus of female voices insisted upon this fact, and Paul's submerged sense of humor noted that almost every one of them was a spinster of no uncertain age. "Unto us a child is born!" they carolled brightly. And the deep voices of the basses boomed, "Wonderful! Marvelous!"

Paul Forrester, in danger of irreverent levity, turned his face resolutely away from the choir and watched the ushers passing the collection plates. He could calculate within three dollars what would go on them, thought Paul. And at this a most irrelevant thought wandered across the runaway mind of the minister of All Saints: if he should decide to marry, how would he support a wife who had been accustomed to making a comfortable income of her own?

He was glad when the ushers stood in a solemn phalanx at the foot of the chancel steps. "All things come of Thee, Oh Lord, and of Thine own have we given Thee—"

He was even more relieved when the service was at an end. Down the side aisle he went to the church door, half hoping, half fearing that Burnett would be there to shake hands with him. But she was not.

"Attaboy," said Skip, when Paul at last came home. "Give 'em the works. If this healing business can be done, seems like a church ought to do it."

"I didn't really mean to give 'em the works," hesitated Paul.

"Well, you sure did," Skip told him cheerfully. "It was worth coming back from the seashore to hear you." And he added, "I bet you stirred up something, though."

This proved to be true. Even though he had swung them with him on Sunday morning, Paul's congregation turned in the opposite direction as the week passed. Veiled glances told him so, the small, tense smiles following the usual remark, "I notice that Miss McNeill was in church."

"Yes indeed," Paul would say with noncommittal heartiness.

The matter would drop from the conversation, but not, Paul knew, from the speaker's mind.

Thursday was the midsummer meeting of the women's guilds, called for obscure reasons a garden party, and preceded and followed by business meetings for the planning of the next year's work. It was an occasion not without hazards to minister and sexton. Paul relinquished the day to it, speaking when called upon to speak and spending the remainder of the time in his study with both doors open, ready for any questions that might be brought to him. But Ambrose disappeared entirely from the face of the earth and if his bleak visage adorned the back room of Doc's drugstore, no one at All Saints was aware of it. He had his principles, did Ambrose, and he adhered to them, keeping clear of the womenfolk at all times.

"Oh, Mr. *Forrester!*" It was Opal, twinkling after him down the cloister.

Paul turned warily.

"Oh, Mr. *Forrester!*" she beamed, prancing up to him. "I think it's so *wonderful*, what you said in your sermon last Sunday. About healing, I mean! So *brave* of you! Especially with *that woman* there! Don't you consider it extremely bold of her coming to church?"

"I see nothing bold about coming to church," replied Paul, a bit snappily. "After all, it's frequently done."

"Oh, Mr. Forrester, you are *so* amusing!" cried Opal, dimpling up at him. "And it's so *big* of you to take her as you do!"

"I really have no idea what you are talking about." Paul turned away. "I'm sorry, but I have an appointment."

"Oh, Mr. Forrester, I did want to say—about healing, you know—*so* true, even if certain *queer people* do it— 'They shall lay hands on the sick, and they shall recover,' " she quoted dreamily. "I found that in the Scriptures only yesterday. Oh, dear Mr. Forrester, you know, I do have the most *frightful* digestive trouble!" Here she batted her eyelashes at him and coughed delicately. "Perhaps if you would lay your hands on my little tummy and say just a teeny-weeny prayer—"

"Lord, have mercy on us," thought Paul, for the idea of laying his hands on Opal's little tummy was altogether too much for him. He bolted into his study and closed the door.

No wonder ministers shied away from the subject of healing, he told himself. Then he remembered Alan Whitacre and gathered together his courage. He had seen Alan once more and he was sure of an improvement in the man. There was less tension in his smile and less hesitancy in his voice. So Paul saw him well once more, as he always did upon remembering him, and said the Prayer for All Conditions of Men with special intentions for his recovery. Once again he wondered whether he should ask Burnett to pray with him for Alan Whitacre. But Al was not an emergency case like Frank. He was under proper medical care, and was already well on the way to recovery.

Nevertheless, he longed to see Burnett again.

"She arouses my curiosity," he told Janet at dinnertime.

"I would like to learn more about—just what it is that she does."

Janet, looking very smug, replied, "Why don't you go back to see her?"

"You think that would be a good idea, do you?" asked Paul.

"I think you'd be showing a gleam of almost human intelligence for once in your life," Janet answered with that grim older-sister wit that had been the plague of Paul's childhood.

"Well, I guess I will," he said.

"Better make it soon, before she goes on vacation."

Now that he had decided to go, he was beset with a great eagerness. Paul never called on lone women in the evening, just as he never called on married women in the daytime. So with difficulty he composed himself until the afternoon of the next day, knowing that Burnett would not receive callers in the morning. He would drop in casually, murmuring, "I was just passing by—"

It was difficult to be casual, especially when his heart pounded in such a ridiculous way. Madeleine met him at the door and he gulped with surprise, expecting Burnett.

"Yes, she's home," said Madeleine. "Just step inside, Mr. Forrester, and I'll tell her you're here."

Paul stood in the hallway, comforted by the indefinable aroma of an old house: apples and burning logs and wood made fragrant by the centuries.

"She's busy, but she says come right in," and Madeleine's pleasant face shone as he stepped down the narrow hall and entered the studio door.

Burnett perched before a painting, a palette in one hand and a brush in another. "Can't stop right this minute," she said without preamble. "Have a seat." She waved her paintbrush toward the one easy chair and added vermilion to the shadowy folds of a lady's dress, making it dance with life.

"Perhaps I'd better go," hesitated Paul. "I was just passing by, and—"

"No, stay." Burnett flashed a smile over the shoulder of her gay smock. "I'll stop in a minute. Soon as I use up this paint I've mixed."

Brief as her words were, her voice welcomed him. His

heart ceased to pound. He settled in the wicker chair and watched her tense profile as she worked; the features a trifle sharp, the mouth drawn down a bit in concentration. A strange face, he thought, a little like an Indian, with its high cheekbones, a little like a panther. An arresting profile, though not a pretty one.

"So you thought you'd drop in," murmured Burnett, leaning back from her portrait and squinting her eyes at it, "and find out why I went to church on Sunday."

What an uncomfortable woman she was, thought Paul, and he wished that she did not always have him at such a disadvantage. "Well—why did you come?" he said.

"I just wanted to see what you have there," Burnett said in her absorbed painting-voice. "I—first I thought, perhaps I shouldn't; people would think it was queer. Then I decided: anybody's got a right to go to church. And there *is* something there: an other-worldly quality. I felt it long ago, when you baptized my brother's baby. Although frankly," she added with devastating candor, "I didn't like the baptismal service."

"And what didn't you like about it?" demanded Paul, wondering why this woman always rushed into combat with him.

"Well, it's on such a moronic level," she said, putting down her paintbrush and facing him. ' "None can enter into the kingdom of God except he be regenerate and born anew of Water and the Holy Ghost.' Now, really. How can a little baby get the Holy Ghost just because you drip water on him? And renouncing the devil with all his works . . . I could just imagine that baby lifting up his hand and saying, 'Get away, you,' and a devil with a red tail scuttling into the rafters!"

Paul was horrified. That a crassly ignorant person with no background whatsoever should dare to ridicule a service instinct with power! "Don't you believe in anything except what you can see with your eyes?" he demanded.

"Of course I do!" cried Burnett. "There's the eternal life and goodness that is God. And we don't have to be dunked to get it. Or sprinkled, either."

What a thoroughly disagreeable person, thought Paul; why had he ever let his imagination dwell on her, just because she had for a moment smiled into his eyes? He got to his feet, his face very red. "There's nothing to be gained from continuing this conversation," he said.

"I'm sorry," she said a little breathlessly. "It was very rude of me. I—I really wanted to learn—that's why I came to church. And there *was* something there, too; something elusive and beautiful . . ."

Paul knew what it was. It was the sacred Presence on the altar. But he did not dare tell her so. What if he should speak the name of his Lord and this dreadful woman should say, "Don't hand me that nonsense?" He shuddered and made for the door.

"Why do I *do* this?" lamented Burnett. "I don't mean to fight with you, and yet . . . I have had such bitter resentment toward the Church because of—the man I told you about. I—I really must get over it."

"It would be advisable," murmured Paul stiffly.

They faced each other in the open door of the studio, hardly noticing the doorbell or the footsteps of Madeleine who answered it.

"Miss Burnett," said Madeleine, and they both turned.

Two Negro men stood on the doorstep. "Grandma sent you a cake," said the taller one, and he motioned beamingly to the basket in Madeleine's hand.

"Oh!" cried Burnett with delight. "She *said* she was going to make me a cake as soon as she got out of bed! Oh, wonderful! Did she really make it herself?"

"Yes'm, she sure did. She had to set down some while she mixed it, but she sure did."

"Let's see it, Madeleine." Burnett's face was as eager as a child's as she lifted the paper napkin from the cake. "It's beautiful!" she breathed; then in a reverent voice, "That's really a resurrection cake, isn't it?"

"It sure is!" the taller man grinned. "Grandma, she ain't been out of bed for six years."

And the other one added, "I never see anything like it, the day you was there. Grandma she whooped and hollered and I come a-running. 'Oh, Lordy!' she say. 'Oh Lord, look at me flap dis-here hand! Oh, my Lord, will you watch me kick dese-here legs!' Yes'm. She pretty near bounced out of bed right then, she did."

"Hands all twisted up for six years," added the other man. "And legs all stiffened up and a misery in her middle."

"That's the truth." Madeleine laughed. "Ever since I've known her she's been like that."

"She's a grand woman," Burnett said warmly. "You tell her so. And tell her thanks a million for this resurrection cake."

The two men, grinning with pleasure, started away.

"How's the baby?" Burnett called after them.

"Oh, he's fine, ma'am. He's fine."

Paul stood and watched her. Her face was lovely with an inner light, all its planes softened into tenderness. Her eyes were full of stars. She was beautiful. Why had he not known before that she was beautiful?

"What's all this?" he asked, smiling.

"That dear old soul sent for me," said Burnett, " 'Are you the lady that was at Madeleine's daughter's funeral?' she asked—"

"Funeral?" Was this another failure? wondered Paul.

"Yes. The child got sick while I was on vacation and died the very day that I returned to town. The first I knew about it was Madeleine rushing here from the hospital. She hadn't even gone home yet, to tell her family . . ."

She said no more. But somehow Paul could see Madeleine crying in Burnett's arms and could hear the words of comfort that Burnett would say to her. What a strange woman, he thought again; so fierce and rude to him, yet so infinitely tender to these little ones in trouble.

"Do you think that it could have been—God's will—for the child to die?" he asked rather timidly.

"It might have been. Susan was born blind. And Madeleine has many other children to look after."

"But didn't you and Madeleine try to heal the blindness?"

Burnett shook her head. "Didn't feel up to it," she said with honesty. "Just couldn't feel that it would work."

Paul was looking about for a lost clue. "But—was the blindness God's will?" he asked.

"I think not," sighed Burnett. "There was no doctor available and no one knew to sterilize the baby's eyes when it was born."

"I don't mean to be insistent," Paul explained. "But there are some things I am really trying to understand."

And he added, in some perplexity, "So you went to the funeral."

"Naturally. To pray for Madeleine and her family. There are other things to pray for besides just the healing of the body." She smiled gently and touched the cake with a loving finger. "The dear old lady," she murmured. "Every time I went to see her she would say, 'Madame, I can never remember your name, but I said to my boys, I said, if that lady that went to the Kimberly funeral was to come to see me, I'd get well, I said.' "

"She didn't know anything about you?"

Burnett shook her head. "Sometimes this prayer-work seems a hard and bitter path—then something like this happens and I am strengthened to go ahead again."

She carried the cake into the dining room, calling out to Madeleine that she must take half of it home.

As Paul stood by the door and waited for her, a disturbing thought came into his mind. This Negro woman had strengthened Burnett and helped her—by an act of gratitude. He, Paul, had taken everything from her and given nothing; he had fought against his debt to her, and the simplicity of gratitude was far from him. "I ought to make you a—a resurrection cake," he said, the slow red rising to his cheeks.

A light came into Burnett's eyes as she stood within the dining-room door, a hand on either doorjamb. But she said nothing.

"I didn't dare—let go and be grateful," Paul added, trying to understand himself. He saw again the boy who was a son to him lying broken on a stretcher dark with blood. And again he saw the boy in church last Sunday, resplendent in tan sports coat and yellow tie, a new Skip, who in his own flippant way knew the reality of God and felt his way toward Him.

He turned to Burnett, his beseeching eyes saying all the words that his tight lips did not dare to say.

And then, for the second time, he ran away from her. If he had stayed there another moment, he would have taken her into his arms.

8

Burnett looked through the train window at a late
September sky, flecks of rose through banks of sombre gay.
Early falling leaves, whirled up by the wheels, darted past
the flying windows, and the shadow of smoke lay dark over
the cornfields. High in the vistadome she watched the night
come down, starlight shining on the silver cars ahead as
they slid through the dark. What if we had never before
known the coming of a night? she thought. What black
despair we would feel, seeing the warm light depart from
everything one had loved ... what terror, to behold the
landmarks of life fading into darkness and we unable to
hold them with our frantic hands! Perhaps some day we
would have lived often enough upon this little earth to
remember, and death would become to us like night, a cozy
interval, a longed-for resting-time, full of gentleness and
stars ...

Alan had called such thoughts as these her "poetry-
mood." It was as if the creativeness that could not at the
moment speak through her fingers, searched for another
vent and blossomed forth in words.

If it were really true that a person sojourned more than
once upon this earth, would she on returning find Alan
again, returning with her, that they might at long last be
together? She smiled and sighed, wondering.

A passing train leaped toward her down the track,
engulfing space and silence in one protracted roar. Then the
night closed shudderingly upon it and it was gone. Burnett
sat up straight, jerked back into reality. And as she thought
about the life ahead of her, the man that filled her mind
was not Alan but Paul. She saw his face as she had last
beheld it, lit into beauty by a warm glow of longing and of

tenderness. What would he have said, if he had not torn himself away and fled up her garden path into the blazing summer street? What would she have said in answering him?

It was good that she had not seen him since that day. Time had been long and had weighed heavily upon her, but it was good. For with the realization that he was verging toward loving her, came the sure knowledge that she was not for him nor ever would be. She, who knew God as a palpitating force, filling every blade of grass and every golden aspen dropping its still leaves on Colorado crags and every far and wandering star—how could she be tied to one who found God in the empty mummery of bells and candles and ancient, morbid prayers and the absurdity of munching bread and swallowing wine? She should never for a moment have let her imagination rest on him. Never!

She reined in her thoughts and looked once more out of the window at the high stars shining softly on the little earth that it might not be lonely in its long traveling through the years. She would be glad to reach her own small home and relax amid pots and pans and rioting fall flowers. She would not even paint for a few days; she would only sink into the deep comfort of earthy things. And Paul would have forgotten her.

But the moment that she entered the prim streets of Mapleton, Burnett knew that Paul had not forgotten. Her brother and his wife drove her home from the great city station, both of them talking to her at once as they turned off the highway and under the maple trees, touched here and there with gold and flame. But when they passed the shabby rectory Burnett's heart leaped toward it with a bound of joy and beyond all reasoning she knew that the desire of Paul's own heart was drawing hers to him. When she had freed herself at last from her family and stood alone in her doorway, a desolation fell upon her. She closed her door and stood with her back to it, her green suit and small amber hat outlined against its white wood. Usually the old house welcomed her, as if her own thoughts had taken smiling form and nestled there awaiting her return. But today she felt as though she were stepping out of the sunlight into a cage.

"What's the matter with you, Burnett?" she whispered to herself in the stillness of the house. *"Get moving!"*

- 118 -

As she stepped away from the front door it opened, and Skip's presence filled the doorway, his brown eyes ablaze with life, his laugh warming the frozen corners of her heart.

"Hi!" cried Skip, and took her in his arms and kissed her, as naturally as if she had been his sister or his aunt.

"Skip!" Burnett rested against him a minute, in the infinite relief of being welcomed and loved. "How did you *know?*"

"Saw you come in. Thought you'd sneak past me, huh? No chance! What's the idea anyway, running out on me and Paul like that? Gee, it's been years!"

"Have you really missed me?"

"*Missed* you?" Skip took her by both shoulders and gave her a little shake. "It's sunup when you come back from the West," he said softly. "Sunup."

"You didn't write."

"Can't write English," Skip explained.

"And aside from being illiterate, how are you?" Burnett said, laughing.

"O.K. I'm pretty dumb sometimes and forget things, but maybe I was always that dumb. I don't know. Anyway, the fuzzy feeling's about gone away. And high time. College next week. I'm kind of glad you came back before that starts."

"You'll be all right." Burnett smiled and added, as a mother might, "Have you been a good boy this summer?"

"Pure as the driven snow, my lass. Pure as the driven snow. I did what you said: I asked the Man Upstairs whether the seventh commandment was out of date or not, and He said 'Not so's you'd notice it, Pal.' Funny, though. I always figured as long as you thought a thing was O.K., it was. Come on. Let's open up." He led the way into the studio, jerked up the window shades, pulled back the curtains and yanked away the sheets that covered paintings. Then his attention was caught by her latest study, done while the rectory family had been on vacation. He stood with its covering cloth still in his hand, studying it. "It ought to be ugly, but it's beautiful."

"Oh no, it oughtn't to be ugly!" cried Burnett. "The desert, stretching wide and wide, with the sun always shining on it and every fold of the blue hills alive and quivering in the brilliant air . . ."

"No grass," meditated Skip. "No trees. Only that funny-looking thing." And he pointed to a cholla, back-lighted, its tufts of prickles silver against the sun, its grotesque shadow stretching dark into the foreground upon the shining sand. "It says something about God, doesn't it?" asked Skip abruptly. "It makes me feel the same way it does when you talk about Him."

"Thank you, Skip. That's the nicest thing anybody ever said to me."

"You don't paint any of the stuff they say you paint," observed Skip, roaming about the studio.

"What do they say I paint?"

"Oh, nudes and things."

"What's wrong with that? An artist has to know the scaffolding of the body."

"Oh, sure, but—" Skip's eyes rested upon her for a moment with trouble in their depths. "You're *not like that!*" he said at last. "You're as cool and hard and clean as a piece of glass."

"Skip, who's been talking about me?"

"Oh, Priscilla and old Birdsong and Opal and—sort of a campaign, I guess. They've been giving Paul a bad time."

"Why? He hasn't even seen me for two months."

"Yeah, but he's been—different. He's been getting people well, same as you do. By jinks, he took the Holy Unction to a fellow dying of heart trouble, and the next day the guy was fine."

"The holy—what?"

"Unction. I dunno. Ask Paul. But anyway, I bet he did a Burnett on the fellow, because he got well."

"Skip, don't be so ridiculous." Burnett scowled. "You talk as if I were the only person who could pray. All your uncle did was to *believe.*"

"Well, that's what he says. 'The Church has always administered the sacrament of healing.' I heard him say it to Priscilla. But she stuck out her chest and claimed she'd been taught to leave such matters in the hand of God."

"Oh, she did, did she?" cried Burnett belligerently.

"Now don't get your back up," Skip said with a grin. "Paul's all right. She can't do him any harm, not really."

"Why does your uncle let the parish know what he's doing?" Burnett asked. "Why doesn't he just keep still about it?"

"Maybe he would, only when they talk about you, he gets mad and lets 'em have it."

At this Burnett's heart turned over.

"Yes," said Skip, answering her thoughts. "I think he's in love with you." He rose and kissed her lightly on the forehead. "So am I," he said, and turned toward the door.

Before he reached it, the doorbell rang. Skip turned the knob and came face to face with his uncle. He stood there, eager and a little shy, pallor on his cheeks and a light in his eyes.

"Paul!" cried Burnett, not even noticing that for the first time she had used his Christian name. "How did you know?"

"I didn't," Paul replied, coming in and closing the door. "I just wondered. I passed by and, somehow, the house didn't look quite so lonely as usual, so I wondered."

"Come into the studio," said Burnett. "Skip has opened the windows and there's sunlight in there."

"There's sunlight everywhere, now."

They entered the studio alone, for although no one had noticed his departure, Skip was no longer there.

"I've missed you," murmured Paul, and his eyes said more than that. "What have you been doing and why did you stay away so long?"

Burnett did not know that her expressive face was lit with joy. If wonderings about the future came to her, she pushed them out of her way. Paul was here, in her own home, that suddenly was warm and welcoming with dancing life.

"It's sunset," said Paul at last. "And your beads are on fire with the light of it. Come down to the rectory for dinner."

"Oh, I'd—I'd better not," faltered Burnett.

"You're coming," Paul told her decisively. "I'll phone Janet."

So Burnett found herself in the rectory, facing a delighted Skip while Janet beamingly carried dishes back and forth and chattered at full speed. She shouldn't be here, thought Burnett; she was a weak, spineless woman. Yet as the evening passed, it seemed completely natural to be at the rectory.

When Paul drove down Main Street to her house, the townspeople stared at them curiously.

"You see," said Burnett. "I *told* you not to take me home."

Paul stood still and grave upon her doorstep and made what was, for him, quite a little speech. "You did the greatest thing for me that anyone has ever done," he said. "And I know no way of saying, 'Thank you.' For a while I did not even dare to let myself feel the gratitude that I owed you..." He smiled a bit tremulously. "I am proud and glad to be seen with you anywhere, always. And if I pay a small price for it, that is—my resurrection cake."

He held her hand for a moment, tight in both of his, then went away.

"This is enough," thought Burnett. "I need no more than this—ever."

As the days passed, her newfound joy continued and increased. Paul was four blocks down the street, in the big dark rectory. But Paul was at the same time very close to her, his warm love comforting the depths of her heart. Hardly a day passed, moreover, that he did not come into her studio and ask her careful questions about the laws of faith. "I really want to learn," he would say. Or sometimes, when her ideas trampled over his theology, "In a way I want to learn, and in a way I find it very painful. I have to remind myself," he added tactlessly, "Out of the mouth of babes and sucklings hast Thou ordained strength..."

Such remarks no longer enraged Burnett. She only smiled to herself and waited for his next question.

"Do you always pray for people to get well?"

"No. I always pray for life, but sometimes I concentrate my attention on the life of the spirit, when a person is very old for instance, or mentally defective... Surely there are worse things than death!" She sighed, suddenly aware of the lifelong pain that was Alan.

"Why are you grieving?" asked Paul, with such deep tenderness that her old brooding melted into her new joy.

"Nothing—nothing!" she said quite truthfully. "Why should I mourn for Alan anymore?" she thought. "When I have Paul here beside me—never mine but always mine? That is enough!"

If she had been ten years younger it would not have been enough. But she had trained herself to find release in her art and in her healing, even in gardening and in cooking. So she had achieved balance. Even her love of Paul was on this higher level, a satisfaction of spirit rather than a craving of the body . . . or so, at least, she thought.

It was not so with Paul. She sat beside him one day at a symphony concert, while the glory of Beethoven filled her with ecstasy. Through that ecstasy she sensed the impact of his passion, so that she did not know whether the quivering tide of feeling that swept her body was from the orchestra or from Paul. "I can't feel like this," she thought, a little breathlessly. "I can't." And she was relieved when the next number turned out to be a modern reflection of a civilization made up of automobile horns and vacuum cleaners, of pneumatic drills and flush toilets. A long flute lifted its head and essayed a faltering tune, only to be leaped upon and torn apart by a furious dissonance of horns and tympani, and still, through all this unrest, she sensed the overwhelming pulse of Paul's desire as he sat in silence beside her.

"He's going to ask me to marry him," she thought. "And I can't—I can't! It would wreck his church and him. I should never have led him on. I should never have looked at him in the first place . . ."

She tried to draw away from him in the days that followed, being too busy to drive with him in the swiftly dying beauty of October, having an engagement when he asked her to concert or theatre.

"I can't stand this much longer," he said one day, when the last dim glow of autumn had sighed and departed over the winter winds. He sat very straight and still in her Windsor chair beside the fireplace, the firelight flickering sharply on his cheekbones, more prominent than usual in his thin face.

"What?" asked Burnett, fighting for time

He did not answer her. Instead he said quite deliberately, as though it were a speech rehearsed, "Burnett, I think you know that I love you. I have very little to offer, and yet I am going to ask you: will you marry me?"

How like him to plan his proposal and make it as planned, keeping his emotions tight in hand, making no move to sweep her into his arms, to kiss her—even to touch her!

Fantastic. Impossible. But there he sat.

"Burnett . . ." only her name, breathed low, while his knuckles stood out white in the clenched fists upon his clerical knees.

Burnett longed to fling herself into his arms, to melt his stony repression with her love. But the inner voice that she had learned to follow said, "No. Not yet."

"I don't think it would be right to marry," she said, quite as though they were discussing a parish project of some sort. "It would wreck your work. Oh yes, it would, Paul! And it would wreck me too; living in the rectory with everyone's eyes on me, cold and unfriendly. Oh Paul! I just don't think . . ."

"If you loved me as I love you, that wouldn't matter," said Paul, his face very white.

"You know I love you!" cried Burnett, moving swiftly to the footstool at his feet where she had sat once before and clasping his hands. "Can't we go on loving each other just like this? This very special and beautiful way—"

"Don't be naive," said Paul sharply, withdrawing his hands. "You are hardly so ignorant of life as to think that possible."

Burnett sat still, her head bowed. "I didn't mean to be stupid," she said at last. "I suppose I hoped that we were—different, being older, being trained in sublimation."

Paul rose suddenly and stepped away, as though he could not endure even the touch of her dress. "I'm a man, I'm not the Holy Catholic Church! And I—I can't—oh Burnett, if only you loved me—if only you loved me—"

Burnett was on her feet and had flung her arms about him before she knew she was going to do so. "I do love you," she whispered against his cheek, crowding down the voice of caution in her heart. "Oh my dear, I do!"

She could feel his heart beating swift and hard beneath her own. And then he kissed her. The touch of his lips was brief and hard, as though he did not know how to let his heart speak through them. Burnett clung to him, delighting in the feel of his cheek against her own, comforted by the pressure of his arms strong and tight about her. "He kisses like an old maid," she thought, now knowing whether to laugh or cry. "If I ever marry him it will take me ten years to melt him down . . ."

Nevertheless she loved him. And after all—she was an old maid herself.

"Then you *will* marry me!" said Paul, his voice from above her strangely deep and low.

"Oh, Paul—"

"Then—*don't!*" gasped Paul, drawing away from her. "To you love is apparently some sort of a sentimental idea. I can't keep on this way. I can't sleep, I can't concentrate. What if it did wreck my church? We could go somewhere else!"

"I would ruin your work wherever you went. Oh, Paul, I'm sorry, but I'd be no good as a minister's wife. If I didn't go to church every time the door was open I'd be a millstone around your neck and if I did I'd be a hypocrite."

"Don't you believe in Christ?" asked Paul, a crust of his old stiffness in his voice.

"Oh, yes! I believe . . . But the way you think of Him—the communion service and all that—I just can't see what it's all about."

The light went out of Paul's eyes and he looked, suddenly, old and worn. He paused for a moment before answering her and sat down, as if he needed the support of the Windsor chair. Burnett sank into the rocking chair. Rather bleakly she looked at him across the fireplace, wondering. Was this all?

"If you can't accept that," said Paul, "you are no doubt right about us. I hoped that if I could make you love me enough, you would try to understand."

"I do try," murmured Burnett. "But I can't bring God down to such a small compass as—the Church."

There was silence, while the fire died away upon the hearth.

"In that case, we cannot go on as we have been doing," said Paul, through tight lips.

"Oh, Paul!"

There was no answer. He rose unsteadily and turned toward the door.

"If only you were not a minister—but a man's work is more important than his love—isn't it?"

"I suppose so," Paul said vaguely, as if walking in his sleep. "Well, I—good-bye."

The door closed quietly behind him and he was gone.

9

"What the heck's the matter with you?" demanded Skip a week later, as he opened the front door at one o'clock in the morning and found his uncle still awake. One o'clock was an early hour for Skip, on a Friday night. But as he had explained to Paul, one roadhouse was much like another and after a while, he got bored. Paul knew that the foundations of his life were shifting. Yet he was not more restless but less so, as though his inner spirit were more content.

"You don't sleep," scolded Skip, sitting on the edge of Paul's bed. "You don't eat. You jump if the phone rings and snarl if anybody speaks to you. What's the idea?"

"Skip, you're a man," sighed Paul. "You ought to know that a bachelor gets jumpy once in a while."

"Just as I thought."

Paul made no answer. He leaned back against his pillows with his eyes on Skip and a moment's fleeting joy at the sight of him, in a flaming scarlet tie and a gay sports jacket. He remembered the night when Skip's latchkey had turned in the front door and a ghostlike figure had padded upstairs. And for the thousandth time, he remembered Burnett . . . He closed his eyes and sighed again.

"It's Burnett, that's what's the matter with you," pronounced Skip. "Well, for crying out loud, why don't you go and get her?"

"It's not quite—as easy as that."

"She turned you down, did she?"

Paul nodded. "After all," he said, "she's—Burnett. And I'm just a country minister."

"Nuts," decided Skip, after due thought. "Girls always

play hard-to-get at first. It's their come-on policy. You don't understand 'em, that's all that's the matter with you. Now look, here's the idea: you don't pay any attention when they say, 'Oh my, keep away.' You just go right after 'em and kiss 'em. That's what they want you to do."

"*Skip!*"

"Well, I'm telling you how to get her. Say, 'You know you love me' and keep right on kissing her. Not just on the face, either—on the shoulder; they like that: kissing them on the shoulder."

"*Skip!*" cried Paul again, in genuine horror.

"Well, it's nothing to jump out of bed about," said Skip in injured tones. "Everybody does it."

What a generation, thought Paul; what a generation! Had they lost every sense of delicacy? "Skip, you—you don't go around petting all the girls like that, do you?" he asked.

"Oh, not all of them!" declared Skip virtuously. "Only when I love 'em. Or almost."

"I can't understand it." Paul shook his head. "And I can't believe that it really makes you happy, all that petting and pawing."

"Oh, it sure does!" And Skip began to explain the emotional reactions connected with this matter.

"Never mind. Never mind!" said Paul hastily. "I assure you that I could solve nothing by rushing up to Burnett and kissing her on the shoulder."

Skip laughed. "I guess you can't," he conceded. And he excused his uncle generously by adding, "There's even fellows in my gang that aren't too good at it. I guess I'm better than most."

"You're just a playboy." Paul wondered if anything would ever sober Skip.

"Sure," said Skip innocently. "Might as well play before this bean of mine passes the draft board. That's the way all of us feel. Sooner or later the army'll get us, and it'll be Korea or some other stink-hole and anybody's guess whether we ever come back or not. So we might as well play now."

And Paul could only close his eyes and think, "What a world we have made for them!"

"Well, now look," continued Skip, not to be turned from his purpose. "Whatever kind of a technique you have, the point is, *keep after her*. Get down on one knee, if that's the way you do things, and say, 'Miss McNeill, again I ask: will you marry me?' But the point is: *don't give up*. The girl's in love with you. She's just acting coy, that's all."

"The trouble is religion," said Paul. "Our ideas on the subject are totally different."

"Heck with that! You're not marrying ideas. You're marrying a woman. Besides, she's sensible. If there's anything to this church business, she'll see it after a while, no matter what she thinks now."

"You may be right there." Quite unconscious of the difference in their ages, because he was humble enough to learn from anyone, Paul gave his mind to Skip's words.

"Sure, I'm right." Skip yawned, rising and looking out at the church tower, silvery in the streetlights, against the blackness of the sky. "You just listen to your Uncle Skip." And he turned for a moment as he opened Paul's door and made the victory sign with thumb and forefinger.

Paul turned off his bed light and looked out at the far stars wheeling past the tower in their silent march toward dawn. Skip was right. Of what importance was a mere difference in religion? The truth, as Skip had said, should in time make itself known. He must win her and convert her at the same time. So he had planned from the beginning— but he had given up too soon.

So on the next afternoon, with his heart keyed high and a fine tremor in every nerve of his body, he went to find Burnett.

"She's in the backyard." Madeleine stood forbiddingly in the front door, reproach in her eyes and in her sensitive brown face.

Burnett had missed him then, thought Paul, as he rounded the corner of the house. She was under her ancient apple trees, raking leaves down to the far end of her sloping lawn. Indian summer wrapped the November day in a dreamy haze. The flowers, had they not been killed by frost, might have blossomed again in this warm, wistful air. Here and there indeed, one of them wakened from its sleep beneath the leaves and lifted a small, hopeful face to the blue sky: sweet alyssum, white and tiny; chrysanthemums, made to match the withering yellows and burnt-out reds of fall; here and there the golden flame of a calendula. Burnett in bluejeans and a navy jacket bent to touch one of them as Paul drew near. What was she saying? he wondered, with a fluttering at his heart... "Don't be afraid to go to sleep; spring will come again?" for she talked to them and comforted them, and they bloomed for her as for no one else.

"Burnett," he whispered with a catch in his throat. For rustling leaves had smothered his footsteps, so that he was very near to her before she saw him.

Did she start a trifle as she heard his voice? He could not tell.

"I—have missed you so," he said, still almost in a whisper. "I tried to stay away from you. I thought it might be better. But I can't stand it."

"All the leaves have fallen since you were here," she said, a little breathlessly. "All the leaves." She leaned against a tree, and looked up into the bare branches. "It always makes me sad—this time of year," she sighed.

"Spring will come again." Paul smiled. "I heard you tell that yellow flower so."

"Why, *Paul!* How did you know—?"

"I'm not so far from your thoughts as you might suppose," said Paul, and he thought, "Skip would be proud of me now." "And—I don't intend to be," he added with great boldness. "Will you go to the concert with me next Monday night?"

"I—yes, I think I can," hesitated Burnett. And the light in her eyes said, "I can't stand it either, without you."

She did not ask him into the house. Instead, she sat down on the dry grass at the foot of her apple tree and motioned Paul to sit beside her. Even Skip would hardly "pitch a woo," as he absurdly said, in full view of the main street. Was this a conscious move on Burnett's part, "playing hard-to-get"? His heart steadied as he watched her leaning against the tree, one red leaf caught in the crown of her black hair. There was such great joy and such deep pain in seeing her again! But he must contain himself and talk about this and that, as she was doing.

"Mrs. Donahue told me about her daughter Betty," he said. "That was an amazing recovery."

"Oh, no." Burnett picked a wandering maple leaf from among the withered foliage of the apple trees and absently traced its veins with her forefinger. "Pneumonia is only an infection."

"But to be well in a *day!*"

"A germ can just be burnt up in God's light and destroyed," said Burnett. "It's the other things . . ."

"What other things?"

"Oh, the mental and nervous cases for instance. Not just the depressed—that's easy too. But the obsessed, the tormented; I can get just so far with them and no farther. There's a key to that kind of thing. There must be! But I have not found it." And she added with a challenging smile, "If you can find the key to that closed door, I will believe that there is something in your ritual and sacraments and all the folderol."

"The folderol, as you call it, are the tools that I am trained to use," said Paul a bit stiffly. And he added, smiling, but with real intent, "Why do you always start a fight with me when you know that I love you so very much?"

"I don't mean to start a fight." Burnett threw away her maple leaf and smiled at him with tenderness in her eyes. "But still I say: if they are your tools, *make them work!* Show me the results!"

"The results are unquestionable," declared Paul from the depths of his knowledge of the unsearchable riches of God. "But they affect the soul, not the body."

"If this Holy Eucharist business is really His life," said Burnett, nose to trail like a bloodhound, "it will affect the body too. His life *does* things."

"So it does. Spiritual things."

"Nonsense!" cried the exasperating woman. "How about Jairus' daughter and the Gadarene maniac? When the Spirit is really working at top speed, it produces results that can be seen on the physical plane as well. Flesh responds. Nature responds."

"My tools *have* produced visible results at times."

"That's fine," said Burnett. And she added inexorably, "Well, then, find out why it happened those particular times and try to reproduce the conditions at other times."

He had brought this upon himself. He had come here expressly to convert her and to win her, and she herself, unwittingly, was giving him the way to do so: not by words, to which she proposed to pay not the slightest attention, but by deeds of faith greater than her own. Paul wondered, not for the first time, why he had not fallen in love with a less demanding woman.

But this was his assignment, and there was nothing to do but master it. How it could be done he did not know, but there must be a way and he would find it. He would choose Alan Whitacre as his special intention for this kind of prayer and would keep him so until he was well. Then he would bring him to Burnett, and Alan himself could tell her the story of his healing.

Thanksgiving was past before Paul could find the time to see Alan Whitacre, and December lowered forebodingly upon a heavy sky. Alan was not out on the chill grounds where Paul had so often found him. Paul strode through resounding corridors, past vacant stares from faces that were sepulchres. "Oh God, oh God," thought Paul in a passion of sympathy, "if there is a way of helping people like this, show it to me . . ."

He located Alan in the occupational therapy room, his square shoulders and brown head bent over the basket that he wove with slow and hesitating fingers. He looked up when he saw Paul but he did not smile. Paul's heart sank. He had felt so sure that Alan was better! But the results that he had seen were all on the surface of consciousness. Beneath them was a brooding darkness that no word could reach, no prayer could lift. And the inner darkness seemed to be spreading. If Al would only talk of his past life, thought Paul, perhaps one could tell how to counsel him and how to pray for him. But this he would not do. Over and over again Paul had tried to bring out of him some information about his past, and had failed completely. The last time Al had turned on him brusquely and silenced him. "I get enough of that from the doctors here," he had said. "I'm glad to have you as a friend. But not as a psychiatrist."

So that door was closed and Paul would not try again to open it. Now would he go to the doctors and make inquiry about him. His delicacy revolted at this. Besides, Alan, for all his broken mind, was surprisingly shrewd. He would know that Paul had information from others, and he would never trust him again.

"You know, you *can* get well," said Paul, as he had often said before. "If you're a little low today, it's only the natural up-and-down course of your trouble. The good days will come back."

"When you first saw me, I was on my way out of a manic period," explained Alan, with that clear perception of himself that made his condition the more distressing. "Now, I'm going down into the depressive stage. It's—the worst. When I'm definitely manic, I'm often extraordinarily happy; happier than a sane person could ever be."

"Well, that's—that's good, anyway," faltered Paul.

Alan lifted his darkened face and the look in his too-brilliant eyes stabbed like a knife. "I throw chairs then," he said briefly. "I take off my clothes."

"Oh," said Paul inadequately. Then he summoned his courage and said, "I'm praying that you never will again."

"But I will, of course," murmured Alan. "I don't mind too much. It's the blackout I'm sinking into now that is—beyond words, beyond words, beyond words..." His voice faded out in the thin scuffling sounds of the room with its half-dozen hopeless ones, patiently weaving straw.

Paul laid a compassionate hand on Alan's knee and tried to look at his averted face. "If you could only *believe* that you can get well," he began.

But Alan bent lower over his basket. "Why should I get well?" he asked. "There's no place for me out there in the world. My parents—I visit them once in a while, in my intermediate periods. But they are old and helpless and they look at me with fear in their eyes. It makes me worse. Everything on the outside makes me worse. Only here is refuge, of a sort. Why should I struggle to leave it?"

"Then you don't even want—"

And Alan said, the inner one of him so desperately hurt that it could no longer feel desire, "No use. No use."

So he was failing after all, thought Paul, driving home through thin dusk in the first flurry of winter's snow. And the cause of his failure was plain enough. Even his Lord had always said, "According to thy faith be it unto thee." Always? No, not quite always. He had not asked faith of the Gadarene maniac, nor of those possessed by demons.

Perhaps it was not so much Alan's lack of faith as his own that blocked the power. He had not said to Alan, "I know that you will be well," because he did not know it. How could he possibly be sure that so great a thing would be? He would describe the case to Burnett, he decided, and see if she could help him. He had hoped to manage this without a word from her, but if he could not—he could not.

So he stopped at the small brick house whose warm lights shining out into the gathering dusk were to him the welcoming lights of home. Burnett met him at the door in her black velvet and her amber beads. Amber pendants burned in her ears and her gray-green eyes shone like stars. It was all that Paul could do to keep his mind on Alan. But he tried, leaning on the mantelpiece, to give her a case history of the man in the hospital. She sat with folded hands, listening with that catlike intentness that was a part of her.

"What would you do in a case like that?" he finished.

"I'd set it aside for a while and try something easier," replied Burnett. "As you see the power work, you will be better able to believe in it."

"How's that?" asked Paul, his eyes on her piquant face. "I—I believe in it *now.*"

"Your conscious self does," said Burnett. "But your unconscious is not yet convinced. So your spirit, or superconscious, is not wholly free to act."

"I don't get it," sighed Paul.

"It's just this: in order to get the belief established in your unconscious, keep practicing on the things that are not too difficult. And leave the man in the hospital until the three of you—conscious, unconscious and super-conscious—are more united in faith."

"But he has already waited so long," worried Paul.

"I know," Burnett said, sighing in her turn. She walked to the window with quick, restless steps and stood looking out, her profile chiseled sharply against the early falling dark of the December night.

Paul yearned over her. What was she remembering, he wondered, that she should look so sad? Was it the man she had loved in China? He strode over to the window and pulled down the shade. Then he drew her back again to the warm glow of the fireplace. "I can't stand it," he said, trembling. "You're so far away—so beautiful."

"Now I know you're in love," Burnett said, trying to

speak lightly. "For I'm not beautiful." But her smile wavered and broke and she swayed a little toward him as she spoke. Inevitably she was in his arms, as though she had always belonged there.

"Oh, my dear, my dear," he whispered against her cheek when the dizziness of sudden rapture had stayed itself and was still. "You belong to me and I to you, and we cannot live without each other... You know it as well as I; don't you, beloved—don't you?"

She nodded, clinging to him, her cheek against his own.

"Then *marry me!*" pleaded Paul. "If you love me, surely you can go to church with me and say, 'These are Paul's tools, and for his sake I am keeping my mind open to them.' And some day, you will feel the power that is in my Church."

"I do feel something," said Burnett quickly. "And last Sunday at the communion service—you know, you told me I might come without receiving—I sensed something a bit different; more warm, more personal."

"That's the Presence!" cried Paul eagerly. "That's Our Lord Himself releasing His life through the sacrament!"

"Then why doesn't He *act?*" demanded Burnett. "I'm not just trying to be difficult," she added gently, seeing Paul's disappointed face. "But the need of the world and my own need is for His power, not just an emotion."

"If you feel something there, can't you marry me and—know that you will understand it better as time goes on?"

"No," said Burnett firmly. "It would not be fair. There are too many things against me as it is. No! I won't have you marry a woman who is criticized and gossiped about unless at least I know that you'll have real cooperation—real understanding. No, Paul, no!" stepping away as he tried once more to take her in his arms. "It would wreck your church and it would wreck you and I won't do it."

"Then I'll resign and you and I can start out in a new place where nobody knows us."

"There are no employment agencies for ministers," murmured Burnett. "No unions, nothing. If you went around ringing doorbells people would say, 'Why did he have to leave his church? There must be something wrong with him.' No! I won't permit that either."

Paul took her face in his hands and kissed her. "I don't care," he said. "I love you."

And Burnett replied steadily "I love *you*. And I do care."

"But someday..." said Paul. "We're both of us growing and learning and someday..."

"Someday," repeated Burnett with infinite tenderness.

The coming of winter was beautiful to Paul. Everything was beautiful—the first snow, embroidering every feathery weed in shining white; doves on the church roof, gray wings circling the tower; the little children of his choir and the kind faces of his vestrymen; even old Hattie Burroughs, wandering into the kitchen in a sweater and a straw hat, looking for the place where she might go to church.

The Christmas season was even more beautiful, with its herald angels and wise men, its shepherds and stars. Early on a Sunday morning Paul entered his hushed church that he might prepare for the services of the day. "Show me what to do," he whispered, looking up at the cross as he knelt by the altar rail. "I know you have a plan for Burnett and me . . . Show me."

He waited, but no answer came to him except the answer that was already in his heart: *"Make the power work;* throw away every restraining fear and go into it, all the way in, giving it everything you have. Everything!"

Hitherto Paul had not done this. True, he had made a few attempts at faithful prayer, as with Alan Whitacre and the parishioner to whom he had taken Holy Unction and who had surprised him by recovering. He had given it a try or two, at his leisure, so that he might know whether Burnett's words were true or not. But to give it every-thing—to take this power in his hands and administer it as carefully as he administered the communion service . . .

Paul was not happy as he thought of this. Of all possible ways of life, this was the last one he would willingly choose. He would lose the deep comfort of following the pattern, standard and exact, of the Church down the ages. He would make himself conspicuous among his fellowmen, and of all things that he hated, this was the worst. The sweat broke out on his forehead as he imagined himself at a clergy conference, shoved into a corner by the polite aloofness of his brethren. He could feel a prickling of horror at the roots of his hair as he imagined overhearing them: "Forrester has gone overboard for this healing business." "Oh? Too bad. I always thought he was reliable; not one to set the river on fire perhaps, but sound. Too bad."

"Oh Lord," whispered Paul, and his lips trembled. "I'm—I'm not a big enough man for that kind of thing!"

But there was no answer.

"I don't suppose You wanted to come into this sorry world either," Paul said. "Born as at this time, for us . . ." And he began to see that as there had been a purpose in that most sacred coming, so there was a purpose in the stern march of events that had brought him to this decision. At long last he rose from his knees, trembling a little and very white and said, "I'll do it. I will go to those who are sick and I will open my mouth without fear and speak. And—Lord have mercy upon me!" He crossed himself and turned to go. Then with a quirk of a smile at the corners of his mouth, he turned back. "This is my Christmas present— to You,' he said. "Show me when to go and I'll go."

Sooner than he desired, the day came.

"Heard the news?" gloated Ambrose, buttonholing him in the cloisters. "Joe McGhann's got meningitis. Bad. Real bad."

"But he was at the children's rehearsal only last night!" said Paul. "And besides—meningitis in winter is unlikely, isn't it?"

"No, it ain't," croaked Ambrose, his smug face falling into lines of complacent woe. "I knew a case just like that. And he was dead in two days," he added with satisfaction.

"Where's Joe?" asked Paul abruptly.

"Home. They're making arrangements to get him into the hospital."

Paul went into the study without a word. This was it. He had offered to speak the word of faith, and now he must.

Paul sat down before his desk and dropped his head into his hands. "Why did You give me such a hard one for a beginning job?" he whispered. "Must I do this?" he prayed. And again there was no answer except the voice of his own heart that said, "You must."

"After all," he told himself, "nobody knows how the germ is carried." But then another fear leaped into his mind: what if he should carry the germ to Skip? Perhaps if

Burnett would help him, he thought, he would not need to go. But Burnett was out of town.

Paul was not aware of having made a decision. He simply arose and went.

"I'm sorry," the housekeeper told him. "Joe is not allowed to see anyone."

"I am his rector," answered Paul quietly. "And he will want to see me. If you don't mind, I'll go right up."

He smiled and brushed past her, walking as though in a dream. All fear and indeed almost all feeling of any kind had departed from him. He was no longer himself but merely a tool in the hands of Another greater than himself.

Once on the second floor, he looked about for a closed door, knocked lightly, and not waiting for an answer, opened it and went in.

Joe lay on the bed, his arms rigid, his eyes terrified. His mother hovered tearfully over him and on the other side of the bed sat his father, white-faced and staring.

"Hello, Joe," said Paul mildly. "Ambrose tells me you're having a little trouble."

"Mr. Forrester!" worried Joe's mother. "I don't think you should have come! You know—contagion—"

But Paul was surrounded by a protection that he could almost feel, could almost see, with an inner visioning that had nothing to do with his senses. "Oh, that's all right," he murmured vaguely. Then he motioned her out of the way and stood beside Joe.

"You don't need to be afraid of this thing, you know," he said in comfortably casual tones. "It's pretty rough at the moment, I know, but it will soon go away."

But Joe McGhann, though only ten years old, had heard about diseases that come to children as quick as lightning out of the sky, and he was afraid.

Paul knelt on the floor to be as near as possible to his little friend. He had forgotten all about germs. He had forgotten Mr. McGhann and Mrs. McGhann and everything and everybody else on earth except the small boy whose mind he must somehow reach. "Joe," he said in his most gentle and persuasive voice, smoothing the boy's hair with a loving hand, "shut your eyes and play like you're carrying the cross to lead your choir into church. Now: do you remember what I told you about that cross?"

Joe tried to nod his head, then opened his tight-shut eyes and cried out, "Mom! It hurts! I can't—I can't move my head . . ."

"There, there, darling," cried Mrs. McGhann, kneeling on the other side of the bed. "The doctor will come soon. Oh Mr. Forrester, it's so fast—so fast—galloping . . ."

"Then it can just gallop away again," said Paul cheerfully. "Come on, Joe. Shut your eyes. Now remember: that cross means that Jesus is near to us. Now when Jesus saw any little boy who was sick, he told the sickness to go right straight away, and it did."

"But He isn't here," whispered Joe.

"Oh yes, He is," said Paul Forrester. "Like electricity is here, in the air, only we can't see it. He doesn't say the words out loud, but He told me to say them for Him and I'm going to do it and tell this sickness to go right straight away."

"Did He tell you? Honest?"

"Yes, He did. Before I came here. So I'm going to talk to Him and then I'm going to say the words. Now close your eyes again and imagine yourself carrying the cross down the church aisle, because that's what I expect you to do next Sunday."

The little boy smiled and closed his eyes.

For one moment Paul was conscious of himself and terror gripped his heart. "Oh God, if I've got to do this, then *give me the gift of healing!*" he prayed, while the sweat stood cold upon his forehead. A picture rose from somewhere in his memories: himself, kneeling in the sanctuary, the hands of many priests upon him and the Bishop saying, "Receive the Holy Ghost for the office and work of a priest in the Church of God . . ." He had already received the gift of healing! For it was one of the gifts of the Holy Ghost and was bestowed upon him at his ordination by the authority of Holy Church. It remained only for him to make it real by using it.

Paul sighed in relief. He laid one hand on the laboring chest and slipped the other beneath the boy. Instinctively, unerringly, his hands found their places as though by a will of their own. It was as if the sword of his spirit leaped from the dark sheath of the flesh and acted according to laws that Paul himself did not understand. "Oh Heavenly Father, send Your light and fire into Joe and burn up the germs right now and make him well," he prayed. "We ask this in Jesus' name because we know He is right here with us—and He is doing it. So we thank You that by next Sunday Joe will be able to carry Your cross before Your altar. Amen."

Something was happening. Paul could feel it like a current of electricity in his hands. He could even detect the quivering of this life in Joe. The strain of channeling so great a power was almost more than Paul could bear. Why his nerves protested under it he did not know. But it was all he could do to keep his hands on the child until the power had run out.

"It feels good," sighed Joe.

Paul sensed a softening and a relaxing in the tight chest between his hands. "What feels good, Joe?" he asked in a voice as gentle as a mother's.

"God's 'lectricity," answered Joe contentedly. "It feels good."

Paul bowed his head in thankfulness. "Oh all ye works of the Lord, bless ye the Lord: praise Him, and magnify Him forever!" the ancient words of the Benedicite sang themselves through his mind.

"I don't know if I want to go to sleep or if I want to throw up," said Joe in a small, meek voice.

"It would be a good idea to throw up," Paul replied calmly. ("Oh ye spirits and souls of the righteous, bless ye the Lord.") He added to the mother, "'Get a basin . . . It would help the germs or whatever they are to hurry up and get out of you. So now I'll go away and you'll probably do that very soon and then you'll go to sleep, and when you wake up you'll be all right."

In the middle of Main Street a sudden realization came to Paul. He had said the word of power! Quite unconsciously, quite spontaneously he had said it: "When you wake up, you'll be all right!"

"Opal's on your trail," announced Ambrose gloomily several hours later. "I tried to shake her for you, but nothing doing. This here's a crisis in her life, this here is, and she's got to see you." And he added on an ominous note, "McGhann's been down here too."

"How's—how's the boy?" asked Paul.

But for once in his life, Ambrose did not know. "McGhann wasn't talking," said he cryptically.

Paul went toward the study with his heart in his mouth.

"Oh *dear* Mr. Forrester! I simply *must* see you!"

Ambushed, just as Ambrose had said.

Paul took her wearily into his study, leaving both doors open, as usual. And he tried to listen to her various nervous symptoms with his mind, it must be confessed, on Joe McGhann.

"So now, I do want a little prayer," finished Miss Oldershaw. "Just a weeny little prayer for strength and courage."

And Paul, doing his best to pray for her, wondered which one of them needed the prayer the most.

Just as Paul succeeded in ushering Opal away, McGhann appeared, lowering down the cloister, hat in hand.

"Oh, Mr. McGhann!" burbled Opal. "Mr. Forrester has been saying a little prayer for me. It's so sweet and soothing I always say, don't you, Mr. McGhann?"

Mr. McGhann, judging by his expression, did not.

"I hear you went to see my nephew today," he said to Paul.

"How is he?" Paul asked.

"Oh, all right. All right. Gave us a bit of a scare, but it turned out to be nothing at all. Indigestion, most likely."

"That's good," faltered Paul.

"Came to see you about the ushers for the Christmas service," said Mr. McGhann. But before he left, he got around to the main purpose of his visit. "About the boy, Joe," he said. "Don't want any rumors getting about. Kind intentions and so forth, but—no need of running around to pray just because a child has a stomachache. Prayer's a good thing, of course, very good thing, but some of us like it better in church where it belongs, you might say."

And he nodded, smiling kindly beneath his gray moustache, put on his hat and went home.

10

So that was the way of it. One took one's courage in hand, venturing greatly, beat against the grim gates of death and overcame.

And those who reaped the benefits of this adventuring decided that there was nothing to it, after all.

Then Paul remembered his own voice saying long ago, "I'll not have that woman in the rectory." Slow red burned into his cheeks. "I'm sorry. I'll learn to do better."

When the Christmas season was past he set himself to study the books that she gave him, hiding the questionable tomes in his bedroom and plowing through two chapters every night, although their theology was distressingly hazy. One realization grew upon him: they insisted most uncomfortably upon the meticulous keeping of the Master's words. They gave no place for righteous indignation, for just resentment founded upon a good cause, for a shady financial deal directed toward a good end. Every one of His teachings must be kept, they said. Every word. Could this possibly be true? Had he really lost power by small habitual annoyances, by resentments suppressed over the years? Was it possible that the gift of healing could be increased in him not by some magic from outside but by the cleansing of the small human channel that was himself?

"Try it and see," said Burnett. And she added with rather a wicked smile, *"Using your own tools."*

That would be, thought Paul, the confessional. But one did not confess such trivial matters as being annoyed with one's sexton! Paul had not found it expedient to teach the Sacrament of Penance in his low-church parish. But according to good Anglo-Catholic practice he availed himself of this holy rite three times a year. Before Christmas, before Easter, before Whitsuntide, he went to a monastery within the city and with much crossing and bowing he stated that since his last confession he had committed the following sins, thinking hard that he might locate certain transgressions of sufficient interest to relate to his confessor. And indeed there were always times when he had eaten meat on a Friday, times when he indulged in a boiled egg before communion, times when he had neglected to pray for his confraternity in the correct manner. He had bewailed these sins and had gone his way with considerable satisfaction. But to try and locate every imperfect thought-habit, every old resentment, every daily irritation—this was a herculean task! However, if this striving after an impossible ideal might cleanse his heart so that the healing power could come in, then there was nothing to do but try it.

He took time for this as the slow weeks of Lent passed by. He went all the way back to the past, bending his mind each day upon a certain span of his life and praying for guidance to remember any unresolved trauma that might be considered an unforgiven sin. Then he wrote down every self-revealing thought that came to him. "Christ have mercy upon us," he thought as Holy Week approached him. "This is a psychoanalysis..." He made no explanation to his confessor as he took the notebook with him into the confessional box and after "I have committed the following sins" read the long list that he had written down. Such was the glory of the Sacrament of Penance: one explained nothing. Here was the form, simple, rigid and direct, and into this form fitted all that was needed of word and thought. Kneeling stiffly in the dim confessional Paul brought forth into the light of day every act and word and thought of guilt that his searching consciousness had drawn up from the memories of a lifetime. It was a rough assignment. With a shuddering sigh Paul murmured at last, "For these and all my other sins which I cannot at the moment remember, I am truly sorry, intend to do better and ask of you, Father, counsel, penance and absolution."

Then for the first time Paul, glancing through the tiny grill on the confessional box, noticed the still profile of the listening priest. It was not his usual confessor. It was a young man unknown to him.

What was he saying? "Although so few people realize it, I know the Church, through Jesus Christ, still has the power and authority to forgive sins. Therefore I am sure that these sins will be forgiven." And he gave the absolution that Paul himself had so often given from the high altar of his church.

Paul knelt once more in a pew and did his small penance of reading a few psalms and saying a few prayers, and then rose and went home. And the man who went out of that church was not the same man who had gone into it.

He went about his work with rejoicing, the power to heal increased within him and the key to some of his perennial problems came into his hands. For instance, there was old Simmons, of alcoholic tendencies, who had been a pest to him for years. Instead of appealing to reason or to conscience as he had so often done, Paul laid his hands on him and prayed for the healing of whatever physical condition tended to aggravate the craving for drink. He felt as he often did a flow of life through his own arms and hands, a tingling in the fingertips, a pulsing in the veins. This did not weary him as it had done when he prayed for Joe McGhann. In some mysterious way his being was expanding so that he could channel the power without so much of nervous strain.

"You'll make the grade now," he said to old Simmons as they left the church.

"I know I will, Parson."

"What's happened to you?" asked Burnett one day in May. "You look younger all the time!"

Paul had found her weeding the perennial bed that stretched beside her back fence all the way to a lone pine at the end of the garden. They sat together on the back steps of the studio in the warm May sunlight. "Spring—and you," smiled Paul, for he shrank from telling her about the strange release that he had found in an ancient rite which he had never before really used.

"It's more than that," said Burnett, studying him. "You're really doing things, aren't you? I hear stories about you all around town. Healings—prayer groups—"

"Well, they just grew. I had to teach people how to pray because they were so many and I couldn't run around and pray for all of them . . ."

"And you did have sense enough not to preach about it."

"Naturally. Then the Bible Class kept wanting to pray for this one and that one, and there wasn't time. So I said, 'Start your own groups,' and they did."

"Bible Class!" smiled Burnett. "For all the world like a Methodist!"

"Heaven knows where I'll end up," sighed Paul. "But after reading all those books of yours I'm trying to study out what Our Lord really did say."

"I bet it startles you, what He said—and what He didn't say."

"I admit that certain standard Church practices seem to have quite escaped His attention," said Paul with a little smile.

"Like fasting before communion. Why didn't He do that if it was correct?"

Paul replied, straight-faced after the New England manner, "Well, Jesus wasn't an Episcopalian."

Burnett laughed in the way that Paul loved. It was a pity, he thought, that there was not more room for laughter in her crowded life.

Paul went on, smiling, his eyes alight as he looked at her, "He didn't mind the children dancing in the marketplace nor the wedding guests drinking the wine. In fact, if He should stride into one of our churches today He might—He just might get thrown out."

Burnett's reaction to this was disturbingly feminine. "You are adorable," she said inconsequentially, and kissed him full on the lips.

"Burnett!" he cried in surprise, trying to catch her and hold her in his arms.

But she drew away from him. "I—I didn't mean to do that," she said with a catch in her voice. "But it's so wonderful to see you like this—free, happy, gay! And you *are* adorable."

This was too much. In spite of her protests she was in his arms and his lips were against her cheek.

"Somebody's in the next yard," she gasped, and with a smothered exclamation he let her go.

"Who cares?" he muttered.

"You'd better care. They talk about you so much anyway that it frightens me a little bit. I almost wish you wouldn't go ahead so fast."

"Well, of all the dumb female women!" Paul laughed. "Who told me, 'Learn how to pray' in the first place, huh? I ask you! What are you afraid of?"

"Priscilla. She's steaming all around town and from what I hear she's up to no good."

"This is a pretty how-de-do," said Paul. "I've often scolded you about living alone and letting all kinds of people traipse through your house day and night, and you say you aren't afraid of what people may say."

"I'm not—for myself," sighed Burnett. "I've always thought that if one walks in integrity gossip cannot hurt one. People will find out the truth sooner or later. But you are so vulnerable, in your position . . ."

"Oh, well. Priscilla's bark is worse than her bite," said Paul, over the faint chill that the sound of that redoubtable female's name always brought to him. "Anyway, now I know you love me, nothing can hurt me."

"I'm afraid my loving you can hurt you more than anything else," said Burnett in a small voice. "I shouldn't have let my heart run away with me like that . . . but I do love you!" she added in a rush of whispered words, her lips very near his.

"Then trust your heart and marry me!"

But her moment of release was over. "I must know it's right, I must be sure—" and nothing that he said could move her from this stand.

But Paul was not disturbed. She was his and some day she would be sure.

"Did you see who was in *church?*" breathed Opal Oldershaw next Sunday, seizing on him with both hands and drawing him away from the stream of departing people. "That dreadful man! You know, he's always rolling about the streets, *most* intoxicated. Don't you think you should *speak* to him?"

"I have spoken to him," said Paul, and it must be confessed that there was an edge to his voice. "I have especially urged him to make his communion with us every Sunday."

"But All Saints "

"Remind me to change the name to All Sinners," snapped Paul.

So, overconfident in his newfound joy, he headed straight into heavy weather.

It was young Margaret Esmond who innocently precipitated his doom. Paul, making a routine parish call, found her sick with pneumonia, prayed for her, and she recovered as rapidly as Joe McGhann had done . . .

But her recovery was not kept a secret. Paul forgot to mention the wisdom of silence.

The next Sunday Paul saw that he was guilty of some misdemeanor in Priscilla McGhann's eyes, but what it might be he did not know: whether he had hung his cassock on the condemned hook again so that it had fallen on the floor, or whether he had used in early Mass certain purificators that she had set aside for a festival occasion, or whether his sister Janet had been in her hair; these matters were hid from him. He avoided her eye as best he could and got himself hastily into his vestments and into church.

But what had happened to his church?

Seven rows of empty pews, a few scattered parishioners and emptiness again. He had not seen so small a congregation in all the days of his ministry at All Saints. Swallowing hard, he followed the remnant of Israel that was his decimated choir into the chancel and went through the service in the strong and steady way that was his to command. He fixed his eyes upon the rear of the church where faces were dim to him and all men were as one. For he could not meet the eyes before him: Burnett's, troubled beneath their veiled composure, Tewksbury's, roving and anxious, Opal's, round and melting like those of Elsie the cow . . . He would not be in ignorance much longer, thought Paul grimly. When church was over he would know what ailed his congregation.

"Oh, *dear* Mr. Forrester!" panted Opal at the church door. "I do think people are *terrible;* not understanding just because you healed Miss Esmond, that doesn't mean *at all* that you are going to speak in tongues or get the Holy Spirit or any such dreadful thing as that! I know it doesn't, and that's what I tell them; and even if you are studying about healing—oh dear, you did leave one of those dreadful books about, you know, and Priscilla found it but I *don't* think she should write the Bishop or—" But at this point Opal gave a squawk, put her hand over her mouth and disappeared.

"Hey! What's the matter over there?" demanded Skip when he entered the rectory for dinner.

"It's just that summer's coming," said Janet with her chin stuck out and a look of tears behind her eyes.

"Nuts! They don't all of 'em go to the shore just because it's spring! All the old standbys ... It's this healing business, that's what it is. It was hurrah for God as long as church was only Te Deums and what not, but when God begins to do things, then they don't like it."

"It frightens them," admitted Paul with a smile. "It isn't *done.*"

"Well, what about it? Better pull in your horns a little, hadn't you?"

"No," said Paul. After all, he had faced all this when he first made his resolution.

"Ask Burnett," said Skip. "She'll tell you what to do."

And Janet inconsistently enough remarked, "Sure. She got you into this. Now let's see her get you out."

"That is nonsense," Paul pointed out calmly, for he was far less disturbed than his family seemed to be. "When I decided to interest myself in this matter, it was purely by my own desire and there is no need of unloading my troubles on Burnett."

"You won't need to unload anything," said Skip. "She was in church. She'll talk."

And she did, driving straight to the point in her usual blunt way. "There's some monkey business going on there," she said the next day, when he dropped in to see her on his way home from calls. "What's it all about?"

"Margaret Esmond, I think." Paul smiled, leaning back in her studio chair and adoring her with his eyes. "She got well too fast."

Burnett shook her head. "There's more to it than that," she said. "Somebody is acting as ringleader, purposely making trouble. And I think I know who it is: Priscilla."

"But why?" asked Paul thinking of Joe McGhann who was Priscilla's nephew, and who had carried the cross the Sunday after his illness. "Why does she dislike me so?"

"Because of me," sighed Burnett.

Paul took her in his arms. "It doesn't matter," he said, his lips against her hair. "There's a joy inside me now, like a light, and there's you and . . . I can endure anything. After all, if I must leave this parish . . ."

"But you won't!" cried Burnett. "I know how to fix Priscilla."

But days passed and Angus McGhann, as heavy as a thunderstorm, called upon Paul in his office, and there was no evidence of Priscilla being "fixed."

Paul had to smile at McGhann's carefully worded arguments, so exactly did they represent his own opinions of a year before. "After all," concluded his warden, "we have so much in our Church. Why do we need any more?"

"Old Simmons needed it," said Paul quite calmly, because for the first time in his life he was not in the least afraid of Angus McGhann. "Frank needed it—and I failed him. Your own nephew Joe needed it." And he thought, looking at his warden's surprised face, "That will slow him down to a walk."

"But it has completely altered the character of the church!" protested McGhann, ignoring the challenge. "All these strange people with no background whatsoever!"

Paul remembered the church of a year ago, a convenient meeting place where one might note the latest fashions and invite one's friends to cocktails later in the day. "Yes, it has," he agreed without expression.

McGhann's eyes flashed beneath his bushy brows. "In that case," he muttered ominously, "I feel that my services on the vestry are no longer needed."

In the morning Paul received a letter from Angus McGhann announcing his resignation from the vestry of All Saints.

This was bad. All Saints Church had been founded upon the solid rock of McGhann and if that rock gave way there was no telling what might tumble with it.

Paul tightened his lips and took the letter into the church. "You see how it is, Lord," he said, for he sometimes forgot, these days, to address the Almighty in the dignity of the prayer book. "Where do I go from here?" He received no answer in words, but only in a deepening of his inner peace. And in that peace he continued calmly on the way that he had chosen, though before the month was out three more of his vestrymen had resigned. And when summer had awakened the last of the slumbering trees, he found himself summoned to the diocesan office to confer with the Bishop.

"Yes, sir," said Paul, swallowing hard and holding the phone in a rather shaky hand. "Four o'clock in the afternoon. Yes, sir."

"Hold everything," he whispered to himself. "You faced this long ago. It's come, that's all."

But his heart was heavy as he turned the car into the highway the next afternoon. Always before he had gone forth eagerly to meet with bishops and clergy. He had been completely at home with them, a perfectly fitting part in a great organization, planned with all decorum to uphold the gracious rituals of the centuries. He had pitied the occasional misfits in this most reverend group: the unfortunates whose ideas were not sound, whose methods veered away from the accepted norm. He had looked on them with compassion and at the same time had thanked God that he was not as they were . . . And now he was stepping into that same most unhappy place.

"Ah, good afternoon, Forrester. Good of you to come," in the hearty boom of a bishop who is up to no good. "Have a seat."

"Yes, sir," said Paul, and he perched himself on the edge of a straight chair.

The Bishop was a large ruddy man, as a Bishop should be, with a kindly eye and a big mouth. "I'm sorry about this," he began, sighing deeply. "I've always considered you a good man. Sound. Not one to set the river on fire perhaps, but sound. Now it seems you've got your congregation all by the ears over some—er, rather erratic—interest in healing."

"Yes, sir," Paul said again, swallowing hard.

"H'm," said the Bishop, cocking one eyebrow at him and drumming upon his desk. "Well, the matter of healing comes to one's attention more and more these days. I do not question the fact that it is an authentic gift of the Spirit—though I deplore the queer people who run up and down the land and shout about it. It is politic, however, for the Church to consider these matters and regulate them before the populace run away with them entirely. The Anglican Church, I understand, has established a commission on healing. We are not ready for that, of course, in this country, but it is time for some of us to interest ourselves in this matter. However," he continued, as Paul sighed with relief and gratitude, "your mistake is in rushing into this thing too fast. There are ways of introducing it into a parish so subtly and so gradually that it offends nobody and helps those who need help. Father Sinclair, for instance, of this city, has woven it into his church in a way that I consider safe and sane."

"Father Sinclair!" cried Paul in surprise. "Why, I didn't know that he . . ."

"Yes, indeed." The Bishop nodded. "He has classes on the subject. Prayer groups. One hears continually of his good work. *And,*" he paused and looked reproachfully at Paul, "he has not in any way disrupted his congregation. I have never received a petition or a letter of complaint about the matter."

"And you have—about me," whispered Paul.

"Look at this." And the Bishop pushed a sheaf of typed pages across the desk to Paul.

"I—don't think I need to read them," said Paul with a little gasp. "I know pretty much what is in them."

"If something is not done about the matter, they will be followed by a definite petition for your removal," said the Bishop heavily. And he added, "There is a place for healing in the Church, I admit. But Mapleton is hardly the town for it, nor All Saints the church. Nor, I might add," said he with a deprecating little smile, "are you quite the man for it."

"I know," sighed Paul, thinking wistfully of Father Sinclair with his great frame and his commanding presence. "I don't have much personality."

"Perhaps I had best look about for a small mission where you might be placed," suggested the Bishop.

"Oh, would you?" cried Paul, who had often thought of asking him to do just that. "I would be most grateful."

The Bishop studied him for a moment, and then smiled. "This means a great deal to you, doesn't it?" he asked in gentler tones.

And Paul, looking up with worried brown eyes, replied simply, "Of course, sir. Why else would I risk everything for it?"

"Then I suggest that you go, right away, this afternoon, and have a talk with Father Sinclair. Perhaps he can give you a few pointers. I'll call him up and make an appointment for you."

"And—the little mission?" asked Paul, as he stepped out of the door.

"We'll set that aside for a while. I have a feeling that in spite of everything, you'll make a go of this."

Paul threaded the crowded streets of the city to Father Sinclair's church. He was not, as he had feared, an isolated figure in a clerical phalanx of unbelievers. There were others, like himself only older and wiser; and there was a bishop who stood between them, verily a father in God that he might help them.

"The answer is," said Father Sinclair, his fingertips together as he smiled at Paul from across his office desk, "let it grow slowly, unobtrusively . . ."

"But I can't! The thing exploded in my face!" And Paul related the story of Skip and Burnett and Frank. "There it was, you see," he ended. "In full sight of the vestry and everybody. That was the beginning, and—"

Father Sinclair shook his head. "Just the same, if I were you I would quiet matters down now as much as possible. Be evasive. Be secretive. Even Our Lord, you know, said, 'Go thy way and tell no man.' "

"I didn't think of that," murmured Paul, remembering Margaret Esmond.

"The matter really is not between you and your congregation but between you and God," continued the priest. "If you increase your own faith by prayer and understanding, the power will more and more heal those you visit. When this happens, you can refer to it as answered prayer, which it is, and take it as something to be expected—which it is. It is not necessary to use the words 'spiritual healing' or even 'faith healing.' These words are true enough, but they are apt to suggest quackery."

"But it's too late for that now, in Mapleton," Paul pointed out. "I suppose the best thing would be to move and start over again."

"You are exaggerating the difficulties," said Father Sinclair after studying him narrowly. "Because you are so deeply hurt you would like to run away."

Paul nodded. He could not speak for a moment. Again he saw Joe McGhann, well and happy, and his warden's lowering face as he muttered, "In that case . . ." and followed his remarks with a letter of resignation. "I've been just refusing to think of it," he said unnecessarily.

"The current changes." Father Sinclair smiled. "The tide turns. If you can ride this out for a while, the time will come when love and gratitude will be poured out on you. That has its dangers too, and the answer is still the same: there is no safe motive for doing this work except the motive of the love of Christ."

"I hope that's my motive," said Paul, remembering Burnett.

"Make it your motive. And do as much of your healing prayer as possible through the communion service."

Paul, arising to go, stood still in surprise. The Holy Eucharist, wrapped in its purple cloud of mystery . . . "How?" he asked.

"The power that heals is there," replied the priest, smiling at Paul's surprise. And he quoted " 'Preserve thy body and soul unto everlasting life.' The body is included."

"My own body, perhaps . . . Though I have never tried to receive for such a small thing as mere healing. But how can that power reach through me to others?"

"There is a great mystery. Perhaps I should not have mentioned it to you at this time. But since I have—read the twelfth chapter of First Corinthians and see what it says to you. There is a key to intercessory prayer in those verses, if you are able to receive it."

"I do know a little bit about the power of the sacraments," said Paul. "Baptism, of course. Sick babies always get well. And the confessional . . ." And as Father Sinclair sat down again to listen, Paul told him the story of his last confession at St. Peter's Church.

"Your confessor was my curate," nodded Father Sinclair. "Very fine fellow."

"Then he believed . . . He understood . . ."

"Oh, yes."

"Then that's why there was such power there!"

"That and your own expectancy. The worthy confession that you yourself made, with prayer and soul-searching. A confession like that amounts to a spiritual psychoanalysis," he went on, repeating a thought that had come to Paul before. And he added, "I have never known a person who made such use of the sacraments to need any other psychoanalysis. That is, if he had a priest with any faith at all. Canonically of course the sacrament is valid whether or not the priest believes in it. But practically, the faith of the priest has a great deal to do with it. For after all, there is the law: one receives or gives—as much as one expects to receive or give."

"And my confessor," said Paul, struggling to grasp these great matters before they should slip from him, "believes that the power of Christ through His Church would not only save my soul in the next life but would also heal me in this life of all the mental and nervous results of past trauma."

"That's it," murmured the priest.

Paul went forth with rejoicing not unmixed with fear. For who was he to administer so great a power as this?

"One more thing," Father Sinclair called after him. "If the key to intercessory prayer comes into your hands, try it first for someone you don't like."

"Why?"

But Father Sinclair only said, "You can't possibly understand that until you try it."

"About time you got back!" Skip greeted him on his return. "Dirty work at the crossroads!"

And Janet muttered, *"That louse!"* and jammed her iron down upon a steaming shirt as though she were pinning her enemy to the ironing board.

"What louse?"

"Priscilla. She's getting up a petition to the Bishop!"

"Trying to boot you out of here," explained Skip, sitting astride a kitchen chair, his arms across the back of it, and glowering at his uncle. "And if I were you, I'd get out—now. While the getting is good. I'd go back to engineering, that's what I'd do, and see how they like that."

"Don't be ridiculous," snapped Paul, suddenly tired and cross after his long day.

"Well, if it isn't engineering, find some other job. Personnel work of some sort, where you're supposed to help people and can do it without a bunch of morons climbing all over you."

So there it was—his blue paper—his dishonorable discharge from All Saints Church. For he could not possibly stay in a church that had requested him to leave.

He could not possibly stay.

He had prayed for Priscilla, in the way he had taught his Bible Class, and apparently it had borne no fruit. He had tried to imagine her weather-beaten features and her gimlet eyes irradiated by the love of Christ—and all the while she had been tearing around the parish working toward his destruction. Suddenly he could no longer keep up his holy pretense. He hated her and he knew that he hated her.

As he lay awake that night, he remembered: "Try it on someone you don't like." And he climbed out of bed and studied the twelfth chapter of First Corinthians, delving deep beneath the surface of its words as he had learned to do in teaching his Bible Class. "Work on it while I sleep," he whispered to his unconscious mind. "There's something there, but I'm too tired to see it now."

And at last he slept.

After a silent and abstracted breakfast, Janet mercifully holding her tongue and Skip asleep as usual, Paul entered the cool dimness of his church and sat in the chancel.

"Give me the key," he whispered. Almost before he had said the words it was there within his mind: *"We are all part of the body of Christ."*

Why had he never before considered that extraordinary statement, with all that it implied of a merging of spirit with spirit? Why had he never connected it with other words, straight and simple but pregnant with power? "Bear ye one another's burdens, and so fulfill the law of Christ." "This kind can come forth by nothing, but by prayer and fasting."

There it was. But did he dare to do it? "Lord have mercy upon us," he whispered as he left the church. "Christ have mercy upon us . . . Lord have mercy upon us."

There was no use postponing this matter. In fact, he did not dare to wait. He was not a very brave man and the only way he could force himself to do a thing was just to close his eyes and do it. "Next weekend," he told himself. "Beginning Friday night and ending at the Communion service."

It proved a difficult three days.

But as Paul merged his spirit with the spirit of Priscilla McGhann, claiming that they were not separate individuals but one in Christ, he saw the woman with new eyes. "This woman is more than my sister in Christ," he whispered before the high altar. "She is myself. So show me, Lord, the original cause of her sins that I may worthily repent of them."

There was a high white peace about the altar, charged with power imperceptible like the blades of a whirling propeller. And in this peace Paul projected his imagination back through time that he might see the small girl Priscilla McGhann had been. "She must have been a forbidding little creature, all jaws and teeth," thought Paul with the hint of a smile. "Isn't it a pity her brother has all the looks of the family?" people would say of her. There would form in her childish mind a bitter resentment and a fear of passing unnoticed through life, so that she overcompensated by trying to dominate.

Paul began to accomplish a small fast for those sins that he had taken to himself. A complete fast was not possible without explanations to Janet, and his delicacy forbade that he discuss this way of prayer. So he evaded and avoided his sister as best he could: "I'll not be home for dinner tonight." "No thanks, just a salad for lunch." And as hunger crept upon him, all the more because of the gruelling effort that his spirit was making, he offered it as atonement for those sins that he had taken to himself.

The effort was beyond all imagining.

Even his words and his actions were not like himself. He found himself snapping at his altar boys on Saturday evening until they looked at him with wonder in their eyes. "Sorry," he said a little breathlessly. "I must have got out of the wrong side of the bed. Let's try again." And all the time of the rehearsal he thought, "What's happened to me? Will I ever feel like myself again?"

When the boys had left him, leaping over the hedge and away with whoops of joy, he suddenly knew what was the matter with him. He had been talking to his boys in the same contentious voice that Priscilla used toward him. It was Priscilla's spirit and not his who spoke thus, who felt thus, who labored thus. He had placed himself under that burden and he was carrying it.

"In that case, it's all right, Lord," he said with a long sigh.

And he carried the burden until the communion service the next morning, when he received for Priscilla McGhann and not for himself and gave thanks for the redeeming power that was at that moment entering her and gave over the burden of her spirit into the hands of Christ.

"What's come over Priscilla?" asked Janet later in the week. "She doesn't snarl, she doesn't gripe, she doesn't rip anybody up the back. What's come over her?"

Paul smiled and made no answer.

On Saturday morning Priscilla paused in her lumbering about parish house and sacristy, came to anchor outside his study and thumped with sturdy knuckles on the door.

"I've been talking to my brother," she began abruptly. "Seems to me like all this resigning and what not is a lot of foolishness. I just want to know: what about that McNeill woman? Are you going to marry her or aren't you?"

"If she'll have me, I am," said Paul gently.

"Well, she's not as bad as I used to think," admitted Priscilla. "As a matter of fact," she added, glaring at Paul as though he were one of the main offenders, "I've got no time for all the clickety-clack that's made about her just because she tries to help people."

Paul smiled behind his hand and said nothing.

"But it's all these fancy ways of praying that I don't like!" burst out Priscilla. "We've got all the prayers we need in the prayer book. Why do we need all that rigmarole? Think this way, think that way, think the other way . . ."

" 'Finally, brethren,' " quoted Paul with a smile, " 'whatsoever things are true, whatsoever things are honest, whatsoever things are just, whatsoever things are pure, whatsoever things are lovely, whatsoever things are of good report; if there be any virtue and if there be any praise, think on these things.' It wasn't Burnett who said that, it was St. Paul."

"Well, he was sort of screwy too," boomed Priscilla, and that disposed of St. Paul. "What I mean is: *we are the Church*. Whatever we need, we've already got." Thus she stood and declared her faith, a great square-rigged woman rooted and grounded not upon an actual power nor upon an actual love, but upon the man-made mechanism for preserving these things.

"The heaven and the heaven of heavens cannot contain

Thee," Paul quoted again, answering her. "How much less this house that I have builded?"

But he was beyond her now.

"Talk sense!" she thundered, lowering her broad beam into a chair and thumping the arm of it.

"What I mean is this," said Paul mildly. "Our Church is very wonderful, I grant you, but there is more that we can learn." And he added with a smile, "A man who thinks he's gotten where he's going is not likely to get there."

"H'm," said Priscilla in a noncommittal voice. Then she came out abruptly with the real purpose of her call. "Did you pray for my nephew Joe or didn't you?"

"Yes, I did."

Priscilla meditated a moment and then asked abruptly, "Meningitis or indigestion?"

"He had meningitis," said Paul softly.

"H'm," said Priscilla. And then, summing up the matter, "Fine thing. Some people around here don't know when they're well off." She went out, shaking her head lugubriously. There was a pause outside the study door. "And I'm going to write to the Bishop and tell him so!" shouted Priscilla in her usual loud and vigorous tones.

That marked the end of the petition to oust the minister of All Saints.

11

If only he could tell Burnett, thought Paul, that the mysterious energy of Christ through His Church had accomplished the taming of Priscilla. For there was no question about the change that had come to that formidable female. "What's happened to Priscilla?" asked Skip. "Sticking her mug in the door wanting to know if you would like some rhubarb out of her garden and a bunch of irises and a lot of other truck. I said, well you didn't have time to plant irises. So says she, all bright-eyed and bushy-tailed, she'll plant them herself, says she. You been jinxing her by remote control?"

"More or less," admitted Paul. But more than that he could not say, either to Skip or to Burnett.

He tried to imagine himself explaining his special altar prayer to Burnett. And he could hear her voice replying, "Certainly. I've been seeing her that way for a long time." No. Priscilla was not the one through whom he was to prove the power of the Church. Professional ethics would prevent him from talking about a member of his congregation. Alan was that one, as he had known from the beginning.

As Paul went out of the kitchen door to the garage, June made soft music in the air and Janet's little garden was rapturous with early summer flowers. Ecstatic birds darted in and out of the ivy that hung upon the parish house and the hemlock hedge of the cemetery gleamed as its polished needles caught the sun, the emerald tips of new leaves as lovely as flowers. The red roses covering the garage quivered as Paul slid back the door, and a mother robin flew out of the bush and scolded him.

"It's all right," said Paul to the fussing little bird. "I'm not interfering with your babies. All I did was to pull them out of the cellar areaway when you kept letting them fall in." And he smiled up at the little bird with a face that did indeed look years younger, as Burnett had said . . . no frown between the brows, no tension around the mouth.

Paul drove to the mental hospital and looked for Alan among the flower beds. It took him a while, for June had lured the wandering patients out into the sun and he must speak to all of them as he went by, but finally he found Alan with both hands in the dirt.

He was not better, as Paul had hoped. There was a wavering quality in his smile, a stiffness in the planes of his face, and he did not speak. Paul eased himself to the warm grass and sat in silence beside his friend. "Hard sledding?" he asked at last, and he plucked a bit of grass and chewed its whitened end as he studied Alan.

"I guess it's no use," said Al tonelessly. "I seem better for a while and think maybe... And then it comes back again. It would really be easier not to—to think 'maybe'" he went on, his voice slow as though the very garnering of the words were an effort.

"Back comes—*what?*"

Alan looked at him out of the corners of his eyes and for the first time Paul saw fear incarnate in a human being. "Never mind," he said gently, as Al did not speak. "You really are better, even though you don't feel it today. After all, you bypassed the manic stage; you didn't throw chairs."

But Alan only replied, "I'm happier when I do."

Paul made no comment. Instead he began to talk casually of little things. "So I had to climb down there and fish out the baby robins," he said, praying within himself. "And what a time I had, teaching them to fly."

Alan said nothing, but there was an indefinable softening in the lines of his face. And when the minister paused he asked a question, irrelevant, but heartening because it concerned another than himself. "Have you been praying for a boy named Harold?"

Paul shook his head. "Why?"

Alan looked dejected. "Oh—nothing. He's better. They said it was the insulin shock treatments but I thought it must be you."

Paul had an irrational feeling that he had let Alan down. "Have you ever had shock treatments?" he asked abruptly.

Alan bit his lips. "Three," he said briefly. "Years ago. That's why my family moved me to a private sanatorium so that I wouldn't have any more."

"Then they didn't help?"

"In a way. Like being hit on the head by a lead pipe."

"But isn't it worth it, if—"

"No!" cried Alan, standing up with a jerk, his trowel slipping out of his hand. "I was just as crazy as ever underneath, but with no way to release those awful feelings. Not even the joy of taking off my clothes and trying to climb out the window. It quieted me; oh yes, it quieted me! But with a thousand tortures underneath the quiet and always the sense of being someone else, not quite myself; never quite myself again—" He broke off and started toward the building, muttering to himself.

"I'm sorry!" cried Paul, catching up with Al's long strides. "I won't ask you any more questions. I promise."

But Alan began to run unsteadily, and Paul let him go.

Halfway to the car Paul stopped short. A thought struck him with such violence that he had to take a deep breath before going on.

He must pray for Alan as he had prayed for Priscilla.

"I can't!" Paul whispered.

It had been hard enough to accomplish this mysterious merging of spirit with spirit for Priscilla. As he fasted for her small sins, claiming her as part of himself in the body of Christ, he had been tormented by feelings that were not his own. He had labored under a burden of darkness, he had lost the sense of the presence of God. It was a dangerous game of the spirit to enter into the personality of another. How could he possibly do so with one who was insane, opening the doors of his mind to take upon himself the horror of great darkness that he had seen in Alan Whitacre?

"I can't do it!" he whispered again.

Through the noises of the highway he seemed to hear the words: "If any man will come after me, let him deny himself and take up his cross and follow me."

The meaning of those words burst upon him for the first time. *"Good God!"* he cried inwardly. This was the way in which a man might share the sufferings of Christ: this and no other. And through the centuries those who might have shouldered that cross and so made reparation for the sins of the world had substituted the small illnesses of the flesh for these most holy sufferings . . .

Another thought leaped into Paul's mind and he whispered through white lips, *"Don't show me any more!"* He remembered that One in the garden Who upon a certain dark night had identified Himself not with the evil in one man's mind but with the sins of the whole world—that One Who had cried out in His agony, "Remove this cup from me: nevertheless not my will but Thine be done."

"If You could take that, I guess I can take this," said Paul Forrester at last in the silence of his own church, holding to the altar rail with his white-knuckled hands. "Only what if I can't get out from under it? What if I land in that hospital in Alan's place?"

There was no answer unless the small words within his mind were an answer. For he heard his inner being say, "What if you do?"

"Too bad I'm not R.C.," Paul muttered grimly. "I'd make a wonderful Trappist monk . . ." And he added in one last outburst of protest, "Lord, You know I *don't like* this kind of thing! I'm not a mystic! I'm just ordinary and I—I want to be just ordinary!"

But when he rose from his knees he knew that he would do it just the same.

"There you go," scolded Janet. "Off your feed again. You need a vacation, that's what you need." Paul only smiled and trifled with his salad. He could not tell Janet—he could not tell anyone—ever.

Saturday was a long and awful day. Paul walked more and more heavily as the hours passed and the darkness deepened upon him. Fear stalked his footsteps; a fear that was not his own; a brooding horror connected in some way with violence and bloodshed. "That can't be Alan," Paul thought. "He wasn't in the war . . ." But it was Alan, Alan's spirit merging so completely with his own that he was overwhelmed by Alan's feelings. He could almost see the great fear at the root of Alan's trouble—almost, but not quite.

Other feelings wandered in and out through the fear and darkness. There was a shifting and sliding of thought, as though at any moment he might lose control. And, most horrifying of all, there were irrational connections of ideas, so that the altar and the cross and the most holy symbols suggested to his shocked consciousness words that were evil and blasphemous. Not for one moment could Paul give way to these things. He must keep his head high and his face quiet, come what might, and by constant prayer he did this. There was no feeling in his prayers, for the face of God was hid from him; but though he received no peace or joy, at least he held to his course without breaking.

Sunday morning was the zero hour. He had awakened with pounding head and pounding heart, feeling the darkness roll over him in great, engulfing waves. As he went toward the church he was aware of conflict in the very air, as though the powers of darkness held him in their hands and struggled for his soul. He felt possessed by rage, he longed to lash out at his servers, to curse his sexton, to sneer at the lumbering Priscilla underfoot with her vestments.

In labored silence he went into church and bowed before the candles lit upon the altar.

Then the fear that had lurked half-seen for three days struck him cold between the eyes.

"God help me!" thought Paul. Then he steadied himself and went on with the service. After all, he had chanced this when he began his vigil for Alan. And he was committed now to that quest, like a scientist experimenting dangerously with the grim secrets of the atom, like a man of research inoculating himself in the hope of saving others. If he landed in the insane asylum, that was where he landed.

He raised the holy vessel into the white light of Christ's love and as never before prayed through the words of the sacrament that the flow of Christ's life might fuse with an invisible power. And as he partook of the sacrament he thought, "Lord, this is Alan! Alan—this is Christ!"

And then came a lightening and a forgetting within him, in waves of joy, overwhelming, relieving, releasing.

The thing was done. And as Paul gave thanks for it, suddenly he knew that he would not always pray after this difficult pattern. He would go beyond Calvary to a resurrection; he would work through the power of joy rather than through the power of suffering.

That Sunday evening when Paul lifted his eyes and saw Alan sitting beside an attendant in his church he was not too much surprised. Only the joy that had surged through him all day rang golden bells in his heart. Alan, quiet and radiant, his blue eyes shining; Alan, his face softened as he watched the minister follow his little flock out of the chancel. "Oh make Thy Church, dear Savior, a lamp of purest gold," piped the small voices as with eyes steadfastly forward the children's choir marched out of the sacristy door, "To bear before the nations Thy true light as of old."

Where was Burnett? wondered Paul suddenly. For occasionally she too slipped into the church of a Sunday evening and sat with her eyes uplifted to his face as Al's had been . . . .

"Alan!" Paul cried, darting back into church and clasping the tall man's hands.

"Something wonderful has happened," said Alan a bit breathlessly. And he added, motioning to the weather-beaten man beside him, "This is Mr. Flanigan, one of our guards."

"Pleased to meet you, Father," said Mr. Flanigan. "Yep. Al here's a new man, all of a sudden like. Don't know what come over him. He wanted to come to church, so they told me to bring him."

"It's gone!" breathed Alan. "The fear—the darkness—gone! I had to thank you, now, tonight. So I came."

Paul smiled. "Why thank me?"

Alan's gaze was steady. "I don't know what you've been doing," he said, "but I know you're behind this."

Paul was spared the need of a response by his small choir bursting in upon him with questions and demands. "Come again," he called over his shoulder. "Come to church next Sunday and stay to dinner."

He would invite Burnett. And she would see for herself the power of God as it had acted through the Church.

Monday, preacher's holiday, was a glorious day with a great, glad sky swept free of clouds by the west wind. Paul was determined to keep it free for Burnett. No, he told Janet, he could not go to Clericus and practice a sung requiem against the time when one of the brethren should pass away.

"But you used to love to go to those clerical things!"

"I used to have time," he said. "Now I don't."

No, he could not have a conference with Opal or attend a Boy Scout troop committee or go over the flower chart with the Altar Guild. As soon as the sun rose high and hot he went in slacks and a blue shirt to find Burnett.

She came laughing down the walk toward him, between her larkspur and summer phlox, her tall delphiniums full of sky-blue blooms. She was like a delphinium herself, in a gingham dress of greens and blues, a scarf in the same close harmony about her blue-black hair.

Paul did not tell her Al's story on the way down through the pines, nor on the plains, mysterious low plateau where land rose to sky and swept in blue waves toward the sea and where the breath of the ocean blew fresh and salty upon one's face. Now that he was with her he felt no need to tell her anything. She was so completely his own, heart of his heart, soul of his soul, mind of his mind.

They reached her brother's summer cottage, changed into swimming suits and ran down to the shining sands. Burnett leaped ahead of him into the sea, cold foam swirling about her knees. Paul would have preferred to venture forth more slowly, but with Burnett's lithe form diving into the breakers before him he could only follow. Always and forever, he thought, she would surge ahead and he would try his floundering best to follow—always and forever.

The wild white chargers of the sea were thundering toward him now. He drew in his breath with a gasp as the rushing waters struck him full in the chest, cold spray flying high into the air above his head. Where was Burnett? Ahead of him, in the deep green trough that yawned ominously smooth before the next thunderhead, her arms upflung, high and wide, in an ecstasy of abandonment. The great wave, gathering into itself the waters of the blue sea behind it, the waters of the green trough before it, rose and towered—towered—three times the height of the small white figure, four times its height—would it never break? A wild uplifted line of foam appeared on the crest. And just as it bowed and crashed with a roar the small white figure lowered its arms and dived through the wall of water...a flash of white bathing suit, a flicker of white feet, and she was gone.

Paul gritted his teeth and dived through the breakers as well as he could because there was no other way to reach her. She lay flat on the water, arms wide, bathing cap submerged, rocking and floating like a sea gull over the swells. She was quite unconscious of him or of anything in the world except the sky and the sea. She was singing, her voice lilting over the breakers.

> "Diamonds, diamonds,
>   Flung against the sky,
> White spray flying
>   Where the wild gulls fly,
>
> "Breaking waves a-thundering,
>   Roaring at my feet,
> Crashing in the shallows
>   Where the bright sands meet,
>
> "Emerald, amethyst,
>   Every shade of blue—
> Ocean that the sun has kissed,
>   Here's my love to you!"

And her voice, sinking into quietness, repeated the last two words of her rocking little tune like an echo: "to you—to you—to you—"

Paul lifted his feet from the ocean floor—indeed it was not possible to keep them on it—gained her side through the powerful waters and floated beside her. At first he wished that she had been willing to swim at a guarded beach, relinquishing privacy for the sake of safety; then he comforted himself in the thought of her brother watching them from the shore; and finally he quite forgot to be afraid and entered in spite of himself into her mood of ecstasy. A breaker forming out to sea would surge toward him, lift him, toss him like a leaf, then thunder toward the shore and break beyond him, leaving a mist of rainbow spray blown cold upon his face. On the horizon one far ship, a silver eyelash under a wisp of smoke, went its mysterious way to unknown lands; overhead the sky glowed with an azure never to be found inland. It was a dream, a fairy interlude between life and Life, too rapturously beautiful to be real. Surely it was a dream, thought Paul, laughing with Burnett for the sheer joy of laughing.

But the ocean towed them gradually inshore until an onrushing breaker tossed them over its top and broke upon them in a welter of white. Choking and blinded they were rolled and ground upon the bottom of the sea until the laughing foam deposited them in shallow waters and hissed back into the trough of the next wave.

"Wasn't that wonderful?" cried Burnett. "Let's rest a minute and then do it again!"

They sat together at the edge of the waters, where the last fine line of foam slithered over the shining sands. Sandpipers tripped comically along the beach, pecking in the sand and hopping away in a tap-dancing little rush when a ripple caught up with them. Sea gulls swooped through the sky, the sunlight dazzling on their silver wings.

"What are you singing?" asked Paul.

"A little poem I remembered."

"And the tune?"

"Oh, that just made itself up inside of me. Tunes do, you know."

No. Paul did not know that tunes did.

"Now and then, I mean. When I don't have a paintbrush handy. *You* know."

"Tell me," he said gently.

Burnett lay down on the wet sand beside him and gazed dreamily up at the sky. Happiness softened her slightly angular features into exquisite planes of loveliness and her smile was as joyous and free as the wide sea.

"I'll try to say it," she murmured, "only it doesn't quite fit the frame of words. It's like this: a certain mood begins to fill me, growing and swelling in here"—and she laid her hand upon her breast—"until I feel that I will burst if I do not let it out. It's like a child that must be born . . . It's—beauty surging in from God and beating through me until I'm forced to give it form. Paints, pastels—only they break the heart because the beauty that I paint is never so radiant as the beauty I see. If I have no paints, then the beauty of words—the beauty of swaying sound . . ."

Her voice drifted away and she was still.

"You're thinking about that other man," he said abruptly.

"For a minute," admitted Burnett. "Only because he once expressed it in blank verse." And she quoted:

" 'Beauty beats upon my heart in ecstasy
    As keen as pain, so that I must needs sing,
    Giving my joy a body and a shape
    With bones of words and blood of melody . . .'

How did you know I was thinking about him?"

"I can't put your thoughts into blank verse," said Paul with a little sigh. "But at least I know your thoughts."

Burnett was silent for a moment. "Do you mind if I think of him once in a while?" she asked.

"Not unless it makes you sad." Paul thought, "If he were to pop out of the grave, it would be a very different matter." And he added to himself, with a leap of fancy, "Then you'd have to do a quick fade-out, Forrester . . ."

Burnett scrambled to her feet with a laugh. "Nothing could make me sad today! Nothing! I have the ocean and you, and what more could I want?"

The wind from the sea blew cold on their wet bathing suits and they went into the house and dressed, lunched with various McNeills and then fled to the sand dunes to be at peace.

"Anybody that wants the Maine coast can have it," murmured Burnett dreamily. "Cold waterspouts on cold cliffs—or else flat water like a millpond, gurgling around the rocks! Or they can have Florida too," she rambled, "the sea shallow and hot like a dish of soup, only the pelicans swimming down the sky to add a touch of drama. But me, I love the Jersey shore—long rollers, piling up, piling up, as far as the eye can see—sand dunes and seashells and never a tree to break the vast simplicity of blue and gold!"

"To most people the Jersey shore means Atlantic City," said Paul prosaically.

And Burnett replied, "I like Atlantic City too. It's silly, but it's fun."

"What of the Pacific?"

Burnett disposed of the Pacific with one wave of her hand. "Fog," she said briefly. "No, give me this. One could hardly be nearer to heaven."

She was a creature made for happiness, Paul thought, and

for the first time it occurred to him that he had never before seen her completely relaxed and that she led a hard and rigorous life. He had fancied himself a bit of a martyr now and then merely because for a few brief months he had faced criticism in order to help his fellowmen. Here was a woman who could have been as free as the waves, as gay as yellow butterflies in the sun, as light and carefree as the shining silver seeds of the milkweed. On this one day he was seeing her as she might be on all the days if she did not walk continually under other people's burdens. Instead of the bright freedom that was her birthright she had chosen a life of rigid discipline and of humble servitude to a town that did not appreciate her; a town unworthy, thought Paul with sudden passion, to tie her shoelace.

No wonder that her smile was apt to be taut, that her shoulders were set at times like those of a soldier marching, that even her walk was a little stiff, not quite the gay, free swing that he had seen on this day of sun and wind!

If only he could keep her forever comforted. He must have her for his own so that he could protect and champion her; he must awaken her to the understanding of his Christ so that she could be really his . . .

Paul remembered the meeting that he had planned and the story that he had to tell her. This was the time, thought Paul, while she was quiet and relaxed, while her mind was still. She sat facing him, arms around her knees, her face sharpened with thought as he talked on.

"But why the communion service and all that business?" she asked at the end. "I don't see."

"It *worked!*"

"Yes, but couldn't it have been merely that your dramatic and difficult way of praying gave you the faith to make it work?"

"I don't think so. I think it was Jesus Himself doing it, not just me thinking positive thoughts." And he added, before Burnett could interrupt him, "Tell me, Burnett, when I talk about Jesus, do you really know who I mean? Have you ever really accepted Him—really given your life to Him?"

"Oh yes," said Burnett, "when I was ten years old and we were at home on furlough. My mother read me the stories of the crucifixion, and I remember how I cried. And the minister, a gentle, kind man who really knew Him, asked me whether I loved Him and wanted to give my life to Him, and I did. It was real! But after some years, as I've told you, I lost faith—not in Jesus but in Christians. They *didn't* give their lives to Him, because they didn't know that He would come into them and do His works through them. They didn't know the indwelling power of Christ, only the historical Redeemer who would some day take them to heaven."

"So—"

"They wouldn't let Him in. They kept Him out by their lack of faith." And she quoted, "For without faith it is impossible to please Him."

"So you lost faith in the established church," meditated Paul. "And I don't blame you. Many people have lost faith in the church, and the time will come when even more will lose faith—and the church will totter and fall," he murmured, as the words came to him from far away, "unless in some way that faith is restored."

"You are helping to restore it," smiled Burnett.

"Well, at least I'm beginning to see that both are true: Jesus Christ is a real Person, outside ourselves, our Savior and Redeemer—but also He wants to abide in us and to do His works through us."

"That's what I mean by the Christ within."

"Abide in me and I in you," quoted Paul.

"But I still wonder," said Burnett, who meanwhile was thinking her own thoughts, "whether it was really His power through the communion service that worked, or whether it was only your own faith."

"It was probably both," said Paul. "But the same thing holds. It worked."

"Then I must try to understand it," said Burnett with honesty. "It's quite contrary to everything that I have believed, so tell me again. Tell me slowly."

Paul told her again, and from somewhere out of the sea and the sky new strength came into his words, new clarity into his thinking. "So as we step into the stream of His redemptive life," said Paul, "He enters into the picture Himself. Hence the uplifted heart and the bowed head as we wait for Him; hence the shimmering presence of the angels and archangels and all the company of heaven."

"You are beautiful," said Burnett with the irrelevance of a woman.

Paul came down to earth with a mixture of joy and of chagrin. *"Burnett!* I'm talking about—"

"Yes, I know. And I'm beginning to get a feeling of your sacramental method, too. But in the meantime, do you know that you are an entirely different person from the man you used to be? I'm going to paint you."

"Don't be an idiot!"

"But I am. The way you are right now, with the sun on your face and that lovely expression about your mouth... No, hold it," she cried with an artist's fury as he tried to take her in his arms. And she half closed her eyes and made small movements with her hand as she studied him. "I'm going to paint you just like that," she concluded. "Framed in sand and crowned with sky." And she repeated absurdly, "You're beautiful."

Laughing with exasperation, he had her in his arms at last. "What I want to know is, when are you going to marry me? When?"

"I never said I—"

But Paul smothered her words with kisses, her lips, her eyes, her hair. "Now I've got a mouth full of sand," he laughed, for she was blown as full of sand as the stiff dune grass half-buried beneath it. "But it's worth it," he cried, "Say it now! Say, 'I will marry you.'"

"I will marry you," murmured Burnett, her gay voice dying into a whisper.

"Oh Lord our God, how manifold, how manifold are Thy works!" chanted Paul as they drove home, too happy for ordinary speech. In his new joy, a childlike thought wandered over the threshold of his mind: how strange that he had never before really believed that God loved him! Every lovely thing shouted aloud of His tenderness toward His small experiment, man, yet Paul had never dared to think that God, like a loving Father, wanted to make him happy. God had not given him the gift of creation, which men called sex, as an instrument of torture to hold his eyes waking during the night with the thin agony of nerves as taut as fiddle-strings. Nor had God given it to him that he might hand it back as a sacrifice, suppressing and sublimating years without end until death should at last rid him of its torment. For the first time Paul dared to believe that this great energy that beat through his body was meant for glory and for joy.

"Do you think that we might ever have any children?" he asked, hardly above a whisper.

"Of course!" replied Burnett briskly. "Thirty-three isn't too old for children. We'll probably get in three, at least; maybe four."

Children! He loved them, yet he had never dared dream of fathering them. "Can't we get married *right away?*" he asked a little breathlessly. "Next week—next month—"

"Well—perhaps not *quite* so soon," hesitated Burnett. "After all, there's the parish . . ."

"Oh, to heck with the parish!"

"They are beginning to see that I'm not a—a loose woman, now that Priscilla has climbed on the bandwagon for us. It wouldn't kill your church now if you were to marry me. But it would still split it. We must wait—"

"You didn't say you'd marry me if the parish approved!" Paul objected. "You said you'd *marry me.*"

"Yes, darling. Because I see which way the parish is swinging. And because I am beginning to understand your tools. And—because I love you."

"But not as I love you," thought Paul. He smiled at her and said nothing. He had always known that he loved her more than she loved him, and he was quite willing it should be so. Even that measure of love was far more than he had ever dared to expect. She would never love anyone as she had loved the other man, long ago. Part of her died with him. Paul knew that, and he was deeply and humbly content to be forever second-best.

"Besides," said Burnett, breaking the comfortable silence as they drove through deepening twilight, their bodies close together and their hearts more deeply and tenderly close, so that the thoughts of each throbbed and broke upon the consciousness of the other, "I need just a little more time to understand; it's still hard to believe the things you've told me."

Paul smiled, thinking of the new Alan Whitacre. "Wait till next Sunday," he said confidently. "You're coming to dinner at the rectory, you know, and I've invited Al to come too. Wait till you see him. Then you'll believe."

12

Alan Whitacre was living in a new world. And he knew precisely the hour of his awakening into it. It was on a Sunday morning at eight-thirty, just as he stepped out the side door of the hospital to do his daily gardening. His spirits suddenly lifted and the sunlight was beautiful, as it had been in his childhood. This might have been a small thing to some people, but not to Alan. Formerly sunlight had filled him with a flood of joy: the strong white light of summer, sharp and keen on the glistening mountains of Kuling; the clear cold light of fall, etching the turrets of the city wall black and silver against the sky; even the pale light of winter, warming itself on the pink pagoda over the south gate; even the sultry sunlight of spring, fighting its way through the steaming wang-mei drizzle.

But for many years sunlight had weighed upon him more heavily than darkness.

Alan stood still on that Sunday morning and looked up through tall oaks into the shining sky. Then he caught his breath. It could not possibly be true, but he saw a figure grotesque and horrible, like one of the idol guardians at the temple gates... the kind of dark spirit that had often haunted his childhood dreams. There was an unnatural shadow in the bright sky and into it the dreadful figure disappeared, as if into the mouth of a cave.

"It's going away from me," whispered Alan. He hardly knew what he meant. He felt alive and free. He stood gazing into the sky until his eyes were blinded by the light. It had not been a real figure, he reminded himself. It was not the first time that his disordered imagination had showed him something that was not there. But just the same, his vision had meaning; his own unconscious mind was telling him something. Alan thought in pictures, and as he bent over the flower bed he saw Paul Forrester's face. In the dark eyes was a deep and brooding compassion such as a father might feel for a child. "He's been praying for me," thought Alan.

For many months Alan had silently resisted the prayers that Paul had made for him, sometimes from unbelief, sometimes from a perverse fear of being well. He did not know how he could endure the struggle of maintaining sanity. Since his eleventh year Alan had been consciously two people, one who acted and one who resisted the acting; one who thought and the other who sneered and scoffed. "So that's the way you think, is it?" the other one would say. "You idiot!" Or sometimes it would speak in Chinese, hissing the s's as it told him to die, hardening the b to an evil explosive as it muttered words so filthy that Alan pushed them into the deep well of his unconscious, as he continually pushed down a certain unbearable memory.

Alan had disregarded this voice at first, being by nature a happy child. He had innocently assumed that everyone thought after two patterns. But it had grown more troublesome, until the strain of making a decision became almost unbearable. He had retreated into a world of fairy tale and of daydreams. He had thus developed something like a sixth sense, so that the ghost stories the Chinese servants told him made sharp, fierce, pictures in his mind and tormented him in his dreams; so that he could see the "little people" in the Canterbury bells beside the compound walls... "But then," he told himself as he weeded, "Burnett could see them too ..." How could the line be drawn between those who were crazy and those who were not? Burnett could only see the beautiful things. Perhaps that was the difference. He saw both, and when the execution ground was in use the spirits of the departed moaned around his bedposts as the ram's horn moaned upon the city wall.

He had been better when he went to school in Shanghai and was no longer alone in the crawling evil of that inland city. He had filled his days with work and play so that he could not think. For a while he had blossomed, like the swift flowers of a northern climate, that hasten to bloom while there is yet time. During those few bright years he had been wildly happy, but never at peace, even though he had everything to comfort him. He excelled in everything: sports, study, drama. He was the hero of the school and most particularly he was the hero of a small, plain girl with eager spirit and glowing eyes: Burnett. But he always knew that if he relaxed his efforts for one moment the old darkness would descend. "I am here," it whispered, "I have not gone away. Wait." When he awoke at night the other spoke, in Chinese, concerning sex and all creativity.

Sex ran strong in Alan, as in every creative person, but his awakening adolescence was made hideous by this inner voice. Denied entrance into his mind, his emotions tunneled beneath the surface to emerge in strange forms. He developed a preoccupation with pain, the thought of it filling him at times with horror and at other times with a wild, unnatural pleasure. "I must be going crazy," he would think, and would strive more desperately to drive away, to bury, the evil thoughts.

It was easier for a while when he went to college in America, away from the ancient, haunted land of his birth. True, he knew an aching loneliness as the months passed without Burnett. But in spite of that it was easier. The air was new, fresh, tingling with life. People were happy, only they did not know how happy they were: no starving bodies to step over in the city gate, no wailing across the execution ground at night, lone late travellers singing in a high weird falsetto to keep away the spirit; no execution ground, no execution ground . . .

If he worked very hard and kept incessantly busy, Alan did not hear that haunting voice at all. And he did work hard, forcing his tired mind to study day and night.

Then in his senior year his mind buckled under the strain. The wheels of thought clogged, grew slow, and stopped. "I can't do it," he would say to his professors when they protested the sudden decline in his marks.

"But you're about to win the Sorbonne scholarship."

"I'll try, I'll try."

But he could not do it. He gave up the struggle and at first he felt a wild hysterical relief merely in giving up. But almost immediately the other self was upon him, urging him toward self-destruction. It was an easy victory. Alan had no fear of pain, but rather a perverted passion for it. The horror of violent death hurled into his childish mind had been perverted into a very longing for the agony he had feared.

They had caught him just in time.

It would not have been an easy death ... under the wheels of a train. He did not want an easy death.

In his lucid intervals he had grieved for Burnett. Never for himself. He was simply too tired to struggle any longer.

After one of his sudden breaks into violence his mother had written Burnett that her beloved Alan had gone away from her into that other world. Burnett had not replied for some time. In fact, Alan was once more lucid when her answer came, wringing his heart with the tears beneath its faltering sentences. "She thinks I'm dead," Alan had said to his mother. "Let her think so." And his parents humored him, seeing that at the moment it brought him peace.

Later, however, it had troubled his sensitive conscience to think that he had lied to one who loved him. But then, he was already condemned to hell, and in hell one more sin made little difference. The loss of Burnett cut the last cord that bound him to real life. There was a certain dull peace in the cessation of effort. And as overstrain had hastened his breakdown, so the removal of strain released his normal healing powers. Slowly and gradually the balance of Alan's mind began to equalize. The manic periods were farther apart and of shorter duration, the blackouts were more endurable. And in the periods between, his vegetable-like existence was not too unpleasant.

When electric shock treatments became popular, Alan had submitted to them with very bad grace and had reacted so violently against them that his parents moved him to a private hospital.

"You wouldn't let the Chinese chain up their insane and beat them," Alan had protested.

"But the shock treatments bring many people right straight out of it," said his mother.

"So did the beatings," said Alan grimly.

"We are told that the mind does not register or remember any distress," his father had pleaded in his gentle hesitating voice.

And Alan had looked at him with shadowed eyes.

"The spirit remembers," he answered.

So the attempt to bring Alan back to normal life by electrocuting part of the brain was abandoned. He had reached a certain halfway point and there remained.

He had liked Paul Forrester from the first moment when the minister had stood behind him and said, "Saint-John's-wort, that's what it is."

Whenever Paul was with him, life awakened and for fleeting moments he would feel free and happy. It did not disturb him when Paul began to speak rather shyly of the possibility that he might recover. He did not believe in that possibility, of course. But he believed in Paul Forrester and loved him. And he knew that Paul loved him, although his friendship was apparently unconscious and utterly unexpressed. There were no long handclasps, no mumbling about the love of Christ such as other ministers were apt to make to Alan's embarrassment. Paul's feeling might almost be called professional. But if so, it was the gentlest of professions: it was the profession of Christ.

Out of love for Paul, Alan had tried in a faltering way to exert his own unsteady faith. And he had failed. Until, on this Sunday morning, the thing had been done for him. The feeling of release grew stronger as the day passed and the tormenting voice did not return. Even the effort he had made to surmount his timidity and attend Paul's evening service had not thrown him back into confusion.

At the thought of Sunday dinner, however, his courage failed him. Thursday morning after the communion service he told Paul so.

The minister looked disappointed.

"I'm sorry," faltered Alan. "But I think I'd better wait until I get more used to seeing people and . . ."

"I thought you were well," sighed the minister, looking up at him with worried eyes. "You said it went away."

"It did." Alan remembered his vision of a dark departing form. "But there's so much else . . . I mean, my mind's been tired for so long that it gets panicky. But *that voice* has gone." He stopped, overwhelmed by the impossibility of explaining to a sane mind the workings of a mind that is not sane. He sighed. "You wouldn't know about that."

"More than you think," said the minister, his eyes upon the ground. And a shadow seemed to pass over his face.

"Well, let me know when you feel up to coming. And in the meantime learn the things of prayer yourself."

"But I can't," Alan replied, his full lips shaking suddenly. "When I try it makes me think of myself and then I get frightened. I wonder what would I do if *it* came back?"

"I see what you mean." And Paul added, "Well, then, don't pray for yourself. But pray for the work of your hands. For anything that you try to do and make. And start praying for someone else."

Alan opened his mouth to say again that he could not. Then he looked at Paul's commanding face and knew that he could. It often amazed him that the minister, skimpily put together, with his nervous Adam's apple and his worried brows, should somehow be vibrant with inner strength. He, Alan, tall and physically strong, was like a child beside him, a scared child who dared not think too much.

On a certain August evening he wandered into the small lounge that shrieked of hospital with its upholstered wicker chairs and its potted rubber plant. A young woman sat there shuffling cards. She looked up at him and smiled. She dealt the cards in a pattern of seven and proceeded to lay other cards upon them according to a system Alan could not follow.

"How wonderful that you can do that!" he murmured.

She looked up at him from dark, brilliant eyes beneath the delicately pencilled line of her eyebrows. "It's very simple," she said. "Sit down and I'll teach you."

"I can't," said Alan in some distress. "When I try to read or write or learn anything, I—" he floundered, gazing at her with his gentle, timid smile. In spite of the stalwart cut of nose and chin, there was an indefinable weakness in Alan's face, a softness; a look of unnatural youth.

"I understand," said the girl, as Alan sat down beside her. "My name is Judith Klein," she added.

"You're new here, aren't you?" Alan asked after introducing himself.

"No," she said briefly. She bent her smooth dark head over the cards in her crimson-tipped fingers. "I have been in Ward Six," as though to say, "You may as well know it now . . ."

Ward Six. Alan knew what that meant. Yet here she sat,

beautiful in a dress of soft rose, able to play a complicated game such as Alan could not play.

"Not—myself at all," she whispered, her head still bowed.

"What's—what's that?"

Judith lifted her head. "Did you ever feel that there was something else in you—not yourself at all?"

"Oh, yes. But it's gone."

"Gone?"

"It's gone," repeated Alan, knowing immediately that this was the one for whom he must pray.

Judith seemed to be considering this. "Did it—" She hesitated and began over again. "Did it tell you to do things that you—that you wouldn't do for anything—?"

Alan nodded. "Sometimes."

"Why did it go away?" asked Judith abruptly.

Alan opened his mouth to say, "Because someone prayed for me." Though Paul had never told him, he knew with certainty that Paul's prayers had freed him. But he could not say the words. "It's hard to explain," he faltered. "I don't quite know, really. Someday I'll try to tell you . . ."

Alan wondered about Judith as the days passed. For although her mind was more alert by far than his own, she was not allowed to set foot out of doors except with an attendant, while he could come and go as he pleased, provided he did not leave the grounds. That was not likely. The very thought of contending with the outside world terrified him. His fear of life was perfectly rational: he knew that he could not cope with it. Nevertheless, as his freed mind regained its energies he knew he must try for Paul's sake if for no other reason. But he would not think of that. Not just yet.

A sound startled him out of his reverie over the delphinium bed. Not far away someone was weeping. He rose and looked about. There on the corner of the terrace above him stood a man, quite openly in tears. Alan had often seen him before. He was not a patient and there was about him a look of power and prosperity that no tears could dim. What could he do, thought Alan, or what could he say?

The man lifted his head and saw him there.

"I'm sorry," stammered Alan.

The gentleman wiped his face with a large linen handkerchief. As he had wept with complete dignity, so now with equal dignity he removed the traces of his tears, making no apology, "Are you a member of the staff?" he asked.

"No. I'm an inmate. But I'm well!" said Alan, a flash of joy in his smile.

"Then why are you here?" asked the large man. And he added, "Wait. I will come down and you shall tell me."

He sat with Alan on a rustic bench beneath a maple tree, where Alan talked briefly of himself and Paul and of the sudden release that came to him of a Sunday morning. It was curiously easy to talk to this man.

"Is this minister a young man with dark, eager eyes and a look of life about him?"

"Yes." Alan smiled.

"Then he has prayed for my daughter Judith at his little Mass."

Judith? Of course. That was why this man was not unknown to him. "You must feel very happy," said Alan. "Judith is almost well, isn't she?"

Judith's father shook his head and sighed.

"She combs her hair and makes herself pretty, she reads and writes and—

"But she wants to kill me."

Alan was silent. Such impulses were not new to him. They might come from hate or from love or from sheer perversion; God knew how they came, but they were real enough. But Judith, so young, with her shining brown eyes and her face as lovely as a rose . . ."

"No one else. Only me," murmured Mr. Klein with a vast, shuddering sigh.

"Such impulses usually go by opposites," said Alan gently. "One is apt to turn against the one most greatly loved. As if the Thing—" He broke off. Why should he assume that Judith was troubled as he had been, by an indwelling evil?

"Do you suppose your minister could help Judith as he has helped you?"

"I don't know," Alan said. "I could ask him."

"If it is a question of money, I am very rich. You may know of me. Felix Klein."

"I'm sorry. I've been out of the world for so long; I know nothing."

"I love money," said Mr. Klein dreamily, as though he gained consolation from the thought of it. "One can do so many wonderful things with it. But this—money cannot accomplish this."

"What do you do with money?" asked Alan with real interest.

He listened fascinated to the story of a factory that had remade a Southern mountainside. "I watched the little children crossing the street," said the big man. "Shivering. No coats. Broken shoes. Shivering. And I thought, 'This is where I will build my next factory.' For always I choose a place where they need me. So now, you should see! They have raincoats and rubbers, they walk to school with happy faces, their fathers, their brothers, their uncles all have work. 'How do you dare to hire so many people from one family?' my friends ask me. 'What if they should strike?'" He looked at Alan with his wide froglike smile and smote himself upon the chest, unconsciously dramatic. "I say, Let them strike!" he shouted. "If they are not happy, I want them to strike! However, as a matter of fact," he added to Alan in a lower tone, "they do not want to strike. They all have a share in the business."

"If every rich man were like you, we would have a heaven on earth!"

"But to help my Judith, my money is no good; no good at all."

Mr. Klein's mournful departing words stayed in Alan's mind. Judith, with her exquisite face and her brooding eyes—how could such a compulsion have taken hold of her? Alan summoned all the strength of his too-vacillating mind and tried to pray for her. And the focusing of his attention upon another relieved him, although he hardly noticed it, of his own introspective tendency, so that the forces of his being moved more evenly toward health.

Judith was restless. She did not sit and stare like other patients. She paced the long corridors, a bright wild bird beating its wings against a cage. And whenever she did sit still, her hands busied themselves continually. Sometimes they flickered about a square of cloth, fashioning daintily patterned lace around its edge. At other times they played with cards, intricate games of Russian Bank and solitaire.

"I see what you're doing," Alan said one day. "King on ace, queen on king, Jack on queen—red on black, black on red."

"Of course! See? You deal out seven cards, face down..."

Concentrating on her instructions, Alan sat opposite and played a game of solitaire. *"I can do it!"* he breathed.

"Why do you doubt that you can do it?" asked Judith gravely. "You seem so well, so strong—"

"I don't know how to tell you," said Alan. For a moment his mind wavered, as it had done for so many years. It was a strange feeling: as if his thoughts were stacked up on two walls in his mind, like two piles of books; and as if they began to slither and to fall, one beneath another, one beneath another, down, down into a wordless blackness... But this time Alan caught them before they fell. He cried out in his mind to Paul and saw Paul's face, quiet, commanding, strong. His thoughts steadied themselves. He took a pack of cards and began to deal a new hand.

"You give me strength," said Judith, looking up at him from beneath long lashes. "Whenever you are with me, I feel like myself. Of course you can play a simple game!"

"But you see, I cracked up because I forced my mind too hard. So ever since, if I try to use my mind even to write—and I used to love to write—I go to pieces again. At least," he corrected himself, hastily changing his tenses, "that's the way it used to be."

"What has made you so much better?" Judith asked.

"Someone—prayed for me," said Alan.

Judith's beautiful mouth was suddenly harsh almost to the point of ugliness. "Are you trying to tell me that you believe in miracles?"

"I'm sorry," faltered Alan. "But I am. Because—one happened to me." And he explained to her the sudden freeing and lightening that had come to him of a Sunday morning; the departure of an old torment, seen by his inner spirit as an evil figure disappearing into the mouth of a dark cave.

"My God," said Judith, for the word fell often as a meaningless exclamation from her lips. "Seeing things, yet.

Is that so important? Everybody in this place sees things."

"But it wasn't like that, because I'm free. The other voice inside of me has gone."

Judith rose, flinging down her pack of cards so that they fanned out over the table. "So you do hear voices," she said.

"I did," Alan said. And he drew in his breath sharply. In his intentness upon Judith he had forgotten to close the doors of his mind and he had almost remembered that thing too terrible to remember. It did not quite cross the threshold of consciousness. But the feelings that surrounded it crept upon him and he closed his eyes for a moment, struggling against that memory and pushing it down again where it must forever stay. "Only my voices were—inside," he concluded, getting hold of himself again.

"Mine are outside," murmured Judith from the window. And she added in a whisper, "Not myself at all. Who prayed for you?" she demanded, whirling about.

"A good man. A minister. If you would talk to him—"

"*No!*"

Alan was startled by her vehemence.

"I don't need him when I have you. Tell me, what can I do?"

As best he could, Alan told her.

"It seems a small tool, to do such a great work," she murmured, doubt in her voice.

"A small key," Alan corrected her. "To open a great door." And he added, "If you will try it, I will help you—the best I can."

Once she began, Judith seized upon the way as a convict might seize on a plan of escape, with blind determination and unflagging zeal. And the darkness about her lightened as time went on. There was no question about it.

"Yes, it's better," she would say to him rather breathlessly, never telling him what "it" might be, never dreaming that her father had already told him. "Any day now, I'll be allowed outdoors."

Before the month was out Judith was placed among the more trusted inmates and came and went as she pleased inside the grounds. But Alan was not happy about her. He looked at her determined face with its set jaws and its tight lips and wondered. Was her compulsion really healed, or was she merely controlling it more successfully, her will stiffened by the hope he had given her? His heart shifted uneasily when he saw her in the bright colors that she loved, walking down a gravel path or sitting in the shade beneath an apple tree.

July with its great heat thundered past and August came to steam and sulk over the countryside. Day after day gray clouds hung low and hot over the cornfields and a man could hardly draw his breath for the heaviness of the air. The weather affected Judith. On the rare days of sun she moved with the light swing of a flying bird. On days when moisture hung in the air yet would not fall, there was brittleness in her voice and in the very movements of her hands, tension even in the set of her slim shoulders.

During the recreation hours when Judith was allowed to wander in the sparsely guarded grounds, Alan made it his business to watch her. If possible he walked and talked with her, trying to answer her fumbling questions about God and life or merely trying to turn her thoughts into the paths of peace.

"Part of this I can believe because it's common sense," she would say. "The rest—"

"The rest you're just trying, to see whether you can believe it or not," Alan finished quickly, not allowing her to say, "I do not believe."

"If only it could be true—all of it!" she would sigh.

There came a day when the air was thick with circling storms. Alan, working among the shrubbery, heard her quick footsteps behind him. It surprised him to see between the rhododendron leaves the glimmer of her golden dress, for three o'clock had not yet struck and here and there upon the grounds visiting relatives waited for the hour. Then he caught a clearer glimpse of her and his heart froze. She was walking with the intent and purposefulness of a stalking cat, and there was death in her face.

In her hands she held a great stone that she had gouged out of a rock garden. She raised it, slowly, deliberately, malevolently.

"Judith!" He screamed the word, he tore through the rhododendrons, gripped her upraised wrists and twisted the stone away from her, so that it crashed through the shrubbery and thudded to the ground.

Mr. Klein rose white-faced from the seat where he had been waiting for the visiting hour to strike.

Alan had not known that a woman could fight as Judith fought. But as her teeth sank into his wrists, one of the guards seized her in practiced hands.

"Judith!" Alan said again, and the word was a low shuddering sigh.

At this she seemed to come to herself, as if arousing from a nightmare. She sank to the ground, the attendant still holding her, and wept.

Her father knelt beside her, tears rolling down his face. "It isn't *you* who do these things!" he cried. "My daughter, my little daughter Judith, it isn't *you!*"

It was true. Long and painfully Alan had practiced seeing Judith released and perfect, but the Thing that he had seen in her contorted face was not herself. What could he do when something beyond herself held her in its teeth? How could he drive the Thing away? He watched her weeping upon the ground and the light went out of his heart.

13

All Saints Church faded every summer into inactivity. The inland heat was too oppressive, the glorious seacoast too near at hand. Mapleton over a weekend was a deserted village, and Paul usually spent an exhausted month in the ancient farmhouse that since his childhood had been the family's summer home.

But this year the slow weeks of August passed by and Paul did not leave Mapleton. Waking in the morning with the heat steaming from the church roofs into his bedroom window and with the perpetual mourning of the doves in his ears he would lie still for a moment, imagining the dewy mornings of the North. The mist would be lying cold and white on the lake below the hill—diamonds of moisture in the shining cups of the water lilies, dragonflies lifting their gossamer wings, a white heron proud and aloof among the reeds of a still cove. And he would imagine Burnett driving with him up the dirt road, crowding into the bushes as the lumberman's team passed by, to the patch of lawn swung like a hammock between house and barn. "Oh, Paul!" he could hear her cry, running to the stone wall that edged the lawn and gazing down over fields and woods and out to the circle of gentle hills. "Oh, Paul, how lovely! And to think it's yours!"

Only it was not his. He had nothing, only himself and the bare wherewithal to feed and clothe himself, no more. Mapleton revelled in a certain school of thought: a minister should give himself wholly to the service of the Lord while enduring the travail of personal poverty that it might make him more holy.

Maybe that was why Burnett, who said that she loved him, had not yet been willing to name their wedding day. Paul remained here in the heat in order to be near her.

On his way home one evening he stopped in at Burnett's. "Why don't you get in there and sweep her off her feet, the way I told you," Skip had demanded.

Burnett refused to be swept. "Your parish is quiescent now," she said. "But that doesn't mean a thing. Wait until fall and see whether they come back to church, whether they start a campaign or what they do. Then we'll decide when to get married."

Paul stood at her studio window, the late breeze lifting his dark hair, and looked at her with shadowed eyes. The joy of loving her was clouded over by the pain of wanting her. She was in blue today; not a pastel shade such as milder women wear but a restless electric blue shot through with light, like rippling waters under a blue sky, and to his longing eyes she was beautiful and chilly like his own New Hampshire lake.

"You don't love me as I love you." Paul spoke aloud for the first time the knowledge that had long been in his heart.

Then suddenly Burnett was in his arms, her cheek tight against his. "Oh, I do, I do!" she cried. "I love you more every day I live. But there's a feeling within me, like an inner voice that says, 'Not yet'...My dear, don't you believe that there is a Providence that guides us?"

"Yes, but is this God's guidance or is it just you—being a little afraid, a little uncertain?" asked Paul.

And in spite of Burnett's warm denial, he went home in wonder and in doubt.

"That fellow from the mental hospital's been trying to get you," said Ambrose, waiting for him at the parish-house door. "And Opal, she's in the chapel again praying away and she wants you to come in and just say a teeny-weeny little prayer for her."

"Lord have mercy upon us," muttered Paul hastily, and he ducked into the study and shut the door. He would have to think how to deal with Opal, for to his mind she was becoming psychotic upon the subject of religion.

Meanwhile—Alan. He knew something must be gravely wrong or Alan would never venture to call him. So he went to the phone. And after long waiting, Alan's voice reached him, low, hesitant, burdened, as Paul had known it would be.

"It's Judith. You told me to try..." Paul's heart

contracted as he listened to Alan's story. Perhaps he had been wrong in turning Judith over to Alan. "I feel that she's your assignment," he had said, when Alan asked his help.

"So she's worse than before," Alan ended. "And now she won't talk to me at all. She hates me for raising her hopes and then failing her. I'm sorry to trouble you, but please come and tell me what to do."

"And you yourself?" Paul started to ask. But did not dare put the question. "I'll come," he said.

There it was. More trouble. And Opal in the chapel again...."Get rid of that woman!" he ordered Ambrose who inserted his cautious face into the study door. "This is the third time in two days, and I can't..." Ambrose closed the door in his surreptitious way and padded down the hall.

With every firm intent Paul tried to pray for Judith. But his mind kept swinging back to Alan. Alan was healed, or so he said, from the disease itself: the "Thing" as he called it. But Paul knew that unless he was set free from the long pattern of depressive thinking which had disrupted his mind, his trouble would come back. A few more shocks such as his failure to help Judith, and he would be all the way down again. "I'll finish what I've begun," thought Paul.

Through the whole long night he prayed for Alan. Remembering his old concern about the value of suffering and his childish wonderment as to whether or not his life was hard enough to please his Lord, he thought grimly, "That's one thing I needn't have worried about." There had been a day when Burnett, seeing him framed in sand and crowned by sky, had called him beautiful in his new happiness. But between the peaks of joy there lay always the valleys of the shadow, and he need not concern himself to seek them out for the demands of life would lead him inexorably into them.

In the gray dawn Paul's mind turned away from Alan to Burnett. He longed for her with an unquenchable longing, as the "hart...after the water brooks," as the spirit of man after his God. Beside the devouring flame of his love for her, Burnett's own love shone pale and thin. Passion had flamed and died in her long ago, buried in the grave of that never-forgotten one whom Paul hated, cringing away from the very thought of him. Would marriage awaken it anew or would he live forever frustrated by her reserve?

When he arose in the late morning he turned his mind resolutely away from Burnett and went to see Alan Whitacre.

He broke short Alan's account of Judith's troubles. "We'll consider her afterwards. Right now I want to know about *you*. Has the—the 'Thing' come back?"

"I don't quite know," hesitated Alan. "But of course I'm feeling wobbly again—you know—I can't concentrate on anything, I can't decide anything, and I'm always afraid I'm going to be afraid . . ."

"You see," said Paul, "what we have done in prayer is not enough. We must heal all of those memories completely. Then we can find the way to help Judith."

"If you think I can ever be any better," Alan sighed, his nervous fingers twirling a yellow maple leaf, fallen too soon. "Maybe this is as far as I can get."

"But if you can't be better than this," said Paul slowly, "then is our faith vain and all that we have been taught about it false."

Alan turned toward him. "You're going pretty far, aren't you?" he asked with a tremulous smile.

"Not as far as the Bible goes. 'As far as the east is from the west, so far hath He removed our transgressions from us . . .'"

"Transgressions?" questioned Alan.

"It's the same thing. Look, Al, here's what it means . . ." Paul leaned forward, his dark eyes flashing with earnestness, his face beautiful as Burnett had once seen it. "It means that every one of those dark thought-patterns can be taken out of your memories; the trauma can be erased as with a sponge. A great deal of that has already taken place," he added, remembering his weekend vigil, "but it can be complete and perfect." And he quoted, understanding old words for the first time, " 'Purge me with hyssop and I shall be clean, wash me and I shall be whiter than snow.' The greatest of all healing miracles!"

"But what is it?" Alan asked, passing his hand over his broad forehead as he did when his mind was laboring. "What do you call it?"

"Christianity!" And Paul flung back his head with a short, breathless laugh. "Only the oldest thing—the original

Good News—the Gospel."

"What do you want me to do?" asked Alan, still bewildered.

And Paul expounded to him the way of the confessional. "I know that it works," he said, holding up a hand to stop him as Alan seemed about to burst into horrified speech. "Because it worked for me. And when I lay awake last night and asked for guidance about you, the confessional came into my mind and it was just as if the voice said, 'This is the way, walk ye in it.' "

"No!" Alan cried, finding his voice at last and leaping to his feet.

Paul, born and brought up in the Church, could hardly comprehend the vehemence of his refusal. "But Al, don't you believe that there *is* power in the Church to forgive?"

"You know I can't—talk about my past," panted Al. "You've often tried to make me and—I can't."

"Sure, I know that. All the more reason why you need to get all that muck out of your unconscious. This is a foolproof way of doing it." He explained that in the confessional there is no spontaneous speech, only a quiet reading of certain statements of past errors, written down in few words.

"But why will that heal the—the fears and—dreadful ways of thinking?"

"Because it will remove from the unconscious all the original causes of those fears and dreadful ways of thinking," said Paul steadily.

"But—so many—so confusing—I can't!"

"Yes, you can." And Paul outlined for Alan a course of daily meditation on his own past life and of writing down the things that the meditation brought to mind. "Fifteen minutes every day, each fifteen minutes to cover five years of your life," he commanded. "Then you can forget what is written, as you will have no further responsibility concerning it. If you can't do this much when I request it, you are hardly worth my time and thought," he finished.

Looking at Alan, he knew that he had won. Then as he studied the pale face and the frightened eyes, his heart smote him. What if he failed? What if his own faith was not great enough to encompass this great thing? What if Alan could not stand the strain of it?

For a brief longing moment he wished once more that he might have spoken of Alan to Burnett. But with her real effort to grasp the meaning of the sacramental life, she was still not within ten miles of understanding it. And Paul sighed, wondering, not for the first time, why he had ever fallen in love with such a woman.

"If you will do this," said Paul, following up his advantage, "then I will promise to make Judith my main concern in prayer and to move heaven and earth to set her free."

"I will," murmured Alan. He sat down again on the garden bench, his head in his hands, his brown hair falling across his fingers.

Why, *why*, thought Paul, driving grimly home, had he ever chosen a lifework such as this? Why had he not remained a topographer? Then if his lines did not close, it meant only a few more days of work. Now if his lines did not close, it meant insanity or death to someone else. "Let go and let God—" the phrase came to him, threadbare with usage. When and at what point did one let go? He had let go of Frank and he had seen the results of his relinquishment. Someday, he thought, he might be able to say one prayer and let go. But that time had not yet come.

Paul went to the hospital on the appointed day to bring Alan to his own church. There he would be sure not only of privacy but also of the power of prayer, increasingly present in All Saints. The day brooded with thunderstorms as though the elements themselves contended with him for the soul of the young man who sat silent and abstracted beside him. Alan had never been so cold and stiff, so emotionless. Paul's heart turned over as he thought again, "What if it fails?" But he set his lips in a straight line and went on.

All Saints Church would have been scandalized at the very idea of the confessional box, humble and handy place of privacy though it is. So Paul placed Alan at the communion rail and seated himself in the chancel beside him.

"The Lord be on thy lips and in thy heart," he prayed, and he crossed himself and waited for Alan to begin.

There was a long pause.

Paul steadied himself and bent all of his heart and all of

his mind on Alan Whitacre.

"I confess before God Almighty..." Stumblingly, in a voice hardly more than a whisper, Alan began. "I have been guilty of the following sins..." And he read from his quivering papers the little sins that can carry the sting of death as surely as a little germ can carry it.

"And I confess that at the age of six I disobeyed my parents and ran away to the execution ground," whispered Alan.

Dropping for a moment the impersonal manner of a priest, Paul turned swiftly and looked at him. He was ghastly white.

Alan controlled his lips and went on in a barely audible voice, "It was—not a usual execution. It was—torture."

So that was it: the cause of everything, laid bare for the first time. That was the horror that Paul himself had felt on his weekend of prayer. That was why Alan had so bitterly fought the idea of confession: he could not face the agony of bringing this half-submerged memory above the surface of consciousness. Paul waited, his heart pounding in agonized sympathy. Alan swayed and clung to the altar rail with blue-knuckled hands.

"Don't be afraid," Paul said in his strong, steady voice. "Let it come. Let it come."

Alan opened his mouth again and stumbled on, bit after bit of that old memory coming out into the open at last.

"Steady," Paul would say when he faltered. "It can't hurt you now. As soon as that memory is all the way out I will pray for its healing and it will be healed and it will never trouble you again. Steady."

And as Alan floundered on Paul lifted his heart continually into the flickering light upon the altar and to all that the light meant to him of the forgiveness of sins. Not the sin of the little runaway boy, more than that—more than that; the sins of a world in which such things could be; and of an ancient country, China—Burnett had lived in China...and a small cold fear closed itself around Paul's heart.

Alan went on through the small tragedies of uncomprehending childhood and of untaught adolescence. But Paul knew that the cause of all trouble had already been told. And he visioned continually the healing power of Christ entering the dim chambers of the unconscious and opening windows to the light of God's love. The power to forgive was not his, thanks be to God. But the faith to make that act not only a valid sacrament but also an actual resurrection—that was his responsibility. And he remembered with a shudder the words, "Whosoever sins ye remit they are remitted, and whosoever sins ye retain, they are retained." "God help me," he prayed, "that I may be a worthy confessor . . ."

"And I do confess," said the low voice beside him, "that for many years I have deceived a certain woman, Burnett McNeill, letting her believe me dead . . ."

Paul gripped the chair and held on tight. The church whirled around him.

He must tell Alan that one did not mention names in a confession. Why had he not known long ago that Alan had lived in China? Why had he not gone to the office and made inquiries about Alan, as many a time he had thought of doing? Why had he never mentioned the name Alan Whitacre to Burnett? Why?

"And I do confess—"

What was Alan confessing now? Paul had not the least idea. *That I may be a worthy confessor.* Did he any longer want to be a worthy confessor? Could anyone blame him if he should give up the act of faith and let this man drift to life or death or wherever he might drift?

The Lord be on thy lips and on thy heart. But there were no angel presences to help him, no lights from above— nothing. He sat alone and in darkness, gripping the chair and fighting the battle of his life.

"Will you then give your faithful diligence always so to minister . . . the sacraments as the Lord hath commanded?" He remembered this question put to him in his ordination service. And he had answered not knowing that the answer would break his heart, "I will do so, by the help of the Lord."

For the first time, he permitted himself a glance at Alan Whitacre. Here he was upon his knees, faithfully and painfully doing the thing that no psychiatrist had been able to make him do. This was not the unknown man whom sight unseen Paul hated. This was his friend. *"Don't let me fail him!"* thought Paul. And a way of powerful prayer swept into his mind. "I refuse to function at this time as a human being," he said within himself. "I am shifting my consciousness into the spiritual body and I shall think as a priest of God and as nothing else."

He did not know from what dim place within himself these words came into his mind, but on these words he triumphed. His plunging emotions steadied. He remembered nothing and thought of nothing except the words that fell from Alan's lips. "That I have hated my doctors and have refused to cooperate with them," and so on and on through little sins that were yet great enough to close a door to light. They ceased at last. "For these and all my other sins that I cannot at the moment remember, I am truly sorry, intend to do better, and ask of you, Father, counsel, penance and absolution," read Alan from the card that Paul had given him.

Here it was: the supreme challenge. Dared he say that most tremendous affirmation under heaven, the words of the absolution? Had he really been a worthy confessor, believing with certainty that these sins and all their ramifications in the unconscious would be taken away and the man Alan go free? "Lord, I believe," he thought, with the sweat standing upon his brow, "Help Thou my unbelief, and my moment of unwillingness forgive." He raised his hand in benediction, and said, "I do pronounce and declare the absolution and remission of all your sins. Go in peace. God has forgiven all your sins."

As Alan rose to his feet, Paul murmured, "And pray for me, a sinner."

It was done. It was finished.

He strode over to the rectory in his cassock, leaving Alan in the pew, prayer book in hand, reading the small penance that had been given. By some merciful providence Skip was home.

"Skip, do me a favor," he said breathlessly, closing the door and leaning against it, his knees shaking. "Drive Alan Whitacre home to the hospital. Something has come up—I can't."

Skip looked at him with the comprehending eyes of youth and said comfortably, "Sure thing."

Paul went into his study and closed the door.

Late that night he dressed and stole downstairs to his car

and drove through the awakening dawn as though to escape the unescapable. As the early morning wind, damp and cool, rushed past him, some sort of quietness settled upon him, and his whirling thoughts hardened into resolution. He would keep to himself the secret that had been given him. After all, he was bound to do so by the very seal of the confessional. For years Burnett had believed Alan Whitacre was dead. Let her continue to think so. Let him be forever buried in the unforgotten grave of her memories. What would it avail to let her know that he walked the earth reborn?

He was no longer the beautiful youth she had loved. Nor was she any more the little elfin girl who had raced with him upon the city wall. Even the land of their childhood with its rosy pagodas, its massive city gates and its ancient slumbering people was no more, its government in exile, its civilization quartered and gone. Let the dead past bury its dead . . .

Dizzy with weariness, he swung the car toward home. And as the sun touched the treetops with dim gold he fell on his bed and slept.

"What's the matter with you?" asked Skip later in the morning.

No one else would have dared speak to Paul when he looked like this, except perhaps Janet. But Janet was away. "No use in all of us stewing down here in the heat just because you don't want to leave Burnett," she had said.

Paul narrowed his lips and glowered at Skip. "It was too hot to sleep, that's all. The thunderstorm only steamed up the place."

But Skip had no fears and no reticences. "You aren't fooling your Uncle Skip any," he remarked, helping himself to a cup of coffee. "It's Burnett. When a fellow looks like you do, it's always a dame. Don't tell me. I've had experience." And he added, "What's she been doing to you?"

"Nothing," Paul said forbiddingly. But as he banged his way out of the dining room he growled, "I'm going to New Hampshire tomorrow."

"Good idea!" shouted Skip, undismayed. "And I'm going to tell Burnett."

"*Skip!*" Paul erupted back into the room. "You are not

to say anything to Burnett."

"Well, but if she's been pushing you around . . ."

"No! This is something quite different. She doesn't even know."

"Then what the heck—"

"You keep still, that's all." And Paul slammed the door.

He was absolutely sure that he should not tell Burnett about Alan, he argued within himself, forgetting that in the grim light of early dawn he had settled the matter once and for all. For as surely as Alan had stood between him and Burnett, so surely would he now stand between Burnett and Alan, and Alan's mind was hardly strong enough to stand the strain of it.

But then, what of his friendship with Alan, a friendship that would draw Alan to his church, where he would inevitably meet Burnett?

There was only one answer, thought Paul, remembering the Bishop's words about a little mission somewhere—and it must be far away, very far away.

Paul took up the telephone and called the diocesan office. Then, in a house now mercifully empty, Skip having departed with his gang, he began to pack—anything, everything, as though he never meant to set foot again in the rectory of All Saints.

Did he? He did not know.

14

"Telephone!" Ambrose shouted in the front hall. What was Ambrose doing there anyway?

Paul in his shirt-sleeves leaped down the stairs, scowling at the sexton who oozed away with hushed footsteps, and picked up the receiver.

"Mr. Forrester—" for though the word "Paul" often trembled on Alan's lips, he never quite dared say it. "This is Alan. Only you've never seen me before, really. This is—a new Alan. I'm entirely different! I—I can't understand it, but I'm—free!"

"Of course," said Paul quite simply.

"When I think of what you have done for me . . ."

"Oh, that's nothing." For though Paul in his loneliness longed for the comfort of gratitude, yet the expression of it threw him into embarrassment. His strained mind wandered a bit as Alan's voice went on. Then a word alerted him: "Judith." He had clean forgotten Judith.

"But—I'm leaving on vacation."

There was silence on the other end of the phone and then, "You promised."

That was true. And there was no way out of it. Swiftly Paul looked forward through the days; Thursday, Friday . . . Could he accomplish his mission and be gone by Saturday? Could he linger in Mapleton two more days and find excuses not to see Burnett? Or could he endure the agony of seeing her? What was he thinking of? he asked himself. Wasn't he planning to keep a still tongue in his head and marry Burnett? He leaned against the wall, dizzy for a moment, and closed his eyes.

"I remember," he murmured. "There have been— complications. I'm sorry " And promising to turn all his thoughts toward helping Judith and to come as soon as he had found the way, he hung up the phone. "What shall I do?" he whispered, still leaning against the wall and dropping his tired head in his hands. His whisper was a wisp of sound in the great stillness of the house, for there was no one there—no one there at all. Paul lifted haggard eyes to the ceiling wondering whether anyone in heaven or earth could help him. For every thought of Judith came up against a blank wall and stopped. He must find an opening in that wall . . .

There would be no use in consulting Burnett. He knew what she would say: "See the Christ in her . . . see the God in her . . . see the good in her . . ." But, thought Paul, answering that dear imagined voice in its innocence, *there was evil in her and not good.* "How can there be evil?" the imagined voice spoke again, twisting his heart. "God made everything, and God is good."

But there was evil.

Perhaps by some merciful chance, Father Sinclair was in his parish and not vacationing. Paul took up the phone. The Father was at home. And leaving a note for Skip, Paul drove to the brick rectory where Father Sinclair lived.

"But you're ill yourself, aren't you, or in need of some kind of help?" interrupted the older priest, leaning back in his chair and studying Paul.

Paul brushed this away with an impatient wave of the hand. "Just tired. I'm going on vacation as soon as this is done." And he continued with the story of Judith.

"If I were you," said Father Sinclair, brows contracted and fingertips together as he studied the matter, "I would try a spot of exorcism."

"What?"

"Thoroughly scriptural. Also churchly. I have an ancient Order of Service for it if I can lay my hands on it."

"But surely you don't believe that possession is an actual fact!"

"She does, doesn't she?" replied the big priest calmly. "Doesn't she say that the impulses to kill 'possess' her at times?"

"It's—confusing," sighed Paul.

Father Sinclair smiled. "On the contrary. It's simplifying. One needs only to believe what Our Lord told us about the

Prince of this world, the Adversary. We can fight much better if we know whom we are fighting. And after all, when you were confirmed you promised to engage in this very warfare, 'And to fight bravely against the world, the flesh and the devil.' "

"But if God made everything . . ."

Father Sinclair looked a little bored. "God made you, didn't He?" he asked, forestalling the question as if it had been asked so many times that he did not need to hear it. "Isn't there evil in you once in a while? Didn't God give you free will, that you might choose good or evil?"

"Of course," said Paul. "But that's a different matter. You speak as though there were an *outside* force of evil."

"Why not? Is there any reason why God might not have also given the angels free will, and why one of them might not have at a certain time chosen evil?" And he quoted, as Paul was speechless, " 'I beheld Satan as lightning fall from heaven . . .' "

"It's a new thought to me."

"It's older than history."

And the two men, facing matters of a world unseen, fell silent for a moment.

"But even if there were such an entity of evil," said Paul at last, "how could it actually enter into Judith Klein and possess her?"

"If there is such an entity," said Father Sinclair, "there could be many who have wandered into his hands and work under his influence. It is quite possible that such a lost soul should force its way into a living consciousness, trying thus to express itself upon the earth-plane, since it knows no other." He added, "I have this from a psychiatrist, not from a theologian." And whirling his desk chair around, he reached into his bookcase and handed Paul *Body, Mind and Soul* by Worcester and McComb, his long finger pointing to a certain passage.

Silence palpitated through the study while Paul read it.

"But the diagnosis for Judith is schizophrenia," said Paul, looking up from the book with doubtful eyes.

"Quite so. And I have this by word of mouth from another psychiatrist: 'There can be disturbance at two levels of the being. On the upper level of consciousness this can be rightly diagnosed as schizophrenia or some other form of insanity. But at the same time there can be a disturbance on a lower level, actually caused by the infiltration of an evil entity. And the latter trouble can be the cause of the former.'"

"So what?" asked Paul bluntly. He did not like all this pseudoscientific hysteria. Yet he had to admit that Father Sinclair looked as little hysterical as a man could look.

The priest came back with sledge-hammer directness to his first point. "So we try a bit of exorcism," he said.

"Psychologically the method is perfectly sound," added Father Sinclair, studying Paul, "whether or not you accept such a theory about the power of evil. After all there is unquestionably a compulsion in Judith's mind, and certainly it is not a good one. Regardless of how it got there, our aim is to get it out. Right? Well then—forget the word 'exorcism.' It is an old churchly word, but I see that you don't like it. We'll start over again: you want to put into her mind a good thought-suggestion, so powerful that it will take the place of the bad one. Right?" he asked again.

Paul nodded.

"Now we can't do this through the reason. The conscious mind is too disturbed to cooperate and the unconscious does not respond to reason. Therefore we try a spiritual shock-treatment. We move in on the unconscious mind with an army of suggestions. The unconscious responds best to things that it can see and feel and touch: hence the effectiveness, incidentally, of the communion service. So we stage a drama for the unconscious. There is the altar, the priest, candles, vestments; most important of all there is the command, the compulsion, given with great force and surrounded with the feeling of authority."

"But can Judith be persuaded to let us try any such thing?" Paul asked.

And Father Sinclair, rising and looking at the clock, smilingly replied, "That's up to you—and your friend Alan."

His friend Alan . . .

For the first time the irony of the situation burst upon Paul's mind. For eighteen months he had used every energy he had toward the healing of Alan Whitacre, in order to show Burnett the power of the Church. Now Alan Whitacre was healed—and it was an empty victory. A bitter twist of fate had tied his hands and sealed his lips. Moreover, he had vexed his soul with fasting to save the very man whom he least wanted to save, the only man able to take Burnett away from him. Perhaps the ancients were not so far wrong after all in their conception of a jealous and cruel Yahweh delighting in the sufferings of man, afflicting those who loved Him in order to test their faith.

Anger began to burn deep and slow in Paul's mind. "You don't need to play tricks on me," he murmured to his God.

Nevertheless, Paul was bound by a promise. He tried to crush down the rebellion in his heart and went to find Alan. "Why did you do this to me?" he muttered to a lowering sky as he drove to the hospital. It was like forcing a man to build his own gallows, to carry his own cross. Old words floated into his mind with a new and sombre understanding: "Whosoever will come after me, let him deny himself and take up his cross and follow me. For whosoever will save his life shall lose it; but whosoever shall lose his life for my sake and the gospel's, the same shall save it." Exactly. The old stern faith that he had been taught from the beginning. Painfully, he recalled the wild bright day of sun and wind, when he had dared to believe for one brief moment that God loved him.

Alan was not among the rhododendrons today nor beside the tall borders of phlox and chrysanthemums. Paul located him at last in the office at a typewriter. He leaped up and strode toward Paul, overwhelming him with the warmth of his strong handclasp, the joy of his smile.

"I'm writing letters for the secretary," he said breathlessly. *"I can think!* I can read a letter, grasp its contents and answer it with no weariness, no confusion! At other times, when I found myself able to write, it was with a boiling-up, fermenting agitation; a terrific excitement; and it always meant that I was about to go manic. But this is different. I can even remember a little bit of my poetry," he breathed, as if in awe. "And I'm to go home almost any day now!"

Let the Bishop move quickly, quickly, quickly find a small mission far away from Mapleton! "Oh God, why did You do this?" Paul thought again. "You could have guided me to help some other man. Why did You choose this one? To teach me that I must not expect joy in this life? Or was it some power of evil and not You?"

Alan was studying him with gentle eyes. "You look so tired," he said. "You do too much for everybody—especially for me."

Paul swallowed hard and hauled Judith into the conversation, repeating Father Sinclair's words.

"I know," nodded Alan. "I was possessed too. Don't you remember the thing I saw, disappearing into the mouth of a dark cave?"

"I still don't know whether that was an entity or the symbol of an entity," Paul said obtusely.

"Does it matter? Whatever you call it, you told it to go away—and it went."

Paul listened with amazement as Alan discussed the power of unconscious suggestion and its relation to the conscious mind. Here indeed was a new Alan. Here was the man whom Burnett remembered. And the sword of Paul's unresting conscience pierced him again as he thought, "Have I any right to withhold such a man as this from Burnett so that she can marry a two-for-a-cent country minister?"

Paul bit his lip and tried to control his wandering thoughts while the man who had feared telephones located Judith's father in the city and demanded that he come to see them without delay.

On the same afternoon the three of them met together, this time in Paul's study.

"But I can do nothing," murmured Mr. Klein, passing his pudgy hand over his bald head. "As you know, I may not see her. Perhaps her mother—"

And they went, the three of them, to the great stone house where lived the family of Klein. Fantastic, thought Paul, fantastic that he should hand his hat to the butler and step into the home of a prince of industry to speak of things not seen in heaven or on earth—fantastic!

But here he was, wading into an unknown sea and no help for it now. Judith's mother came upon them, gliding into the vast drawing room: a large blonde woman with a face like a cat and coiled hair too smoothly perfect to be real. He had seen her before, in the hospital, he remembered now.

"I have not been able to visit my daughter recently," she

murmured as though reading his thoughts. "I have not been well. Please sit down, Mr. Forrester, and tell me why you have come."

So Paul, wishing that he were anywhere on earth except here before her secretive and stony eyes, swallowed his nervousness and recounted to her the unbelievable things that Father Sinclair had said. "I don't know whether it's true or not," he faltered in concluding.

But Alan said in a strong quiet voice, "It is true."

Mrs. Klein looked from Paul to Alan, and though she did not smile there was a grave approval on her face. "It is true," she echoed amazingly. But bitterness was cold in her eyes and harsh on her tongue. "You needn't look at me as if I were crazy!" she said to her husband. "My father used to do such things as that. He was a chaplain in an army hospital," said Mrs. Klein. "And finding out that prayer worked, he set himself to learn the secret of it. He had no particular ability. He was just an honest man, humble, sincere, that is all. He had no other purpose except to help people."

"And what happened?" asked Alan eagerly.

"His church withdrew their support of him and he was fired. It seems that it is a fine thing to pray so long as you are sure it won't do any good. But if prayer really heals, then it is a dubious practice."

Silence fell upon the little group.

"You are thinking," said Mrs. Klein from out the ambush of her enamelled face, "that this is why I married out of my own church. It may be—among other reasons."

"Surely a thing like that wouldn't happen today!" faltered Alan.

Mrs. Klein replied with silence, the lift of her eyebrows and the twist of her mouth saying more than words. "Do I understand that you are a minister of a regular church in good standing?" She seemed to leap at Paul with the question.

Paul nodded.

"And how long do you expect to remain so?"

"It—doesn't matter," Paul said.

"That you should sacrifice yourself!" Mr. Klein sighed. He touched his eyes with a vast linen handkerchief, flourished it in the air and tucked it once more into his pocket.

"But I'm not sacrificing myself!" Paul insisted, feeling small and foolish on the pedestal of their admiration. "Will you help us?" he appealed to Mrs. Klein. "Will you try to persuade Judith to see me?"

"I don't know whether she will be willing or not," mused Mrs. Klein, her eyes on the floor. "But I'll try."

"It must be soon," murmured Paul. "Very soon."

And Mrs. Klein, nodding gravely, said, "I will call you up tomorrow."

But tomorrow when it came found Paul in a torment of doubt and fear. How could he, in his present frame of mind, help Judith or anyone else? And yet, how could he fail his friends who trusted him? He must and he could not—he could not and he must!

Before he had finished his lonely breakfast in the kitchen, James Morse appeared, casually drawing a chair up to the table and helping himself to a cup of coffee. "Got to worrying about you," said James. "We're a bunch of bloodsuckers, telling you, 'Don't go away.' You're all in. You work too hard anyway, and where will the rest of us be if you crack up and leave us? Better take off on vacation and let us all go to hell in our own way."

"I'm planning to go tomorrow."

"Good!" said James. But he did not take his eyes from Paul's face. "It's not only being tired," he decided at last. "You're off the beam, Parson, you're off the beam."

Paul longed intensely for a moment to speak to James of Burnett and of Alan. But he could not break through his lifelong reserve, overlaid as it was with a crust of ministerial dignity. He put Burnett out of his mind and told James the story of Judith Klein instead. "I really hope she will refuse to see me," he finished. "I just don't feel up to it."

But the telephone rang at that moment and the purposeful voice of Mrs. Klein said, "Come."

"Is she really willing?" hesitated Paul, while James in his shabby work clothes leaned against the door and studied him.

"She will be," said Mrs. Klein grimly.

"I'm in for it," sighed Paul to James. "Four o'clock this afternoon."

"Better put it off till you get yourself squared away with God," James said gravely.

Paul went into the chapel when James had gone, slipped into a pew like one of his own congregation and knelt. But his prayer rose not so high as the altar. He could feel his words drop dead beside his feet.

"What shall I do?" he whispered in despair.

More than Judith Klein hung upon his decision. He knew that. His little children, who would miss him, his boys in Korea, who even over the miles would feel him wavering, his depressives and alcoholics . . . and there was not enough power in his spirit to lift a single one of them.

"What shall I do?" he whispered again.

"Get yourself squared away with God." That was it. He needed no voice from the skies. The words of a plain working man were quite enough, if only he would heed them. His crooked ways must be made straight. He must break his engagement to Burnett, bring Alan to her and leave her free to follow the dictates of her own heart. This was not breaking the seal of the confessional. It was merely living in honesty.

He saw the truth at last with sorrow and yet with deep relief. One could endure all sadness. But one could not endure the dark confusion of trying to live contrary to the will of God.

"Forgive me," he whispered, his shadowed eyes upon the cross. "I really knew all along that I would have to do this. I just couldn't face it right at first."

The sunlight filtering through the stained-glass windows gathered about the cross like a faint gray mist, like a shadow, like an enfolding light. And in the chapel there was peace.

Burnett on the phone . . . Burnett! "Paul!" Her vibrant voice exploded with anxiety. "What's the matter? I haven't seen you for two days."

"Two days?" thought Paul. "An eternity . . ." "Yes, I know," he said, trying to keep his voice quiet. "Things have been rather thick around here. I'll tell you all about it when I see you."

"When?"

Not yet, thought Paul, for he dared not see her again until he brought Alan with him. "I don't know," he said, his voice unconsciously stiff and cold with the pressure that he put upon himself. "I'll have to let you know, soon."

Bang—the receiver was set down with a thud.

"God is good and God is all . . ." A child's concept, Paul decided, with no more truth to it than a dream upon awakening. On the contrary, one carried one's cross and so grew strong. One walked a narrow path and a steep one, seeing no summit and no goal, only climbing.

"Why did You do this?" Paul asked the question for the last time.

Suddenly he remembered his own prayer on a certain weekend: "Al and I are one in Christ, so let me carry his burden for him . . ." He had not meant *this*. No, he had not meant this! He had been playing with fire, tampering with a way of prayer too great for him. "I don't understand," he said to his God. "But it's connected somehow with that prayer of mine, and I'll just have to take it."

The next step on the narrow path ahead of him was Judith. As he thought of her, the tumult of his feelings settled into quietness. The power of prayer flowed back into him in such a flood that he could actually sense it, like a spiritual breath filling heart and chest. It was not sorrow, he realized, that had cut him off from God. It was his own inner spirit, created in original holiness, refusing to tolerate anything else. In other words, it was a guilty conscience. The judge was not an irate Being on a far white throne but himself, his very self, made in that Being's image and likeness. And with this knowledge a strange high joy mingled with the sorrow. As never before, he knew and sensed his real self. And for a moment the radiance of that Far Country where he really lived lifted him into an unreasonable ecstasy.

He would go to Judith as a spiritual being and as nothing else. Even as he had been confessor to Alan, not as a human being but as an agent of the Most High God, so in the power and authority of God he would speak to Judith. And he knew of nothing that could stand against that Word.

He returned to the rectory and found Skip at the kitchen table, drinking warmed-over coffee.

"Look more like yourself," said Skip observantly.

Paul ignored this remark. "I thought you were having a vacation at the seashore with the gang," he said. "When are you going?"

"Not until you stop ramping back and forth, dragging suitcases all over the place," said Skip, pouring cereal out of a box. "Somebody's got to keep an eye on you."

Paul perched on the kitchen stool. "So you've decided you're my boss, have you?" he said in the teasing voice through which he was apt to express his affection. "Looking after the old man, huh?"

"Somebody's got to," said Skip again. And he added, "How's Burnett?"

"All right, I guess." Paul's voice unconsciously stiffened.

"You *guess*. What do you mean, you guess?"

The clock ticked on the kitchen wall and the teakettle sang on the stove and there was no other sound.

"What's up between you and Burnett?" demanded Skip.

"I am making some decisions," said Paul slowly. He added hastily, knowing that Skip was quite capable of going straight to Burnett, "I want to be sure of them before I mention them to her."

"The heck you say," muttered Skip. And in his capacity as spiritual adviser to his uncle he remarked, "Now look; if there's any funny business brewing in your mind about congregations and bishops and vestries, you just cut it out, see?" He muttered darkly into his cereal, "We've got to have a little common sense around here."

Paul rose abruptly and made for the door.

Nothing daunted Skip shouted after him, "And don't think I can't do anything about it, because I can, and I will, too!"

Heaven defend us, thought Paul, another problem in his path: Skip.

But as the time drew near for his meeting with Judith, neither Burnett nor Skip nor any other being entered his mind. This was to be an adventure of life and death, and of more than life and death.

"Therefore with angels and archangels," thought Paul as he drove to the hospital, "we laud and magnify Thy glorious name..." And he imagined the hosts of heaven filling the bare hospital chapel with their serene presences.

He had asked permission to use this chapel for his private prayers. So he went there at once, vested and lit the candles upon the altar. Then he knelt and waited and there was no longer any fear in his heart.

Footsteps. Judith, between Mrs. Klein and Alan. Paul had expected to find unwillingness upon her face. But he found more than unwillingness. Sheer, stark terror glared from her eyes, even as her feet led her to the altar.

"There is nothing to fear," said Paul gently to the real Judith, the spark of personality that he felt rather than saw behind her frozen face. "You will just kneel here, your mother and your friend beside you, and we will hold this little service that will set you free. And afterward, you will begin to feel like yourself again." He spoke tenderly as to a child, and Judith, stiff with terror, knelt before him at the altar rail.

Whereupon Paul raised his commanding hand and there in the presence of the altar he spoke not to Judith but to the evil compulsion in her mind. In the name of Jesus Christ he commanded any influence that was not of God to come out of her and to depart from her.

Then he prayed for God's heavenly protection and for His guardian angels to stand around the girl and shield her from any return of the dark shadow that he now dismissed. He spoke with a power and an authority that he himself did not understand. And quite without volition he found himself praying, "Receive, oh Lord, the soul of this Thy servant and grant her at long last to be received into Thy heavenly kingdom and to Thy dwelling-place."

Why was he saying the prayer for the departed? The words had come unbidden to his lips . . .

There was a small strangling sound from Judith's throat. She swayed. Out of the corner of his eyes Paul saw her mother and Alan reach out to support her. But he did not look upon her face. He dared not see her; not yet. Instead he knelt before the altar and gave thanks that all darkness had departed from Judith's mind. "Come quickly, oh Lord Christ," he prayed, "and fill with Thy love every empty place in the unconscious mind."

Paul had desired that this inner one of Judith should have a sign or a symbol of its new freedom. He would have liked to bless a cross for her, as he did for servers when they departed overseas on the service of their country. But remembering Judith's heritage, and knowing that to the human family of Christ the cross was not a symbol of peace, he had chosen another object in its place. Her mother had bought her a little ring, a circle of tiny diamonds, which Paul laid upon the altar and blessed. And he prayed that the power of God might enter into it, so that as Judith wore it, the ring would be to her a circle of light in which she would walk in safety. Then he placed it upon her finger and said, "Whenever you see your father, put your hand upon this ring and say, 'I am standing in the circle of God's light and nothing can come through it into my mind.'"

Judith bent her head over the ring and her left hand closed on it and held it.

"Now in the name of God the Father..." And Paul gave the benediction, making the sign of the cross above her. Then he turned and knelt before the altar, suddenly conscious of a great weakness as though all the strength of his body had been drained out of him. With bowed head he waited there for a return of God's upholding life, and that life came to him. He rose and left the chapel, removed his surplice, returned to extinguish the candles and found the three still kneeling before the altar. Then Judith raised her head and smiled at him. And as Paul looked at the new expression in her eyes and at the softened contours of her face, he knew that the darkness had gone.

15

"Tomorrow?"

Madeleine stood in Burnett's front door in the sultry sunlight of late August and surveyed a row of suitcases in the small front hall.

"Tonight," said Burnett grimly, coming downstairs in her white shirt and red shorts and flinging a coat and a wide straw hat on top of the suitcases. "My brother's driving me down."

"What about Mr. Paul?" Madeleine's brown face was concerned.

"I have not seen Mr. Paul for three days. If he wants me, he can come and find me."

"Men!" offered Madeleine sympathetically. "They're more trouble than anybody in this world." And she sighed and went into the kitchen. "Shall I take the ironing home?"

"Yes, take it home. Madeleine! What do you suppose is the matter with him?"

"Men get notions," said Madeleine, pausing broom in hand at the living-room door. "Maybe the congregation or the Bishop or somebody has upset him. Now, Miss Burnett, you've taught me how to pray about things like that! Let's both do it, and he'll come around all right."

Burnett sat down at her grandmother's desk and rummaged through its pigeonholes, not knowing what she sought. "I'm not angry—really," she whispered to the unresponsive wall. "I'm frightened. But I can't tell him so. He doesn't like clinging vines. He has plenty of them around his church." She smiled a little at the thought of Opal Oldershaw. Then another face came into her mind. "There's a girl in his church who's in love with him," she said. "A girl who would be just perfect for him and for the congregation . . ."

"Now, Miss Burnett, Mr. Paul isn't that kind of a man. He don't run around after this one and that one like some men do. He's like a rock wall, he's that immovable." Then she glanced out of the front window and started. "Look!" she cried, pointing.

Burnett looked. There was the travel-worn rectory car drawing up beside the house. "Tell him to wait until I . . ." she gasped. And she fled upstairs and came down again in her yellow linen dress.

He stood in the living room looking out the window. One glance at his despondent shoulders and Burnett's heart fell into her shoes.

"Paul?" The word was low and questioning.

Paul turned slowly, not in his usual eager way. Burnett braced herself and drew on all her inner resources for support.

"You look as if you hadn't slept for days," she said abruptly.

With a brief, flickering smile, Paul replied, "I haven't."

"What's the trouble?" Burnett sat down and motioned him to another chair. Her swift hand did not touch him, but returned in quietness to her lap.

Paul sat stiffly on the edge of his chair, as he had done the first time he had called on her. "Burnett," he began, his voice cold and strained, "what I have to say may shock you at first, but I think that when you have considered it, you will be glad."

"Well?"

"I have come to see that you are right—about us," said Paul, all of the old worried lines back upon his face as he glanced at her and away again. "In—in postponing our wedding, I mean. We are not growing closer in understanding, as I had hoped. You do not and cannot understand the Church, though you have tried. And I am not satisfied with your ways of thought, though I have tried. Moreover—I haven't said much about this, but I—I can't really support you. I mean—there would be no money for Madeleine, for instance . . . And you wouldn't be happy," said Paul, rushing toward the end of his speech, "to leave this sunny little house and live in the rectory—to have babies and wash and cook instead of painting—"

Surface things, thought Burnett, her mind still functioning in spite of the pain in her heart. There was something beneath them.

"Are you—jilting me?" she asked in a small voice.

"I could hardly do that. You have never been willing to announce our engagement or even to let me give you a ring."

"That was—for your sake. I felt that if we just waited a while your congregation would accept me and—" Burnett could say no more. Tears choked her throat. She rose and started for the door.

"You have told me that before," said Paul wearily. "If you had loved me as I love you— But never mind. That's past history." He paused, swallowing hard, then said with a little gasp, "Besides, there's—there's another complication. Have you ever wondered whether the other man—the one you have always loved—might not be dead after all?"

"I don't understand."

"Alan Whitacre."

For a blinding moment Burnett saw Alan again, quite clearly, as though he were standing before her in the flesh. "Alan has been dead for years," she whispered.

"Many a man has been believed dead and has been found again."

Burnett felt her way back to her rocking chair and sat down, trembling. "But—his mother wrote me . . ."

"Has it ever occurred to you," Paul went on, "that it would be quite in keeping with Alan's nature to let you think him dead, so that you would be free to marry a well man?"

"No," whispered Burnett. "No."

"But it is," said Paul, his voice unconsciously gentle. And he watched her narrowly, as a doctor might watch a patient, as a father might watch a child.

Burnett's stunned mind rallied to grasp the import of the words. *Do you mean to tell me that Alan is alive?"* she cried.

Paul nodded and reached out his hands to support her, for she swayed as she rose to her feet.

"Insane?" she asked in a stunned whisper.

"No. He has been making a slow recovery over the years and lately he has—he has become completely well. He has very recently been discharged from the hospital. Just today, in fact. I wouldn't have told you about him if he had not been well."

"But I—but I don't know what to do . . ."

"Your heart will tell you that," said Paul with a certain sternness. And he added, "Only one thing: he must never know about you and me. He is well, but he cannot stand another shock at this time and it might upset him. It might even undo the work of years. *Promise me!*"

And before his compelling eyes, Burnett replied, "I promise." Then she cried, *"Where is he?"* flinging off Paul's hands as though they were dead leaves fallen upon her, as though they were chains.

"Here. In my car, waiting." Paul laid his rejected hands upon her shoulders and gently pushed her down into the chair. "Pull yourself together," he commanded. "There's no need for hysteria. He's well, he's happy, he's come to see you. You are free to take up the old love where you left it off."

"I feel so—strange." Burnett looked up to him for comfort, as a bewildered child might look to a father.

"It is joy that you feel," stated Paul, and he smiled at her with the tenderness of one who has completely forgotten himself. "Such great joy, such infinite relief, that at first you can hardly bear it."

Burnett sat still, her eyes on his strong, steadying face, and knew that it was indeed joy: the lifting of a burden carried for years. *"Oh-h, Paul!"* It was a long-drawn sigh, her voice shaking with the quick relief of tears.

Paul stepped hastily away; she might have wept on his shoulder . . . in his arms . . . "Shall I bring him in?" he asked.

Burnett nodded, the cloudburst of her tears lit by a smile. Her heart shook her with its pounding, so that she could only sit still, while Paul's footsteps died away and after a breathless century returned again, other footsteps behind them—footsteps that she knew.

She managed to reach the hallway before he came. He stood in her front door, sunlight framing him in brilliance, touching his tall head with a gleam of gold.

"Alan!" And she was in his arms.

The front door closed gently behind them and Paul's forgotten footsteps died away down the front walk.

"Forgive me," said Alan's voice against her cheek. "If I had ever dreamed of being well again, I wouldn't have hidden from you."

"Are you—quite, entirely well?"

"I am most perfectly, most unbelievably well!" cried Alan. And before she could question him again he held her away from him and said, "Burnett, listen. You don't have to take me back just as we were before. Years have rolled over us and . . ."

"But you do still love me?"

"I do. It has smouldered within me all this time, all this time . . . an unquenchable fire, burning low; sometimes perceptible and sometimes not, but—always there."

"And I . . ." The restraining voice within Burnett said *"Wait."* But she had waited too many years. "I love you," she said recklessly.

"Oh, my dear!" The words were full of longing. "If I had known, if I had ever dreamed that you could still love me . . ."

"Then what?" asked Burnett, as Alan paused.

"Then I might have been well months ago. I never told Paul, but for a long time I wasn't sure that I wanted to be well. I couldn't bear the thought of facing real life without you."

"You never—told—Paul?" Burnett repeated stupidly.

She had forgotten Paul.

How many hours had passed? Burnett did not know. But it was late. Even the drugstore across the street had turned off its lights and pulled down its shutter. Burnett had not heard half of Alan's words as he talked on of Paul and of his own plans for the future, of his resurgent joy in writing, of his desire to serve as he had been served, to help as he had been helped. Conflicting pictures flitted through her mind: Paul in the strong sunlight by the sea, beautiful in the simplicity of his goodness; Alan saying to a homely little girl, "I have always loved you and nobody else, and I always will."

Paul and Alan—Alan and Paul—why must it be Paul out of all men upon the earth who had brought Alan back to life?

"Oh Lord," thought Burnett as Alan talked, *"what shall*

I do?" And when he had at last departed she still asked, *"What shall I do?"*

The telephone rang. "Burnett!" Her brother Ian. She had quite forgotten him. Hours ago, or ages ago, he had come to drive her to the seashore. At the sight of Alan Whitacre his brows had lowered and his face had paled and he had bolted out of the place as fast as he decently could. *"Burnett!* Has he gone? Well then, pull yourself together and come with me!"

"I told you not to wait. I—I can't go now."

Ian's voice was sharp and expletive at the other end of the line. She must not be a fool of this kind or of that kind.

"I can't. I—I must see Paul first. Alan said that he's going on vacation the first thing in the morning, and I must see him!"

For one moment a wave of relief flooded her heart as she thought of Paul. She darted to her car and turned it toward the rectory as a lost child might turn toward home. Then another memory rose into her mind. She saw herself kneeling in a cold church and saying aloud, "If You will give Alan back to me I promise You that I will spend the rest of my life taking care of him. This I will do, no matter how difficult it may prove to be." And remembering grim stories from the Old Testament read aloud at the Whitacres' family prayers, she had added, "This solemn vow I make to the Lord. The Lord do so to me and more also if I ever forget it."

Burnett drew up by the sidewalk and sat still for a moment, her head in her hands. Then she started the car again and drove to the rectory. Promise or no promise, she must see Paul. And late as the hour might be she could not wait, since Paul was leaving at sunup.

"He didn't even tell me that," she thought. "I had to find out from Alan . . ."

Alan had talked a great deal about Paul. "When Paul Forrester speaks, the powers of darkness obey him," Alan had said. "He's a great man."

Burnett had been startled for a moment. Great? He was lovable and good, and there was in him a sturdy, homespun strength that would hold in life or in death, but she had never thought of him as great. "Alan loves him very much," she thought as she drew her car up beside the shaded ground. And she cried out again in her mind the old unanswered question: "Oh God, why? Why? Why couldn't somebody else have helped Alan get well? Why of all people on earth did it have to be Paul?"

Light in the rectory bedroom, the office dark and closed. Burnett rang the doorbell—no answer. A slow flush crept to the roots of her hair. But she bit her lip and rang the doorbell again. Footsteps quick and sharp bounded down the stairs and Paul in shirt-sleeves flung open the door. His face darkened when he saw Burnett. He almost glared, as though to say, *"You* again!"

It was not a good beginning.

But Burnett, started on her path, was not to be turned aside. She stepped resolutely into the house and closed the door behind her. "Paul," she began without preamble. "I must know, so please tell me the exact truth. When did you find out about Alan?"

"It doesn't matter," said Paul, standing belligerently in the middle of the front hall, his head up and his lips tight.

"I think you found out about the middle of this week. And that was why you said all those things about you and me." Her voice broke a little. "Isn't that true?" she insisted.

"No," said Paul, categorically.

"Well, then—what is the truth?" asked Burnett, hardly knowing what she wanted him to say.

"The truth is, I'm fed up with this business," snapped Paul. And certainly he looked "fed up." He was strained, he was irritable, he was cross.

"It's made nothing but trouble from the very beginning," Paul went on, standing his ground with no welcoming gesture toward living room or chair. "It gets in the way of my work, it disrupts my church and I am *tired of it.* It's never been really satisfying, never! One day you'll marry me and the next day maybe you will and maybe you won't unless the vestry send you an engraved invitation and . . ."

"Paul!"

But Paul went on, biting off the words with bitter lips. "No man likes to be kept dangling. He can stand it just so long and then he's through. Even before Alan was—alive—I knew that you loved him as you never would love me. Now if you think that I want to marry you with him hanging around the back door, you can just think again."

"Paul, I . . ."

"And where your happy God comes into the picture I do not know," Paul snapped.

Burnett did not know either. "Why didn't you tell me his name?" she breathed.

And Paul only replied, "Why didn't *you* tell *me* his name?"

"I can never forget what you did—for him—for me. How can I just accept your sacrifice and . . ."

"Sacrifice my foot!" shouted Paul inelegantly. "I tell you, I'm through. I'm fed up with the whole thing. I'm tired of struggling with problems too big for me. Evidently I was meant to be married to the ministry, and there's no use bucking it. So . . ." His voice softened a little as he looked at her, standing in front of the door in her yellow dress, her proud, dark head held high. "You've been very kind to me," he said. "And I've learned a great deal from you. I'm grateful. But—it's finished." And he added in a lower tone, "God planned it this way, leading us on together just so far, that I might learn and that Alan might be set free for you—just so far and no farther. Everything is working out as it should, and I—I wish you every happiness."

Well then, this was the end, thought Burnett, the sharp sting of tears behind her eyes. Here was Paul, irritable (in a foul mood, as Skip would say) but obviously able to control his life, with her or without her. And just emerging into life was Alan, who needed her. She had always been a perplexity and a trouble to Paul, as he had just pointed out. To Alan she had always been a joy and a comfort. Moreover—"If You will give Alan back to me," she had said; and He had given him back.

"Thank you," whispered Burnett to Paul because she did not know what else to say.

Paul shuddered away from the two paltry words as though they were a whiplash. "Now—sorry," he said with a little gasp, "but I really must pack."

And Burnett, somehow unable to say, "Good-bye," turned and left him in silence.

It was finished. And determinedly she faced her thoughts toward Alan.

As she unlocked her front door Burnett stood still for a

moment, looking down the front walk to her picket fence dimly outlined against the darkness of the street. She remembered Paul eagerly hurrying up the path. She remembered Paul standing on her doorstep and saying with a little smile, "That is my resurrection cake . . ."

She closed the door firmly behind her. "There is no turning back, ever, in this life," whispered Burnett McNeill to the stillness of her listening house. "No turning back."

16

Birds were singing in the hills, and all the laughing air was filled with their happiness. Paul sat on a terrace of rough stone, in the corner between the farmhouse and woodshed. He and Janet had breakfasted there, the sun hot on their faces, the breeze cool about their feet. Janet had carried the dishes into the house, and he could hear her singing above the sound of the ancient pump as she drew water for washing them. Janet did not like to be still. But Paul's frayed nerves longed for quietness, and he drew the silence of the hillside around him like a comforting cloak. There were flutterings and chirpings from the apple trees that spread their gnarled branches over the low stone walls, there was the small perpetual singing of crickets and grasshoppers, but there was no other sound in all the great outdoors. Paul leaned back in his garden chair, sinking into the friendly quietness and for the first time in many days beginning to relax. He could see only sky above the parapet, and a bit of the gentle circle of hills that cradled the lake, for the hayfields sloped downhill and out of sight; only sky, blue and comforting, and the air sweet with the breath of new-mown hay.

Paul sensed it all with a sick man's feeling of life ahead, to be enjoyed on some fine day, but not now, not now.

"What's the matter with you?" cried Janet sharply. He had not seen her coming out of the door, broad-bottomed in her bluejeans. She walked barefoot across the dewy grass to scatter bits of his uneaten toast on the stone wall for the chipmunk.

"Nothing," said Paul.

But Janet was equally obstinate. She sat down on the

stone doorstep beside him and demanded to be told his trouble. "Mooning around here like a dying calf," she stated. "It's Burnett, of course. Nothing else could give a man such a hangdog look. What's she up to now?"

"Nothing." But he sighed and finally said, "Remember that Alan Whitacre that I used to go to see?" After all, he thought, Janet must know some time and he might as well tell her and get it over with.

"Yep. One of the crazies."

"Well, he turned out to be the chap from China that Skip told you about, the one man Burnett ever really loved."

"Stuff and nonsense!" commented Janet rudely.

But Paul was in no mood to laugh. "It happens not to be nonsense," he said stiffly.

"But certainly and undoubtedly Burnett loves you!"

"She never pretended to love me as much as she used to love him. And as soon as he recovered . . ."

"Well, you sap! Why didn't you let him stay in that asylum out of harm's way?"

"I didn't know, until the very end."

"Well then, at the very end, that's when you should have kept your mouth shut. No good can come of his marrying her. He'll never be able to keep up her pace!"

"Certainly he will, with her to support him."

"So you're pulling the noble hero act and turning her over to him?"

Silence.

"Well, of all the darned foolishness I ever heard in my life."

"Not at all!" snapped Paul. "I don't want to marry a girl who's in love with somebody else."

"Well, all I can say is, if she prefers a nut out of an insane asylum to you, your best bet is to forget her."

"That's just what I'm trying to do," said Paul grimly.

"But Burnett isn't like that," exploded Janet, unable to accept this twist of fate. "She's got lots of sense!"

"It is not stupid to love Alan Whitacre. He is a very exceptional man. You show a childish and ignorant point of view, Janet, when you call him a nut just because he has been mentally ill. Especially in these days," he added with some bitterness, "when a mental hospital has become a normal resting place for so many of us."

"Where is he now?"

"In a sort of Halfway House run by a church. But very soon—"

Janet, as usual, paid no attention to him. "Does Skip know?" she asked.

"Yes," Paul said, remembering the stormy scene when he had returned from Burnett's house and Skip had forced the story out of him. "Skip took a dim view of the whole thing," he admitted with a wry smile.

"It's a wonder he wouldn't go to Burnett and . . ."

"I think I settled that," said Paul sharply. He had told Skip the same unconvincing lies that he had told Burnett, and when Skip had flatly refused to believe them he had said, "Burnett did believe that and will believe it, no matter what you may say to her—because she wants to believe it. You have my orders, Skip: you are to stay out of this."

"Well, if you could settle Skip . . ." said Janet dubiously. She sat on the doorstep, her mouth pulled down, scowling fiercely at a butterfly in the tall hollyhocks that crowded the doorway.

"I'm thinking of resigning from All Saints," said Paul abruptly.

Janet looked stunned. *"Oh, Paul!* Where would you go?"

"I don't know."

He had asked for a transfer and his request had been refused. "I have considered the matter carefully," the Bishop wrote, "not only in the light of your statements but also in consultation with certain influential parishioners, including Mr. McGhann. The church books have been brought to me and I find there a decided increase in church finances. Also I find that the attendance record, after the sharp drop that you brought to my attention, is climbing back to normal. I think you have weathered the crisis and that you will find both vestry and congregation increasingly understanding of the power of prayer. In fact I took the occasion to visit your morning service one day, as you may remember, and was impressed by the sense of life and power that pervaded the church. You are just embarking on a very fine work and it would be disastrous to leave it at this time. Your discouragement is, I feel, merely the result of weariness, and I trust that your vacation will rest you sufficiently so that you will look upon this matter from the viewpoint of common sense and duty."

"I don't know," Paul repeated, as Janet sat in silence. "Back to engineering, maybe."

"A minister who throws in the sponge is finished," Janet pointed out.

"You said it." Paul lifted himself out of the chair. "Going down to the mailbox," he muttered. He went around the house and across the little lawn swung like a hammock between house and barn.

"Get me a quart of milk while you're down there," Janet shouted after him.

Paul went past the great clump of lilacs that shrouded the well, past the old apple tree that grew horizontally from the steep bank, down the dirt road to the tiny settlement that was their entry to the world. Here an old mill straddled the brook, where the black road swept around the corner of the millpond-lake. Two farmhouses filled the hollow with their barns and corncribs and their rambling gardens, and a row of mailboxes perched unevenly on posts beside the road.

Paul did not really care about the mail. He did not care about anything, not even that Angus McGhann, influenced by the Bishop and probably by Priscilla, was apparently swinging toward him again. A week ago this victory would have brought him joy. But now it was too late. Neither that nor any other message the mail might bring him from the wide world was of any importance. Nevertheless he turned into the black road and over the little bridge to the mailbox just as an excuse to move, to walk, to be soothed by the rhythm of action. He could not enter into the pleasures of swimming or fishing, and the effort of smiling and talking with people was more than he could manage. It was easier to do chores about the farmhouse, to run errands for Janet.

In the mailbox was a package of forwarded letters, among them, surprisingly, a note from Skip. "What's the big idea?" wrote that young one. "I dropped into the rectory to pick up my camera on account of we were in Mapleton for Pinky's wedding. There were your books all over the place and a steamer trunk from the attic, half-packed. I shoved the books into the bookcase and lugged the trunk back into the attic before Ambrose got wind of it and told everybody in the place you were pulling out.

What's up? You're not really thinking of leaving Mapleton just on account of a dame, are you?"

Paul shoved the letter into the pocket of his slacks and started sombrely to the farmhouse to get the milk. What a fool he had been to leave behind him the telltale traces of his midsummer madness about a woman who had never really loved him! The sooner he got away from that unhappy town the better. But where in the wide and desolate earth should he go?

He opened the back door of the ancient farmhouse, sweet with the comforting smell of apples and new milk and firewood.

"Morning," said Uncle John, the hired man, wiping his grizzled mouth as he went back to the barn.

And Paul said "Morning" with equal brevity, took his milk bottle from the refrigerator and plodded back up the hill to the little house that was as much like home as any place on earth.

After all, he thought, until he knew where to go he could stay right here, and cut wood and work on the land and do odd jobs for the farmers round about. He would not return to Mapleton, not even for a day. Skip could bring his trunk down from the attic again and pack his books and Janet could make whatever disposition of his meager furniture she pleased.

Not until evening did he remember the rest of his mail, unopened, in the deep pocket of his slacks. There was one in James Morse's handwriting, neat and rounded like James' pleasant face. It was a long letter. Paul sat in the garden chair with his feet up on the stone parapet and read it. The rich gold of sunset touched the encircling hills and brightened the bits of lake that shone between the trees.

"Dear Parson," wrote James. "We're glad you're having a rest. But it sure will be one great day in Mapleton when you come back. The whole town feels empty and kind of insecure. And when Jimmie runs up a temperature and I remember you're not around, I get butterflies in my stomach. We ought not to be like that, ought we? Give us another ten years and maybe we'll stand on our own feet. Right now we are standing on yours. No wonder you looked awful tired when you went away.

"You know, sometimes I get to thinking, what would

happen if you were to leave All Saints? I don't know why I think that, but I do, and I wake up at night dreaming about it and scared silly. You wouldn't go away, would you? Not now. You've given us something real to hold on to and we're just learning how to hold it. I know we're a poor lot. We don't even tell you how much you've done for us. It isn't that we don't feel it. We just don't know how to say it. Please don't hold it against us, and please stand by till we learn. Maybe you think, 'Any other rector would be as good.' Parson, that's where you're dead wrong. I've never seen a preacher who could give what you can. You didn't use to do it but, boy, you sure do now. When I first knew you, you were a nice guy but that was all. And now you're a powerhouse. When I see you walk into church, all the lights come up.

"So long now. I don't know why I'm saying all this, unless it's those dreams."

Paul sat beside the parapet with James' letter in his hands while the shadows grew long across the fields and cowbells tinkled in the distance. In his mind he saw not James but Frank, whom he had failed, being at the time but a lost shepherd. It was for Frank's sake that he had sought the way of power. Holding in his hand the letter from Frank's brother, he knew, beyond doubt and beyond reason, that he could not leave All Saints until he had established there the thing that he was building. He must steel himself to the sight of Burnett and live above the pain of it. He must be a friend to Alan and never let him know by word or look the feeling that he had for Burnett. He must lie to him if others disturbed him with gossip. This he must do—for Frank.

He stumbled through dinner with Janet, trying to talk of this and that, but always thinking: how could he endure going back? Seeing Burnett, casual and gay among her zinnias and chrysanthemums. Seeing Burnett in church, tailored and exquisite in her green suit and her amber beads. Seeing Alan beside her...how could he endure it? He remembered thinking at that agonizing moment during Alan's confession, "I choose to function not as a human being but as a spiritual being: a priest of the church." And he remembered the shift of his feelings that had followed this thought. Could he at all times rise to those difficult heights? Perhaps such an arising was "surrender," the giving of one's self to God, which people spoke of so lightly and which nobody did. And perhaps the way of surrender led to the path of power. He had prayed for power, and here was a way to attain it, not without effort, not without tears. "To be married to the Church." He had said those words to Burnett on that dark night when he was fleeing from her and when her intrusion into his house was more than he could bear. He had said anything to her, anything—to protect her from hurt or to hurt her, he did not know which of the two had been his aim. But he had not really believed it. He was only an ordinary man, with an ordinary man's desire for human love. But perhaps those words that desperation had put on his lips were in very truth God's plan for him . . .

"You're getting hold of yourself," Janet remarked the next morning when Paul came in from the wood lot with a wheelbarrow-load of logs.

Paul gave her a little smile. "About time," he said.

Twilight was the most difficult time during the days that followed. The sad light of departing day oppressed Paul's spirit so that he could hardly pray the constant prayer that he had set himself. All day long he tried to pray to his Lord, "Abide in me more and more, teaching me both to will and to do Thy good pleasure." Sometimes this prayer was in the conscious mind, and sometimes in the unconscious, an undercurrent to other thoughts, so that when his mind returned to himself it came to rest upon this prayer and was held in a kind of peace. But as the darkness of evening descended, even this was not enough to lift him above the engulfing waters of despair.

He could not deny this darkness of soul. He could only face it and offer it to God. "Here is this grief of mine; use it as a channel for power, and through it lighten, somehow, the sorrows of the world." He wondered sometimes whether anyone was really helped by this constant and humble work of prayer. There were times when above and beyond his own grief he felt a certain restlessness of spirit, a dark uneasiness of mood, as though someone were calling out to him. When this feeling came, he would send out the healing power of God to those who needed it, asking God Himself to guide the prayer in the right direction.

"You sure are on the beam," wrote James Morse. "My

sister's kid was awful sick. I just called out, 'Hey, Parson! S.O.S.!' And by George, I could feel it right away: the same feeling a fellow has when you walk into church. And the kid was O.K. in no time. It was five-thirty on Wednesday. What were you doing then?"

Five-thirty. Yes, that was his zero hour. There was no question about his being in prayer at that time. He *had* to pray. Apparently in the economy of God this very weakness had been turned into power.

But in spite of all this, Paul was tense with foreboding as the time for his return to Mapleton drew near. They left the hills in the early morning, sunlight gay among the maples and the birches, touching here and there a spray as red as the red apples that shone on the trees. Down from the sparkling air fragrant with mown hay, into the steam and smoke of cities and out again, through the stately parkways of tall New York with its ocean liners nosing into their docks, through the stink and grime of north Jersey and down into the country that they knew so well. Rather a tired country it was, pounded flat by summer heat, its cabbage fields faintly odorous through the dank night air. It was dark night when they arrived and there was no light in the little house on Main Street where Burnett lived.

Skip was at home to greet them, boisterous and joyful at the front door. "Boy, you sure threw a scare into me! Thought you were never coming back."

"Well, here we are," and Paul sighed a little as he entered the rectory.

"I talked to Burnett," said Skip darkly. "Oh, I kept your orders! I didn't tell her anything about how you felt. I just said what the heck, and words like that."

"Well, what did she say?" asked Paul with a faint smile.

"Said it was none of my business."

"Some truth in that, isn't there?"

But Skip replied, "No! Everything about you is my business. I can't help feeling a sense of responsibility for you."

"I'll manage," Paul said briefly, and patted him on the shoulder and went upstairs. He longed to say, "When is she coming home?" but he did not.

Skip, however, answered his thoughts. "She's staying down there till the end of October," he called, gathering up suitcases. "And that nut's down there with her."

Paul should have reproved Skip at this point, but he was too tired to concern himself. He set down his suitcases, looked at the big, bare room with its nondescript furniture and tightened his lips with determination. He would put Burnett entirely out of his thoughts. He would do more than rise above his grief for her, he would have done with it. He could master himself and he would turn all his energy into his work.

He had thought deeply about this work while cutting wood and mowing hay in the mountains. And he now began to carry out the plans that he had conceived. First of all, his children. He had long felt that they should be taught the power and the reality of Jesus Christ instead of lessons in cooperation from the ants and lessons in obedience from the birds. "Mamma bird says cheep," as James Morse had once bitterly observed, "and all the little birdies pick their bugs out of the ground just like she says. So when Mamma and Papa speak we should obey them right away. Heck with that. Jimmie knows he's got to obey right away or I'll warm his pants for him and that's a darn sight better reason than because a mamma bird says cheep . . . And if it ain't that," James had added, "it's all about Tiko and Miko and Mexico and how somebody gave Tiko a toothbrush. When are they going to teach them about God?"

Paul had tried to write out lessons on God and had failed. Who was he, he decided, that he should outline these things? There was a book in which they were already given and there was a Teacher, the Holy Spirit speaking through that Book.

He would teach his children the Bible, adding nothing and taking nothing away, but merely verifying the truths that were there and putting them into modern words and modern thought so that they could be understood.

So with painful care he studied the Gospels and wrote out for his teachers the thoughts that came to him—explanations, illustrations, applications. "And if any of the teachers don't like it, they can quit," he thought.

The teachers did like it. The church school grew until it overflowed into the rectory living room into the dining room, even into the cellar where a temporary classroom was erected with plywood.

The children also liked it. Paul's small parishioners knew that they were his friends, but they knew also that he was in authority over them and would tolerate no whispering or romping but would promptly remove the offender into his study, there to sit until church school was over. Paul had even forced them, in his stern past, to memorize Bible verses until they were released. But with some uneasiness he discontinued this practice.

"Burnett says it's not good psychology," he had explained to Janet. It was more and more difficult to speak of Burnett as the slow days passed and she did not return. But he forced himself to do so; he must learn to see her and smile and hide his heart.

"Psychology's all right," said Janet indulgently, "but you have to use your head once in a while."

Paul wished that he would not remember things like this while he was trying to tell his children about Christ. "Verily, verily I say unto you, he that believeth on me, the works that I do shall he do also," he quoted one day. "Do you think that Jesus would tell a lie?" he asked, with the grave simplicity of a man speaking to an equal and a friend.

Half a dozen voices answered, "No!"

"I don't think so either," said Paul. "And yet, we don't do the works that He did. It must be that we haven't yet learned how to do wonderful things by prayer. Anyway, we haven't that much power all by ourselves, do we? He knew that, and so He went to the Father to get help for us. And He comes back and is with us, only we can't see Him. It's like the wind. Did you ever see the wind?"

Paul waited until the children had thought this through and shaken their heads. "But you know when the wind is blowing, don't you, because you feel it and you see what it does. In the same way we can see His power when we ask for it, and we can see what it does."

All this was very difficult for Paul. He drew a deep breath and wiped his brow. Then he looked up and saw Angus McGhann standing in the back of the auditorium, his arms folded, his brows drawn together. His former senior warden had been more friendly since Paul's vacation and had even hinted, just as the Bishop had foretold, that if there should be a vacancy upon the vestry some fine day he might be prevailed upon to fill it. But he would surely think that Paul was going too far in teaching the children of the church to actually believe the words of Christ. A year ago his presence in the auditorium would have terrified Paul. But now it was a matter of minor importance. Paul went quietly on explaining to the children the way of creative imagining as Burnett had explained it to him.

"So you see," he ended, "we play a pretend game and then we say, 'Thank You, God, that's the way it's going to be.' And after a while we know that it isn't a pretend game at all, it's only a way of teaching the unconscious—that's the other one that lives inside of us, remember—to think with faith."

"Don't you think your children are rather young for that sort of thing?" asked Angus McGhann, catching up with Paul as he left the auditorium.

"No," Paul said quietly, "I think they're just the right age. 'Whoso shall not receive the Kingdom of God as a little child shall in no wise enter therein.' "

"But their fathers and mothers wouldn't understand, and the children might become disillusioned."

"That is a very real danger," replied Paul, smiling. "We must consider how to meet it."

So he said to his children on the next Sunday, "Lots of grown people don't really believe what Jesus said, because they don't know Him. And they don't know Him because they have never tried to do the things that He commanded them to do. This isn't the grown people's fault, because when they were children everybody told them that the age of miracles was past. They thought, 'How can we believe what Jesus said when we don't see miracles happen?' So they decided that He must have meant something else. Now we know that the age of miracles isn't past." He looked at Joe McGhann sitting before him uneasily and smiled, for he knew the heart of a boy too well to call on him. "All of you know how fast my nephew Skip got well. That was a miracle. The doctor said so. So we are trying to learn all over again the things that He taught us. We are explorers, like Columbus, looking for a new world of prayer. But we must not mind if our fathers and mothers are not Columbuses, and we had better not talk about our exploring to people who do not understand."

A hand went up and a voice said, "Why don't you tell

the grown people about it too?"

Paul reeled a little at this challenge. "I've told some of them," he said, for he saw no reason for saying other than the truth. "But it's hard for grown people to believe it because the other one inside of them, you know, the unconscious, that takes care of the memories, it's full of doubts. In order to believe it they have to teach themselves all over again and that's not easy. But probably I haven't explained it to them well enough," he added, quite willing to learn from the children. "I'll try again. And it might help if some of you would come to church and pray for me."

This slipped out quite unintentionally and Paul forgot it. Therefore he wondered a bit, on the next Sunday, to see the small heads between the taller ones in the pews. Until he stepped into the pulpit Paul did not remember the reason for his children being there. Then he looked at them and smiled, and the light of his love illumined his plain face into beauty. He preached about the love and power of Christ and about the truth of His words and about the spiritual value of proving that truth, much as he had spoken to his children. And he was surprised himself at the words that came from him. He found himself saying things that he had not known he knew, putting the mystic reality of Jesus Christ into words that clarified even to his own mind the present and glorious power of that unseen Friend.

He was trembling a little when he finished, spent with the power that had been flowing through him. He wiped the perspiration from his brow and returned to the chancel. But before the offertory anthem when he might sit down and rest, he made an announcement: "There will be a confirmation class, meeting after the evening service on eight Sundays, beginning next Sunday. In this class we will endeavor to study together the things of God and the power of Christ. Any are welcome to the class, whether or not they are desirous of being confirmed."

And he sat down during the singing of the anthem, resting his head against the carved back of the clergy seat and closing his eyes. "You were wonderful!" That was Opal, recovered from her fit of hysteria and fast heading, thought Paul grimly, toward another one.

"Great sermon, Paul, great!" Thayer Tewksbury beamed, with a vast engulfing shake of the hand.

But Paul kept his feet on the ground and his eyes on the other door where those who did not care to speak to him slipped silently away.

Paul was amazed at the number of people who came to his first confirmation class. He began his lectures at the very beginning, assuming that his class knew nothing. "Is there a God?" he asked, and he built simply and logically the foundation of faith on which a man might erect his house of life.

"Hot stuff," commented James Morse afterward. And he added, "It sure is different from the line you handed out a while back, when me and Frank came to your classes."

"What did I talk about?" asked Paul.

"Church symbols," said James grimly.

"And if I had lectured on the reality of God and of His power, instead of on the Church and the prayer book, Frank would be alive today."

"I didn't say that, Parson."

"I said it. And you know it."

"I'm sorry," said James. "I shouldn't have brought it to your mind."

Paul entered his study with slow steps, praying his constant prayer, "Abide in me more and more."

There in his leather chair was Alan Whitacre. So—they had returned, the two of them. And Burnett had not spoken to him, or called him up, or come to his church. Of course she had not, Paul told himself. But he realized that he had allowed himself an occasional flicker of hope—that she could not forget . . .

"Ambrose said I could wait here," said Alan, as Paul, trembling a little, closed the door in silence. "I didn't know about your confirmation class or I'd have been there."

"Glad to see you, Al!" cried Paul a bit too emphatically. "How's everything?"

"Everything is wonderful."

"And Burnett?" Paul forced himself to say.

Alan leaned back against the chair, his appealing face relaxed, his blue eyes dreaming. "Do you remember when you first told me that she still loved me?"

Paul remembered.

"It is true," said Alan in the deep tones of perfect contentment. "Every day I am more sure of it."

"Good," said Paul through stiff lips.

"Do you think I am well enough to marry? Or would that never be quite safe?"

Paul had faced this inevitable question long ago and had made up his mind. Yet it was not easy to give his answer. He leaned his head on his hand for a moment, gathering strength. Nevertheless he did not think, "Why should such grief come to me?" He knew that grief could come to anyone, the Kingdom of Heaven being so far away.

"Yes, I feel sure that you are well enough to marry," Paul said steadily, and if his voice was brittle his friend did not notice it.

"Not just yet, of course," added Alan hastily. "I must be sure, first, that I can earn a decent living. Right now I'm working in a greenhouse. It isn't much of a job, but I must earn some money right away. My mother and father have spent every cent of their inheritance keeping me in a private institution. If I had only had sense enough to realize what they were doing, I would not have permitted it."

Paul looked at his purposeful face as he talked of his work and of his family and of Burnett. Here was indeed a new Alan, reclaiming his original inheritance of strength. Even the planes of his face had changed, stiffening intangibly into manhood.

"But your writing?" asked Paul with real interest.

"I write in the evenings. My teacher—for I'm taking a correspondence course in commercial writing—says I'm a 'natural.' " He smiled, but the joy faded out of his face. "I can only write a little while at a time," he said hastily, as though it hurt him to admit the fact. "Then my thoughts begin to slip and slide and . . ."

"That's only because your mind has been inactive for so long," said Paul gently. "If you had worn your arm in a sling for years, it would take a while for its muscle tone to return. But it *will* return."

Alan's face cleared. "You always help me," he said simply. "Thank you. I must retrain my mind as a man must go into training to strengthen his body. I will do so. And as soon as I have sold my first article I will ask Burnett to marry me."

Paul had no words.

But Alan did not notice his silence. "Judith is doing

wonderfully," he said. "Did you know that?"

"Yes. I see Mr. Klein once in a while . . ."

"He says that she misses me," murmured Alan. "He tells me that I am able to help her, as you help me. Nothing in the world makes me so happy as that; to know that I can help someone else!"

"Good!" Paul said heartily. And he thought, "Oh Lord, make him go soon, while I can still like him . . ."

17

Burnett was at home again, four blocks down the street. Her little house dreamed amid falling leaves and pungent chrysanthemums as when he first loved her. It was one thing to decide to have done with that love while she was out of sight and out of range. But when he need only walk down her brick path with its edging of sweet alyssum in order to see her again, it was quite another thing. He could hardly bear to pass her house. Burnett, in her blue jacket, raking leaves under the apple trees. Burnett, leaning against a tree trunk, one scarlet maple leaf caught in her black hair, her eyes reflecting the tender sky.

"Forget it, Forrester," he would tell himself grimly, driving past her house with his eyes straight ahead. "It's not for you anymore, that look in her face, not for you."

No it was not for him. It was for the man whom he had saved. Oh, bitter victory! Was there no way of life except through death, no way to power but through sacrifice? He did not know. He could but go ahead using the faith that he had and teaching the laws that were established to him, leaving the rest in the hands of a power beyond his ken. With infinite care he worked out for his confirmation class the understanding of God that had come to him, the ways of contacting God that he had learned. And when he reached the horizon of his knowledge he simply admitted it.

Sunday by Sunday the class increased. And on the Sunday next before Advent, when November had seized the earth in savage teeth and shaken every leaf to death, Burnett herself entered the church and sat by Alan Whitacre in the last pew.

He paused for a moment. He could not help it. The class paused too. People turned to the chapel door and smiled and nodded at her as she slipped into the pew. They were accepting her, as she had said they would. He remembered. Wind in the high pines and Burnett's voice, "If you walk in integrity, people know the truth about you at last ..." He swallowed hard and said, "We're glad to have you with us, Miss McNeill," and went on with his lesson.

But the thought of her ran like deep waters beneath his mind, even as he taught with that controlled authority that was becoming more and more a part of him. If it were not for her, the class would not be here now. If she had not had the courage to keep to her path in an apathetic and critical town, he would not be teaching this class now. He would have clung to the shell of his own dwarfed personality and there he would have remained. If it had not been for her . . . How thin she was, how pale . . . A long engagement was hard for one so tempestuous as she ... After the class he would have to speak to her . . .

It was over at last. Paul stood by the door shaking hands with those who spoke to him.

"Burnett!" He could find no other words to say.

"You're amazing!" said Burnett rather breathlessly. "I've never known you to speak with such power!"

"You are tired," Paul said gently, noting the dark shadows under her eyes.

And Burnett replied in a voice hardly more than a whisper, "I am tired."

For a moment the defences wavered about Paul's heart. She looked so little, there beside tall Alan, so little and so spent. "How's the writing coming?" he asked, turning abruptly to Alan.

"Better. Thanks to you, everything in my life is going much better. But the most exciting of all my adventures is Judith. Have you seen her?" And when Paul shook his head Alan went on eagerly, "She's just wonderful! I suggested that she express herself in music as I try to do in writing, for I knew the therapy of creative action. And I wish you could hear her sing!"

"There's nothing that makes Alan so happy as helping Judith," said Burnett, and Paul could not read her thoughts.

"It strengthens a man to be considered strong," Alan replied.

"Oh, go quickly, *go!*" thought Paul within his barricaded mind.

At last they went away and a Sunday was ended; Early Communion, Sunday School, Morning Prayer, a Baptismal Service, Evensong, Confirmation class—all was over. Sighing deeply, Paul went on slow feet to his study where he was apt to quiet himself with bits of bookkeeping before seeking his bed.

But the light was on in his study, and a large figure arose from the easy chair as Paul went in.

"Your man told me to wait here until you came," Mr. Klein said, beaming. "Who is he? Sort of a holy butler?"

"A very good name for him." Paul smiled, visioning the sexton's unctuous smirk and his pompous manner of ownership.

"It's late and you are tired," said Mr. Klein as Paul dropped into his desk chair. "I will only keep you a moment. I want to tell you: Judith is well, thank God, well. And as for me, I—I must thank you. I have been thinking of ways to make my gratitude real, and I will find one. So—forgive me if I ask you: what do they pay you here?"

Such an odd question to ask of one who is supposed to live above money! Paul stared at him for a moment before he could collect his wits and answer.

"Forgive me," said Mr. Klein again. "But I want to know."

After all, it was no secret, thought Paul. Anyone who pleased might look it up in the Diocesan Journal. So with a little smile he answered the question as simply and directly as it had been asked.

"What?"

"I have a rectory too," said Paul apologetically.

Mr. Klein settled himself again, for he had leaped half out of his chair in surprise. "But that is not good business!" he spluttered, and with waves of agitated hands he explained that fact to Paul.

"I know all that," Paul interrupted, his face rather red. "But . . ."

"Well, then, tell them! Tell them!"

"I can't."

"Why?"

"I don't know why. I guess I'm just no good as a money-raiser. I feel that they must have reasons . . . They are used to living on a different scale from mine, and I don't know what demands may be made on them . . ."

"That is nonsense," said Mr. Klein with finality.

Paul tapped with a pencil on the desk, his face flushed as he fought the old battle against the pain of ingratitude.

"And you must have a housekeeper," ruminated Mr. Klein. "Your sister—and if you should want to marry and have children . . ."

"That, fortunately, is unlikely," said Paul drily.

"You have done so much," mourned Mr. Klein. "When I think how I am grateful . . . Have they no gratitude?"

"They see no need of gratitude," Paul remarked with a touch of bitterness. "I'm supposed to delight in serving them."

"So they shortchange you, thinking, 'He is a Christian, he must not complain that I cheat him.' Do you not think that your God will be annoyed with them for that? For their own sakes, you should tell them."

"I can't," said Paul again.

"Ah, well." Sighing deeply and shaking his head, Mr. Klein stood up. "You will see me again," he said. "I have not finished."

Paul, at last alone, lay back in the big chair and permitted himself to relax. As he did so, he felt himself sinking into darkness.

He could not stand under the pressure of his life. Burnett, Alan, Judith, a vestry that congratulated themselves on getting so much for so little, a congregation that squeezed the last ounce of strength out of him. After all, he told himself, there was no reason why he should kill himself for these people . . . remaining here grimly in the sinking ship of his own overstrained body, taking aspirin in order to sleep at night . . . He imagined himself selling encyclopedias from door to door while people said, "Poor fellow, he used to be a minister." He imagined himself driving a four-wheel drive truck through desert sands and his employers muttering, "Lost the knack of it. Never closes his lines any more." He imagined himself in the Bishop's office murmuring, "Yes, sir, I know you warned me, but . . ."

He was still brooding on the night of the November vestry meeting, when twelve men sat around the sacristy table, oozing good fellowship and keen business management.

"Pretty good returns for the every-member canvass!" Thayer Tewksbury beamed at him. "Pretty good!"

"How much did the Simpsons pledge?" shrilled old Birdsong, holding his hand to his ear.

Silence around the table, while Paul, looking into the treasurer's eyes, remembered the usual fifteen cents a week.

"The same," nodded Thayer, and went on with his speech. "Three-fourths of the budget is already raised, which is much better than we usually do by this time of year."

"We can use the Christmas offerings to cover the rest of it," said Angus McGhann, whose Christmas gift to his wife was apt to be double the Christmas offerings.

"We won't need to do that," said Thayer, determinedly getting on. "A number of families have not yet been heard from and we are sure to raise it all eventually. Gentlemen: I have talked with several of you informally and I think I can say that we would like to do something for our rector to show our gratitude for his excellent work over the past year. I have looked over the attendance books and find a marked increase, both in church and in the church school. And the offerings . . ."

A deep and comforting warmth stole into Paul's heart as Thayer boomed on.

"So I hereby move," said Thayer at last, "that with the cooperation of the Woman's Guild, we raise the money for the game rooms that our rector desires."

Game rooms. He had forgotten that there were such things.

"It's very kind of you," he said, over the sinking of his heart. "But I no longer need a recreational center. As I recall, my thought was to draw our young people to the church. Now another power draws them. We can't take care of any more unless we build a new church—and engage a curate."

"What's the matter?" chirped old Birdsong, for the matter of game rooms had been shouted into his ears. "Don't he want the young men to play games?"

"Not particularly," said Paul drily.

"Well, I dunno," said Thayer with disappointment in his voice. "The Woman's Guild is planning to hold a couple of rummage sales to help."

Paul bit his lips and swallowed an unministerial expletive. "What I do need is more room for the church school," he said. "At present classes are meeting all over the rectory. The next rector might not like that."

This passed completely and totally over their heads.

"Wonderful idea!" cried Thayer. "Sunday school rooms!" And before Paul went home to the rectory, the matter was concluded.

"Two cakes," announced Janet as Paul came into the dining-room door. "Two of 'em!" And she led him into the kitchen and pointed. "That one's the Young's and that one's the Peterson's. Both of 'em grateful as all get out."

Paul touched one of them and smiled, remembering Burnett's "resurrection cake." They solved nothing. But at least they showed him that some of his people wanted to make him happy.

"Why don't you go to the Clergy Conference?" asked Janet two days later. "You used to love those things and you never get to them any more."

"I haven't time."

"Well, it's too bad you don't go," Janet insisted. "Maybe you could teach them something about helping people."

Her brother paused with his soup spoon halfway to his mouth. "Me?" he asked. "Teach? Who would listen to me?"

"Someday people will listen," said Janet. "I've never known anyone get as far in one year." And being his older sister she had to add, "It's a poor idea too, if you ask me. You ought to go slower, like other people, and take maybe ten years to it. You put me in mind of one of these plants that's forced too far so that it topples over. What have you got to do tomorrow that you can't go out and enjoy yourself once in a while?"

"There's a young couple I've been trying to bring together. I must find the girl a place to stay, because her mother-in-law is throwing her out. Then I must locate the fellow and bring them together somehow."

"How do you know you can find him?"

"I'll find him. Then there's old Higgins in the TB sanitorium. He's making a comeback."

"He isn't worth two hoots when he does come back."

"He will be," Paul said, smiling. "And my old lady in the county home . . ."

"You don't expect to make *her* well, for heaven's sake!"

"Not in this life," agreed Paul. "I'm not trying to." And as Janet removed the soup plates he saw in his mind the departing one in the nursing home. Her wandering spirit knew him whenever he came to her. He would sit by the bed in silence, not seeing the decaying body nor allowing himself to be sickened by the odor of it. In a way that he could not have told he would merge his spirit with hers in order to comfort and reassure it as it started on its long journey to eternity. When he did so, the sunlight of that far land would shine upon her and there would be peace in her fading eyes and the shadow of a smile on her ancient lips. "Don't be afraid," Paul would whisper to the spirit too long clinging. "He is with you, taking care of you. Look up and find Him!"

"Why you want to waste your time sitting beside that horribly, smelly old woman, I wouldn't know," fussed Janet.

But Paul replied gently, "We're working on an experiment together."

He had sought the power of God that he might help people to get well, and that same power was of inestimable value when the time came for them to graduate into the next life. Through life to Life this power worked, irradiating the gates of death so that the visitation to the dying was no longer a grim duty but was softened by a mysterious contemplation of eternity through the spirit of the departing one. "Maybe I'll postpone my call till morning and take her the communion," said Paul. For she knew the communion, her dim faculties rallying and participating in the sacred act. "I've got to get up a talk for the Bible Class and make out some notices for the Men's Breakfast Club."

"It's Monday. And it's supposed to be your day off," Janet reminded him.

But Paul had not taken a day off since he returned from his vacation. What could he do on it? He could not afford to play golf, his father's farmhouse in the hills was too far away and the blissful solitude of the sea was lost to him for it was filled and pervaded with the spirit of Burnett. In every wind, in every laughing bit of blown grass, on every sand dune, there she was, in her gay dress of blue and green, "framed in sand and crowned with sky," as she had said of him. No. It was best to stay in his parish and work.

Burnett came to his next confirmation class. His heart gave a great leap as he saw her there. It was not so easy as it had been to live above the thought of her. Not that it had ever been exactly easy . . ."

"You don't look well," she said abruptly after the class, her eyes searching his face. "Are you all right?"

"Of course." And Paul added, abrupt in his turn, "Why do you come?"

"Because I want to be confirmed," answered Burnett quickly. "What else?"

"You have missed several lectures."

"I'm sorry. It was a little difficult to—to take the first plunge."

"You always looked down on the Chruch," persisted Paul.

"Alan has taught me to look up to it."

Alan, towering behind her, smiled warmly. *"You taught me,"* he said to Paul. "All I did was tell Burnett the things that happened when you prayed through your sacraments."

"You tried to explain those things to me," added Burnett, "but I couldn't quite take it in."

"You couldn't quite—take it," Paul corrected her.

Burnett nodded. "I couldn't quite take it. Not from a minister. But Alan made it clear to me."

Oh, no doubt, no doubt, thought Paul. Alan made it clear. Precisely this had been his hope in the old days before he knew who Alan Whitacre was. Why then the resentment that tried to rise in him and must be quickly smothered in the tide of his constant subterranean prayer? Paul kept his eyes on the floor and murmured to Burnett, "We will be very glad to have you with us." And he added severely, "I am holding make-up classes on Tuesday nights for those who missed the first lectures."

"Well, now, this is nice," boomed Priscilla McGhann,

ambling up to Burnett with a broad smile. Priscilla was always the last save Paul to leave the house of the Lord. "I just dropped in to see what's going on here," she said rather apologetically to Paul. Then she turned again to Burnett. "Yes, indeed, it's nice to see you getting some real religion at last," she said in her bull-in-the-china-shop way. "Time was when we thought maybe you'd be our minister's wife. He needs one, too," she added severely. "Looks more peaked every day." And away she blundered, leaving an awkward silence behind her.

"People are always saying that," Burnett said with a smile.

And Alan, in a rather strained voice, remarked, "Yes. I've heard it before."

"You'll hear it again," Paul said, gathering himself together so that for the sake of loving-kindness he might tell one great and gracious lie. "Only, it will probably be about a different woman next time. An unmarried rector furnishes the parish with a constant guessing game."

"You used to see her very often," hesitated Alan, waiting to be convinced. "You don't, anymore."

"I was her pupil. A very eager pupil, on her doorstep every couple of days like the milkman until I had learned the thing I wanted to learn."

"And now I am his pupil." So Burnett supported him, her glance on him as casual and cool as the autumn wind.

Alan looked from one to the other of them, his face lightening with relief.

"Like as not they'll pick out Margaret Esmond next," added Burnett.

Paul glanced at her sharply.

"Well, why not?" Burnett answered herself. "I watched her in the class tonight and I thought, 'There! That girl's made to order for Paul.'"

"You aren't being very subtle," said Paul shortly.

"I guess subtlety isn't my strong point," admitted Burnett. "But it's the truth, just the same. I know what she thinks of you, just looking at her face while you were lecturing."

"I might do worse." Paul tightened his lips as a slow anger rose in him.

"You might," said Burnett, and mercifully departed.

But the next confirmation class threw him even more

into her presence. She intercepted him at the door when he would have fled from her. "Anna Wilkins has asked me to direct your midnight Christmas pageant," she said.

"*Why?*" demanded Paul, horrified. "And it isn't a pageant. It's the introit to the communion service."

"Because Anna is going to Florida. And you needn't bite my head off, either."

"Burnett!" protested Alan, laughing.

"Miss Wilkins should have consulted me before appointing her successor," said Paul.

"Well, I'm consulting you now," snapped Burnett.

Alan murmured, "Why do you two always pick a fight with each other?"

Paul forced himself to smile but anger seethed. Would he ever teach the women of his parish to consult him before they appointed each other to do this or to do that? However, there was no reason why Burnett should not succeed Miss Wilkins in directing his Christmas service except that her presence in the church would disturb him.

"Of course, I'm glad if you feel that you can do it," he managed to say. "It's just that these women really should consult me first. One never knows when they may choose some utterly unsuitable person and put me in a very embarrassing position."

And he thought as he went dismally home, "I'm beginning to sound like a fussy, crotchety old bachelor."

But how could he help feeling fussy and crotchety in his parish house? He would find her rehearsing the shepherds at the Sunday School piano. He would find her trudging down the steps from the costume closet, her arms full of robes of scarlet and purple and gold. As Christmas Day drew near he would find her even in the church with the electrician, going over the schedule of lights. And always on finding her he fled.

But the rehearsals themselves he could not escape. He too must be there, to shepherd crucifer and acolyte down the aisle with flags and with tall candlesticks and with prayer. For Burnett, gathering her seventy choristers in the pews before her, gave them a program of prayer as well as a program of song.

"This is not a show," she said. "This is an act of worship. Therefore what we think in our minds is just as important as what we sing." And she explained to them, her head high and her face very white, the dynamic of prayer that was theirs to use.

"It's more difficult than I thought it would be," she said to Paul afterward with a little gasp. But still she did it. Some of her choristers listened with their hearts and some did not. There were high school girls, their faces cryptic and closed. There were women who had been her enemies, eyeing her dubiously. There were men who hearkened with perplexed faces as though to an unknown tongue. But half of them heard and believed.

"As brave as banners flying in the sun," thought Paul as he sat in the third pew and watched her with his heart in his eyes.

"So during the first episode," Burnett instructed them, "as the captive Israelites come down the aisle singing, 'Oh come, oh come, Emmanuel,' pray for all the captives of the world—in prisons and in concentration camps—and imagine God's power reaching them through your faith and setting them free. And during 'He shall feed His flock like a shepherd' imagine the love of Christ finding the lost and desolate and comforting them until an awakened world can find a place for them." So she outlined the program of prayer that would walk beside their program of song. "And now, before beginning—Mr. Forrester, will you lead us in prayer?" she ended.

And Paul rose and stood beside her in his cassock and prayed, "Direct us Oh Lord in all our doings with Thy most gracious favor . . ."

He sat down in the pew, his knees trembling. Here they were, the two of them, leading his congregation in an act of worship. "It will work out," Burnett had said in the old days. "Give them time." And it had worked out, but in a way that broke the heart.

More and more as the rehearsals proceeded, his people accepted her and followed her. It amazed Paul to see her increasing command of them as she brought in her processions here and sent them out there, as she muted or swelled their singing with a wave of her hand, as she lifted them through prayer into a high consciousness of the Prince of Peace. For she made not only the final service but every rehearsal for the service an act of worship and of prayer.

And as the church throbbed with beauty, people began to wander into the rehearsals and sit in the back pews and listen. Opal, inevitably, twittering and beaming; various of his alcoholics and depressives, finding there strength and comfort for their souls; old Hattie Burroughs, tottering uncertainly down the aisle among singing shepherds and wise men: "Yes it *is* time to come to church. Look at all the people! What makes them traipse up and down the aisles and sing all the time? That's a funny way to have church. And there's one of them singing way up high where the others can't reach her. I wish she wouldn't do that."

Paul spoke firmly to the shaky old lady whose piercing voice disturbed the lovely descant on "O Come All Ye Faithful." "Now Miss Hattie," he said, gently putting her down in a seat, "this is a different way of having church. It's a Christmas way. You may sit and listen to it, but you must be quiet. You and I will just kneel here and have a little prayer and then we'll be still and listen. And we won't make any noise at all, will we?" he said in the gentle persuasive voice that he used to little children.

He had done his part in the rehearsal. He need not stay to the end. But watching Burnett in her Christmas dress of soft red wool, her face alive, radiant, expressing every mood of the service, he could not leave. So he sat down in the back seat, with a lump in his throat and a stinging sensation behind his eyes.

Paul Forrester no longer asked, "Why?"

There was a power greater than all Burnett's creative thinking, and it was the power of a sacrifice willingly offered. There was a greater prayer-lever than the lever of joy: the patient enduring of a suffering, voluntarily assumed. Even so the Apostle had "rounded out what was left of the sufferings of Christ," for these were the sufferings of Christ. He did not suffer the pains of illness, for He was so instinct with spiritual power that no illness could have fastened itself upon Him. No one could ever have said of Him that Satan had bound Him for eighteen years, for in the purity of His life He had given no opening to the power of evil. He did not suffer for His own sins but only for the redemption of others.

And he himself, Paul, not knowing what he did, had dared to step into the stream of this redemptive love. He had offered to take upon himself the sorrow of Alan Whitacre and so to set him free. And if his offer involved more than the weekend travail that he had undertaken, what right had he to complain of it?

"You trusted me to do this job for You," he whispered beneath the throb of the singing voices. "And I'll not let You down. But I can't take much more! Even You didn't stay in the valley of the shadow. You passed through it and went your way. Please show me where to go ... because as soon as Christmas is over I am going to resign from All Saints Church."

18

"Paul." Burnett's voice on the telephone, cool and crisp like dew on sharp grasses.

All morning long he had felt her calling him, an inner tug as if by an invisible cord. The feeling was so strong that several times he had gone to the telephone to speak to her. Then he had sighed and straightened his shoulders and turned away.

"May I drop in to the study and see you a few minutes?"

Strange how the deep timbre of her thinking sounded in the voice. Paul Forrester perceived that this was to be no casual dropping-in. "I'll come to see you instead if you like," he said, perhaps a shade too eagerly, the shadowy body of his thoughts passing already down the brick pathway to her door.

"Thanks, Paul, but I'd rather come to the study. I think that would be—easier."

As the time of her arrival drew near Paul could not sit still. He moved here and there, opening drawers aimlessly and closing them again. Finally he could no longer endure the cage that was his study and burst out of it. He stood at the window beside the parish-house door and watched for her. Snow clouds had marched down the sky from the far west, their gray battalions flanked by fog. But the brooding Atlantic had met them and tempered them, and rain now fell from the black sky in silver sheets. Women splashed down the sidewalk from the Asco and the A&P, struggling with umbrellas and paper bags. Ambrose of All Saints, hands in coat pockets, trudged home after his usual comfortable hour in Doc's back room. Schoolchildren scampered happily down the sidewalks, their pet dogs frisking at their heels. Would she never come? And could he all his life stare out of windows with his heart in his mouth and a thousand butterflies in his stomach merely because this one woman was on her way to his church?

Here she came, like sunlight in the dark, raindrops dancing from a merry umbrella of red and green. The tension disappeared from Paul's mind and joy swept over him in a wild, irrational flood. What had he feared? he wondered: that she would never come? That a car would fell her on her way to him? That she would take wings and fly away, her red and green umbrella parachuting her to heaven? With a wry grin at his own foolishness, Paul darted back to the study and closed the door before she should see him there, nose on pane, gazing out into the rain like a deserted child.

"Well! Good to see you again, Burnett!" The hearty ring of his voice deceived not even himself as Paul swallowed down his surging desire to seize this will-o'-the-wisp in his arms and hold her there forever. He motioned in a casual way to the big chair facing the light.

Burnett stood against the door for a moment, her scarlet scarf and dark green coat framed against the wood like a brilliant flower in an earthen vase. Her open hands behind her pressed the panels as if clinging to them for protection. Rain glistened on her crown of coal-black hair and her gray eyes rested on him sombrely as they always did when she was hiding her inner feelings.

Paul's heart sank as he looked at her. He sat in the chair beside his desk and talked about the weather for a while as people do when they dare not wrap the cloak of silence about them and be at peace.

"Paul, Alan and I have decided to be married the last Saturday in January."

Here it was, then. He might have known. He found himself wondering, foolishly, whether she noticed his too prominent Adam's apple riding up and down above his clerical collar. Then he wondered why he should be thinking at this moment about his Adam's apple. It was as though his inner self, refusing to contemplate Burnett's marriage to another man, turned away and hid its face from reasonable thought. He leaned forward in his chair, elbows on knees, nervous fingers intertwined. He did not dare to meet the level gaze of her eyes. "The—last Saturday in January," he murmured aimlessly.

Through the sudden roaring in his head the five words separated themselves, over and over again, louder and faster as they went, like an express train sweeping toward him, crashing down upon him. Beneath them he heard the words that came from her, light and casual words about Alan and his work, Alan and his writing, Alan and an article on mental institutions that he had just sold.

"You remember? He asked you to say a prayer that it might find the right publisher."

Paul remembered. He could see Alan now, with that new light in his face, saying, "If you'll pray for it—just once!" And he remembered his own sudden rage, hid behind a taut and silent face, and his inward cry, *"No, I will not!"*

But he had done so just the same.

"Paul!" cried Burnett sharply. "Put that pen down and listen to me!"

"I am listening," Paul managed to say. "I—well—congratulations."

"Thanks. So then, will that date be convenient for you?"

Paul raised dark, stricken eyes to her face, the pen still in his hands. "What do you mean—convenient for me?"

"I mean, can you marry us then, of course."

At this the fountain pen was on the floor and Paul was on his feet. *"What!* You don't expect *me* to marry you?"

"Of course..." The words breathed out into a thin whisper and there was silence in the room. Slowly the light faded out of Burnett's face and it was set and still, as he had seen it many months ago—Burnett hiding behind it and looking out like a cat, crouched and hiding, staring warily at an uncertain world.

"Of all the consummate *nerve!"* exploded Paul Forrester. "I step out of your way and let you have this man because you want him," he panted. "But that's not enough. You expect me to stand up before everybody and actually say the words... *What do you think I am?* A holy automaton? An india-rubber doormat for you to trample on day after day and expect it to spring up and be just the same? 'Step on me again, do; step on me again...' *No!* I'm through! I'm finished! I've taken all I can take!" Paul reached out, as it were, within himself, to stem the flow of these wild words;

but they would not be stayed. "I will not marry you! Nor will I come to the wedding and give you away! I've given you away already, God help me! Now have the decency to take him and get out of my sight!"

"Paul." Her voice was hardly a sigh, the smallest possible sound, like faint wind stirring the grass. And it brought him back immediately to his senses and to his chair.

"I'm sorry." Paul pulled back desperately on the wild horses of his wrath. "I'm sorry."

"But it was *you* who decided . . ."

"After Alan appeared on the scene," snapped Paul.

"But you said—that we were not meant for each other, that it only made trouble in the church . . ."

"What did you expect me to do?" Paul leaped up again as if the chair were too hot to hold him, and strode to the window. "Smite myself on the chest and put your hand in his, turning away to hide my tears?"

"But you've gone steadily ahead with your life, always cheerful and firm, with your hand on the helm of things . . ."

"Poor taste." Paul flung the words over his taut shoulders, his eyes upon the cemetery, veiled in rain. "I should have drowned myself. Or at the very least, taken to drink."

The last sound that Paul expected at this time was a laugh, but that was the sound that smote his ears; a small laugh ending in sudden tears like April's sun.

Here, now, he told himself sternly, this is enough. Another moment and he would have her sobbing in his arms. He was after all a man, with power to order and control his own emotions. There was silence behind him while he studied the mantle of rain that fell upon the brown turf of the cemetery.

His sombre gaze lifted to the cemetery wall and life awoke in it. For a small boy walked that wall, as small boys do. Paul opened the window, letting in a shower of drops from the ivy that hung over it. "Come down from that wall, Bobby," he called in the gentle, authoritative and half-humorous voice that he reserved for children. "Come—*right—down.*" And he watched the boy clamber down the other side of the wall and disappear.

"The ruling passion," murmured a voice from the midst

of the leather chair.

"What's that?"

"Shepherding your little flock," Burnett explained with a wavering smile, her eyes still bright with tears.

"Well, it's about time I remembered," agreed Paul, closing the window and coming back with steady footsteps to his chair. "Sorry for my—outburst." His own smile, rather stiff and forced, broke the drawn lines of his face. "A flare-up of an old emotion, that's all."

"Is it possible that you still love me?" Burnett's voice was hushed.

"Since I am about to marry you to someone else, I consider that question unnecessary," said Paul. "Now let's see. What was the date you mentioned?"

"It's too bad to ask you to marry us if it would really disturb you," Burnett worried. "But you know, it would look funny if anyone else performed the wedding."

"Yes indeed," said Paul grimly, and he thought it would look a sight funnier if the minister rammed the ring down the bridegroom's throat and choked him. "I think we can manage that." And with steady hand the Reverend Paul Forrester marked on his Phillips Brooks' calendar the day on which he would marry the woman whom he loved to the man he had saved.

Paul went to the dinner table in raggedness of soul and body.

"What's the matter?" asked Janet. "Don't you feel good? Here it's almost time for your lovely Christmas service and you don't have a word to say."

The Christmas service. Burnett's service, with Burnett herself darting in and out among shepherds and wise men and holy angels like a sweet wild bird among still flowers...

Skip studied him with wise young eyes but Paul did not see sympathy in their depths.

"Where were you Sunday?" he snapped to his nephew.

"Football game—pros."

"Sunday morning?"

"Sure. Begins at one o'clock. It's a long way into the city and you've got to go early to get a seat."

"Haven't I told you that as long as you live in the rectory you can't skip church and go to games?"

"Well, see," answered Skip, not at all disturbed by his

uncle's ferocity, "the way I felt that day, I just didn't give a darn. Here we go, praying like heck and all the rest of it, and things work out wrong just the same."

Ambrose inched open the door and pushed his homely face into the dining room. "The women are on the prowl again," he announced in a stage whisper. "Fixing to decorate for Christmas. Into everything and under everything. They want to know why it isn't dusted on top of the mantelpiece. And they want to know where their flower baskets got to. And they say the cocoa-pot is gone again."

"Heavens!" Janet darted into the kitchen, coming out somewhat red in the face with the kettle in her hands. "It was the Altar Guild," she claimed. "They met in the rectory this month, and you know, Paul, I've been begging you for ages to let me buy some new pots and pans for the kitchen and you said they cost too much."

So he had. That was in the old days when he would sit, pencil in hand, trying to figure out how he could support a wife . . .

"Well, get one for heaven's sake," he snapped. And when Ambrose spoke again about the flower baskets, he leaped up and flung down his napkin in disgust. "I'll go look for them," he growled.

"Now see what you've done," said Skip to Ambrose, as one might say, "You've waked the baby."

"If you can steer clear of the womenfolks in this world, you'll get by all right," grumbled Ambrose, shuffling after him. "That's what I always say."

Janet kept Paul's dinner warm in the oven and produced it hopefully when he returned. But at that moment Hattie Burroughs appeared at the front door, negligently clothed in a cotton dress, a sweater and an old straw hat. "Where's everybody?" she quavered. "I can't find anybody. I've come to church. And I can't find anybody at all."

Paul pushed back his plate and rose.

"Eat your dinner!" Skip ordered. "I'll take her home."

But Paul had gone for the old coat that he kept on purpose for Miss Hattie and with an expressionless face he wrapped it around the confused old lady and started her home. Then plodding back through the wet December night he set his face toward his study and toward work. One could always work. He was thankful, looking back over the wearying years of his life, that he had always worked; thankful for foundries and summer hotels and surveying gangs, for swamps and deserts and all the other places where he had labored to earn his daily bread while his father's salary dragged months behind and the parish treasurer went to Florida on vacation. At least one learned to put one's mind on one's job and keep it there no matter what distress lay sick upon one's heart.

He was counting the money from the children's Advent boxes and rolling it into neat rolls when there came a kncok at the door.

"Come in," he called, and Skip strode over to him and put one hand gently on his shoulder.

"You know, Paul," he said, his deep voice resonant with sympathy, "I've had these things happen to me. You forget the dames after a while. Honest you do."

"Thanks, Skip," said Paul, smiling in spite of himself.

"Tell you what: why don't you do a spot of praying about it?"

Paul hesitated. "I can't pray in a way that would hurt Alan."

"Well, but God must know how to unscramble things, mustn't He?"

"I'm afraid I'm pretty badly off the beam," confessed Paul.

"Sure, sure." And Skip patted him on the shoulder consolingly. "Well, it's a large order, but I guess I'll have to do some work on it myself."

He left, leaving a bit of comfort in Paul's heart. For Skip's sake if no other reason he must find again his lost current of subconscious prayer and must abide in it.

But he had no time to think of these things now. There was another knock, heavier than Skip's and the door opened without waiting for permission. There stood Angus McGhann, now reelected to the vestry upon the retirement of old Sammy Birdsong.

"Going to be a fine service Christmas Eve," rumbled McGhann, oozing friendliness and Christmas cheer. "Wonderful service. A great little woman, that Miss McNeill. At one time I thought—well—" he glanced at Paul, coughed delicately and swept on to the business of the evening. "Probably be a good offering," he hazarded.

Paul, knowing Mapleton, had his doubts.

"Now let's see, you had in mind some project for the church school, didn't you?"

"The offering has been promised to the church school since the October vestry meeting," Paul stated specifically. "The proposition is to build three new classrooms in the parish-house basement."

"Well, I don't know," began Mr. McGhann apologetically. "The budget has not been raised as fast as we had hoped it might be. It would be a big help to the treasurer if we could throw the Christmas offering into general expenses." He paused and looked hopefully at Paul, his gray moustaches lifted in a genial smile.

"I'm afraid I cannot consent to that," said Paul rather stiffly. And he added, greatly daring, "I believe the vestry said that it was a special act of gratitude."

"I see no need of gratitude," said Mr. McGhann.

Sadly, Paul studied the man. What could he say to him?

A strange thing, gratitude, so baffling that a man may tell himself he does not want it. Yet what is gratitude after all? Only the swing of kindness in its eternal orbit, a giving of love in return for love, a spontaneous action of the heart, which opens a door so that one may receive more love. And since a man is made to swing in this orbit of love, there is in the human heart no deeper need than the need of gratitude.

But none of this could Paul say to Angus McGhann. And mumbling something about considering ways and means, his warden gathered himself together and took his departure.

No more, thought Paul, no more. As soon as he could find a place where he could work, there would be no more squeezing of the collection plate, no more commotion about cocoa-pots and flower baskets, no more Opals around his neck, no more sitting for endless hours in a study whose loneliness cried aloud to him of the presence of Burnett, where sorrow lay like dust upon his heart—no more.

"Paul!" He must have dozed, for he woke with her voice calling him, with her presence in the room so real that he leaped up and turned to the door, half expecting it to be flung open by her hand.

But there was nothing at the door; only the wind from the far sea blowing in the rain.

He felt her presence again in his study the next day, as real as if she stood there, somewhere between the shelves of ancient books that lined the room: his father's books, his grandfather's, his uncle's; theology and sermons and more theology, gathering dust. Again and again he glanced about as though to see her shining eyes, her flashing smile. He had known in the old days when her presence called to him, that her love was drawing him with a thread invisible but real. Now it could only be his own love that he had tried so hard to bury and that had leaped into rebellious life during the last month.

He closed his mind to the phantom of a thing long dead and telephoned Priscilla about the altar flowers to avoid having her steam into the sacristy the next morning and explode at the sight of the arrangements he had made.

"Poinsettias in *pots?*" screamed that worthy on the other end of the line. "I don't think that would be pretty *at all*. Besides, Mrs. Matthews has always given the Christmas flowers. She gets red roses and she comes down there and arranges them herself."

She did indeed, crowding the sacristy with her heavily upholstered form while the Altar Guild girls, white veils upon their little heads, waited for her chattering voice to fade away so that they could work in prayer and silence, as they had been taught to do; while the committee on decorations visited in the rectory kitchen with Janet, their evergreens choking the cloisters, until the way was clear for them. With a dexterity worthy of a foreign ambassador Paul soothed and reassured Priscilla. And all the while a little voice said in his mind, "It will not be for long, not for long."

He had written his letter of resignation, and he carried it in his inside coat pocket, for it comforted him to have it there. Even though he did not know where he would find work and the thought frightened him, still he carried the letter in his pocket.

As Priscilla's last feeble plaint simmered into acquiescence, he hung up the phone and answered a gentle knock on his study door.

There stood Felix Klein, a wide smile irradiating his froglike face. He sat down in the red leather chair and beamed. "Christmas present for you," he said, "Christmas present." He thrust an envelope into Paul's hand. "But tell me first: are you well? Are you happy? You do not look so."

"I'm all right. I didn't sleep too much last night, that's all."

"We are not happy either." said Mr. Klein with a prodigious sigh. "My daughter Judith . . ."

"She's not—disturbed again, is she?" asked Paul, snapping to attention.

"Alan, whom she so much loves, is marrying Miss McNeill within the month," said Mr. Klein with all candor. "So she is very much disturbed."

"Does she love Alan in *that* way?"

"In every way." And Mr. Klein spread out his hands and lifted his shoulders in a gesture that said, "What can one do?" "And I had hoped . . . Well, one cannot have everything. Judith is at home and she is well. Alan may marry whom he likes, I will still be grateful to him for bringing you to Judith. And you—I have no words to express my gratitude. It is too great for words. But I will find ways. One way I have already planned and it is good. Listen to it!" He sat up straight in his chair. "You intend to leave this church," he began.

"What?" cried Paul. How could his secret thoughts have leaped into the mouth of his friend?

"I know. I cannot say how I know these things. I look at men, I listen when they talk, I know their hearts. That is why I am a genius," he added modestly. "That is why my business is so good."

"But you haven't even talked to me!"

"I know what you are paid. And I know how much you do for men. And I know the sadness of your heart. Therefore adding the three together I advise myself that you are planning to leave this church." And while Paul still looked at him in amazement he cried, "In some churches I can understand. Only music and loud words and nothing else. But here, so much! There is Judith; she lives, she is well, she no longer tries to kill me. And why? Because here is a man, a humble minister with a white face, but when he speaks, it is the rod of Moses! How many like Judith there may be in this church, God only knows. What do they owe this minister!" He flung out wide, expressive arms. *"Every-*

thing! And what do they give? No. You do not want to stay. I see it in your face. Your eyes are sad. Your smile fades. I see. So, I have a plan, for there is need in the world for a man like you. I offer you the position of personnel director in my Southern plant. I will pay you a salary of fifteen thousand a year."

"Fifteen thousand!"

"That is nothing, that is nothing! I am after all a business man. I do not pay a man more than he is worth. To my company doctor I give the same, but he cannot heal the troubled heart, the mind that Satan has entered. You can. They will go into your office, these people, as they come to me. 'Boss, I'm worried,' they say. 'I can't sleep at night, I can't work...' And what can I do for them? I give them a little kindness, a little cheer, and that is something, for life is so empty and so dark. But it is not enough. They go out on beaten feet, as they came in. But they will come to you with darkness on their faces and they will come out with the head on high and new light in the eyes. In my mind I see it already!"

Paul could see it too. Freedom to work, to help people, with no concern about money or cocoa-pots of ironing boards or Sunday school rooms or Christmas offerings ... "Tell me something about the work," he said with his usual caution.

"It is entirely a work of helping people as you do here; the alcoholic, the depressed, the suicidal, those who are ill and beyond the help of doctors, those who are burdened with family problems—everything. You can help in any way possible according to your own judgment, and you can teach them how to help others."

"May I teach them—how to pray?"

Mr. Klein threw out his hand dramatically. "Listen!" he said. "Do you hear the wind?"

Paul listened and heard it, blowing low in the cemetery over the little graves.

"It is free to go where it likes," said Mr. Klein. "You are free like the wind, like the air. It is true, you will have no church. Only a consulting room and an office, and a classroom, if you like. But you will have the freedom of money—and it is a great freedom. And if some day you should want a home and family ..." He paused, with a bright look, but Paul turned his face away and made no answer.

"You accept," Mr. Klein stated.

Paul drew the letter of resignation out of his pocket and spread it out before Felix Klein. "I did not know where to go," he said briefly. And he added under his breath, "God sent you here."

"My boy, my boy," said Mr. Klein, his hand on Paul's shoulder, "God sent you to all of us."

19

The last rehearsal for Christmas Eve was less difficult than
Paul had imagined it would be. A person can stand
anything, if only he knows that it will some day come to an
end.

Alan Whitacre was the second server, standing directly in
front of Paul as he read lessons and prayers from the
chancel steps, four acolytes around him with tall candles in
their hands. Glancing at Alan's square shoulders and
uplifted head Paul was able to smile within himself. He
could remember the day when the very back of Alan's head
proclaimed his disturbance. But here he stood, steady and
strong. And Paul knew that he himself through God's
power had given birth to this man's soul.

He closed his book and followed the five young men
down the dim church to his own seat beside the choir; for
they sang tonight from the rear of the church, so that those
who enacted the ancient drama of the humble and holy
birth might have the chancel to themselves. From there he
watched Burnett, up the aisles and down, sending out the
captive Israelites, bringing in the shepherds from front
door, from sacristy, down the side aisles and out of the dim
chancel while the choir sang the story of their coming in
"The First Noel." He watched Burnett, lithe, tense,
absorbed, her quick mind in complete control of every one
of her seventy choristers, and he even smiled a little
remembering how he had once said, "Burnett—a name like
a whiplash." Why should he not smile? He would soon be
far away in the mountains of the South. And she would be
at long last only a memory sharp and sweet of a love that
was past.

When the last weary caroller had gone home, Paul sought his study. And there in the red leather chair, awaiting him, was Alan.

"I know it's late," he said apologetically. "But I do want to talk to you for a minute."

Paul sighed and composed himself to listen.

"It's about Judith," Alan said hesitatingly. His face was veiled with sadness and there was a pallor beneath the warm tints of his skin. "She's not happy."

And Paul, remembering Mr. Klein's words, replied shortly, "Well, there's no use in worrying about what you can't help."

"Do you think Judith ought to be baptized?" asked Alan surprisingly. "In order to be healed?"

"The centurion's son was not baptized. The Cyro-Phoenecian woman's daughter was not baptized. The Gadarene maniac was not baptized."

Paul had no intention of discussing baptism with Alan while Burnett, he knew, was still somewhere about the place working with costumes. At least he could see her and store his mind with these last pictures, to take them with him to the Southern mountains.

"If Judith's unhappy at this juncture," continued Paul crisply, "it has nothing to do with being baptized. It's you."

"Yes, I know. That's my problem. What should I do about it?"

"Nothing!" exploded Paul. "After all, you can't console all the women in the world." And if the voice within him remarked, "And I don't know why they all want you," at least he did not put in words that errant thought. "You can't marry both of them, and that's that." And he whirled his revolving chair slightly toward the desk, as though to close the interview.

But Alan made no move to go. "Yes," he whispered, not raising his eyes. "But the question is—which?"

"What?" Amazement and fury chased each other through Paul's mind. But when he opened his mouth to speak, the words which came to him were quite other than those he had thought. *"Alan! Look at me!"*

Alan fixed on him a level gaze. There was no terrifying iciness about his look and no hysteria on his face, pale, still and veiled.

"There is something you are not telling me," said Paul slowly.

"There is a great deal I have not told you," murmured Alan, dropping his eyes again as though it were an effort to keep them on Paul's face. "For a long time now Judith has meant more to me than I have cared to say."

"But you're marrying Burnett within a month!" cried Paul, and leaped to his feet, his slight form towering over the large, grave man in the leather chair. "What kind of a Don Juan are you, anyway?"

At this Alan's reticence broke and he too rose, his eyes flashing. "I am a *man*, after all!" he said. "And so it pleases me that one person in the world looks up to me, not down! 'Think this way, think that way, think the other way . . .' "

"But *Alan!* You've loved Burnett since you were a child!"

"I am a child no longer," said Alan, and only his clenched hands, thumbs within fingers, showed the tension of his mind. "And yet—I still love Burnett. But I also love Judith." He sat down again and after one long scrutiny of Paul's white, startled face he sighed and bent his gaze upon the floor.

"Would it be too much to ask *why* you are telling me this?" Paul inquired with an ice-edge on his voice—while he crowded down within him a singing thing which must not be faced until later.

"Not at all," said Alan mildly.

Once more Paul noticed the pallor of his face and his averted gaze, and the doubt that had almost departed from him raised its head again.

"You have been my friend," said Alan, and the voice was hardly more than a whisper; a sorrowing whisper like low wind over the pines when the sun has gone away from them. "More of a friend than anyone on earth. You have already done enough for me and too much. And yet I want to ask one more favor of you, because no one else can do the thing but you. I want you to talk to Burnett and find out whether she would be too much upset if I married Judith instead."

"Isn't that rather a fantastic suggestion?" asked Paul,

after a moment of stunned silence. "A girl would normally be upset if a month before her wedding day the bridegroom decided to marry someone else."

"Normally, yes. But there are times when both man and woman go through with the wedding because each is afraid of hurting the other, when really—both of them have changed their minds."

"Both?" breathed Paul.

"I said both." The last word clanged with the solemnity of a funeral bell. "Because within the last week Burnett has been different."

It was a week exactly since Burnett had sat in that same red chair filling the whole room with the light of her tingling presence, and he, Paul, had of a sudden burst all bonds and shown his love. Paul sat still, hardly noticing Alan's murmured words as he turned away, closing the door gently behind him.

Paul leaped up and rushed to the parish house, searching for Burnett. She was not there. He called her home, eager, trembling. There was no answer. He stilled himself perforce and steeled himself to wait.

The next day was Christmas Eve, a day of light snow and of brilliant sun, of heaven and hell, of torment and rapture. What if Alan were right and Burnett had changed, she too seeing over the long months that she was no longer the same person who had loved this brilliant and unstable man? At one moment Paul would cling to this idea and unbearable joy would sweep him from head to foot. Then again he would call this the notion of a fool and would grimly shake himself into his mould of stoical gloom. Meanwhile Christmas Eve filled church and parish house. James Morse was in the church, putting up the platforms that he had made to fit beside the chancel steps. "No use having a flock of shepherds and what not if you can't see 'em." The women of the parish scurried here and there with evergreens and poinsettias, with scissors and wire; the Altar Guild worked as best they could in all the excitement, Ambrose hovered about supervising everything; the telephone rang all day long and the study was continually full of those who came to bring Christmas gifts.

One was Phyllis Morse, bearing a sweater that she had knit for him, while Jimmie and Caroline behind her carried a bedside table constructed by James. "He's too shy to give it to you himself," said Phyllis. "But he loves you."

"Well, look here! Well, for goodness' sake, Jimmie! What do you suppose this is?" Paul addressed himself to the children in the rush of sudden tenderness that threatened to break through his Yankee calm. And as he did so, the letter of resignation that he had written burned against his heart.

The next visitor was Opal, tender and twittering. "Here's a *very special* Christmas present that I had made *just for you!*" she panted dramatically. "You know, I've been telling you about it for ever so long!"

She had indeed. And since she was well supplied with this world's goods, Paul had been human enough to wonder once or twice whether it might be something really useful.

It was a portrait of herself, looking soulfully over an uplifted shoulder into the camera.

"How very thoughtful of you!" Paul said, trying hard to sound sincere. He added it to the pile of calendars and handkerchiefs upon his desk.

And all the time, the thought of Burnett burned like a steady, torturing flame within his mind, and he ached to see her and could not. "Not today, Paul," her voice cool on the phone had said. "I really and truly don't have time. Last-minute jobs on costumes and Christmas presents, company coming from the West . . ."

So there was nothing to do but wait and try as best he could to keep his mind on the work of Christmas Eve.

"The Boss is in a queer mood today," he heard Ambrose say. "Can't figure him out."

"He's excited," boomed Priscilla, ironing vestments in the sacristy with everyone climbing over her. "We'll have to say a little prayer for him."

This would never do, thought Paul. When the women took to praying for him, it meant that he was jittery indeed. So in the evening when all the carpenters and electricians had left the church, he went in and tried to still the tumult of his heart. Quietness stole upon him as he knelt by the rail flanked by the pedestals on which his angels soon would stand, appearing out of the darkness as the lights came gradually on, as though they might have flown down from the skies.

He was able to go with calm to a dinner that Janet had

prepared for some half-dozen choristers from a distance, shepherds and captive Israelites and a wise man from the East, all very gay in their sports coats and their brilliant ties. And in spite of everything, the intoxicating joy of Christmas Eve began to awaken in him as he listened to their foolishness.

"Oh boy, do I love Christmas Eve!" shouted Skip, above a general gay clamor of young voices. "Sometimes I think it's tough, living in a rectory, but on Christmas Eve, it's swell." He looked out of the French window as people scurried by in the starlight on their way to the parish house. "Here they come!" he cried. "The makeup men from Van Fleet's. First thing you know, everybody'll be piling into the church. And the second congregation will be waiting on the sidewalk before the first one's out. It was that way last year and heaven knows what it will be this year."

"Why do you say that?" asked Paul, coming out of a reverie.

"Well, there's something different. The church has got life. Even Sunday mornings. I don't mind going there myself, anymore."

This was a victory toward which Paul had labored for years. But he did not linger to sense it, for a magnet drew him to the parish house in which Burnett, he knew, was beginning the labor that would last till dawn.

The main hall of the parish house was draped in evergreens, crimson candles blossoming here and there among them. For the women, seeing that those of many churches came here to give a loving Christmas gift to the Heavenly Babe, prepared a bit of food to stay them between the one service and the other and made the place beautiful in red and green for their joy and comfort. A hundred people gathered in the parish house: vested choir and costumed choir, makeup men and ushers, organist and electrician and those who helped in costuming; and center of everything, Burnett herself, in red and green as she loved to be, a dress of soft red wool with a green belt around her small waist and her black hair taken out of its severe roll and curled high on top of her head. There she was, with a piece of an old sheet bound about her waist for an apron, her face tense with absorption, doing makeup with both hands. Paul watched her as she made beards out of crepe hair and disguised his vestrymen till he himself would not have known them; he watched her as she wiped her hands casually on her apron-sheet and darted into the classroom to fill her mouth with safety pins and anchor the angels' wings more firmly to their tall shoulders. Paul almost forgot her for one moment as he marvelled anew at the beauty of these angels' costumes that she had made long ago. Their towering wings were of glimmering gold and purple, green and blue, shining fold of some bright fabric laid on shining fold. Their robes, modeled after Fra Angelico, were of metal cloth in the same colors intertwined, so that each costume repeated the color of each other costume and the four together created an iridescent loveliness clear and cool and heavenly.

The hall was filling as more and more of the large cast arrived. The shepherds, dark with beards and grease paint, costumed in the dun colors of the earth, gathered about the piano and sang together, "Oh come let us adore him, oh come let us adore him," while the soprano from out in the choir room joined in with a descant as high and slender as a dream. The Madonna sat alone and prayed, overwhelmed with the greatness of her role; for was she not, without a word or movement, to convey to the audience the truth: that the light of love had dawned upon the world this day, a light to lighten the Gentiles and the glory of His people Israel? One of the wise men, very young and gay, flung himself about the hall in a laughing dance, his scarlet robe floating about him as he lifted his great golden voice in song.

And Burnett, in the middle of it all, smiled on the one who prayed and on the one who danced.

"Nearly time," murmured Paul at last, showing her his watch.

"Call them together then," said Burnett. And when Paul had raised his voice and all over the great hall they were hushed before him, she spoke. The captive Israelites would now go roped together as they had planned, along the sidewalk to the main door of the church; Isaiah would stand at the sacristy door, ready to sing his prophecy; the shepherds would take the places assigned to them, outside various doors; all of them would wait until the angels and the Holy Family had entered on a blackout and were planted in the darkness, the first behind great cedar trees in the chancel, the others back of a screen which would later be removed; the choir and the acolytes would arrange themselves under Mr. Forrester's direction in the cloisters; and everyone, everyone would remember that they were performing an act of worship and would follow the pattern of prayer that she had outlined for them.

As in every rehearsal Paul gathered each heart to himself and prayed, "Direct us, oh Lord, in all our doings with Thy most gracious favor..." And the great singing pageant swung into life while the silence of tears filled the crowded church.

The captive Israelites mourned and departed; "By the waters of Babylon we sat down and wept, when we remembered thee, O Sion . . ." And following the mighty words of "Unto us a Son is born" an unseen voice poured forth the compassion of "He shall feed His flock like a shepherd." As the melody pulsed through the hushed church Paul knew that the choir and the captives, the shepherds and the wise men waiting outside, the angels hidden in the dark chancel and Mary and Joseph behind their screen were every one of them praying for the lost and lonely people of the world. He could feel the power of it in the still church. Never a service like this, he thought; never like this, never like this. It was a power that could not be confined in the church but flowed forth into the world and gathered the world into itself. Not only angels and shepherds did Paul see as the service progressed, not only wise men in robes of glory laying their gifts before the manger, not only the light that shone on the lovely face of Mary and on gentle Joseph brooding behind her: but Paul felt that Light, an active, living Power, flowing forth into the world.

Bits of the great world floated into his mind from here and there as he prayed among his people· his own New England, shining meadows beyond dark·water, sunlight through white birches lighting the tall ferns; Southlands warm with Negro laughter, fields ruddy beneath the burning sun, forests blazing in chill fall evenings and little barefoot boys searching for ripe persimmons by the roadsides; the fantastic wastes of the Far West, a thousand miles of desert lavender and coral in the sun, its soaring mountains laced with pines and tipped with snow; the cities, steaming with humanity, where every subway is a battleground and where the tall buildings with a million twinkling lights outshine Orion and the Pleiades and make a fairyland of night: America...a living entity that was his own.

Why? The service had always hushed the heart with beauty, but never before had it taken the nation under its wings. Why?

Burnett. With quiet, fierce intensity she had declared that the Creator knew no bounds of space or time and that in His name they could evolve a power that would go forth into the world. So she had said, and he who knew her and loved her understood what it had cost her to throw out these valiant words to the small, half-open minds before her: shopkeepers and bankers and schoolgirls and the youthful veterans.

"Lord, now lettest Thou Thy servant depart in peace," sang the costumed choir at last, filling the chancel and the platforms and the chancel steps. "For our eyes have seen Thy salvation; a Light to lighten the Gentiles and the glory of Thy people Israel."

"Israel." Mr. Klein came into Paul's mind and with puzzlement and deep repentance, because he had never before thought of doing so, he prayed for the remnant of Israel scattered over his vast country from East to West, from North to South.

It was over at last. They all came singing down the aisle to group themselves in the rear of the church, and there was no one left in sight of the congregation except Mary, her young face still with a deep meditation, Joseph behind her and the angels, descended from their high pedestals and grouped about the manger with reverent faces and with outstretched hands. There were no lights in all the church except the light that shone from the manger and from the hearts wherein the Prince of Peace was born anew. "Silent Night, Holy Night" sang all of them together upon their knees in the trembling dark.

It was over, the congregation surging out, the later congregation, for whom this service would be the introit to the midnight Mass, waiting on the sidewalk, just as Skip had said, and filling the church immediately with an hour to wait.

Where was Burnett? The only one of all of them unseen, unheard...Paul made his way to the parish house, where joy and laughter held high festival. Shepherds, their robes pulled up over their knees, were holding their beards aside in order to eat sandwiches. The makeup men, unwilling to go home, stood by the door. "I never knew a church could be like this," one of them said when Paul came in. And the other one only smiled and sighed, the light of another country in his eyes.

"Where's Ruth?" shouted a young man darting past. "I owe her fifty cents. I told her I'd pay her at the half..."

"Sing a good tenor?" called Skip to a stranger wandering in, as he was once more bound to the next captive. "Latch on!"

Youngsters, beside themselves with joy that Christ was born, expressing it in the only fashion that they knew...

And Burnett, darting here and there, a ruby hummingbird among tall flowers, tying girdles, adding spirit gum, murmuring an occasional reminder: "Remember, just a little farther over toward the pulpit; don't kneel quite so soon; exit a little more quickly on 'Come all ye shepherds...'"

Burnett everywhere—but he could not talk to her until the last chorister had departed, until he had driven half a dozen people home, until he had helped take down the platforms so that the church would be ready for the morning service. Then at last he found her in the classroom that had been a dressing room. And he found her in tears.

"What is it?" He stood before her, his hands unconsciously reaching toward her. *"Crying,* after all that joy?"

"You—are going away," whispered Burnett beneath her tears.

Paul had forgotten. He was going away. Never again would he know the rapture of a Christmas service such as this...never again.

"How did you know that?" he faltered.

"Mr. Klein," said Burnett. "Via Judith. Via Alan."

"And you're—you're crying about that?"

"Paul, I can't bear it! Ever since you told me—ever since I saw that you still loved me—"

"I didn't tell you that. I said that it was a flare-up of an

- 267 -

old emotion," declared Paul. "I just forgot myself and blew my top because I'm not the kind of person who changes lightly—even if you are," he added on a sudden note of bitterness.

Burnett, amazingly, accepted the rebuke without comment. She leaned against the classroom wall, both hands against it as though for support—or as though to keep them away from him. "Paul, a year ago I—I couldn't love as I can now," she said breathlessly, her face very white. "Part of me was buried along with Alan and it took Alan to bring it back to life. But Alan isn't the same and I'm not the same. He hasn't had time to mature and I've grown far too old, far too old. My affection for him gets more maternal every day. I find myself telling him to put on his rubbers and not to forget his wallet. I thought: 'Well, this is my bed. I've made it and I'll lie on it. I must try my best to make Alan happy.' But when you broke down in the study and I knew that you loved me—oh Paul, Paul! All the passion that Alan awoke in me belongs to you and to nobody else on God's earth!"

Ever since Alan's visit Paul had hoped for this. But the joy of it made him a little dizzy just the same. He gripped the edge of the classroom table and leaned against it speechless, his heart pounding too fast for words to be possible.

Burnett came close to him, bewilderingly close, intoxicatingly close. "Do you know when I fell in love with you?" she asked, her voice low and infinitely loving. "Nearly three years ago, when you baptized little Patricia. My brother's baby; remember? Light from the stained-glass window shone on your face and it was beautiful with love of your Lord and of that little baby, and—I saw you, what you are. *Oh Paul, believe me!*" she cried, as Paul could only gaze at her, too unsteady to take her in his arms and still too choked with happiness for speech. "Why do you suppose I consented to make those angels' wings? Only to be in your parish house, in hopes that you would notice me! Which you wouldn't do—you would only scowl and stalk past as though to say, 'That woman again . . .'"

Paul was laughing a little now. "You're—you're making that up," he gasped.

"No, beloved, I'm not. I never meant to tell you. But I

want you to know—I want you to believe that I have always loved you. I loved you long before you ever looked at me."

"One more thing—" she said, raising her hands, palms outward, as though to hold him away from her until she had said all that was in her heart. "I told you that Alan helped me to see the reality of Jesus in your sacraments—but actually it was *you*, what you did for Alan. And Paul, at your last confirmation class I saw Jesus! At least, I think I did! There was a light around the cross; there was a light! And He was real to me as a Person, as He was when I first gave my life to Him when I was ten years old. He came back to me!"

"He had never left you, not really—just as I never really left you."

She held his face between her hands and studied it with eyes full of tears.

"What are you doing?" asked Paul, trembling only a little as he put his arms about her.

"Just storing your face in my heart," she whispered, the tears springing anew into her eyes. "So that I'll never forget—never forget."

At that their lips met and heaven and earth were blotted out in a blinding ecstasy.

"How can you forget me," murmured Paul at last, his lips against her cheek, "when my face will be across the breakfast table from you every morning?"

"But—Alan?" faltered Burnett. "I must marry Alan."

"Alan is going to marry Judith Klein." And as nearly as Paul could remember it he told her what Alan had said.

"Are you sure that he loves Judith?" Her words were shaky with hope and fear.

"Not quite," Paul admitted with all candor.

"He's probably seen the truth about me. Because during the last week I couldn't keep it up, the forced affection, the pretense... Then one day he came in unexpectedly and caught sight of my portrait of you ..."

"What?"

"Yes. From snapshots and memory and love. Framed in sand and crowned with sky, just as I said. It's beautiful."

"Now I know that you love me," Paul laughed, holding her tight. "Because a portrait of me couldn't be beautiful."

"But it is. It's a picture of—*you*. Your spirit. Yourself.

Alan saw it and . . ."

"Listen, my darling. You try so hard to carry the burden of the whole world, but you don't need to carry Alan's any-more. He will be happier in the long run with Judith than he could be with you. He has grown away from you, and he knows it. And if you really think you could be happy with me . . ."

"Oh, Paul! Will you marry me soon—next week?"

"Next week?" Paul laughed. "What about wedding invitations and dresses and . . ."

"Oh, what do I care about wedding dresses and invitations! All I want in the world is you."

Several moments passed before Paul could answer her. He could only hold her tight against his heart, her dark head against his cheek, while the warmth of her love flowed over him and every cold and lonely spot in all his heart melted and glowed in the light of it. "We could marry right after New Year's and—and have a honeymoon in Bermuda," said Paul, gratitude flooding his heart as he remembered Mr. Klein's Christmas present. "Then we could go South and . . ."

"Paul! You don't have to run away now! There's no reason now why you should work in a factory, is there?"

"There's a very strong financial reason," Paul said soberly. "I would like to be able to take care of you properly."

But although he laid the facts before her, he did not move Burnett. "Money's nothing!" she cried. "You can learn to manage it by spiritual power, if it's in His service. Everything is in His hands; everything. You haven't learned how to release it, but you will. Then it will begin to flow toward you through your vestry and congregation. Or another church will call you."

"But I can't wait for that."

"We won't wait for anything. Not for anything! But your heart is here in your church, although you may not know it."

"But I've accepted . . ."

Burnett ignored this. "Come into the church with me a minute," she said. "Please."

"Why?"

"Never mind. Just come."

So in the last hour before the dawn they lit the chancel lights and seated themselves far back in the church, in the very pew from which Paul had joined in the service that was really hers, the very pew where long ago Frank had lain on the cold floor.

"Now imagine what you have just seen and felt in this place," Burnett said softly, her hand in his, her gray eyes like candles in the dark. "Remember."

"Small chance that I'd ever forget," murmured Paul, who could find no words in which to clothe the Presence that had come that evening into his church.

"Could you do *that* in a factory?"

"Well, hardly, but—"

"Could you do *anything* as personnel director of a plant? You could help individuals with their problems, surely. So could a social service worker or a psychiatrist. But being a minister is more than that. It's *building* something! An entity, a corporate Being, a dynamo!"

"The Body of Christ on earth," Paul whispered.

"Well, yes. I'm beginning to understand now what you mean by that. I—I can feel it now when He comes into the church. Well! To build a dynamo like that, you need lots of people working together, like the different parts of the body; Opal and Priscilla and Mr. McGhann and poor old Hattie Burroughs and Ambrose and James. And you need your tools. What would you do without the communion service and the choir and all the little symbols, every one of them an act of mysticism in its way?"

"Before you came I had all those things. But the power wasn't there."

"Of course not. You thought the things were God. But now that you have both God and your tools, you would not be happy to give up either one of them. Why, Paul, you'd be a lost shepherd indeed without even a sheepfold for your little flock!"

Paul remembered the lonely feeling that had come over him whenever he thought of leaving All Saints, as though there were two of him and one of them wanted to resign and one did not. Of course. There were two. The man desired to leave the place that had become for him a vale of tears. The priest within the man grieved at the thought of leaving those who trusted him and who were not yet strong enough to stand alone.

"You are right," said Paul. And he took the letter of resignation from his pocket and put it into her hands.

"Listen!" cried Burnett, lifting her head.

Paul listened. Christmas Eve was past, and Christmas morning dawned in faint, far light. And from the street, the sound of youthful voices rang through the air: "There were shepherds, there were shepherds . . ."

"Some of my young people, still traipsing around the streets," said Paul severely. "They ought to be home in bed."

"The ruling passion," Burnett said as she had done once before. "Shepherding your little flock . . ."

And down the street the laughing voices faded away into the still night air: "There were shepherds, there were shepherds, keeping watch over their flock by night."